"You're still staring."

"I'm wondering how many times I'll need to dance with you and drink tea in your drawing room before you let me kiss you again." It was said so casually, she took an extra moment to fully comprehend his words.

A tingle shivered down her arms. "Do you think about kissing me often, then?"

"Kissing you often, or often think of kissing you?" That damned eyebrow raised again and it did something low in her belly. Sweet Lord, she was becoming aroused by his *eyebrow*.

"Either, I suppose." Her voice trembled, so she gulped her punch until she hit the bottom of the glass. There wasn't supposed to be alcohol in her drink, but the longer he looked at her, clearly in no great hurry to do anything else, the warmer she grew.

"If you're nearby, I'm thinking of kissing you."

Praise for Bethany Bennett
and the Misfits of Mayfair series

"Packed with disguises, debts, and debutantes, this delightful Regency does not disappoint."
—*Publisher's Weekly*, starred review on *West End Earl*

"Delicious, sexy fun."
—*BookPage*, starred review on *West End Earl*

"Filled with gripping drama, strong characters, and steamy seduction, this tantalizing story is sure to win the hearts of Regency fans."
—*Publishers Weekly*, starred review on *Any Rogue Will Do*

"Everything I adore in a Regency—wit, steam, and heart!"
—Grace Burrowes, *New York Times* bestselling author on *Any Rogue Will Do*

"A beautiful tale that weaves second chances, genuine characters, and heartfelt emotion into a satisfying happily-ever-after."
—Kelly Bowen on *Any Rogue Will Do*

"This is a fast-paced and spicy debut, with likable characters and a feel-good finale that boasts a just-right blend of tenderness and groveling."
—*BookPage*, starred review on *Any Rogue Will Do*

"This debut novel has everything Regency fans love—wit, drama, loveable characters, steam, and romance all in an entertaining story." —All About Romance on *Any Rogue Will Do*

DUKES
DO IT
BETTER

BETHANY
BENNETT

FOREVER
New York Boston

Forever
Hachette Book Group
1290 Avenue of the Americas, New York, NY 10104
read-forever.com
twitter.com/readforeverpub

First Edition: May 2022

Forever is an imprint of Grand Central Publishing. The Forever name and logo are trademarks of Hachette Book Group, Inc.

The publisher is not responsible for websites (or their content) that are not owned by the publisher.

The Hachette Speakers Bureau provides a wide range of authors for speaking events. To find out more, go to www.hachettespeakersbureau.com or call (866) 376-6591.

ISBN: 9781538735725 (mass market), 9781538735732 (ebook)

Printed in the United States of America

OPM

10 9 8 7 6 5 4 3 2 1

*For Ben, who never expects me to share my drink,
but always offers his.*

holds up three fingers

Acknowledgments

Writing is my kind of team sport, because there's always wine, and no one expects me to look presentable when it's down to the wire. There's tremendous joy in knowing your team is the best, and this is my chance to toot their horns.

The Let's Get Critical group does so much more than redline my writing. You ladies are my people and I love you. Thank you for being a safe harbor for me and my imaginary friends, and trusting me with yours.

Thank you to Rebecca Strauss, the queen of agents (all hail the queen)! I wouldn't want to do this without you. Thank you isn't enough.

The amazeballs creative and talented people at Grand Central Forever continue to assemble my jumble of words and make books from them. A special thank-you to my editor, Madeleine Colavita, for answering my emails with smiley faces and brilliant insight. This book is a million times better than the draft because of you. Thank you for taking a chance on my Misfits.

Special hugs go to my older sister, Alexa. As a reader, you can assume she will be in every dedication or acknowledgments somewhere. It's the least I can do as thanks for keeping me writing on days when words are hard.

Remington, if you read this when you're older, yes, you were as adorable and precocious as Alton. And that's why I haven't gotten you a goat.

And finally, a personal note. I was a single parent for many years and I admit to harvesting heavily from my emotional experiences for this book. If you're a single parent/guardian, I see you. You're doing a great job.

DUKES DO IT BETTER

Chapter One

Somewhere in the Baltic Sea
February 1825

On days like this, the fantasy of you brings me comfort. Well, you and a glass of brandy. I've been chasing a small child all day, and although a lady shouldn't drink brandy, we both know I'm not a perfect lady. With you I am simply myself, and you love me anyway.

Malachi shifted in his bunk, the mattress ticking giving way beneath him until it cradled his body the way it had for countless nights before. It had been a hellish day. Definitely worthy of reading one of his favorite journal entries for the umpteenth time. He tucked one hand under his head and used the other to tilt the book to catch the light from a swaying lantern.

I imagine you sitting beside me now, as I write this. You're so handsome, you take my breath away. I make a habit of staring at you when you aren't looking. Others might not think you are good looking, but yours shall be the kind of face I want to watch age. The kind of face I want to see first thing in the morning.

You'll love everything about me. Not because you can't find fault, but because I'm yours. I'll have no secrets with you. Lord knows I have enough to burden my soul, so knowing I have nothing to hide from you will be a relief.

Besides, I miss sex.

God, I miss sex.

Whoever she was, this woman was damn near perfect.

Perhaps you are only a fantasy, but I think we can both agree a fantasy is safer for the heart. I can't imagine opening up to anyone other than you. Which, yes, means I will never remarry. The dream of you keeps me warm. The idea that somewhere out there is someone who could love me. Maybe not even despite my secrets, but because of them.

In my mind, the firelight in this parlor reflects off your smile—that smile you save for only me. You have your own glass of brandy cradled in your hand, because I hate to share. When I kiss you, the brandy will linger on your tongue, making you doubly delicious. The flavor of you is something I miss, although I've never tasted it.

The wind is howling outside the cottage tonight, whipping up from the waves and tearing across the top of the cliff like a wild thing. But this fire, the brandy, and the dream of you keep me warm.

Malachi closed the book, content for the moment. The author of the journal may be a mystery, but the book had been a comfort this voyage. No matter how much a man loved the sea, there were days when the tedium of being stuck on a floating piece of wood in the middle of endless water, with the same group of unwashed sailors, wore on one's sanity. Even though he was the captain of those smelly men, and considered them to be the best version of family he had, he'd escaped into the entries in this journal over and over again.

He'd found the book abandoned on the beach about a hundred yards from the mouth of the cave he called the vault, where he stashed treasures collected from his years in the Baltic.

The bloody Baltic, where action was minimal, the risks were low, and his father's reach in the government had effectively placed his career in the doldrums.

Most captains had prize money tucked away from their years of service after living through the war. But not Malachi, whose meddling father had ensured he and his crew wouldn't see any action of note. The Russian treasures he'd collected with meticulous attention to resale value were the closest thing he had to a nest egg, since he was determined to not live off the duchy's funds. After his father deliberately financially damaged him, he wouldn't give the man the satisfaction of accessing family money.

Which also meant that Malachi didn't have a home in which to store his treasures until they found new owners willing to pay a generous price.

One only had to look around the average high society London drawing room to see evidence of decorating crazes. Egyptian, Chinese, Indian. At some point, a dowager was going to fall in love with the gilded opulence of Russian art, and Malachi would be ready.

If nothing else, the British Museum remained an active buyer of artifacts and art from other cultures. Unlike many contributors, he could provide documentation and provenance. The existence of the Elgin Marbles was proof enough that the museum tended to be...flexible when it came to certain details.

Stumbling upon the journal had been an unexpected gift during the trip in October to the sleepy village of Olread Cove on the coast of England. The second unexpected gift, to be honest.

The first had been the delightful armful of a blonde he'd enjoyed the last night before he'd sailed.

After the first month at sea, he'd nearly memorized the entries, so it wasn't as if what happened next was a mystery. The following letter detailed the writer's baking projects and the bread she'd finally mastered. Each time he read about her kitchen adventures, it made him hungry.

But tonight, he needed the longing in this entry. It came through so clearly in her writing. Sometimes, when he needed to think about something other than his duties on the *Athena*, he imagined the letters in the journal were to him. Pretended he was the man sitting beside her in a snug parlor, listening to the wind howl outside as the waves crashed below. More often than not, the fantasy included the blond widow from the village as the woman beside him, and the image always calmed him.

Outside his window the waves never stopped. Gulls and water were constants. Had been for the last fifteen years. Up here at the top of the world, being at sea meant beating ice off the lines, biting wind, and a cold that seeped into bones and never left. But there were also moments of breathtaking beauty. The first time he'd seen the aurora he'd stood on deck, utterly entranced by the swirls of magnificent color painting the sky, dancing to music heard by only those waves and creatures of myth.

In his breast pocket the dispatch from this morning crinkled as he shifted. No need to read it again. Those words floated behind his lids each time he blinked, and would likely haunt his sleep.

The discharge papers were short and to the point. Due to the demands of taking over the title Duke of Trenton, Malachi Harlow was relieved of duty and ordered to the port of London from his current service in support of relations between England and Russia.

Mother must have raised hades at the admiralty to get his orders changed. But he'd expect nothing less. She did what she wanted, and wielded her coronet like a weapon, with the unerring ruthlessness of a seasoned soldier. Odd to have her championing a cause for Malachi, but decidedly in character that the cause stood at cross purposes with his wishes.

It was a hell of a way to find out his brother, George, was dead.

Orders were orders, and thanks to his mother, the only way to challenge these was to march into the offices of His Majesty's Royal Navy and demand reinstatement to his ship. Plenty of aristocrats held positions of command in service of the king. Mother hadn't needed him home when he was the spare son, so demanding he return now was ridiculous. The duchy would have to continue without him. With Mother around, he'd be no more than a figurehead anyway.

The circle of lantern light swayed across the ceiling with the rocking of the ship. He was due on deck in a few hours, so despite the news of the day and the riotous thoughts demanding attention, Malachi reached up and snuffed the light.

Tomorrow would come no matter what. Georgie would still be dead. Malachi would still be stuck with a title he didn't want. But, if he slept now, he might be able to dream of the woman who'd written the journal.

Clutching the leather book to his chest, he let the sea lull him to sleep.

e

Olread Cove, England
Late March 1825

Emma Hardwick opened her journal, flipping by habit to the back pages. But no. She stopped. New journal. Fresh pages, with plenty of room for all her thoughts. The old journal seemed to have disappeared into the ether months ago. No doubt she'd find it under a cushion or tucked into a wardrobe one of these days. Alton enjoyed hiding things, because five-year-old boys were made entirely of mischief and some mystery substance that made them smell vaguely of wet dog.

Things always seemed clearer after she wrote them down. She'd never kept a journal as a child, but since moving to this cottage at the edge of England, free of the usual social distractions, she had begun to write out her thoughts. No one else was around to hear them, after all, and holding in all those emotions wasn't an option. Some days she'd thought she would explode with the suppressed feelings. This journal, and the ones before it, was the one place she could be wholly honest. Free to be herself without risk of consequences.

The leather of this journal hadn't sufficiently softened yet, so the book stood open and stiff, like a soldier at attention, as she flipped to a blank page closer to the front.

"At ease, obnoxious book," she muttered, smashing the cover flat on her table. A smear of flour from her hand marred the brown leather, and she brushed it away, which only made the smudge worse. She'd thought her hands were clean, but in this kitchen, flour lurked everywhere.

It might be something she complained about on a daily basis, but Emma adored her kitchen. Over the years this room, with its perpetual scent of yeast and baked sugar in the air, had become her favorite place in the world.

She rubbed her fingers together, rolling the residual flour into a slim snake of white goop. Holding the journal in one hand, she painted the spine of the leather with the flour paste. Eventually the cover would soften from frequent use and exposure to natural oils. Or in her case, smears of pie crust. The old journal had been perfectly soft, falling open to the back pages as if awaiting her words.

Pinning the cover down with her left elbow, she dipped her pen in ink and wrote.

Frankly, I'm more upset about losing my journal than I am about Father's passing. What kind of person does that make me? Father is dead. The mourning period is nearly over. Yet I can't seem to cry, no matter how hard I try.

One should cry when their sire dies, right? Instead, my mind skims over grief and focuses on the to-do list I need to accomplish to make the journey to London.

A— is over the moon to be there for F—'s birthday this year. No doubt the boys will raise hell as usual. When my brother visits the Cove, the boys essentially run feral. The potential for disaster is substantially increased in London. Which might be why we typically celebrate the summer birthdays here on the coast.

To think, once upon a time, I thought London the most glamorous city in the world, and here I am already missing my cottage.

The words stopped flowing from her brain to her fingers, so Emma slumped in the chair. A piece of hair had escaped her simple coiffure. She tucked it behind her ear and stared out the window over the counter while she fiddled with the edge of the paper.

How her old friends in society would laugh to see the woman once hailed as the diamond of the Season dreading going to London. My, how time changed things.

Beyond the glass, the lawn stretched toward the sea, where it ended abruptly at the cliff's edge. Along the cliffside, the grasses grew tall enough to sway in the breeze. Closer to the house, the lawn stayed short thanks to Leonard the goat, and Titan, her horse.

As if called forth by her thoughts, Leonard wandered into view, round belly swaying. Emma suspected Leonard might be female and expecting a blessed event. Although who Leonard had found to rut with, Emma had no idea.

Like her, the goat found a mate, then was left to deal with the consequences alone. Lady Emma Hardwick, daughter of a marquess and a much praised beauty, had married a nobody, then disappeared from society.

Not that the accolades mattered much now. To her knowledge, a widow had never reclaimed the title of diamond. Diamonds, after all, were pure, sparkling, and precious. Not dangerous liars. The thought sent a dark twist through her belly.

She drew in a calming breath and set aside the familiar thought. There was a bright side. Widowhood came with certain undeniably enjoyable freedoms. She never needed to marry again. Which, considering the piles of evidence pointing to her being exactly like her mother, was probably for the best. Emma had taken a lover out of wedlock, lied to everyone to cover her tracks, and eventually run away to a place where everyone accepted the lies as truth. Mother would have approved. Her passionate, manipulative mother had wielded her dimples as weapons to get her way, heedless of how her choices impacted others. Father hadn't been much better, truth be told. When Emma had arrived in Olread Cove at the age of eighteen, she'd already been well on her way to upholding their legacy.

It wasn't something to be proud of.

A pair of eerily pale hazel eyes flashed in her memory, making a rueful smile appear.

The man with those eyes had been compelling enough to divert her from the restrictions she usually lived under. And what happened? Emma let loose for a few hours and landed in a sailor's bed.

If ever she'd questioned whether she was her mother's daughter, that encounter—delicious as it was—laid any doubts to rest. Flirting at the local assembly rooms had been the first time she'd been out in years, and just like that, Emma had reverted to old behaviors.

She'd intended to stop at a kiss.

But damn, it had been a spectacular kiss. No wonder she'd thrown caution to the wind and spent the night with him.

Even now, months later, knowing she'd never see him again, Emma couldn't fully regret that brief flight into merry widowhood. It was one time, and only one time. At least now, when she lay in bed and it was just her hands and the darkness, her mind had clear pictures to fantasize about. Those memories were more than enough to keep her warm through the winter.

People would say a mere sailor wasn't a suitable match for the daughter of a marquess—even the notorious Marquess of Eastly, famous for his countless affairs and scandals. A twisted version of a smile tilted her lips. There was quite a bit of her father in her, in addition to her faithless, long-dead mother. Not many would miss him.

She rolled the quill pen between her fingers, then returned to her journal.

C— is the marquess. How odd to think of him with Father's title. And P— shall have to adjust to being a marchioness, instead of a countess. Lord knows how much she twitched and moaned about being a countess to begin with. If nothing else, hearing her complain about changing titles will

*be grand entertainment. I can hear her voice cursing in
my head already, and it makes me smile.*

"Mama, Mama, Mama, Mama…" Alton's voice carried down
the hall.

"In the kitchen, little love," she called back. He repeated her
name until he found her, and by the tenth *mama* her nerves
had frayed.

Alton's curls peeked over the back of the wooden chair beside
her. Goodness, he was getting tall. The chair scraped against the
plank floor as he pulled it away from the table, then clambered
up onto the seat. "Is there pie?"

Emma moved the inkpot out of reach before his little hands
could make their inevitable grab for it. "Pie is in the oven." His
pout made her chuckle. "Baking takes time. These things don't
happen by magic, you know." At his age, she'd thought the
kitchens produced delights like a djinn from a lamp.

Wish. *Poof.* Pie.

She'd had no concept of the labor and time each pastry
and loaf represented, and hadn't wrapped her mind around the
reality until nearly six years earlier. Even in the womb, Alton
had craved pie, and thus Emma's love of baking had been born
a few months before her son.

Alton sagged in the chair like his bones were turning to jelly.
He lolled his head in her direction with beseeching eyes. "Can't
it go faster? It smells so good, and I'm hungry." As if on cue, a
gurgle sounded from his tummy.

"Some things are worth waiting for. Have a glass of milk and
some bread with cheese to tide you over."

He blinked his big, dark eyes at her. Dark eyes, gold hair. No
one could deny Alton was her son. When she met his impression
of a starving orphan waif with an unblinking stare, he sighed
and climbed off the chair.

"Fine," Alton grumbled, then moved toward the cupboard for a glass.

The milk jug was too heavy for him, so Emma rose to slice the cheese and bread, then pour his milk. The plate trembled slightly and tipped at a precarious angle as he carried it back toward the table. Her fists clenched with the need to step in, but instead of taking the plate away, she hovered, ready to make a grab for the stoneware before it hit the floor and they lost another place setting. Alton's independent streak had been making an appearance during the last few months, which meant more chips, cracks, and crashes than were good for their dishes.

He was growing up right before her eyes. So many changes since the weather turned cold.

Maybe she had been too busy and distracted to grieve Father. When she was back in London, wrapped in the easy life of her brother's house with its army of servants ready to see to her comfort, the reality of Father's death might crash into her.

Or she might find that London changed nothing, and the part of her that should mourn her last parent remained cold. Exactly like Father had been when Mother died. After a lifetime of drama and heightened passion over every damn thing in their relationship, Father's reaction to his wife's death had been unexpected. As if she'd taken all the emotions with her when she died. Father hadn't cried, and he hadn't mourned in any discernable way. The next week he'd found a new mistress and was back to his old habits.

Alton scurried over to the open window and yelled, "Leonard! Don't eat that!"

A muted bleat from the goat was probably Leonard's way of telling the tiny tyrant to go to hell, and the sound made Emma smile.

She'd miss their home, but the need to see Calvin and Phee was stronger. Alton would love seeing his cousin again, and the merriment of celebrating Freddie's day of birth as a family would be worth the travel. It was only a few weeks, after all. It wasn't as if she planned to stay for the Season.

She knew her place now, and it wasn't in glittering ball-rooms. Although this life, as sweet as it was, could feel solitary. Especially late at night, when loneliness settled over Emma heavier than blankets, the memory of a pair of hazel eyes and a wicked smile reminded her that no matter how hard she tried to suppress it, her desire was alive and well.

Maybe she needed to take a lover. To enter into the relation-ship thoughtfully and methodically, and not on impulse. Choose someone decent and kind who would be around for longer than one night, but wouldn't expect marriage or access to her secrets.

Yes, perhaps a lover was worth considering. If Leonard the goat could manage it, surely she could too.

Chapter Two

I sometimes wonder what life would be like if I'd received everything I thought I wanted. I'd have missed so much. Not a bit of my day-to-day existence would resemble my current reality, beyond the presence of A—. No cottage. No crashing sea. No midnight baking sessions, or overly familiar household servants. Worst of all, I would have married HIM.

— Journal entry, May 12, 1824

London, England
Early April 1825

For the love of everything holy, if Roxbury didn't release her arm, she was going to do the man some serious harm. Here, in Hyde Park, where anyone might happen by, Lady Emma

Hardwick would raise a fuss the likes of which London hadn't seen since King George barred his queen from attending his coronation.

"You shall unhand me at once, and never touch me again. Do I make myself clear, Lord Roxbury?" The words had to work past her clenched jaw. Out of the corner of her eye, Emma spotted her sister-in-law, Phee, chattering animatedly with Alton while leading him farther away. Bless her. Phee knew Emma's top priority would be keeping Alton away from the scene her unwanted companion seemed determined to create.

Roxbury released her arm with clear reluctance. "I've called twice this week and your prick of a butler says you're not at home."

It took every ounce of her self-control to not roll her eyes. "I have no interest in renewing an acquaintance with you, Lord Roxbury." She made a note to thank Higgins when she returned to the house. The aging butler had had his hands full these past few weeks. Not only dealing with houseguests and the young master's birthday celebration, but keeping unwanted callers like Roxbury at bay.

He grinned, and for a second, she glimpsed what had caught her eye so many years before. Devon had a great smile. Charming, persuasive, and distracting. Many women besides her had been taken in by his smile while he lied through his teeth.

"So formal, my love," he said.

Emma couldn't help grimacing in disgust. A week prior he'd been dancing attendance on a well-dowered wallflower. The girl was young and sweet and didn't deserve to be stuck with this reprobate for the rest of her life. After an anonymous note to the girl's father, the match everyone had been expecting fizzled abruptly. The resulting speculation in the gossip pages had made her smile into her coffee cup.

Sending that note had been Emma's good deed for the week.

Unfortunately, the interference had unexpected consequences. Namely, Roxbury's full attention was now focused on her, instead of divided between two women with money and empty ring fingers.

Emma tucked a lock of hair back under her bonnet as she wished her former lover to the devil. "I'm not your love. I'm not your anything. If you call on me, I won't be at home. You and I have no relationship, no ties."

Roxbury's smile turned flinty, with an edge that threatened to slice her world apart as he tilted his head to study her, then glanced toward where Alton stood near the river. "I'd say we have quite a few ties, Emma. Pity the boy is so small. The men in my family are usually strapping lads from a young age."

She swallowed a wave of acid back down her throat, forcing her expression into something neutral. "Adam wasn't a large man, but he was a good man. I'd be thrilled if his son grows to look like him." She'd lived the lie for so many years, it no longer tasted wrong on her tongue, but throwing it so blatantly in Roxbury's face sent a spike of anxiety straight through her.

His smile disappeared, and he wrapped a hand around her arm, dragging her close enough that his hot breath hit her face, ripe with stale liquor. "You stole my fiancée—I know it was you. And you stole my heir. Next time I call, you'll receive me, or everyone in London will see who his father really is."

The pressure of his fingers sent panic tightening her chest as doubt crept in. Devon Roxbury, biological father to her child and all-around rotter, sounded earnest in his threat. Unlike her, he'd been in London all this time and had a full roster of friends, allies, and dupes. If he spoke against her and her son, people would believe him. He could ruin Alton's future with his twisted version of the truth.

Why couldn't she have left well enough alone and let him marry his wallflower? She winced under the pressure of his fingers and forced a breath into her lungs. Memories of how Roxbury had sneered at, shamed, and then abandoned her when she'd told him she was pregnant, rose to the forefront of her mind. The wallflower deserved happiness, and Roxbury hadn't changed. That's why.

The truth stiffened her spine until Emma jerked free of his hold. "She deserves better than a man like you."

She braced as he opened his mouth for a no-doubt scathing retort.

"There you are, darling. So sorry I left you to the wilds of the park. I didn't realize there were so many dangers about." The deep voice from behind her sent a wave of gooseflesh rippling down her back. The last time she'd heard that voice, it had rumbled in her ear with aroused disappointment as she'd crept from his bed at the inn in Olread Cove. The sun had been peeking over the windowsill, and knowing Alton would be awake soon drove her from his arms and back to real life.

Captain Malachi Harlow, in the flesh.

And what mighty appealing flesh it was. His rough palm, warmer and more solid than her memories, seared her lower back as he slipped into place beside her. The hard chest she'd explored with her hands, and those wide shoulders she'd clung to, blocked the sun and cast a shadow over Roxbury's wide eyes. Harlow did make quite an impact on the senses. Rather like a blunt force blow to the side of the head—enough to scramble your wits and steal a breath or two.

Emma loosed her sweetest smile on the captain. "Lord Roxbury was just saying goodbye. You returned at the perfect moment." She turned to Devon. "You were preparing to take your leave, weren't you, milord? I'm certain a gentleman such as yourself wouldn't want to intrude on our private outing." For emphasis, she stepped closer to Captain Harlow's firm heat. Bay rum, made more potent by the man's body and the sun's warmth, hit her nose, flooding her with a feeling of safety. Even if for one moment, it was a relief to not face Roxbury alone.

"I don't believe we've been introduced." Malachi slipped one hand around her waist and offered the other to Devon.

The men shook hands in a parody of civility. "Lord Devon Roxbury. Former *friend* of Lady Emma." The man's chest puffed like a peacock, as if he could somehow claim her by proclamation alone.

"Captain Harlow of His Majesty's Royal Navy, and the Duke of Trenton. Current friend of Emma," the man beside her said.

Duke? Emma shot him a glance, but saw only a distractingly hard jaw and heavy brows bisected by a scar.

The two men stared at one another long enough that no one could mistake their exchange as friendly before Roxbury stepped away and cut a shallow bow in her direction. "Good day, Lady Emma," he said, then turned on his heel and made a hasty retreat.

She and Malachi held their cozy pose until Roxbury and his mount rounded the curve and disappeared.

"*Duke of Trenton*?" She whirled around in his loose embrace.

"*Lady* Emma?" he countered, arching his scarred brow.

At the base of her spine, his fingers flexed, urging her to sway closer. "I don't use the honorific in Olread Cove. It would have made a fuss."

His pale hazel gaze flicked toward the path Roxbury had taken. "And he's part of the reason you didn't want a fuss, I take it."

A shrug would be the only answer he'd get from her. Emma wrestled her wits back from the pull of emotion he'd created by standing so close. They were in a public park, and their physical relationship had been months ago—even if their night did show up in her dreams on a regular basis. She blew out a breath and backed away. He let her go, but a frown twitched at the corner of his mouth.

"Thank you for stepping in. Roxbury overstayed his welcome." Moving from the solid heat of his body hit her as a loss the instant she shifted. The day was clear, with blue skies and fluffy white clouds, showcasing brilliant spring weather. She shouldn't be cold. And yet. Wrapping her arms around herself did little to retain his warmth.

The big man in front of her seemed to suffer the same momentary awkwardness, if the way he shifted his weight and twitched his hands was any indication.

His fidgeting made her smile, as if his discomfort soothed hers. Of course there would be a few moments of not knowing what to do or say. After all, the last time they'd seen each other, they'd been naked and dewy from a final bout of enthusiastic sex. Now here they were, in Hyde Park, facing one another in the light of day under rather strange circumstances.

"Mama, who's this?" Alton's voice came from behind them. Emma turned to see Phee chasing Alton and mouthing "Sorry." Little legs must have outrun his aunt.

Emma glanced at Malachi, assessing. How a man interacted with a child said so much about him. Did he squat down to their level or raise his voice into a higher octave? Did he ignore the child entirely or frown at the interruption?

Malachi did none of those things. He held his hand down for Alton to shake and looked him in the eye. "I'm Lord Trenton, but you can call me Captain."

Alton shook hands with a serious expression. "Pleasure to meet you, Captain. I'm Alton Hardwick and I'm five." Still holding Malachi's hand, her son looked to Emma. "Did I do it right, Mama?"

Emma couldn't contain the smile. "Yes, little love. Very well done."

"This is Aunt Phee, but you have to call her something different," Alton said, pointing to the redhead behind him.

Phee sent Malachi a nod, but the blatant speculation in the look she shot Emma made it plain there would be a conversation happening at the first opportunity. While Emma had written about her torrid night with the captain, now that the man was present, Phee clearly had *thoughts* on the matter.

"Your Grace, this is Lady Eastly, my sister-in-law. Phee, may I introduce the Duke of Trenton," Emma said, her finishing school training coming to the rescue.

"Your assistance was well-timed, Your Grace. Thank you for helping with Roxbury," Phee said.

The captain glanced down the path Roxbury had taken. "Happy to be of assistance. It's a pleasure to meet you, Lady Eastly." He turned to Emma. "May I call on you soon, Lady Emma?"

Almost against her will, Emma's lips quirked into a smile. Playing at manners seemed a little ridiculous given their history, but she dipped a shallow curtsy. "I'm staying with my brother on Hill Street, off Berkeley Square. You may call on me there."

When he bowed over her hand, his pale gaze flicked up to hers at the last minute. Malachi placed a light kiss on the sliver of skin above the cuff of her glove. A shiver, followed by gooseflesh, raced up her arm.

Emma smiled in response to the kiss. The manners were purely superficial, but her response to him was far from it.

⟲⟳

The next day, Malachi was at his wit's end. His first lieutenant had written this morning, briefing him on the status of the *Athena*'s dry dock repairs and news of the crew. Not that the officer had to, but the man had become a friend, and knew Malachi's desire to resume his place on board ship.

When they'd returned to England, luck had been on his

side in one way—the *Athena*, while technically no longer his responsibility, would remain for a while in England for repairs and maintenance. If Malachi could convince the unexpected luck to remain long enough to see him back to command and his men, it would be a miracle. But he had to try.

After the encounter in the park the day before, he'd tried yet again to meet with the Admiralty.

When he'd reported in upon his return to London, the Admiralty hadn't outright denied the request to reinstate his command of the *Athena*. But there'd been clear reluctance on Admiral Sorkin's part to consider the matter further. The disheartening meeting left Malachi with endless piles of paperwork and an appointment two weeks hence.

Today, he'd gone to what was no doubt the *real* source of the order to relinquish his command.

Which turned out to be a mistake. Because only one person could so thoroughly ignore a question while evoking this unique blend of frustration and emotional impotence. His mother—who had somehow managed to shove the Admiralty of the British Royal Navy into her pocket, but damned if he knew how.

"Your brother was prepared to do his duty to the title by marrying and siring an heir. It's not unreasonable to expect the same of you." Marjorie Harlow, Dowager Duchess of Trenton's tone signaled both her conviction of her position on the side of moral right, as well as her refusal to be swayed by things like common sense or another person's free will.

Malachi stifled a groan. "George was raised to hold the title and had settled in this role. He had everything in order. You can't judge me by his life. Frankly, I have too much going on right now to bother with chasing some skirt." He caught himself too late to call the words back. A pair of dark chocolate eyes and gold hair flashed through his mind and Malachi cleared his throat of an unexpected lump of guilt. Calling Emma a skirt didn't sit well. "Pardon me. I meant I have other priorities at the moment. Dealing with the dukedom is more important than finding a wife."

"You'll never find a wife with such a mouth. Please remember you aren't on a ship anymore," Lady Trenton huffed, setting her teacup down with the faintest *clink*.

Oh, the things he could say in reply. His mouth had won him quite a few fans in several countries, but some comments weren't for a mother's ears.

The bitter reminder that he wasn't on board the *Athena* or in command of anything—much less his own life—slapped him in the face, yet again. Malachi clasped his hands behind his back and turned to stare out the window at the square of green below.

Outside, a maid in a starched uniform walked a puff of hair one had to assume was a dog, stopping along the wrought iron fence bordering their green grass. It was hard to tell given the indeterminate body parts covered in fur, but judging by the maid's expression, he was pretty sure the dog was relieving itself on their front gate.

A foggy memory surfaced, bringing a smile with it. He'd done the same thing years ago while on a rare week of shore leave. After discovering the full extent of Father's meddling, he'd drunk to numb the humiliation of his family undercutting his career in such a way. In his alcohol-induced haze, Malachi had thought literally pissing on the ducal home was a grand statement regarding his feelings toward his family.

While other Englishmen won glory fighting Napoleon on land and water, Malachi and his men rode forty-foot seas in the Baltic. With command of a frigate built for speed and maneuverability in battle, the *Athena* was a valuable asset to the crown, and Malachi had been ready to prove it.

Nevertheless, he had to obey orders, and hadn't realized his father was pulling strings at the Admiralty to keep him away from the fighting. Those orders meant watching helplessly while the war passed him by. His men, trained and foaming at the mouth for battles and prize money from captured ships, had to sit back and wonder why the *Athena* was left to bob like a cork in the frigid northern waters.

When he'd raised hell with the Admiralty, they'd made him shuttle convicts between England and the penal colonies for four years.

Then came orders sending him back to the Baltic, where Father's post with the diplomatic service meant Malachi couldn't break wind without his parents hearing of it.

Mother joined George in London not long after Father passed two winters ago.

He glanced over his shoulder at the woman who'd fallen silent. Black crepe from head to toe reflected her genuine state of mourning. She'd probably wear her blacks for many months longer than Malachi, before moving on to half mourning. Perhaps she would never set aside her blacks. After all, Mother had lost her two great loves: Father and George.

Lady Trenton's unfailing adoration of her oldest son would never be in question. Since birth, George had existed as the center of her world. Grief etched deep grooves between her dark brows and dug canyons around her mouth like parentheses, framing her disapproving tight lips.

"I'll be returning to sea as soon as possible. A wife won't be part of my life for a good long while, I'm afraid." His announcement fell on deaf ears. Without acknowledging he'd spoken, his mother refilled her teacup and picked up the day's paper. Flipping to the society pages, she perused the columns of text and seemed to ignore Malachi entirely. He closed his eyes and tried to simply breathe instead of sigh. This was her way. It had always been her way. But that didn't mean he had to stand here and wallow in the icy silence.

"I have things to do today. Do you need anything while I'm out?"

Silence.

All right. He bowed his head in polite farewell. "Good day, then. I'll see you at dinner."

"Some friends will be joining us tonight for the meal. I expect you to be clean-shaven, Malachi."

That suppressed sigh escaped, but Malachi didn't trust himself to speak, so he closed the drawing room door behind him and leaned against it for a moment. Being home shouldn't be this hard. Even with George's death, it shouldn't be this hard. The walls of the town house seemed to press in on him, as if the house itself were wringing every last drop of happiness from its inhabitants.

Ivan, the butler, handed Malachi his hat with a silent, pitying look.

"*Spaciba*," he thanked the old Russian retainer. Fresh air and sunshine would knock these doldrums loose. That, and looking for a place of his own. If he continued in the family home, he would never survive this time in London. Visiting a property agent today became a priority, right after he visited the Admiralty. Again.

The stones rang beneath his feet as he dodged around a vegetable seller's cart and a hackney carriage. He needed answers, not excuses. It was time to dig for gossip, and there was one reliable source for that within the Admiralty's walls.

⌒〜

"Explain to me again how the machinations of my mother, who doesn't give a frog's fart about me, has somehow overrun common sense in the Admiralty." Malachi heard the growl in the demand and Simon must have recognized it as well.

Simon Wilshire, also known as Lord Marshall, rolled his eyes and rose. Malachi's tall, lanky friend squeezed past him, reaching for the door to the tiny room the Admiralty called an office. With power came floorspace, and apparently Simon's status didn't warrant adequate square footage for two men to stand in front of the desk. At least he had a window, otherwise there would be little to differentiate it from a jail cell.

Simon leaned against the heavy wood door and sighed. "You're a pain in the arse on the best of days, Harlow, but coming in here demanding answers without so much as a hello is hardly a way to make friends."

"You're my best friend. I didn't think a greeting was needed. And as much as it pains me to correct you, it's Trenton now, not Harlow."

"Lucky for you, the Duke of Trenton has more pull around here than plain Captain Harlow ever did." Simon bit his lip, catching the subtext of his own words too late. He might have blushed, but the pitiful light of the room hid the flush on his dark complexion.

Simon wasn't wrong. He and Malachi had been friends and worked with the government for long enough to have the lay of the land. The Duke of Trenton, the golden lord of the diplomatic service, close friend and confidante to two kings, and all-around managing father had overshadowed Malachi's career from the beginning. It was ironic that the name he'd come to resent so fiercely was now his, and may be the only power he could wield.

Running a hand through his hair, Malachi cursed when the long strands snagged on his fingers, forcing him to pull out the ribbon tying the mess off his face. This would be the third queue of the day. Although calling it a queue implied a certain level of order he lacked.

"You should cut it short like mine." Simon grinned. He'd worn his thick, tight curls shorn close to his head for as long as the men had been friends.

"Had lice so bad on one of the voyages to Australia, I did shave it. My head isn't nearly as well-shaped as yours." Standing in the room made him feel like a looming animal in a cage, so Malachi pulled a plain wood chair away from the wall. It had to move all of three feet to be in place directly before the desk, and he couldn't sit, otherwise it would block Simon's path from the door. "If I were locked in this room all day, I'd go mad," Malachi commented.

"Better tell your mother that. She's pushing to get you a desk down the hall. I overheard her discussing it with Lord Clarey's clerk. Apparently, my presence here and our friendship are reasons enough for settling you in this wing. Apologies if our relationship results in you being stuck here." Simon shimmied sideways to get around Malachi, then resumed his place behind the desk.

Another growl broke free. His mother. Sure, as a duchess, she held a certain amount of power. But enough to reasonably hold over the commanding officers in His Majesty's Royal Navy? "How is she pulling strings to this degree? That's my question."

Simon dropped his voice to a whisper, and Malachi had to lean forward to make out the words. "Your father's bank book."

The edge of the chair caught Malachi as he sat with a thump. "I'm sorry, what did you say?"

"He made a career of doing favors, covering tracks. The highest currency in the diplomatic service is secrets, and your father's code name was the Banker. When George died, your mother met with Clarey behind closed doors. Ever since, there are whispers of your father's bank book. A journal filled with information. He recorded everything. Names. Dates. Specifics about the favors. There are pages and pages of government secrets, and the duchess is playing the same game your father played. Dealing in the only currency they respect."

A cold ball of lead settled in Malachi's gut, pinning him to the chair. "Are you telling me Mother is blackmailing the Royal Navy to get me pulled off sea duty?"

Simon shrugged and picked up his teacup for a leisurely sip. "Surely not all of the Royal Navy. But certain members? It would appear so."

There were so many curses hovering on his tongue, it was hard to choose one. Instead, Malachi forced himself to focus on the important details. "Any idea if she shared specifics?"

"None at all, although I doubt outright threats were made. That's never been your mother's style. She's more of a smile and drop chilling hints over tea kind of woman. I've rarely spent time with her without walking away feeling unsettled."

"Yes, Mother has that effect on people. Myself included." So she had found Father's little book of secrets and thought to use it as a weapon to force the hands of everyone into doing her bidding.

The plan was alarmingly in character, but Lord, the woman was exhausting.

Simon's expression wasn't without sympathy. "She's walking a delicate line, Malachi. If those threats are too overt, or pointed at the wrong person...well. You're familiar with how the diplomatic service works."

That ball in his gut grew heavier, rushing foreboding instead of blood to his vital organs. Agents of the crown would eliminate her if she made herself into too big a threat. Snuffing out one woman to contain her secrets wasn't a particularly original tactic, but tried and true.

"Thank you for telling me."

"I'm not sure it helped, but you're welcome."

"It both clarifies the situation and makes everything a tangle." This time, Mother had gone too far. Not only had she interrupted his career, but she'd put herself at risk. Whatever she held over the government, Mal would need to get his hands on it to clean up the situation.

Mal rose from the chair, then plucked his hat from where he'd set it on the corner of Simon's tidy desk. "It was good to see you. I'll make sure I stop by again before I return to sea."

As he turned into the hallway, Simon called, "*If* you return to sea, Lord Trenton. And get a damn shave—you look like a pirate!"

Chapter Three

Explain to me using logic and reasoning a woman would agree with, why ladies are to be demure, helpless, and proper? We aren't supposed to have hobbies that wouldn't be appropriate to discuss in a drawing room, our opinions are formed by the men in our lives, and we aren't expected to enjoy sex. Meanwhile, men have all the fun. Utter rubbish if you ask me. But no one did, because I'm a woman.

—Journal entry, March 23, 1824

The candelabrum in the assembly room of Olread Cove had played over the Widow Hardwick's features, deepening her dark eyes and creating sensual shadows on the delicate bones of her face. The sight had fired his blood and he'd been unable to resist attempting to charm her.

In the drawing room of a London town house, where Emma

was sitting in a shaft of light like a cat warming itself in a sunbeam, Malachi couldn't ignore how bloody young she looked.

He'd thought to find the room filled with people when the aging butler inspected Malachi's calling card and said these were her at home hours. Instead, the room was empty, except for Emma.

His fingers tightened around the flowers he'd bought for a pretty penny from a hothouse vendor. After all, no matter what a man's intentions, when one called on a lady a certain amount of wooing was expected.

He'd fully anticipated making an appearance, perhaps getting her to smile a time or two, then weaving back toward the door through a mob of eligible bachelors and chattering society ladies. Then he'd repeat the process as often as necessary until he determined if she'd like to move their acquaintance beyond her drawing room to somewhere a little more private. But to find her alone was an opportunity he hadn't expected.

It struck him that this was the first time they'd been alone since she kissed him goodbye in the soft morning light back in October.

In the park a few days ago there'd been several sets of watchful eyes, including a child's. Their audience meant Malachi couldn't say everything he'd wanted to...just as well, since the whole thing would have turned into an awkward sort of confession. *I've thought about you. So much so that I haven't been with anyone else since. I tried in Riga, and couldn't manage more than a kiss before walking away.*

Now a question hovered on his tongue, but he bit it back. *How are you lovelier than I remembered?*

Malachi crossed the threshold, but she didn't look up from the sketch pad in her lap. A plush patterned carpet muffled the sound of his steps, and she was so focused on her task, she must not have heard the butler announce a visitor. He was a few feet away when she dropped a gum eraser.

"Damn it," she muttered, shifting her skirts aside to search the floor, flashing an enticing view of delicate ankle in the process. The sight quickened his blood and made his palms itch to touch her. Once upon a time, his hands had encircled her bare thighs, and here he was admiring an ankle. His fingers flexed at the memory of smooth skin over lean muscle.

The eraser rolled to a stop between them, marred by smudges of pencil and carpet fibers. He plucked it off the floor before his hand could betray him entirely and reach for her.

Emma rolled her eyes. "You heard that, I suppose."

Their fingertips brushed and Malachi cursed the barrier of his gloves between their skin. "I've heard worse. If you want to offend me, you'll need to work harder."

Lady Emma offered a tinkling laugh, sounding nothing like how he remembered. "Apologies for my less than ladylike tendencies, Captain. Or should I say Your Grace?" She waved him toward the space beside her on the gold silk sofa.

Thrusting the bouquet of flowers at her made him feel like a young lad charming a maid with a fistful of daisies, but she took the flowers with a smile wide enough to make the corners of her dark eyes crinkle.

"Thank you. These are lovely," she said, setting them aside.

Their shoulders nearly touched when he sat, balancing his hat on his knee. The edge of her gown—a cobalt blue thing, trimmed in simple but no-doubt expensive lace—was trapped under his thigh. Flashes of memory coursed through his limbs, as he remembered what it had been like to have the entire woman under him, and not just the edge of her dress. Damn, he was staring at the sliver of fabric peeking from under his leg. Malachi cleared his throat and shifted, but didn't free the gown.

An enameled clock on the mantel chimed the quarter hour

in the silence as he tugged off his gloves and searched for the conversational thread. She'd asked about his name. Specifically, the title. A reminder that while they shared a past, they weren't in a coaching inn on the edge of England anymore. This was London, and she wasn't merely a merry widow who'd turned his head.

But then, he wasn't merely a sailor either.

And they were sitting in her brother's drawing room. Bollocks. Not an ideal place to bring up their history and ask for more time with her. But when would he have another opportunity to speak freely without an audience? Besides, if she turned him down flat, there would be no one to witness it.

"Would you prefer formality in London?" he asked, not sure what to expect from her in this environment. Emma seemed different here. More uptight, refined. She—the woman who'd used the word *fuck* in bed—had apologized for her mild language, for God's sake.

Emma tilted her head toward him conspiratorially, and he caught a whiff of her vanilla scent. "I suppose it would be disingenuous to stand on formality at this point." The dark brown of her eyes warmed and a charming blush covered her cheeks. "I, ah, didn't expect to see you in London, Malachi. I thought you were at sea, occasionally visiting ports to drink vodka with Russians."

A sigh rumbled out of him, infused with dramatic flair to break the tension between them. "I miss vodka. You can't get decent vodka in London." Icy cold, followed by a fiery burn to warm a fellow from the inside out, a good Russian vodka would change a man's standards for alcohol forever. And God knew after the newest developments in his situation with his mother and the Admiralty, a frigid slide of vodka would be just the thing.

The rustle of fabric as she shifted in her seat brought him

back from his musings. Beneath his thigh, the fabric of her gown was tugged but didn't break free of the weight of his leg, which made him perversely happy.

Dancing around a topic had never been his style, so he asked what was on his mind in plain terms. "Is it uncomfortable to see me now? Are you regretting our night?"

Emma had been boisterous, warm, and flirtatious back in the village. This woman, with her perfectly coiffed hair and fine gown, wasn't the same one who'd laughed aloud and shimmered with a fine sheen of sweat as she raucously joined in a reel across the floor.

"Our encounter in Olread Cove was…"

He waited, but she didn't seem inclined to finish the sentence. The heat of her so close to him sent tingles of awareness up his leg as if his skin could feel the silky smoothness of her gown beneath him.

The gold and yellow furnishings in the room seemed designed to complement her elegance and coloring. Like living inside a Fabergé egg. The perfection of it all made him want to muss her a bit. See if that passionate woman who laughed a little too loud was still in there somewhere behind the polished exterior.

Malachi crossed one ankle over his knee and teased, "Exciting? Enticing? Entertaining? Enthralling? Erotic? Our encounter in the village was erotic as hell."

So erotic she'd haunted him for months. The ink on the lease to his new house was still wet, but his bedchamber was now miles away from his family home and, more importantly, his mother. Malachi finally had the privacy to pursue more than a single night with Emma.

Either Emma was open to an affair, and he could burn this attraction out of his system, or she would reject him, and he could cling to that instead of her sweet kiss goodbye, and the memory of watching her get dressed in the faint morning light.

A blush spread across her chest as she met his eyes with the boldness he remembered. "It was erotic."

"I'm happy to see you again, Emma. Even if it is a surprise."

"A pleasant surprise, milord." With one finger, light as a feather, she traced the line where her skirt disappeared under his thigh and sent him a sly smile.

Mal hoped the smile was intended to be encouragement, because that's how he was taking it. "If you're amenable to the idea, perhaps we could see more of each other while we're in London." He shifted slightly, canting his body toward hers to rest an arm across the back of the sofa. For a moment, he lost his point when her tongue darted out to wet her bottom lip. Sweet heaven, he missed those lips. In October, she'd tasted like wine and happiness and passion, and he wondered if this polished version of her would taste the same.

"Let me make my intentions clear. I want you in my bed again," he said, voice rough.

"We agreed to one night." Negating her own words, Emma reached out and smoothed her fingertips down his bearded cheek. Neither rejection, nor agreement.

"And it was spectacular." He turned to kiss her palm. Her breath caught, making him smile. Yes, that crackle of interest they'd experienced to explosive consequences at the assembly room ball was alive and well. What a relief to know she felt it too.

Heat sparked in her eyes. "I've thought about you," she confessed.

"I've thought of you often." An understatement. He'd thought of her lips and the husky laugh he'd teased out of her, more times than he could count. Those memories kept him warm on frigid nights bobbing in the Baltic. The journal he'd found had entertained his brain, but mental images of Emma brought him to pleasure, alone in his cabin, so often his fantasies always began now with dark eyes and gold hair.

"How long are you in London?" she asked.

Malachi sighed, some of the budding arousal leaching from him at the question. "I'd love to know the answer to that as well. A few weeks, probably. My mother bewitched someone in the Admiralty and pulled me home, but I'm handling it."

Her finger brushed the black ribbon around his biceps. "I'm sorry for your loss. My father died several months ago. The family recently came out of mourning."

"My condolences." The polite words were automatic, but not insincere. A low current of grief over George swept away the lingering attraction he'd been enjoying.

"You are moving about in society, though, correct?" he asked.

"Yes, but I'm picking and choosing events. My departure date isn't set in stone as of yet, but I doubt I'll be in London for much longer, Lord Trenton."

The title should have made him flinch, but her tone, low and intimately teasing, brought back a simmering shock of heat to his belly. Malachi leaned forward, until their faces were close enough to smell the bergamot on her breath from the pot of tea cooling on the table nearby. "I like it better when you call me Mal," he said, angling his mouth to steal a kiss.

She lifted her chin to meet him, dark lashes already swooping down.

"Em, have you seen today's edition of the *Times*? I set it aside at breakfast and it seems to have disappeared." A blond man wandered into the room as he spoke.

Malachi jerked back, clambering to his feet like a child caught stealing sweets. A glance down showed Emma biting her lip, blinking as if waking from a daydream. There was no doubt she'd been ready for his kiss, with her pink cheeks and rosy flush peeking from her fichu. Emma recovered quickly, straightening her shoulders as she raised a brow as if to say *don't just stand there*, then nodded toward a nearby chair.

"Phee had it last. Calvin, would you like to meet my *guest*? Calvin, Marquess of Eastly, may I introduce Malachi Harlow, Duke of Trenton. This is my brother, Your Grace."

Malachi cocked his head. He'd always had a memory for faces, and he was certain he'd met her brother before now. It was only a matter of placing where he knew him from.

The blond man froze for a second before his darker brows met into a solid line across his forehead. "The pirate captain is a duke?"

Emma jerked her head to look at Malachi. "Pirate?"

"Captain, yes. Pirate, no." Malachi shook his head toward her, but eyed the man.

Like a puzzle coming together, pieces of memory clicked into place. They'd done business several years before, while Malachi had been running convicts to the penal colonies. Where had he picked up the prisoner? Scotland? Yes, the Solway Firth. He and the man she called Calvin had struck an under-the-table deal to transport someone with forged papers. It hadn't been the first time he'd supplemented his crew's income with creative transactions.

He offered the newcomer a handshake. "A pleasure to see you again, milord."

The man stalked across the room to stand between Malachi and Emma, ignoring the proffered greeting. "What the hell are you doing with my sister?"

"How do you two know each other?" Emma rose to her feet, eyeing Malachi and her brother with suspicion.

Malachi asked Calvin, "Would you like to tell your sister what this is about, or should I?"

As quickly as he'd marched over, full of protective indignation, Calvin deflated, slumping into a chair by Emma's side of the sofa. "My sins have come home to roost, I suppose."

Emma put her hands on her hips and studied the two of

them. Although her face was composed, her mouth was hard, daring the men to attempt a lie so she could squash them like a bug.

Another current of desire flared. Before now, Malachi hadn't realized this combination of strong and adorable would shoot straight to his groin, but here he was. Silently counting backward from fifty, he willed his body not to betray him.

When Emma turned that expression on Malachi, he shifted from one foot to the other. No matter how much he'd prefer to take a seat for whatever lecture was imminent, he wouldn't sit while Emma stood. He shot her brother a condemning look, although the man ignored him.

"It seems to me, whatever sins Cal refers to are shared by the two of you. Now somebody had better explain."

Calvin stared at the toes of his boots but didn't offer words right away.

Malachi shrugged. There wasn't anything to hide. While not technically legal, he'd provided a service, which he'd been paid for. Nothing too sinister there.

"A few years ago, your brother had a problem. I helped solve it in the form of taking a bad man off his hands and delivering said bad man to the penal colonies in Australia. Simple as that."

Calvin glanced at Malachi with a look he couldn't define. Relief? Puzzlement?

"Who was the man? Cal, why haven't I heard of this before now?" Emma's attention focused on her brother, eyebrows meeting over the bridge of her fine nose.

It was almost comical when her brother was the one being interrogated. After all, *Malachi* hadn't paid to have a man shipped off to the end of the world. He'd only been the one to take out the trash, so to speak.

Calvin's heavy sigh echoed in the room. "It was the year before your debut, Em. It's not as if I deliberately hid it from you." He waved a hand at her. "Sit down. Stop looming like you're going to take a switch to my hide."

Emma sat, folding her hands in her lap primly. Malachi took his seat, observing the exchange between the siblings. He and George had never been so relaxed, yet confrontational, with one another. As children, they'd been playmates until their mother drove them apart with cruel favoritism. As adults, they'd been polite. These two? They were friends.

"The man was a horrible person who hurt a friend, and I took care of the situation to make sure he couldn't hurt her or anyone else again," Calvin said.

Emma cocked her head. "Does Phee know about this?"

Calvin frowned. "Of course she does. If I kept secrets from my wife, she'd murder me in my sleep."

The triumphant look Emma shot them sparked an alarm in Malachi's head. "So it wasn't Phee the man hurt. Has to be Lottie, then. That's the only other woman for whom you'd dispose of a whole man in her defense. And you'd do anything for Ethan."

Malachi swiveled his head to watch Calvin's reaction to her deductive reasoning, then returned to the much more pleasurable option of staring at Emma. Seeing her ferret out the information was appealing to him on a level beyond his fascination with the plump mouth he'd nearly kissed again a moment ago. Emma was clever, and the longer Malachi sat in this Fabergé egg of a room, the more he enjoyed her company beyond the possibility of ending up in bed together.

Emma pressed, "Did you and Ethan hatch this plan together, or was this a solution you came to on your own? No, he has to know. I can't imagine you keeping a secret from your best friend. You and Ethan are so inseparable you practically share a brain—tiny as it sometimes appears to be."

Calvin's cheek worked, and Malachi suspected the man was literally biting his tongue.

"If you don't tell me, I can always shout out the window and ask." Emma turned to Malachi. "Their drawing room window mirrors ours. Lord and Lady Amesbury live next door when they aren't in Kent. Their knocker is hung, so I know they're home."

Calvin pressed his palms over his face, and a pang of sympathy tugged at Malachi. Any hope of Calvin keeping the truth to himself died as they watched. Her brother leaned back and sighed, giving in to the inevitable.

"No need to shout across the lane like a hoyden. Ethan knew." Calvin said the words with clear reluctance.

Emma clapped. "Ha! I knew it!" She turned the whole of her attention on Malachi. "Don't look so smug, Captain. Or Your Grace. Whatever you are." She wagged an admonishing finger at him, but her eyes sparkled with mirth. "He called you a pirate, and you somehow made an entire *man* disappear at my brother's request."

"A *bad* man," Malachi and Calvin said in unison, then exchanged a surprised look.

Emma rolled her eyes, and Malachi glimpsed how she might have been as a young girl. This woman must have run circles around her brother with her wickedly quick mind.

"Fine. A bad man. The fact remains, you made someone disappear. What'd you do with him?" She straightened on the sofa and turned to her brother. "Is he dead? Calvin, did you pay a pirate to kill a man?"

"Again, not a pirate," Malachi protested, a thread of amusement threatening to make him laugh inappropriately. "And I didn't kill him. He survived the voyage."

"Did he?" Calvin asked. "Pity."

"Taking money to make someone disappear sounds distinctly piratical to me," Emma said with a teasing grin.

"I was stuck with the prisoner route because I'd annoyed

someone at the Admiralty. England wasn't at war, so His Majesty wasn't compelled to pay the sailors under my command. I was on half-pay, which is bad enough, but my men often went without wages altogether. Under those circumstances, one must get creative to see one's crew compensated for their labor. Such as doing paid favors for people like your brother. See? Nothing piratical." Malachi spread his hands in a gesture of innocence.

Emma again swiveled her head between Malachi and her brother.

Calvin threw his hands in the air with a short laugh. "Imagine walking up to all...that...in a gloomy pub in Scotland, then handing over a bag of gold for a shady favor."

Emma's gaze turned speculative, and by reflex Malachi glanced down at himself. Breeches, polished boots, a coat over a patterned waistcoat. The only remarkable thing was that he'd managed not to spill breakfast down the front of himself this morning, so his cravat wasn't spoiled by even one drop of coffee. Before calling on the pretty widow, he'd made an extra effort with his dress to appear as respectable as possible. Possibly to balance out the unrespectable thoughts she inspired. "I see nothing amiss."

"I don't think he's talking about your clothes, Mal," she said. "You are rather a lot to take in. Which is a compliment."

The clock on the mantel chimed. Calvin said, "Is your call over yet, Sir Pirate? I still need to find the *Times*, and the way you two look at each other is distressing me."

Emma stood, shaking out her skirts. "I'm a grown woman and a widow, Calvin. I may look at Lord Trenton however I choose."

Her brother rose with Malachi. "You mean you really are the new Duke of Trenton?"

Malachi blew out a sigh. "I almost prefer being called a pirate to the title."

Emma dimpled at him and offered her hand. "You'll get used to it, Your Grace."

He bowed and gave her fingers a brief squeeze. Her nails were short, filed smooth. A white paste marred the crevice where nail met cuticle, but her fingers were long and tapered. Delicate. There were quite a few delicate parts of her. She was just a little bit of a thing, although the direct speech and healthy laugh he'd witnessed in the village made her seem larger than she was.

Acting on impulse, Malachi brushed a thumb over the white paste. The movement made her chuckle, but the sound held a touch of embarrassment.

"I didn't realize I had dough on my nails. Flour gets everywhere, doesn't it?"

When she removed her hand from his clasp, Malachi frowned. Embarrassing her hadn't been his intention.

Flour. Dough. "You bake?" Malachi stared at the adorable blonde before him. She was the daughter of a marquess. Why the hell was she in the kitchen? The thought wasn't distasteful—just the opposite. Certainly a surprise.

She picked at the dried dough with her thumbnail, then straightened her shoulders as if admitting to baking was an act of defiance. "I find it relaxing. Not to mention rewarding to eat something you created with your own hands. Pies are my favorite, but I'm proficient in baking most things these days."

An image arose in his mind of her in a kitchen, rolling out dough, surrounded by the scent of baking sugar. In his fantasy, a dusting of flour—no. Sugar. It should definitely be sugar streaking her smooth cheek, begging his mouth to kiss off the sweetness. If her damned brother wasn't looming five feet away, he'd have risked bringing her fingers to his mouth for a taste.

"What were you making this morning?" he asked, instead of telling her she was extraordinary.

"Ginger biscuits. They're Alton's favorite. Cal finished off the last batch, so I made more to appease the tiny tyrant." She said it with such a sweet smile, the love she had for her son temporarily stole his breath.

Malachi's mother had never spoken of him in such a way. And she sure as hell had never baked his favorite biscuit in the massive, ancient kitchens of Stonewill Hall. If pressed, Mother might confess to entering the kitchens on official business a half dozen times over the years. But to actually bake? Preposterous.

Some response seemed called for, as a basic rule of conversation if nothing else, but it took two rough swallows to make room in his throat for words. "You're a great mother to do so, Emma."

Going from burgeoning desire to thoughts of his mother within such a short time was a journey he didn't want to take twice. While he'd arrived with thoughts of seduction—or establishing the opening for it, anyway—now his mind filled with images of her baking biscuits for her son. Merging the two together in his head was a new experience.

"May I call on you again? Or perhaps I'll see you at an event soon and we can further our acquaintance." Out of the corner of his eye, Lord Eastly slumped back in his chair.

"I don't get a voice in this questionable friendship, do I?" Calvin asked, staring up at the ceiling in comedic defeat.

"No," Malachi and Emma said together, exchanging a grin.

Damn, her dimples could fell a man. Take him out right at the knees if a gent wasn't careful.

"You're always welcome to call." Those dimples deepened; her plump bottom lip was shiny after she swiped her tongue across it, distracting him for a moment. An instant zing under his skin reminded him of why he'd chosen to visit this morning.

Emma was a dangerous beauty in a slightly chaotic package. Alarm bells signaled in his brain like the warning cries of centuries of sailors who'd fallen to sirens before him. With a nod of farewell to the siblings, he left.

Sliding his gloves on, Malachi donned his hat and stepped into the bustle of Hill Street.

A smile slipped over his face as he paused to let a carriage roll past. His personal life was a mess, his professional life was teetering on the brink of extinction, and the blond widow in the house behind him made him smile despite it all.

Emma was temptation personified. And Malachi? Well, he never had been keen on resisting temptation and didn't see any reason to begin now.

Chapter Four

~

If you'd told me five years ago my closest friends would be a cook, a maid, a reluctant countess, and a goat, I'd have sent you off to Bedlam. I'm particularly fond of the goat.
—Journal entry, February 22, 1824

*M*adame Bouvier greeted Emma, Phee, and Lottie with the wide smile of a woman who knew her purse would be heavier by the end of the hour.

"Lady Amesbury, I have the most divine garnet silk that would set off your coloring to perfection. The bolt isn't even on the sales floor yet." The modiste snapped her fingers and an employee hurried to join their group. "Jillian, please fetch the red watered silk from the latest shipment." Madame Bouvier turned back to the ladies. "Lady Eastly, your order is ready if you want to look it over before I send it out with the deliveries. Although, this morning I received a length of satin the exact color of spring onions, and I thought of you. Now, there isn't a lot of it, so I thought to fashion it into accessories. Since this green would complement so many items in your order, I simply had to mention it."

Phee grinned, no doubt at the obvious sales pitch. "I trust you, Madame. Add the accessories to my order."

Not that Emma faulted Madame for it. This was her livelihood, and she was an artist. When Emma stepped to the side to let her friends take care of their business, her eye caught on a flash of color tucked into an orderly stack of fabrics against the wall.

A bolt of apricot shot with copper threads seemed to glow in the sunny shop. It was impossible to resist running a finger over the smooth surface. Satin and decadent. Heavy enough to drape beautifully. A wistful sigh escaped before she could catch it.

Phee sidled up beside her. "That would be a beautiful ball gown. Imagine candlelight on those threads. You'd sparkle, Em. Citrine and gold pins in your hair, I think, but minimal jewelry. Let the dress be the statement."

Emma chuckled. Once upon a time, she'd had to beg and plead to get Phee into a modiste's shop, and now her best friend was instigating a ball gown purchase for a woman who lived in the middle of nowhere. "It is gorgeous. But I have no need for another ball gown in Olread Cove."

"How fortunate you aren't in Olread Cove, then," Lottie said, joining them. "That is exquisite, isn't it?" She stroked the bolt of satin. "Emma, if you don't make a ball gown from this, it would be a crime."

"I'm leaving this week," Emma reminded them. Freddie's birthday celebration had come and gone. Fun was had by all, and she'd been enjoying the time with her family. But she hadn't intended to spend more than a couple weeks in Town.

Phee and Lottie exchanged a look, and Emma raised an eyebrow in question. "I smell a rat. You two have concocted a plan."

"Just hear us out," Lottie began.

"You've been hiding in your cottage for years, Em. *Years*," Phee said in her usual direct manner.

"Not that the cottage isn't lovely, because it is," Lottie hastened to add. "But is it enough? When you debuted, society fell at your feet and you *loved* it. We worry you're staying in the village for the wrong reasons."

"You're hiding," Phee repeated.

"I've visited London. You make it sound like I'm a hermit living by the sea," Emma grumbled.

"Never during the Season. Even now, you're leaving right as society is returning." Phee crossed her arms and cocked her head. "We've discussed it and we think you should stay for the Season. Let the old Emma out to play. Don't you miss her?"

An unexpected pang of panic hit Emma's chest at the words. "The old Emma was a spoiled brat who made awful decisions and took advantage of everyone around her." And accidentally killed Phee's awful uncle. Self-defense, but still. Old Emma was dangerous, willing to lie, cheat, and apparently kill to protect her own interests.

Lottie nodded. "But what about the rest of it? You thrived in the social whirl. You loved to dance and drink champagne until the wee hours of morning, and you adored dressing to perfection."

The apricot satin beckoned, and Emma couldn't stop touching it. "Life is different now. I'm different," she whispered. Or rather, she hoped she was different.

Phee slid her arm around Emma's waist and pressed their heads together. "In all the best ways, Em. But you're still a woman. Not just a mother. Please stay with us for the Season. Dance and laugh with your friends. We miss you."

Emma leaned into the sideways hug and sighed. If she stayed honest with her family, and didn't do anything she'd have to hide, it might be different. No lying about where she'd been or who she'd been with. After all, she wasn't a debutante anymore. She was a widow. What could it hurt? Besides, it wasn't as if her spring schedule was terribly pressing back home, and Alton would love the time with his cousin. "Fine. We'll stay. But only for the Season."

Phee grinned as Lottie grabbed the bolt of satin and held it aloft. "Madame! We need a gown, posthaste, if you please. We will take all of it. It wouldn't do to have anyone else wearing this fabric."

The modiste crossed to them with a wide smile, motioning for a clerk to take the apricot satin. "Lady Emma's gown will be one of a kind. If you wouldn't mind waiting, I'll sketch a few ideas."

An almost forgotten excitement stirred, fizzing like the fresh pop of bubbles hitting her nose from a glass of champagne. Madame's creations were stunning. There was something magical about wearing a garment designed to make you feel beautiful.

The modiste's shop was wall-to-wall fabrics, trims, and premade gowns. Paler fabrics were in the front of the store, where the bleaching sunlight couldn't do as much damage, and the richer, deeper colors inhabited the far walls. The last time she'd shopped here, Emma had been eighteen and forced to stay up front with the pale colors.

She had to wonder how Malachi would react if she showed up at an event wearing something vibrant and luscious like the apricot. Or perhaps the garnet shade Lottie was ordering.

That man's eyes would burn right out of his skull with lust, and she wanted nothing more than to see him hungry for her the way he'd been in October.

"If I'm to stay for the Season, I'll need more than a single ball gown, won't I?" Emma grinned at her friends and headed deeper into the store toward the alluring colors along the back wall.

"There she is. I knew the old Em was in there somewhere," Phee laughed and followed with Lottie.

Midway across the store, Lottie stopped beside a young woman shopping alone. "Not to meddle, my dear, but with your skin tone, I'd suggest using that color in limited amounts. Not a whole gown."

Emma glanced back. Beside her, Phee sighed good-naturedly. "Lottie is fixing people again. Should we wait, or rescue the poor girl?"

The young lady didn't seem to know what to say to someone offering commentary on her shopping.

When Emma spied the fabric in question, she winced. "She's right though."

"Or course she's right. It's Lottie."

Upon closer inspection, the lady struck Emma as familiar. It could be because the woman had one of those faces someone would struggle to describe after an incident. Medium-brown hair, pulled under a straw bonnet adorned with a wide brown ribbon. Brown pelisse, darker brown walking dress. Brown eyes sparked with intelligence, keeping her from looking like a human impersonating a sparrow. Also reminiscent of a bird, the lady cocked her head, studying Emma in return as they approached.

"Lady Emma, what a pleasant surprise," the lady said. "I hadn't heard you were back in Town."

Emma's smile froze. They were supposed to be acquainted, then. Her gaze flew to Lottie's, hoping her friend could offer a clue as to the lady's identity.

The woman in brown laughed. "Don't look so panicked, I beg you. I apologize. You may not remember me."

"I'm so sorry," Emma began.

"No, please don't. I shouldn't have put you on the spot like that." She offered her hand to shake, like they were men sealing a business deal. "Adelaide Martin. I went to Saint Alban's with you, although I was a year behind your class and rather terminally shy."

Emma shook her hand and fixed her smile to show more warmth. The recognition still didn't come. This floundering sensation was unlike her. Typically, in social situations she felt at ease, yet since arriving in London she'd struggled to slip into the old skin she'd once inhabited so effortlessly. Even entertaining Malachi in her drawing room hadn't gone the way it should have. Instead, he'd shown up without her noticing, and then heard her swear at an inanimate object. They'd quickly set aside proprieties to some degree, but there was no denying the manners that used to be instinctual were now *work*.

And she'd just agreed to stay for the whole Season. Lordy goodness.

"It's a pleasure to meet you again, Miss Martin. Or is it missus? I've recently returned to Town and am still catching up with everyone's news."

The corners of the other lady's mouth tightened, but she maintained her smile. "It's still plain Miss Martin. The grace with which you move about in society never came as easily to me. Mother despairs that I'll die a spinster."

It felt like she'd misstepped. After talking about Old Emma only moments before, she realized Miss Martin likely expected to be speaking to *that* Emma. Especially since they'd gone to school together. Had Emma been kind to her? Or dismissive? Oh, dear. The possibilities were endless given the kind of young woman she'd been.

There was only one way to handle this. Emma took a breath and forced herself to do the exact opposite of what she would have done during her finishing school days. "It's funny you say that, because I'm realizing being in society isn't as easy for me as it once was. I'm a bit like a fish out of water, to be honest. I'd love some company at events should our paths cross, Miss Martin."

Beside her, Phee squeezed Emma's hand as if to say *well done*.

"Lady Emma"—Miss Martin's face softened into a conspiratorial smile—"if you're a fish out of water, you're welcome to flop on the dry pavement next to me. Or dance floor. There's always room with us wallflowers."

Lottie and Phee appeared to be following the exchange with great interest, but Miss Martin's words gave Emma pause. Years ago, she'd been the belle of the ball. That illusion of success had been glorious in its way, but those days were gone. From Miss Martin's tone, Emma didn't believe the offer to sit with the wallflowers was meant cruelly, but as a genuine gesture of friendship.

"Miss Martin, I shall take you up on your offer. Another friendly face would be welcome. In fact, I find myself a bit peckish. Would you care to join us in getting something to eat after we finish our shopping?" Emma asked.

Lottie made a moue of disappointment. "That sounds like a lovely idea, but I'm afraid I'll have to bow out. Ethan and I have a meeting with brewery investors. They're all in a tizzy about something, and we need to smooth ruffled feathers. But you three go on and enjoy yourselves."

Emma's eyebrows pinched together. "Is everything all right? Whatever could the investors have to worry over?"

Lottie waved away the concern, but Emma could see a shadow of worry in her dark eyes. "I'm sure it will be fine. It's just business. But I will need to get going shortly, after I check in with Madame about the garnet silk she mentioned."

"Lottie, do you mind if we share a hack? We can leave my carriage here with Emma and Miss Martin," Phee said.

Turning to the tall woman in brown, Emma said, "Miss Martin, it appears to be the two of us, then. Surely you won't leave me to eat by myself? Let's get to know each other better. One flopping fish to another."

"Thank you for the invitation, Lady Emma." Miss Martin nodded.

"Just Emma, please."

"Then I'm Adelaide." She offered a wide, lovely smile that transformed her face from quietly appealing to remarkably beautiful. "Are you making an order with Madame today, or having a fitting?"

Emma grinned. "Oh, you have to see the fabric we found for a ball gown. Speaking of fabric, unfortunately, Lottie was right. Put down the one you're holding. We can find you something better. And then we'll go eat."

Madame Bouvier appeared with a sketch pad. "Lady Emma, are you ready?"

Emma looked around her circle of friends, old and new. "Yes, Madame. I'm ready."

*

"Explain to me why we're here again," Simon said.

"Because you're always hungry, I'm thirsty, and it's too early to drink properly. Besides, I hear this place is new, so maybe we can talk without anyone overhearing." Malachi scanned the room of the cozy tea shop and prayed they had decent coffee.

"The walls have ears in my office for sure." Simon craned his head and rocked onto his toes as he glanced around. "There's a table back by the wall without anyone sitting nearby. This all feels very clandestine, Lord Son of a Spy. Certainly the most excitement I've had in a while."

"Then you should get out more. And Father wasn't a spy. Not exactly."

Simon took a seat at a wood table and shot him a disbelieving look, complete with an arched brow. "Of course. My mistake. He simply worked for the diplomatic service, held closeted meetings with rulers of nations, and made secret transactions for peers and kings that he recorded in a journal that's being held over the heads of the Royal Navy. Oh, and had a code name. But that's drastically different from being a spy. Silly of me to mix up the two."

"Bloody hell." Malachi chuckled despite himself. "He was a royally endorsed agent of the crown."

"Kind of reminds me of the fine line between pirate and privateer. They do the same thing, one just does it without paperwork." Simon picked up the menu printed on a card and perused it, so Malachi didn't waste the effort of rolling his eyes.

"This pirate thing again?"

"I told you to get a shave. Your beard is scruffy, your hair is overlong, and don't think I missed the flash of ink at your wrists."

He tugged his cuffs down to conceal the tattoos that ran up his arms and met in the center of his chest. A damned pirate, of all things. The irony. A career at sea, with blessed few prizes taken from battle. He'd have liked to have been a privateer. It was every boy's dream—or, at least the boys he'd met. Fortunes were made, lost, and stolen during war—except those of Malachi and his crew.

Simon brought him back to the conversation when he said, "Before we get to whatever it is that couldn't be said in my office, let's order. You're buying." He raised a hand to call a waiter, who scurried to their corner of the room with a speed Malachi didn't usually command.

Malachi rubbed a hand over his prickly jaw. Simon by comparison sported a clean shave on an annoyingly sharp jaw and defined cheekbones. Perfectly turned out in a well-fit coat, with a crisp white cravat contrasting with his russet skin, Simon looked every inch the gentleman. But then, he always had taken care with his appearance, while Malachi tended toward a more lackadaisical approach. Simon followed fashion. Malachi favored utilitarian clothing. After all, you couldn't raise sails or break ice off lines when your coat was so tight you weren't able to even scratch your own nose.

The waiter turned to him with an expectant expression. "Coffee. And more of whatever food he ordered," Malachi said.

The waiter dipped his head in a strange nod-bow, and left as quickly as he came. Across the room, a large group arrived and spread out over three tables in the middle of the restaurant.

"If I had to hazard a guess, I'd think your appalling beard remains on your face because it annoys your mother to see you unkempt. Am I right?"

"In my defense, my face doesn't like a blade. If I shave every day, my jaw turns into a mass of painful red bumps." He rubbed the tangle of facial hair again, because frankly, it was starting to itch. Maybe it was getting out of hand. "When Mother called me home, I deliberately let it go. Juvenile of me, I suppose."

"You sharpen the blade every time? And use a good quality shave soap?" Simon asked. How like him to focus on fixing a problem while ignoring the confession of immaturity from a friend.

"I've tried everything I know. If you have any advice, I'm open to it. I suppose it could use a trim. Clean it up a bit."

Which would defeat the overall purpose. When he tweaked his mother's nose by looking rough, he controlled the things she complained about. Left to her own devices, Mother's chosen conversational topics hurt far more. Malachi crossed his arms and glanced over as the door opened, admitting more patrons to the shop.

George had never experienced the critical side of their mother because in her eyes, George could do no wrong. When she sniffed disapprovingly over Malachi's appearance and commented on how George had never left the house without being well turned out, Malachi could agree with her. George had been a perfect son, a perfect duke. Bit of a pain in the arse sometimes, but he'd also been a good brother, if not a close friend. Given more time, could they have forged a friendship as adults? Malachi had been at sea, and George on land, so the chance had never materialized.

Heat gathered in his throat, and Malachi coughed to clear it away. He wasn't going to cry in a bloody public tea room. "To get to the point, I asked you here to discuss the—shall we say materials—my mother claims to have in her possession. Do you have any idea what this book looks like? Over the last two days I've begun to search the house, but it would help to know what I'm looking for."

The waiter arrived with their order. Another group wandered in the door, filling most of the remaining seats. Their private table wasn't so private anymore.

Any chance of speaking uninterrupted dwindled to nothing. It grated, until he saw a familiar smile across the room. Not directed at him, because she hadn't seen him yet. No, Lady Emma chattered animatedly with a tall woman. Just then, she broke loose with a laugh that made him grin even though he couldn't hear what had sparked her amusement. The woman standing beside her was nondescript in nearly all ways but one—she'd made Emma laugh.

"Do you mind if I ask someone to join us?" he asked, not taking his eyes off the pair, who appeared to be searching the room for a place to sit.

Simon swallowed a large bite of sandwich before answering. "Not at all. We can't safely discuss crown business in this crowd anyway. But the sandwiches are bloody fantastic. The perfect bread-to-filling ratio, I think. To answer your question, I don't know what the book looks like. There. Conversation complete. Who are you inviting over?"

"You'll see. She might decline." Malachi stood. It would be hard to miss the largest hairy man in the room, and sure enough, Emma caught sight of him right away. The way her eyes lit when she saw him did something to his insides similar to the unsettled feeling he experienced when riding out thirty-foot seas. Like the moment when they'd met in the assembly room, her smile was all for him, and he rolled with an emotional swell that threatened to capsize his composure entirely. His hand rested on his abdomen as if it would help calm his response. Those dimples were loaded with a lot of potent charm to throw around so casually.

On High Street outside the shops in Olread Cove he'd thought her pretty as she conversed politely with the baker. When the baker's wife had joined them on the cobblestones, Emma had greeted her with a wide smile. Back then he'd thought it transformed her into an otherworldly thing comprised of lips and dimples and a kind of bubbling joy that spread to everyone in her vicinity. So, when he'd spied her across the room of the local assembly, he'd crossed the dance floor without thinking twice. By the end of the night, he'd discovered exactly how right his first instinct had been—Emma's lips could easily be the center of one's universe.

This time he beckoned, gesturing with a jerk of his chin and raised brow. She said something to her companion, who glanced his way and froze. After a moment, the two wound their way around tables and through the press of bodies filling the room toward where he stood with his back to the wall.

Across the table, Simon wiped his mouth on a serviette and stood to greet the new arrivals.

"We've chosen a popular spot. Although it wasn't this much of a crush a quarter hour ago," Malachi said by way of greeting.

"Is it always this busy?" Emma asked the woman with her.

Her companion shot a glance at the men before answering. "It wasn't this crowded when I visited before. Perhaps we've caught them at a rush. Or all of London suddenly needs sandwiches." The young woman surveyed the room with wide eyes, looking everywhere but at their table.

"Then it speaks to the quality of their wares," Emma said. "An excellent recommendation on your part." She squeezed her friend's hand where it clutched a rather ugly brown reticule.

Emma turned toward him. "Miss Adelaide Martin, may I introduce the Duke of Trenton? His grace is in His Majesty's Royal Navy, and recently returned from the Baltics."

Miss Martin's gaze settled on the black ribbon around his biceps. "My condolences on the loss of your brother, Your Grace. He was well-liked, as I'm sure you know."

"Yes, everyone loved George. Thank you. Ladies, may I present my good friend Lord Marshall. Simon, this is Lady Emma Hardwick." Oddly enough, Simon didn't appear to be as enchanted by the petite blond woman as Malachi. In fact, he had yet to look away from the brunette, who stood eye to eye with him.

"Ladies, would you care to join us? I'm sure the waiter can find two more chairs." The smile Simon offered was familiar— it had won more than one heart over the years. "It might be a bit of a crush, but I'm sure we can muddle through if we are all fine with being friendly."

Simon somehow made it sound like a grand time to huddle around a table the size of scrap wood with strangers. If Malachi had said those words, he'd have come across as a gruff giant propositioning damsels.

Within moments, the ladies were settled in, and, as predicted, it was a tight squeeze. But with Emma's knee pressed against Malachi's, and her vanilla sugar scent teasing his nostrils over the smell of the coffee steaming at his elbow, he had no complaints. Spending the rest of the afternoon like this sounded like a fine idea.

However, it was hard to ignore Miss Martin's discomfort. She held her shoulders stiffly, sitting close to Simon but keeping her elbows pinned to her sides as if to make herself as small as possible.

"Miss Martin," he said, modulating his voice so he wasn't using his captain-on-deck tone, "have you known Lady Emma long?" Out of the corner of his eye he spied Emma opening her mouth as if to answer for her friend, but Malachi stalled her with a brush of his finger against hers under the table.

"We attended the same school. Although not in the same class. I was a year behind Lady Emma. We reconnected only this morning."

"How fortunate you've been able to reignite your friendship. Lady Emma and I are renewing our acquaintance after a time apart as well. And, of course, Lord Simon and I are longtime friends but used to maintaining a friendship over a vast distance. Letters and very short periods of time face-to-face."

Simon piped up, "If you stick around, we might decide we hate each other."

Miss Martin smiled, and it changed her whole face. She was not plain by any means, merely unassuming. The monochromatic brown ensemble wasn't doing her any favors either. But her smile was sweet. Simon, bless him, appeared to forget how to breathe. With open lips, he resembled a gaping fish while the ladies laughed at his joke.

Malachi glanced at Emma and found her raising a brow at him. He winked and turned back to their friends. Something significant was happening with Simon right before his eyes. It was hard to define—a change in the air, or a shift in a person—but it was there nonetheless.

Their waiter appeared, took the new orders, and refilled Malachi's cup. Emma requested coffee, while Miss Martin opted for tea.

"Have you been in Town long, Miss Martin?" Malachi tried to get the woman talking, since Simon clearly was having an uncharacteristic quiet spell.

"I usually come to London for the Season. Father takes his seat in the House quite seriously. While he's doing his duty, Mother and I enjoy the chance to renew acquaintances." She smiled at Emma. "And London offers so many entertainments. One hardly has time to get bored."

"So I'll see you at the usual balls and soirees?" Simon asked.

"Mother enjoys them. I'm expected to accompany her. For myself, I prefer museums and exploring the city more than balls and routs. But if you see me at one, please do come say hello. I tend to stick to the edges of the room, I'm afraid. Look for a potted palm, and I'll likely be nearby." It was said with a charming self-deprecating humor that had Simon smiling along with her. The longer Miss Martin sat at the table, the more she relaxed, and the more Simon was charmed. If Malachi had to hazard a guess, he'd bet Simon would be searching the foliage in the next ballroom they entered.

"It would be frowned upon to dance while in mourning for my brother. But my mother insists being unwed is of higher consequence than strict mourning rituals, so I'm still expected to attend events. However, Simon loves to dance, so you may have to abandon your potted palms should we meet one of these evenings." It was as close as Malachi could get to throwing Simon at her feet.

"Will you be around for a while, then?" Under the table, Emma nudged his leg with her knee.

"My plans are unchanged. As usual, I exist at the whim of my admiral and the king. But I'm here for now. How about you?

Will I have the pleasure of your company in Town, Lady Em, or are you going to leave me to wander the wilds of the city without you?"

She hummed a low laugh. "I've been persuaded to stay through the Season. So any wandering of the city must be placed squarely on your head, not mine."

Interest surged at her words. "That is the best news I've heard all day. Simon and I will look for you. Are you willing to give a hint at your schedule so I may monopolize your attention?"

A considering expression settled on her lovely features, then she moved nearer. When she closed the scant inches between them to whisper in his ear, the brush of her warm breath caressed the side of his neck, sending a quake rippling over his skin, chased by a trail of gooseflesh. The minx did it on purpose, he was sure of it.

"Is Lord Marshall a good man? If he breaks her heart, so help me, I shall take it out of your hide." For emphasis, she jabbed his thigh with a finger.

He hooked the poking digit with one of his own and closed his hand. Not quite holding hands. Just one finger, connected under the table, where no one could see.

Somehow, that one finger was attached to every nerve ending in his body. They were so close, if he turned his head, he could claim her lips. Damn their public location. Canting his mouth toward her, he gave her ample time to lean away, but still, his lips grazed her cheek on the way to her ear. Lord, she was sweet. In Olread Cove she'd made noises in the back of her throat when they kissed. The memory of those noises had haunted him since. Denying himself the opportunity to kiss her, to taste her like he wanted to, and to hear those sounds again had his muscles tightening under his coat, until he was hard all over.

"Simon is the best of men. I give you my word. He's taken with her, I can tell."

"In that case, Adelaide and I will both attend the Vanfords' ball next week."

Sharing her schedule wasn't an outright agreement to an assignation, but it was a step in the right direction. Anticipation made his breath catch, then draw deep, filling his senses with delicious edible things, and a maddeningly appealing woman. Malachi wanted to bury his nose behind her ear, where a stronger scent of vanilla lingered. "You smell like biscuits topped with vanilla icing, and you're making me hungry."

When she smiled, the apple of her cheek pinked and shifted near his face. "You already ate, Malachi. There's half a sandwich left on your plate."

"That's not what I want to eat." The raw whispered confession would have sent any gently bred young lady flouncing away after a resounding slap to his face. However, their shared history, while brief, had been passionate. Emma had to know what he meant. And there it was—her breath shuddered out on a shaky exhale.

"I use vanilla instead of perfume," she said, voice gone a bit thready. "I never took to the heavier scents. In some things, simpler is better."

"I like it," he said. The table hid exactly how much he liked it, thank God. Simon and Miss Martin had settled into their own conversation and were effectively ignoring everyone else's existence, which was probably for the best.

"My mother always wore scent. You could smell her before you saw her in a room, and it lingered in the air after she left. She claimed it was her signature, but I always found it cloying. After she died, everything she owned still smelled like it for weeks afterward." Emma tucked a strand of hair behind her ear and gave him a sheepish grin. "Sorry. I'm not sure why I told you all that. I don't mean to bore you with my life story."

Under the table, Malachi tightened his finger around hers.

"You're never boring, Emma. Your life story is fascinating. You have nothing to apologize for."

She looked away from him as if uncomfortable with his scrutiny, then offered her cup when their efficient waiter arrived. When she sipped the fresh steaming brew, the line of her shoulders relaxed and she sighed. It *was* decent coffee. A kindred spirit. He brought his own cup to his lips to wet a suddenly dry throat.

This woman tied him in knots, and he wasn't keen on the idea of untangling from her any time soon.

Her finger flexed around his under the table, but she didn't let go.

Chapter Five

Dear Future Lover,
    On days like today, I wonder what kind of
life I'm offering you, if indeed you ever turn
out to be real. I'm doing my best, but the
parlor still smells like burned goat hair, and
my son went to bed without his supper.
                    —Journal entry, June 12, 1824

Parenthood taught one the value of sleep, over and over.

Emma kept her eyes closed, but shifted to make room for Alton's body. If he thought she was still asleep, he might curl up and drift off. Exhaustion threatened to pull her under again as her son squirmed beneath the covers.

It couldn't have been that long since she went to bed. She'd taken some time to peruse the latest issue of *La Belle Assemblée* until the itching under her skin couldn't be denied any longer.

Sitting so close to Mal in a public place where she couldn't act on the needs he stirred up had been a sweet torture. Bay rum and coffee had filled her nostrils, then moved to her memory, where she could later use those sensory phantoms to imagine he was close. Linking fingers and feeling his breath caress her cheek weren't enough. Not when she knew exactly what kind of pleasure those fingers could create. On top of that, the anticipation of seeing him again at the Vanfords' ball left a fizzing sensation in her veins that made her twitchy and restless.

Thankfully, she had Phee's solution to the problem of an empty bed for the foreseeable future. When she and Phee had first moved to Olread Cove, back before Cal showed up and begged convincingly enough for Phee to marry him, Emma discovered her friend's talent for whittling. The rest, as they say, was history.

Roger the Dildo was the result. Long, smooth, thick, and polished with wax to a fine sheen, the best part of Roger was his innate inability to get a woman pregnant. As benefits go, this was pretty compelling for a woman who'd found herself pregnant, unwed, and abandoned by the penis responsible several years ago.

For years, Roger had been enough. Last night, with Mal so fresh in her mind, she'd needed Roger's perfectly formed length three times. The hour grew late before her body would settle down and rest. Wildness paced inside her like a feral animal, until she finally pacified it for one more night.

As her body had cooled from another orgasmic rise and fall, her mind returned to what Mal had said in her drawing room. *I want you in my bed again.*

Tempting as it might be to ponder his words further now that she was awake, she couldn't. Alton wiggled again, tossing from his belly to his back, then rolling to bury his head in her shoulder. Emma slipped her arm under his sturdy little shoulders and held him close.

"Did you use the chamber pot before climbing up here?"

"Yes." His voice wobbled. Not the drowsy response she'd expected.

Emma opened her eyes and tried to make out the pale contours of his face in the darkness. "Did you have a bad dream?" A brush of her thumb over his cheek came away dry.

The head resting on her shoulder nodded, then paused and moved in the other direction. "It wasn't scary. It made me sad."

If it wasn't a scary dream, then she probably didn't need to light the lantern, but she asked anyway. "Do you want the light on while we talk about it?"

He murmured no, then brought the covers up over his shoulders. "I dreamed we were home. Mrs. Shephard made honey cakes and we ate them outside by the cliff on the woolly yellow blanket we keep in the upstairs cupboard. The water was gray with white tops, and the gulls were stealing the cakes from our plates. Polly was shooing them away and we were all laughing."

Their housekeeper made excellent honey cakes. Emma hadn't learned her secret yet, and the older woman refused to give it up. Their maid, Polly, would absolutely chase away the birds in defense of Alton and said honey cakes. The image made her smile into the darkness.

"That sounds like a lovely dream, darling. Why did it make you sad?"

Sniff. "I want to go home. I miss Mrs. Shephard and Polly. And what if Leonard had her babies without us?"

Ah. An echoing ache made itself known near her heart at his words. Yes, she missed Polly and Mrs. Shephard too. The servants were enjoying time with their families while she and Alton were in London. Jimmy, the caretaker, stayed on-site full time to deal with the livestock. And yes, Leonard the goat had probably given birth by now.

If Phee had any idea her pleas for them to stay had won over the chance to see adorable tiny goats bouncing over the lawn, her friend would be insufferable.

"But aren't you enjoying your time with Freddie? It will be months before we see him again."

He shook his head. "Freddie is mean," he said against her skin.

Emma started at that. "What did Freddie do?"

"Tonight he said my papa was dead and I couldn't get another one, because getting a new papa wasn't like getting a new pair of boots after you ruin your old pair, and now he's not my cousin anymore because I hate him." The words tumbled out, one rolling over the other without a breath in between. Purging the explanation seemed to calm him, because Alton quieted on the pillow beside her.

"Oh, little love," Emma whispered. "Frederick should never have said such a callous thing about your papa. We should always try to consider other's feelings, right? You can be upset with him, but he won't stop being your cousin because you're cross."

"All I did was say I wanted a papa like his, because Uncle Cal is capital. Then he said I couldn't just wish for a new one since mine died. But Papa died before I was born, so how is that my fault?"

A dagger through the ribs would be less breathtakingly awful. Emma closed her eyes and tried to breathe through the pain, willing her tears to remain unshed. She'd thought she was doing the right thing when she and Phee had concocted their plan.

Phee had been impersonating her brother, Adam Hardwick, in those days. When Roxbury showed his true colors and left Emma pregnant and alone, she and Phee made their own solution.

Emma married Adam Hardwick on paper, then she and Phee moved to Olread Cove for the pregnancy. While there, they published Adam's death announcement and Phee began again with a new female identity as Adam's cousin, Fiona. Somewhere in there Phee and Cal fell in love, and Emma was able to keep her new best friend around. It worked out beautifully for everyone involved.

Everyone except the sleepless boy in her bed.

"I'm so sorry. Papa dying isn't anyone's fault. Maybe someday we could find a new papa. Who knows what the future holds? At least we have Uncle Cal in the meantime." It was an empty suggestion—she was unlikely to marry again—but a valid distraction. Alton had a wonderful example in his uncle, which lessened the guilt somewhat. It helped to focus on the good. Which in this instance, was her brother.

Alton lived in a world where Adam Hardwick had been a real man. A father who never parented. A newlywed taken from his young bride too soon. While Emma's and Phee's conniving provided legitimacy for Alton, she feared their plan served her more than it did her child.

The freedom of widowhood was hers to enjoy, while Alton walked around with a hole where his idea of a father should be.

"How will a new papa find us if we're not home?"

Emma sighed. Alton's little heart was so tender. She brushed her fingers through his fair hair, the ends sticking up in all directions like soft hedgehog quills.

"I think, if we are to get a new papa, he shall have to find us. If he's meant to be ours, it will all work out." That must have satisfied him, because Alton didn't argue. "Do you want me to walk you back to the nursery? Freddie shall miss you in the morning if he wakes and you're gone."

"Can I stay in here? Pleeeeeeease?"

She rolled her eyes, grateful he couldn't see. "Very well. But the minute you kick me in your sleep, you go back to the nursery. Agreed?" He giggled, then rolled over to face the edge of the bed.

It took her longer than expected to fall asleep again as her mind continued to roll over each word of the conversation with Alton.

Consequences had a way of finding a person. She'd once been a selfish, willful girl. Alton paid the price for that, much as it pained her to admit it. Just as she and Cal had paid for their parents' scandals, affairs, and battles. For all they'd put their children through, their parents had been remarkably uninvolved in actual parenting.

Which was one way she could do better. Be better. As soon as she looked into Alton's eyes, she'd known this was one way she differed from them. Emma would be an involved parent and a loving mother. Her gratitude for Cal's providing a reliable, affectionate role model for her son was bottomless.

A twist of unfamiliar grief rolled through her chest at the thought. No, Father hadn't been a particularly good parent, although he'd loved her in his shallow way. A sigh released some of the tension under her ribs, but no tears came to wash away the lingering ache.

Finally, the soft piggylike snores from beside her lulled her back into dreamland.

In the morning, she awoke when her son jabbed her in the side with what had to be the sharpest little elbows in the country. Rolling away, Emma sat up and glanced over her shoulder at the sleeping little boy. Their conversation in the middle of the night had haunted her dreams, until each one starred a scene in their cottage on the cliff. Homesickness settled around her heart. Before her feet touched the chilly floor, a plan had taken root.

She needed coffee and her brother—preferably in that order. But first, Emma leaned over and gently nudged Alton's shoulder. "Wake up, little love. Momma needs coffee." His face scrunched and his eyes stayed stubbornly closed. "Fine. Be like that. But don't wake up wondering where I am."

"Breakfast room," Alton mumbled.

"Yes, I'll be in the breakfast room." She kissed his cheek and he scrubbed at the spot with a grumpy hand. Donning her wrapper, she padded out the door.

In the hall she stopped the first servant she saw. "Could you tell the nurse that Alton is in my bed? I'm getting breakfast, but he wants to sleep awhile longer."

There. Someone would be there when he woke.

Maybe having an army of servants was convenient after all. This was an informal household, evidenced by Phee and Cal, also in their banyans at the table sipping coffee with twin tired expressions. Or rather, Phee was in a banyan she'd stolen from her husband years ago and refused to give back. Cal loved clothes, so it wasn't a hardship for him to visit his tailor on a legitimate errand to get a new one.

Emma poured a cup of coffee and sat. "Calvin, I remember when you refused to leave your room until you were fully dressed and polished to perfection."

Her brother raised a brow. "That sounds bloody exhausting now. So much effort to appear perfect in my own home."

"It's a good change. I like it. Besides, after the night I had, getting coffee and food is more important than vanity." Emma took her first sip and sighed as the warmth poured through her veins.

"Was Alton restless?" Phee asked as she rose and refilled her plate from the sideboard.

"He's homesick and ended up in my bed. But it gave me an idea I'd like to discuss with you, brother mine."

"I'm on my third cup. We can talk whenever you like," he said.

"I'd like to buy the cottage. I've lived frugally off my dowry interest, as you know. Are the funds accessible as one lump sum? I'm not sure where the Eastly fortune stood when Father passed. Honestly, I don't know the first thing about buying a house."

Phee resumed her seat, holding a plate loaded with toast, fruit, and bacon. As soon as she sat, Cal swiped a piece of her bacon, then held it out of reach until she gave up and let him have it. "I love the idea, Em, but why now? Why not keep renewing your lease?"

"Alton doesn't have an inheritance unless we leave him something, and you have your own family to worry about."

Cal raised a finger and interrupted. "You and Alton *are* my family."

Emma continued as if he hadn't spoken. "If I buy the cottage, at least my son has land and a house when he's older. Besides, I think maintaining his childhood home would go a long way toward helping him feel secure."

"Him, or you?" Phee speared a strawberry off her husband's plate, ignoring the pile of fruit on her own.

Damn Phee's observant nature. Emma blew out a frustrated breath. "Fine, not just Alton. I want to buy the cottage." To have someplace safe to return to if being in London was an unmitigated disaster. To belong somewhere, when it sometimes felt like she didn't fit in anywhere except her little house on the cliff.

Phee nodded and didn't push further. After years of friendship, Emma knew the intent was never to harm, but to shove Emma toward admitting the truth. For her own good, naturally.

Cal sat back, cradling his cup between his hands. "As you often remind me, you're an adult and make your own decisions. If you're sure about buying the house, the capital for your dowry is untouched. I protected it from Father when I took over the accounts a few years ago. Do you want to go through this process yourself, would you like my advice, or would you rather I handle all of it?"

Phee reached over and laid a hand on her husband's arm, then squeezed. A silent look passed between them, and Emma knew enough of their history to interpret it. Cal wanted to take over and fix the situation, but he was trying to give her options, and Phee was praising him without words.

"It's tempting to throw the whole thing in your lap. But I need to do this. It's my house, after all. If you won't mind a bit of hand-holding, I'd appreciate you advising me through each step."

"When would you like to begin?" he asked.

"As soon as possible. I imagine the first thing would be to contact the leasing agent, Mr. Williams, and make an offer, correct?"

Cal smiled. "We can write a letter this morning and make our initial offer. If your landlord is willing to sell, they'll likely counteroffer, and then we'll see where we stand. But you aren't using your dowry to pay for it."

The cup rattled on the table when Emma set it down. "That dowry is my money. I should be allowed to spend it how I wish."

"You live off the interest of the dowry, so I'd rather not touch it. We will pay for it out of Father's estate." A protest rose from deep within her, but Cal cut it off with a hand in the air. "Father was a horse's arse and we both know it. He didn't fund your debut. He didn't even pay for your fancy finishing school—I did. Let him pay for your house. The man owes you."

Silence sat heavily on the table between them, a tangible thing.

"He's dead. He doesn't owe me anything." Now would be a brilliant time to find tears for her father, but besides a tightness in her throat, Emma's eyes remained dry. Goodness, she truly was an unfeeling daughter.

"Let him do this one thing right by you," Cal said. Phee smoothed the groove between his brows with one finger. He caught her hand and kissed her fingertip, then visibly relaxed.

Emma stared down into her cup to avoid the intimacy across

the table. The chances of finding what they had were nil, especially for her. Unable to look away for long, Emma peeked through her lashes at her brother and her best friend. They held hands and continued to eat, completely confident in their place with each other.

When she let herself dream and write to her imaginary lover in her journals, that was what she imagined. The comfort and acceptance.

Since Calvin had found it, Emma knew such a thing was possible despite their upbringing. One difference between them held her back from outright hope: Calvin was a moral person. If anything, he put too much effort into helping others. Fixing their problems.

Fixing *her* problems. Because she wasn't the upright person her brother was. But she was trying to be.

Their parents hadn't been good for much. It was her brother who had always taken care of her—financially, emotionally, socially. Cal cleared the way, ensuring Emma had every opportunity.

"I'll find you later, after we're all dressed, and we can write the leasing agent. Thank you for helping."

"I wonder how much longer we have until the children join us," Phee mused.

Emma shrugged and rose to make a plate for herself. As she sat down again, with breakfast in hand, the echo of young voices carried down the hall, growing louder as they approached.

"You summoned the little devils," Cal muttered, but he was smiling.

"We could make them eat in the nursery," Emma said.

"Where's the fun in that?" Phee asked, opening her arms to the little redheaded boy barreling through the door.

The mood in the room changed when a giant of a man followed Freddie into the breakfast room.

"Ethan? What's wrong?" Cal jumped to his feet, concern etched across his face as he wiped his mouth with a serviette and threw it on the table.

Ethan waved a piece of paper in the air, clenched in his fist. "'Tis deliberate. All of it. The investors. The issues these last few months. Our bad batches of brew. Not a bit o' bad luck after all."

Yesterday in the modiste's shop, Lottie had mentioned a meeting with investors, which must have gone poorly. Claiming deliberate problems was another matter altogether. "Are you talking about sabotage, Ethan?"

The giant Scotsman rounded the table and shoved the paper at Calvin. "Here. Read."

Phee scurried out of her chair to read over her husband's shoulder. Emma kept an eye on them, dividing her attention between the adults and their news, and two mischievous little boys who were stuffing their pockets with breakfast foods.

Emma snapped her fingers at the boys, shaking her head. At least they listened. In part. Evidenced by shoving sausages and bacon in their mouths instead of their pockets.

The other adults, meanwhile, were clustered at the end of the table with the crumpled piece of paper and expressions of concern on their faces.

Emma joined them and asked, "How bad is it?"

"'Tis not good, I can tell you that," Ethan said.

Cal's answer was more concise. "It's a blackmail note. The writer claims responsibility for the issues the brewery has been having, and threatens more extensive damage to the business."

Emma glanced around at the faces. "Unless? You said blackmail. What's the price to make this go away?"

Ethan's face was carefully blank. "Too much. We've worked hard tae make Amesbury Brewing a success. If we pay, it takes us out at the knees. Which means sacrificing the economy of

the village. The locals have only recently begun tae fully trust
Lottie and me."

"You won't be sacrificing anything, Ethan. You're family.
Family takes care of each other. We will deal with this. There
has to be a solution," Cal said.

"Bloody Kent," Phee grumbled. "I don't have any contacts in
Kent near the brewery. If the blackmailer was near the docks,
we'd have information within the day." Phee's league of child
spies and informants served their family well when she and Cal
dug in the underbelly of London for information on their investors. But Lord Amesbury's estate, Woodrest, and the brewery
were in Kent, not the city.

Ethan slumped into a chair, which gave an ominous creek
under the sheer mass of him. "I don' have much choice but tae
ask for help. I hate that. But I can't let the village suffer." A sigh
rattled out of him.

Emma placed a consoling hand on his shoulder. "I'm sorry
this is happening. Does the letter writer give a timeline for
payment or any indication as to why they're doing this?"

Phee plucked the letter from the table and thrust it toward
Emma. Emma's eyes widened. Lordy goodness. Such a hefty
sum, and the blackmailer gave Lord and Lady Amesbury only
one week to come up with it. A single clue as to motivation
came from a vague line at the end of the note. *You'll pay. Either
with funds or with everything you hold dear. The world will
know exactly what you are.*

Chapter Six

❧

I dream of it sometimes, you know. London.
But I miss you more. I've had London, but I
haven't had you.
—Journal entry, January 1, 1824

This was the magic she remembered. At eighteen, the events among the *ton* had an aureate quality to them, as if everything gleamed with the shine of youthful enthusiasm and the undeniable acceptance she'd found in London. That gilded edge had been lacking in visits to Town since, and only partly because she had avoided genteel society.

Until tonight.

Soft music drifted through the rooms of the Vanfords' elegant townhome, carried on the waves of laughter between finely tailored men and women in satin gowns. The tune was vaguely familiar, low to allow conversation, but still loud enough for the dancers to pick their way through waltzes and minuets without straining to keep time.

Champagne sparkled in her glass, and strands of diamonds and citrines glittered from Emma's throat—her mother's necklace she'd borrowed for the evening. Most of her dances were spoken for shortly after arriving. Since every man was a friend of her brother's, single, and respectable, she suspected Calvin was launching a counterattack for her affections after meeting Mal in their drawing room over a week before. Either that, or he was simply being, well, Calvin, and smoothing the way for her first official Season event in years.

"Emma, may I present Lord Mason. Mason and I went to school together and he's heard so much about you." Cal swept a hand toward a decent-looking fellow with very little hair and a bright smile.

Lord Mason bowed over her hand, but didn't go so far as to kiss the top or squeeze her fingers, which she appreciated.

"Lady Emma, I've been looking forward to meeting you. Would you care to dance?"

And so it went.

Lord Mason, cheerful and unassuming.

Lord Dawson, dashing and flirtatious.

Lord Hamilton, light on his feet and attentive to every word she said.

Mr. Percy, shy and endearing.

Her brother was, if nothing else, thorough. As one dance ended and she returned to her original place in the ballroom, the next man stepped forward. By the end of the second dance, she motioned to Cal to pass along the gentleman to Adelaide for the next turn around the room.

Thank God Adelaide could dance, otherwise it would have been an awkward moment for everyone. As it was, Adelaide hadn't taken too kindly to Emma forcibly removing her from the foliage along the edge of the ballroom. Now on her third partner, Adelaide's smile had overtaken the initial discomfort of leaving the cover of the palms and ficus.

Madame Bouvier had created a brilliant confection of a gown from the apricot satin. And as predicted, the rustle of slippery material shot through with gold lent a fantastical quality to gliding around the room on the arm of one eligible man after another.

Emma was curtsying to a dark-haired viscount at the end of a quadrille when it occurred to her that this was only the second time since Alton was born that she didn't have to be a mother for the night. Not in this exact moment, anyway. Alton was home, safe, and able to be tucked away for an hour or two from the forefront of her mind. The one other time she'd handed off her responsibilities to this degree, she'd landed in Mal's arms.

She scanned the room for him, for the tenth time since arriving. No matter who Calvin sent to dance with her, Emma couldn't help being on the lookout for a tall, dark-haired piratical duke who'd told her in no uncertain terms he wanted her back in his bed.

Adelaide met her as she exited the cluster of dancers lining up for the next set. "I'm parched. I don't think I've danced this much in years. Do you want to find the refreshment table with me?"

"I'd be happy to fetch you a glass of punch, ladies," Lord Hamilton said, letting go of Adelaide's arm and stepping away.

Emma stayed him with a gentle touch on his coat sleeve. "No need, milord, but thank you for offering. Miss Martin and I shall find our way."

He stuttered, "Are, are you sure?"

Emma confirmed with her friend through a silent glance, then smiled. "How else do you expect us to steal a moment and discuss what charming company you've been this evening?" She winked and linked her arm with Adelaide's, then headed for the double doors leading out of the ballroom.

"I love not having a chaperone. Being a widow is fantastic," Emma whispered, and Adelaide giggled.

"I can hardly wait to be married so I can do whatever I want. Within reason, of course."

"And what would you do with your day if you had no one to answer to?"

"I'd spend so much more time in the British Museum. I'd get involved with charities—and not by sitting on a committee and donating money. But actually helping. I want to finally matter, if I can say such a thing without sounding maudlin." Adelaide smiled tightly. After a moment, she shook it off, then offered a real grin. "Thank you for passing along your partners. I truly haven't enjoyed an evening so much in years. Maybe ever."

They entered a less populated hall and followed the next rise of noise toward conversations in the refreshment room. There, tables were laden with beverages and bite-size things to nibble. The Vanfords' annual ball was a showcase of elegance and exquisite taste all the way from the decorations to the delicate cakes nearly too beautiful to eat.

"Was there anyone noteworthy tonight? Someone you'd like to encourage?" Emma asked.

Adelaide took a cup of punch from the footman minding the table and sipped.

"You're avoiding looking at me and haven't answered the question." Emma bit her bottom lip to contain her grin. "Did you like one of them? More than Lord Marshall..." She wiggled her eyebrows suggestively. Over the last week, Adelaide had mentioned Mal's friend more than once, and always in glowing terms.

The brunette rolled her eyes. "I haven't seen Lord Marshall

yet. And all those other men are your suitors. I can hardly poach one before you've given them adequate time to win you over."

"I'm not in the market for a husband. And if I was, I'd only need one of them to stick. If I have extras, why not give you the chance to enchant one? Or two. Let them fight a duel over your favors and the last one standing gets your hand," Emma joked, and took her own glass of punch from the footman, who appeared so stone-faced, she had to assume he was pretending he wasn't listening to their exchange.

Adelaide blinked.

"What? If I had an extra set of gloves and you needed gloves, I'd share." Emma shrugged.

"I'm trying to imagine what it's like to have such an excess of interested men that I could compare them to pairs of gloves," Adelaide wondered aloud and Emma snorted.

Behind them, a deep familiar voice said, "Not much difference, really. Like gloves, you can choose color and size, but we all essentially do the same thing."

It would be foolish at this point to be surprised when yet again she'd said something slightly appalling, and the captain appeared to witness it. Her moments of impropriety were like a whistle, and he showed up every time. Then again, he seemed to enjoy when she wasn't a perfect lady.

"Mal, you do have the most fantastic timing." The power of his grin hit her as she turned around. Blinding white against the dark shadow of a beard, loaded with enough mischief that some instinct warned her to run away from the inherent danger of his roguish smile, while the rest of her swayed closer.

After the experiences with Roxbury, she should run. She'd been taken for a fool by a rake once, drawn in by wicked charm. Left pregnant, alone, and rejected. Surely primal instinct should force her to some semblance of self-preservation for her heart.

But then, it wasn't their hearts involved in this budding relationship, was it? Mal hadn't hurt her like Roxbury had, and frankly wouldn't be able to unless she fell in love with him.

To keep heart and body separate, she need only remember that she was her mother's daughter, and therefore cursed in love. So, remove love from the equation.

Besides, putting Mal and Devon Roxbury in the same category felt as wrong as claiming a dog and a fish were brothers. That would make Roxbury the slimy fish, and Mal the dog. It was worth noting—dogs made great pets.

She licked a drop of punch from her lip. Sure enough, his eyes narrowed to stare at her mouth and she smirked in a silent reply. "Are you enjoying the evening, Captain?"

"With you here, things are looking better by the second," he said.

Lord Marshall stepped around Mal, flashing a bright smile. "Oh good, reinforcements have arrived. I've been entertaining him all evening to no avail." It wasn't her imagination when his smile warmed and lingered on Adelaide.

"It's so nice to see you again, Lord Marshall," Adelaide said. Which, for her, was the equivalent of writing "come and get me" on her forehead. Emma dearly hoped he received the message.

Lord Marshall said, "Miss Martin, if you have any dances unspoken for this evening, I'd love to claim one."

Adelaide blushed, but raised her chin. "I have the next dance free, milord."

Setting his glass on the nearest tray, Lord Marshall held out his hand. "Well, then. Shall we?"

Emma and Mal watched the pair leave. Conversations carried on around them, but they stayed silent, facing the open door to the hall and the ballroom beyond. After one moment turned to two, she wondered if he planned to stand there all night saying nothing, like a particularly attractive tree. Body heat radiated toward her, carrying his bay rum scent and igniting sparks in her blood. Lordy goodness, the nearness of him did more for her pulse than dancing with an entire line of men had all night.

She stood there, blood simmering, while he did nothing to earn or merit such a reaction. Finally, she huffed out a sigh and glanced over. At some point, he'd turned to watch her.

"How long have you been staring at me?" she asked, before she thought better of it.

The left side of his mouth quirked up and he arched his scarred eyebrow. She would dearly love to trace that line and ask to hear the story of how he'd received it. In a barroom brawl perhaps, or in battle aboard his ship.

Who was she fooling? The man had probably walked into a door when he was ten, and now made up lies to make the scar sound like a war wound.

"You're still staring," she said.

"I'm wondering how many times I'll need to dance with you and drink tea in your drawing room before you let me kiss you again." It was said so casually, she took an extra moment to fully comprehend his words.

A tingle shivered down her arms. "Do you think about kissing me often, then?"

"Kissing you often, or often think of kissing you?" That damned eyebrow raised again and it did something low in her belly. Sweet Lord, she was becoming aroused by his *eyebrow*.

"Either, I suppose." Her voice trembled, so she gulped her punch until she hit the bottom of the glass. There wasn't supposed to be alcohol in her drink, but the longer he looked at her, clearly in no great hurry to do anything else, the warmer she grew.

"If you're nearby, I'm thinking of kissing you. Right now,

I'm remembering the noises you made when I sucked the skin on your neck beneath your ear, and the way you liked it when I licked the crease at the top of your thigh and hip...and between those thighs." The growled confession made the warmth flare.

If she didn't do something with her hands, she was going to reach out and touch Mal in front of God and everyone. A few steps away, a table was piled high with intricately decorated pastries. When she wandered in that direction, he followed, then stood by as she took her time selecting a tiny cake topped with a candied violet.

Hearing him say such wicked things in public, while pretending to be politely conversing, sent a thrill through her. Like the verbal equivalent of doing those things he mentioned. The way he brushed her back as he leaned around her to pluck a cherry pastry from a towering display made a shiver travel up her spine to the spot on her neck he'd talked about sucking. Oh yes, she knew exactly what spot he'd referred to.

Somehow—one or both of them shifted closer—his arm brushed hers and stayed there, until a brush became a press. The meat of his biceps under the coat cradled her shoulder. Instead of pulling away, she leaned against him. Not enough for anyone in the room to notice. But enough for him to feel it.

"You're awfully bold for a man in a public room, surrounded by the *ton*," she murmured. Every inch of her skin was alive, waiting for the next whisper of stimulation. Mal dipped his head toward her ear and his breath brushed her cheek, sweet with the fruit he'd eaten.

The cake in her hand disappeared in two bites, so she wouldn't turn her head and chase that mouth of his. Next, he'd probably say something else titillating and daring. Emma braced herself for a sensual onslaught of words.

Instead, he said, "You like it."

He was right. She did. The casual press of his arm, the bold, raw, sexual words spoken in low tones while they stood in the middle of a ball, of all places...she liked every bit of it.

A footman passed close enough for her to grab a glass from the tray he held. Champagne, not that she tasted it. Cool liquid chilled her fingers through the crystal and tiny bubbles exploded on her tongue, yet didn't quench the desire building within her.

"If you're bold enough to talk like this, you're bold enough to do something about it. You want to kiss me again? We're at a ball in Mayfair, not a dark garden outside a country assembly or an anonymous inn in the middle of nowhere. There are eyes everywhere, Captain."

"Unlike you, I'm not expected to dance. And except for Simon, I don't want to talk to anyone. So, I've wandered a bit."

"You've poked around in the private rooms, you mean."

"Absolutely. Out this door to the right and around the corner is another hallway. Third door on the left is a study. It isn't locked, but the lights are off to discourage guests."

A tremble rippling the surface of her champagne gave away the excitement coursing through her. Maybe he didn't notice. Schooling her features into a bland mask, Emma scanned the room and said, "When would you expect me to use this information?"

"If you leave first, I'll follow in a few minutes."

He left it at that. The choice was hers. It wasn't much of a decision. If she were a better person, perhaps she'd tussle with it more. Find some moral code to hold her back, or dig deep for the shame she had been taught should be the result of a gently bred lady encountering tingles in her feminine bits.

Shame was certainly familiar, but not something she was particularly fond of. Especially when she knew in her heart of hearts this was why she'd come tonight. She'd hoped to see him, to get more of him. It didn't make sense to keep standing there sipping champagne when she knew damn well that she was going to search for the snug dark room he'd described.

Still, curiosity and a general need to poke at him made her ask, "And if I say no?"

He shrugged, the wool of his coat brushing her bare arm. "Then we stand here and enjoy each other's company. Or we go our separate ways and I'll probably call on you sometime this week."

Emma turned to stare. "You'd still call on me?"

"Of course. Each night, I imagine taking off whatever dress you were wearing when I last saw you. Undoing it button by button." Mal brushed a finger over a blond lace ruffle at her shoulder. "I like this one, by the way. Pinky orange looks good on you."

He grinned, and it reminded her of her earlier comparison to a dog. Had she thought to make him a pet, like some loyal retriever or lap pup? More like a wolf. And her pulse thumped at her neck like a rabbit ready to run.

"Apricot." Her voice was hoarse.

Mal winked. "I like apricots. Especially when they're soft and sweet and the juice drips down your chin."

That wasn't even remotely subtle, but few would describe this tall, broad man with a direct manner as subtle. Judging from the way her thighs clenched at his words, Emma's body was voting yes to what he offered.

Up until now, her merry widow status had been embraced only once. That ended tonight. Without another word, she headed for the door.

There were perfectly nice gentlemen in the ballroom down the hall, along with a brother who would happily introduce her to more if the ones on offer didn't satisfy.

But none of them gave her this rush. Like the delightful

tingling feeling one experienced when one awoke from a long sleep and stretched, and every nerve ending felt like it was smiling.

Was she built for a short affair? She *was* her mother's daughter.

One foot into the hall, Emma glanced back at him, grinned, then turned right.

Chapter Seven

I sometimes wonder if I'll recognize your kiss the first time. Or will the knowledge of you sneak up on me? Shall I be confident in us right away or have to learn the art of loving you, and being loved by you, before I can be fully myself in your arms? Or perhaps I will, indeed, be alone forever. These are the things I ask myself when I'm in bed and the wind howls at my window like a wild animal.

—Journal entry, March 4, 1824

It was the smile that did it for him. The juxtaposition of the merry widow with the society lady, with dimples added... he was done for.

Standing in the middle of the room was a trifle awkward, so Malachi took his drink and leaned against a wall while he counted to one hundred. Which didn't seem long enough to avoid the appearance of him chasing after her like a dog after a bone. So he counted again.

He was revisiting the seventies for a third time, and mentally halfway down the hall toward the lady waiting for him, when a familiar man walked in.

The scoundrel Emma had been quarreling with at the park didn't seem to be faring better this evening. In the light of day, he'd seemed a bit worse for wear around the edges. Tonight, he'd clearly been in the bottle before arriving at the ball. What had she called him? Lord Roxbury.

Roxbury clutched a glass in one hand half full of an amber liquid normally served by the finger width, if Malachi wasn't mistaken. A sway dominated the man's gait, much like a sailor on his first days back ashore. Except, as far as Malachi knew, he hadn't seen the deck of a ship anytime recently.

The man was drowning in drink and wandering about unsupervised. Where were his friends? Everyone should have companions willing to shepherd their acquaintances home when they'd had too much. As if on cue, another inebriated man entered the room and called out. Roxbury stumbled as he turned.

"Damn it all, you spilled my drink, Coswell." Roxbury shook liquor off his hand, then wiped the drops on his coat. The friend taking the blame, although he hadn't touched Roxbury, apologized and whipped out a handkerchief to help, which the other man ignored.

What a mess of a human. And Malachi had dealt with his fair share of drunkards.

He shook his head. Enough of this. Emma was waiting. Malachi pushed off the wall and headed for the door.

"You! Raggedy-looking chap. Where's Emma? I wanna dance."

Malachi paused and spoke over his shoulder. "If you want

a partner, I suggest putting down your glass and looking in the ballroom."

"Ss-is she there?"

"I'm not sure what gave you the idea I'm her keeper, but I assure you, if Lady Emma wished to speak with you, you'd already be talking to her."

"Of course you're her keeper. You're her new *friend*, aren't you? Have you met the little bastard yet? Doesn' even look like me, does he?" Roxbury slurred the words, but the meaning was clear.

In three steps, Mal crossed the room and invaded the man's space. Roxbury might be wide, but so was Malachi. And he not only had several inches of height on the nasty little bugger, but after years of climbing lines and clambering about a ship, his bulk was solid.

This could get one of them kicked out of the Vanfords' home, and fast, so Malachi clenched his hands to stop himself from reacting the way he wished to. Even if he'd love to wrap that damned fussy cravat around his fist and tighten it around Roxbury's neck, Malachi wouldn't lay a single finger on anyone except the gorgeous blonde this worm had just insulted.

"You may be drunk, but that's no excuse for maligning a woman and her child."

Roxbury opened his mouth for what Malachi assumed would be a rebuttal, and a blast of hot alcohol-scented breath hit the air between them.

"You're foul, Roxbury. Inside and out. It's time for you to leave. And if I hear a single word about you spreading your vicious filth about Lady Emma, I'll come for you."

"Is that a threat?" Roxbury puffed up like a cock ready to fight, bumping his chest against Malachi's.

"Damned right it is." Malachi showed his teeth in a growling, almost-smile of anticipation at the idea of taking out this particular piece of rubbish. "And when you wake up tomorrow with a splitting head, I need you to remember this, so concentrate. I have the means to take you to the Baltic Sea, where the wind cuts to the bone and tears freeze on your face." The sound of Roxbury swallowing hard was music to his ears. "When you go overboard, icy water will invade your lungs while you scream for mercy. But you won't find mercy with me."

He turned to the one called Coswell. "Lord Roxbury needs to find his bed. You're responsible for getting him there. Do I make myself clear?"

The red-faced Coswell nodded so vehemently his head was in danger of rolling off his shoulders.

Without another glance, Malachi left the room. But he wasn't a fool. He turned right, then leaned against the wall, putting his body between Roxbury and the hall leading to Emma. Sure enough, after about three minutes Coswell and Roxbury exited the refreshments room.

"No one threatens me," Roxbury slurred, while Coswell tugged him toward the front door. With any luck, their grumblings would be dismissed as drunken nonsense.

As Malachi stood watching the flurry of movement in the front hall with servants fetching hats and accessories for the gentlemen, Coswell checked over his shoulder repeatedly to see if Malachi still had them in his sights.

It was damned near impossible to not examine the things Roxbury had said.

In the park, when Malachi had approached Emma, his goal had been to intercede if needed. He hadn't meant to overhear certain things, and had tried to dismiss them from his memory. Tonight, Roxbury's slurred sludge of words repeated the same troublesome accusations. Even thoroughly intoxicated, he'd stuck to his story, despite his general arseholery.

An entry from the journal he'd found on the beach ran through his mind.

> *I learned young that consistency was an attribute no wise woman should expect from a man. First my fickle father, then the man who ruined me. I still have nightmares about how he laughed when I told him I was expecting. How he claimed he couldn't be sure the baby was his.*
>
> *Yet I can't shake a hope that somewhere out there you exist. And you are trustworthy.*

What were the chances that Emma and the journal writer were one and the same? The question wouldn't go away after thinking it. Olread Cove, where he'd found the book, was a tiny community. He didn't know where Emma lived, but how many unwed mothers with a young son with a name beginning with A could there be in the village?

Except Emma was a respectable widow. He'd heard the tragic story of how her husband passed away before the birth of their son. Surely, if a man were married to a woman like her, he'd react with joy and gratitude when discovering he'd be a father, not the way described in the journal.

Unless someone was lying.

Or Emma wasn't the journal author.

But what if the mysterious writer who'd kept his brain engaged this past voyage and the widow who inflamed his desire were the same woman? Such good fortune would be entirely out of place in the life circumstances in which he found himself.

At the front door, Coswell shot Malachi one more worried glance, then dragged Roxbury out into the night.

Right, then.

Abandoning the casual pose, Malachi slipped around the corner and counted doors in the increasingly dim hallway. The latch clicked under his hand, quietly allowing entrance to the dark room. Leaning against the door to close it, he barely registered her saying, "It took you long enough" before his arms were full of warm vanilla-scented woman.

Roxbury, the Royal Navy, and secrets would have to wait.

ℯ◌

"Honestly, did you go woo a wallflower while I waited—"

Mal's mouth cut off the rest of Emma's words, and then speech felt superfluous. Who needed words when they created their own language of pressing lips, tongues, sighs, and the eager quest of fingers reacquainting themselves with each other?

Emma's bones might have turned to jelly entirely if not for the desire roiling through her. Like flames dancing up a chimney on a windy night, the simmering heat Mal inspired in her flared into an entirely different beast the second they touched. The tips of his fingers were rough against her arms and neck. The sandpapery slide against her skin woke up every nerve ending. Sure, she wanted to eat the man up like a decadent dessert, but she also just wanted those hands to touch her. If she could strip on her bed and have him lightly caress her from head to toe with those working hands, Emma would happily stay there until she expired from contentment.

"God, Emma, you're so soft." His voice was ragged as his fingers slid from her shoulders, tracing her collarbones, thumbs dipping to the tops of her breasts.

It had been so long. Months since their night together, and right now, her body was telling her exactly how many days, weeks, and months she'd been without a man. Especially this man.

Pulling her head back enough to speak, Emma gasped, "You're still leaving soon?"

Mal froze. "That hasn't changed. I'm going back to my ship and you'll return to the coast. Like last time, this isn't forever."

She raised to her tiptoes and then sank back on her heels, enjoying the delicious slide of her body down his hard frame. His erection dug into her belly like an iron pike. Her fingers clutched his biceps, and the wet heat between her thighs demanded satisfaction.

"How long do you think until you leave?" She could enjoy him for a month, then let him go. One blip of time in the grand scheme of things. A short affair.

Mal smoothed his delicious hands over her shoulders, then down her arms. "Probably a few weeks."

Emma ran a finger down the soft bristles of his beard. "Will you give me those weeks? No more. No less. No one else until you leave, then we go our separate ways." The bulge of his Adam's apple fascinated her and she couldn't resist scraping her teeth over it. The responding purr of pleasure vibrated under her lips.

He bent to place an open-mouthed kiss along the side of her neck and growled. "I found the vanilla."

Emma giggled. "Is that a yes, Captain?" Wrapping her arms around his neck, she tried not to squeal when he lifted her off her feet and walked them toward the nearest piece of furniture, which turned out to be a desk. Something tipped, then rolled away and fell to the floor when he sat her on the top. It didn't sound breakable, so any concern disappeared when his mouth moved down her neck, to her shoulder, then to the swells of her breasts above the neckline of her gown.

One of Mal's hands wrapped around her ankle, then slipped under her skirt until he found the ribbon garter and end of her silk stockings. "I won't share you. You won't share me. We walk away satisfied when I return to sea. Those are your terms?"

"Those are my terms. I also expect us to do all we can to prevent pregnancy. I'll take measures during future meetings, but I don't have anything with me tonight. I require your agreement. On this matter I won't budge," Emma said.

His hand traveled higher up her leg and paused on her thigh. "Agreed. I give you my word as an officer and a gentleman."

Emma grinned, then lifted her skirt higher to spread her thighs and make room for his body. "Well then, permission to come aboard, Captain." She caught her breath when he brushed a thumb along the wet slit between her legs.

"Good. Because I have the fiercest craving for apricots."

She laughed, then lost her breath entirely when he knelt and laid an open-mouthed kiss on her most intimate place. Mal kissed with confidence, no matter where he happened to lay his mouth. The man didn't ease into anything. He barreled forward, and her body wasn't prepared for the onslaught of sensation. A shuddering moan finally returned with her gulp of air.

Goodness, he was good at this. Not that she had much to compare him with. Roxbury hadn't been interested in this position. He far preferred to receive than give, which wouldn't surprise anyone who actually knew the man. The one time he'd kissed between her legs had ended with Emma changing position to make him stop. The jab, jab, jab of his tongue had been annoying, not arousing.

Thoughts of her only other lover acted like a splash of cold water, and she stiffened on the desk, while her thighs instinctively tried to close, clamping on the sides of Mal's head.

"Where'd you go, Emma?" His question blew a hot breath of air against her inner thigh.

She blew out a sigh and forced her knees to fall open. "Nowhere you need worry about." Thinking about the cad in her past would have to wait for later, when she wasn't so pleasantly engaged.

"Want me to stop?" His hand slid along her calf, then up her thigh, gently massaging the tension out of her muscles.

"Don't you dare." Emma shook her head so hard, a hairpin fell to the desktop with a tinny *tink*.

Mal placed a gentle kiss on the inside of her knee. "You can stop me at any time. If you're not enjoying it, I'm not enjoying it. Clear?"

She closed her eyes, grateful he likely couldn't see the details of her expression in the low light. Dissecting the utterly foreign sweetness of his statement would have to wait as well. This was about seizing the moment and feeding her body the sensations it desperately craved, not *feelings*. "As clear as crystal, Captain. Now get to work."

His huff of laughter blew against her core. "Aye, aye, ma'am." And he did.

Emma sighed as a wave of pleasure rippled from her core, down to her toes, and up to her chest to settle in a fizzy feeling under her breastbone. Leaning back on her palms, she used the faint light available to watch the dark head between her legs. More shadows than anything, but somehow the lack of sight heightened every other sense.

The musk of her arousal mingled with his bay rum scent and the tang of lemon wood polish from the desk under her.

Mal's tongue did something that sent a lightning bolt to her toes and she gasped. He did it again, then added a gentle scrape of teeth and a flick of his tongue to sooth the slight sting.

Large hands gripped the soft flesh of her inner thighs, keeping her open to his mouth. The pressure holding her to the desk was barely enough for Emma to let go of her carefully guarded control. The illusion of being pinned made her hips soften and her spine go weak, even as her breath shortened into panting little gasps.

For the first time during sex, Emma wished for more light.

She'd like to see if his pale eyes darkened with desire. As it was, she relished the heated breaths against her tender flesh, the luxuriously soft tongue contrasting the firm, long-fingered hands keeping her hips in place. All of it combined to make the tension gather low, shimmering under her skin, until her nerves paused, waiting for one final push over the edge into oblivion.

Mal seemed to know. When he sucked her clitoris lightly, in rapid pulses, it destroyed any remaining calm she might have been clinging to. Even as her bones turned to jelly and her thighs quivered against his ears, Emma refused to stop watching the dark shadow of him until the final quake finished within her.

Slumping back to rest on her elbows, she closed her eyes on a contented sigh, letting her heavy head loll back as the release settled over her like the softest blanket. Lord, she couldn't tell if she wanted to run laps around the garden or sleep for a month.

The soft silk of her skirts shifted to cover her legs, then she heard Mal rise.

"Give me a minute to catch my breath, then it's your turn," she said.

The warm presence of his body overwhelmed her senses. With her eyes closed, Emma focused on the many ways she felt him. His cologne carried on the stir of air as he leaned close, a butterfly-light brush of a kiss on the plump top of one breast, then the smell of her on his lips and the soft bristle of his beard on her chin when he hovered at her mouth, waiting for her to meet his kiss.

They tasted good together. Emma licked into his mouth lazily, welcoming the rise of desire again.

"Can you come to me tonight? I'd hate to meet your brother in the hallway outside your bedroom," he said.

The idea made a snorting laugh burst out, and Emma covered her mouth to call back the indelicate sound. "Cal would kill you. As if he was any better with Phee. But yes, he'd kill you."

If she was going to keep to her plan for the Season and not hide things from her family, she'd probably have to be open about where she spent her nights. Eventually. Maybe. If asked.

That line of thinking made her close her eyes and take a breath. No. No lies to Cal and Phee. Besides, they'd need to be available to run interference with Alton. Because no way would she bring this affair to her bedroom, where her son could wander in and see a strange man in her bed. "I'll come to you. First, I need to leave instructions at home in case Alton wakes and I'm not there." Mal made a grunting noise she took as consent.

"How long do you plan to stay at the ball?" she asked.

"About thirty seconds longer than you. I'll find Simon, say my goodbyes, and we can share a carriage if you like. We'll stop by Hill Street first."

"Then on to your house?"

"Then on to my house. The carriage is at your disposal to return home whenever you choose."

Emma straightened, putting her bodice to rights, although it hadn't shifted too much during their interlude. "I'll tell my family I'm leaving early and meet you out front in ten minutes, shall I?"

She'd reached the door when she paused and turned. "Wait. On second thought, I'll take the family carriage and send it back for Cal and Phee. Give me your direction and I'll take my own transportation to your door later."

That felt right. To not be beholden to anyone to get home whenever she chose. Perhaps by the end of their affair she would be comfortable with him having such power. But now? No thank you.

His kiss acted as a poker stirring the coals on a banked fire, and Emma sighed happily against his lips.

"You go first," he said ruefully. "I need a few more minutes to get my body under control."

Emma grinned, then ran an appreciative hand over the front of his trousers.

"Not helping, milady." He laughed, then gave her another short kiss and nudged her toward the door. "Don't dawdle. I'll see you shortly and we'll finish this."

At the door, she glanced back. "These few weeks will be delicious, Captain."

"Plan on it."

Chapter Eight

⌒

A—'s hair is a sweaty mat on his head, and he simultaneously wants all and none of the blankets on him. Nothing satisfies his discomfort. This terror as a parent is overwhelming. I'm so awfully aware of my loneliness tonight. Which is why I write this by the light of a single candle as I sit at his bedside. I need someone to write to. In this way, you can be scared with me.

—Journal entry, April 3, 1824

The lingering effects of the release she'd had at the efforts of Mal's talented mouth fizzed under her skin like bubbles in her blood.

Charles the footman opened the carriage door and offered his hand down to the steps. "Welcome home, Lady Emma."

"Thank you, Charles. Could you make sure the staff eats before returning the coach to the Vanfords'?"

Charles nodded. "Of course."

Inside the hall, the butler took her outerwear.

"I trust it's been an uneventful evening, Higgins?"

"I wish I could say so, Lady Emma. I believe Nelson has a more thorough briefing of tonight's events when you go upstairs."

That didn't sound good. Emma picked up her hem and took the stairs at a run. Surely if there'd been an emergency, the staff would have sent word to the ball. No amount of dancing, punch, and desktop liaisons were more important than Alton and Freddie.

The mother in her wanted to call down the hall so she could get a report a few seconds sooner. But the *smart* mother in her noted the late hour and didn't want to wake children who should be sleeping—and apparently had enjoyed an eventful evening themselves.

As it was, the footman met her at the door. "They're sleeping now, but they've been asleep for only about a half hour," he said, closing the door behind him so they could speak in the hall.

"What happened?" Emma clutched her hands together, knitting her fingers around one another at her waist. "How is Alton?"

"We think it was the fish," Nelson said.

Emma paused. "The fish?" The meaning settled over her and she curled her lip.

Nelson grimaced. "Quite right. The staff and nursery ate fish this evening, and several members of the house have spent the night indisposed."

"I take it you didn't eat the fish tonight."

"No, milady. I'm a butcher's son. I'll take a slab of beef any day, but I've never been fond of fish." Nelson paused, listened at the door, then resumed speaking. "Miss Lacey is down with it as well. I sent her to bed a couple hours ago and stepped in."

Things must be rough if the nurse was abandoning her post.

Emma closed her eyes and tried to take a calming breath. "I'm so glad you were here. How are they now?"

"Their stomachs are empty at this point. Alton and Freddie teamed up as usual and comforted each other through it all. I was going to send word to the Vanfords', but then they finally nodded off."

"Thank you for taking care of everyone up here. Give me a moment to change out of this gown, and then I'll take over for the night."

Emma hurried back to her room, shedding the layers of her evening wear as soon as the door closed behind her. It wasn't until she'd changed into a comfortable old cotton dress and warm wrapper that she remembered Mal.

"Damn, drat, and double damn." Her shoulders slumped and she stared at the ceiling. Huffing a sigh, she grabbed a sheet of paper and dashed off a quick note. No matter how long or short their acquaintance, Mal would have to learn he wasn't the top priority in her life. Alton would always come first.

Back in the nursery, Emma closed the door behind her softly so as to not disturb the boys sleeping in their slim beds by the far wall. Nelson stepped into the room from the direction of Miss Lacey's chamber.

"Everyone's asleep. Let's hope they stay that way," he whispered.

"Find your bed for the night, Nelson. But could you please ask Higgins to send this out before retiring?" She handed over the folded missive with Mal's direction inked on the front.

"Happy to, milady." Nelson tucked the letter in his pocket and bid her good night.

Emma waited until the door closed again before darting to Alton's bedside. The half-moon fans of his dark lashes rested against pale, chubby cheeks and she smiled. He was beautiful;

her heart never failed to flutter in her chest at the sight of him sleeping so peacefully. A tuft of wheat-colored hair stuck straight up in front, and one arm had been flung over his head. She tugged the blanket up under his chin, and he stirred.

"Mama?"

"Shh, little love. I'm here now."

"Feel icky, Mama. I don't like fish."

An entirely inappropriate chuckle threatened to break free, but Emma managed to stifle it. "No, I don't imagine you'll want fish for a while after this. How does your belly feel now?"

His eyes drifted closed and he spoke through a yawn. "Better now. Nelson gave us ginger candies."

God bless Nelson. "Try to rest. We'd hate to wake Freddie."

"Freddie spewed two times after my last one. He won," Alton said, half asleep already.

The laugh burst out and Emma slapped a hand over her mouth. They'd kept score how many times they'd vomited. Of course they had. Because boys. Attempting to not giggle, she said, "In this competition, I'm glad you fell behind. Now sleep. I'll be right here if you need me."

Miss Lacey's bedchamber was in an adjoining room, but they kept a sleeping cot in the corner for circumstances exactly like this one. Emma gathered a pillow and blanket from the cupboard and made herself a bed. Alton's breathing settled back into dreamland, and little Freddie hadn't stirred since she'd arrived. When she checked on him, Phee's son lay sprawled on his belly, full lips slightly open on a tiny snore, and one arm hanging off the bed with fingertips clutching the rim of a metal basin.

Fish. Ugh. Nelson deserved a raise.

Hours later, Emma jerked upright on the cot, sending the soft quilt tumbling to the floor. Pushing her hair off her face, she panted, finding her way back to true awareness.

The dream didn't terrorize her often, but when it did, the

scene played out the same way. If the nightmare were simply a mashup of her fears, it might be easier to shake off. Instead, this memory wormed past her defenses when she slept.

Across the room, gentle snores rose from the two boys. Pale light illuminated the yellow curtains, setting the room alight with a glow, disguising the exact hour beyond a general impression of "early." Emma's breath wheezed as she tried to wrestle the dream back into the corner of her mind where such memories lived.

Yet the scene remained. Pushing Phee's uncle Milton away, yelling for him to get his hands off her while Alton fluttered in her womb, then the resulting crack of his skull against the heavy wood desk—the sound had reverberated through the dream like a gunshot, jolting her awake.

Killing a man in self-defense was still killing a man. Calvin and Phee had barged in a second later, in time to see the life drain from Milton's eyes. This secret, like the truth about her marriage and Alton's paternity, were burdens.

Before she'd fully considered the matter, Emma's feet were carrying her to the door, then down the hall, then through the dressing room of the master's chambers. Listening at the door to ensure she didn't walk in on something embarrassing, Emma waited to make sure the room was silent before knocking gently. She counted to ten slowly just in case, then knocked again as she eased the door open.

In the bedroom, early morning light sliced through the narrow gaps in the curtains, revealing enough of the room for Emma to find her way to the massive bed. Calvin always slept between the door and his wife, so Emma made her way around the foot of the four-poster bed to the other side. Phee's wild red curls were a stark contrast against the pale pillow.

"Pst. Phee. Phee, wake up."

Her closest friend in the world cracked open one eye. "It's

early, Em. What's wrong?" With a strong blink, Phee bolted awake. "Is it the boys? I checked on them when we came home, but you were already sleeping with them. Are they all right?"

Emma touched Phee's shoulder to calm the maternal panic. "They're resting comfortably. I'm not, though."

Phee settled back against the pillow. "You had the dream again?"

"Yes. And I can't seem to shake it."

On the far side of the bed, Calvin stirred and said sleepily, "Mmwhoisit?"

"It's me," Emma said.

"Bad dream?" her brother asked, as he'd been asking since she was old enough to toddle down the hall to his room after a nightmare. Going to her parents had never been an option. But Calvin? He'd always been there. And now Phee was too.

"Mm-hmm," Emma's breath caught on the affirmation. These two, the other guardians of her secrets, were such a gift. No need to elaborate, or to relive it, or to explain. They just knew.

Phee shifted over in the bed closer to her husband. Cal rolled to face them, then slid an arm around his wife, snuggling her close and resting his chin on Phee's shoulder. "Milton again?"

Emma flung a wrapper and a wooden duck off the nearest chair, then grabbed a lap blanket off the footboard of the bed. Tucking the blanket around herself, she settled into the chair and rested her feet on the mattress. "I'm not sure why. It's been ages since that bastard has haunted me. But this time it looped over and over. The sound of him hitting the desk was so loud, it woke me."

"Did you do anything out of the ordinary tonight? Anything to spark the memory?" Phee asked.

Emma searched her mind. Out of the ordinary? Well, she'd been on a desk herself—climaxing with a man's face between her legs. "Uh, I kissed Mal. Lord Trenton, I mean. More than kissed him."

"I thought you said your visit to the inn last autumn was only a one-night thing?" Phee asked.

Cal groaned. "That's my cue to go get coffee."

Phee wiggled her eyebrows at Emma and they giggled, like little girls telling secrets.

"You're comfortable with me talking of killing a man, but not sleeping with one, brother mine?"

Cal shrugged into his banyan and cinched the tie closed. "The difference here is that I've already disposed of the body of one man in question. Frankly, the pirate is a behemoth and would be an absolute beast to get rid of." Cal gave Phee a short and sweet buss loaded with affection. "Phee, my love, I leave you to talk about boys without my judgmental presence. I'll return with coffee shortly."

The door closed behind him, and Phee sighed. "I love that man. Now, tell me all about your captain. Was last night the beginning of something or were you merely scratching an itch? *Again.*"

Remembering the thrill of having the burly sea captain alone in a dark room, Emma grinned. "A little of both, I think. He's in town for only a few weeks. We've agreed to enjoy each other while he's here."

"You had fun last night?" Phee asked.

A warm sensation crept through Emma and she sighed. "I did. For the first time in years, I felt the magic I remember from my debut. The gentlemen lined up to dance with me, I had you and Adelaide to laugh with, and Mal quite turned my head. The night was going to end with me in his bed, but when I returned home the boys were ill."

Phee was quiet a moment. "I wonder if that's the answer."

"Vomiting children are rarely the answer to anything, Phee."

Her friend nudged Emma's toes with a grin. "No, silly. You enjoyed yourself. Like you used to before Roxbury, before Alton. Before Milton. I wonder if the guilt you harbor served up the nightmare in an attempt to kill your joy."

Emma stared up at the dark, plaster ceiling. "The theory has merit." Phee would know. Not only had she been there the day Milton met his end, but Phee carried her own burden of guilt over accidentally pushing her brother out of a rowboat when they were children. Her brother, Adam, had drowned that fateful day and set Phee on a path that eventually led to Calvin.

What if it wasn't only the guilt? What if it was her fear of making all the wrong choices *again*, and her mind was warning her of dire consequences? After all, her parents had never learned their lesson. Never learned to do or be better than their endless cycle of passionate declarations of love, then the inevitable yelling, name calling, and dramatic parting when one or both of them betrayed the other. Over and over, never caring who they hurt or embarrassed as they chased their sexual desires with the focus of a dog after a rabbit.

When Emma debuted, she'd taken one look at Devon Roxbury's wide shoulders and confident grin and had proceeded to lie to everyone who loved her while she snuck around with a man they'd all warned her against. And for what? He'd shamed and abandoned her when their activities caught up with them. Like her parents, she'd fled and lied some more to hide her pregnancy. In the process, Milton had found them, and now years later he still haunted her. "Does the guilt ever lessen?"

Phee's sigh was loud in the quiet room. "It changes. You need to forgive yourself. Not only was it self-defense, but he tripped. Knocking his head on a desk was sheer awful luck. And it goes without saying, Milton deserved worse than an accidental death."

He had been an awful man. "How would you have preferred your uncle die?"

"Pecked to death by ducks."

Emma snorted at the image.

When Phee continued, her voice held a smile. "Covered in honey and staked out in the sun atop an anthill. Stung a million times by wasps until his body swelled up like a balloon."

Emma laughed outright. "Good lord, you're a bloodthirsty wench." The laughter subsided. "We're awful to find humor in this, aren't we?"

"Gallows humor helps to deal with the situation, I think. Milton was a horrible human being. He deserved to die for his sins. And I'm grateful he's dead. You need to forgive yourself. Be happy. Allow yourself to be the belle of the ball and kiss a handsome man."

"How about allowing myself to be thoroughly compromised atop a desk in a dark room at the ball?"

"Oh, well done, you. I take it Roger is doomed to rattle about all alone in his drawer for a while?"

"Lord, I hope so." Emma sighed contentedly and rolled her head on the back of the chair to look at Phee. "Have I thanked you recently for being the best friend a woman could ask for?"

"Not nearly often enough. Feel free to sing my praises until your voice goes hoarse."

The bedroom door opened and Cal entered, pushing a cart. "Are we done talking about boys?"

"Yes, now we're discussing dildos," Phee said.

"Sweet Christ, help me." Cal shook his head and closed the door behind him. "I brought coffee and irritated the staff by insisting I do it myself. Didn't want to risk a servant overhearing you two."

"Annoyed the household staff *and* talked about boys? All in all, a morning well spent." Emma flung off the blanket and poured herself a cup of coffee, then took a bracing sip. "Different topic. Any word on the situation with the brewery? The deadline is today, isn't it? Besides seeing you and Ethan hiding in your library more often, I haven't heard anything since the Amesburys got the note. What could someone possibly have to hold over Lottie's and Ethan's heads?"

Phee and Cal exchanged a look, and a ripple of alarm raced up her spine. "What is it? What don't I know?"

Cal poured himself a cup of coffee and another for his wife, avoiding Emma's gaze. "They lost another investor. Three days ago."

A curl of unease sent goose pimples over her skin. "How big of an investor?"

"Significant," her brother said. "This blackmailer, whoever he is, means business. As we understand it, the investor received a letter full of accusations and slander, destroying their faith in Lottie and Ethan. Whatever this is about, it's personal. Ethan and I are meeting with the gentleman today. We will attempt to change his mind. Perhaps then we will have a better grasp of what we are dealing with."

"You're going to pay the blackmailer, aren't you?" Emma asked, already knowing the answer because she knew her brother.

Cal climbed back into bed, holding his coffee cup aloft as he settled next to Phee against his pillows. "Paying to make problems go away and hide scandals is what I did for years. However, this doesn't strike me as a single-payment situation."

"But?" Emma moved to the foot of the bed, and Cal shifted his feet to make room for her.

"But, yes. I am going to pay this once. Ethan is livid about the whole thing, but without more time to determine the full scope of what we're up against, we can't make it go away. I'm buying us time."

Emma and Phee exchanged a glance. "Is there anything we can do? We will help however we can," Emma said.

Her brother smiled, but it didn't have his usual carefree air. "If I think of anything you can do, I'll certainly let you know."

Draining her coffee cup, Emma stood. "Thank you. I'll go check on our boys." She crossed the room but stopped at the door. "I love you both, you know. Thank you for everything."

"We love you too, Em. Once I finish this first cup and kiss my wife properly, we will join you in the nursery. I told Cook to give them only porridge until their bellies are settled."

Emma closed the door behind her and smiled at the muffled sound of Phee's laugh coming from the room. Sighing, she returned to the nursery, wrinkling her nose at the lingering, faint odor. Ugh. Fish.

Chapter Nine

❧

I received a letter from London today. How I
ever managed without a sister, I don't know.
P— brightens my days immeasurably—even
if I do have to share her with my brother.
　　　　　　　　—Journal entry, August 6, 1824

Malachi wasn't in a foul mood per se. Because pouting about a woman prioritizing her sick child over shagging him would be the move of a lout. But the disappointment was there. The concern over the sick child was there as well, wrestling with a disconcerting annoyance over the fact that although he knew Emma's taste, and could recognize the noises she made when she came apart, he wasn't entitled to know if her son had recovered.

The lad had been with them in Hyde Park for mere moments, a couple weeks ago, but Malachi cared about Alton's well-being because he cared about Emma. Even though thinking of her in her role as a mother caused an entirely different sensation in his chest from when he merely considered her charms as a woman. The soft ooze of sentimentality was such a striking contrast to how Malachi thought of his own mother. Who, conveniently, had planned to be out most of the afternoon on calls. After Simon sent a note this morning reporting no change in Malachi's status with the Admiralty, Malachi became even more determined to find that damned book and turn it over to the Royal Navy and leave London in his wake. All of the petitions, urgent requests, and the accompanying stack of paperwork hadn't moved him any closer to returning to the *Athena* and his men.

As he searched the house, a gnawing unease churned in his gut. What he'd labeled as disappointment at the canceled rendezvous with Emma didn't go away. In fact, the longer he tried to ignore it and keep busy, the worse it got.

Sun streamed through the window of the study, spilling gold light over the honeyed wood of the desk. Malachi rested his hands on his hips and surveyed the shelves. But instead of books, his brain rolled over thoughts of Emma. With a sigh, he tilted his head back and stared at the ceiling.

Fine. There was some conflict here, but nothing he couldn't manage.

Yes, he wanted to get back to sea. Of course he did. The Royal Navy was his life. All he knew, and he was damn good at it—unlike the flailing incompetence he'd likely exhibit as a duke. The men who'd worked in this room for decades had been raised for this. Trained, educated, and prepared to sacrifice their dreams in service to the title.

The fact that he couldn't imagine spending his days in this room, or sacrificing a damned thing for the dukedom, only reinforced the truth he had already accepted.

He was never supposed to be Trenton. He knew it. His mother knew it. Now if he could convince the Admiralty, that would be grand.

Amid that darkness, the one shining light was Emma. They'd begun something last night.

There was more conflict. But as he mulled it over, some of the tension in his gut eased. He blew out a sigh and let the feelings come.

Truth: Malachi needed his command back.

Second truth: he wanted time with Emma—more than one night.

Third truth: getting one meant losing or delaying the other.

There was no simple solution he could see. No clear way forward beyond doing what he could with the time given.

And today, that meant searching the study again.

That damn book had to be in the house. It had to be.

In this room, Malachi felt like an interloper in a way he didn't anywhere else in the house. Grief was impossible to hide from here.

George was everywhere. Notes in his hand scattered over the desk. A stack of books he'd last read rested in a basket near the closest bookshelf. Mother had told the staff to leave the room alone, except for the basic dusting needed to keep the fine layer of coal in the London air from settling on the furniture. Not knowing what else to do, Malachi inspected the basket of books, then found their places on the shelves. On the far wall, beside the globe, their ancient atlas stood open to the two-page world map.

As Malachi ran a finger over the familiar image, he noted the faint pencil checks over the cities where they'd traveled as a family.

Madrid had been a wonderful time.

The post in Calais had been short-lived because of Napoleon.

Athens had been pleasure, not business. Weeks spent rambling with his brother over sun-bleached ruins etched against impossibly blue skies.

A town on the western English coast was marked in ink, and
Malachi smiled. That trip, just Father, him, and George, had
been idyllic. Imagining George circling the town in ink made a
warmth bloom in his chest.

"Yes, George, that place was special. I'm glad you thought
so too," he murmured.

George might have been a bit of an uptight perfectionist, but
he'd been a good brother. A good man. A good duke.

Malachi was a captain. George was Trenton. To take his
brother's title felt wrong in every way.

With a shaky finger, Malachi flipped the pages of the atlas over
until he found the map of the Baltic region. As before, pencil
checks showed where Father served in the diplomatic office.
Except there were additional marks where the family hadn't
been stationed. All coastal towns, following the edge of the sea,
then along the waterway to the North Sea and Atlantic.

They'd never been stationed along the coastline of Sweden.
But Malachi had taken port there several times. He'd posted
regular letters home to his brother, sent from whatever water-
front town he'd been closest to. With new eyes, Malachi studied
the map and its many checkmarks. Slowly, a ball of grief
loosened in his chest, replaced by a bittersweet ache. George
had tracked his voyages.

His brother had loved to travel, but once their mother
returned to London after Father passed away, George's world
had been reduced to this atlas, books, and these four wood-
paneled walls.

And Malachi's letters, apparently.

Sitting in this study living vicariously through letters was an
awful thought. And if he didn't convince the Admiralty to let him
return to the *Athena*, his life might end up exactly like that.

Closing the atlas, Malachi went to work searching the drawers of the desk.

The task was tedious, monotonous, and methodical. Every seam of every drawer needed to be inspected. Each book had to be opened, searched, and replaced.

After a solid half hour of carefully setting each item back exactly in its previous location, it dawned on Malachi that he didn't need to hide his tracks. Technically, this was his study now. These books and this desk belonged to him. It still felt wrong to claim the space. Especially when he didn't want it, or anything it entailed.

He rubbed a palm over his beard and shoved his hair back. Patting his waistcoat, he curled his lip. Damn. The scrap of ribbon he usually kept at hand to tie his hair back was gone. The wide, shallow drawer in the middle of the desk had some bits and bobs rattling about, and a black leather-bound volume with gold foil edges at the corners. The drawer didn't offer up a useful piece of string, but the black book had a red ribbon marker inside he could appropriate for the task. As he reached for it, excitement teased the edges of his fingers. Was this the bank book? Had it been here in this desk all along?

He flipped open to the page with the ribbon and read. Disappointment replaced hope. George's writing filled each page in what appeared to be the world's most boring journal. A business diary, perhaps? Malachi scrunched his brow. Why would a man need a record of which Monday in September he'd paid the butcher, when the account books were *right there* with the same information? Leave it to George to double up on the record keeping. At least his brother hadn't left Malachi with a financial disaster to reconcile.

Taking a seat at the desk, he tugged the ribbon free and tied back his hair, then flipped to the middle of the book to read a few more pages. Dull and not terribly noteworthy, overall. These pages would be his life if he couldn't convince the Royal Navy to give him back his ship.

Yet, these neatly documented pages were a reflection of
George's world, just as the atlas was Malachi's. Here and there
a personal note jumped out, warm and lifelike amid the dry
recording of business tasks and chores.

An amusing line about a conversation at a dinner with Lady
Amesbury and Lady Carlyle last year. Lady Carlyle, wife to
Emma's brother, would now be Lady Eastly. Strange, and yet not
unexpected that they socialized in the same circles. "Charming,
hilarious, and genuinely good" was how George had described
the women.

Earlier in the spring, George's horse, Gallant, threw a shoe in
the park, resulting in a grousing line beside the farrier appointment record. The expense was annotated with a complaint of
his horse needing heavier shoes with which to step on him.
Malachi grinned, but it faded when he skipped a few pages and
ran across another appointment record.

In May of last year, George had visited his solicitor and
drawn up a new will. Good thing he had, as tragically, the will
had been needed within a year.

At the bottom of the page, George had written a single line.
Father's secrets die with me.

The house was too quiet. At sea, there was always noise. Even
if it was merely the constant *shush* of waves, there were noises.
Usually there were snores from the sailors off shift belowdecks,
footsteps, rumbling laughter, and curses from the men. And that
wasn't even factoring in the crying gulls adding to the overall
sounds of the sea.

This house? Silent as a tomb. The lease included staff, but
other than maintaining the house and keeping the larder full,
Malachi didn't need them—much to the consternation of the

housekeeper. For the first week, she'd waddled around muttering about feral bachelors, but now focused on managing the staff schedule. As long as Malachi held the lease, the servants had more frequent days off, and absolutely no one was upset about that.

After leaving the Trenton town house he'd made yet another fruitless visit to the government buildings. Admiral Sorkin's secretary had been firm in his assertion that no earlier appointment was available, then promised again to send word to Malachi's residence if the schedule changed.

He'd ducked into his solicitor's office, but the man had been out. When Malachi had thrown the Trenton title around and demanded a meeting, the assistant had offered an appointment for later in the day.

All Malachi had to do was wait at home until then. Which was all well and good, but the only sound in the sitting room was his own breathing, and that was beginning to get on his nerves.

A messenger arrived with a note, and he welcomed the interruption. The wax seal hadn't been stamped, so when he broke it, the blob of dried wax fell to the carpet. Out of habit, Malachi squatted to pick up the wax and throw it away as his eyes scanned to the signature.

Emma. He settled onto the carpet with a thud and read the note through, then studied it a second and third time.

Alton was much recovered and should be completely fine by tomorrow. She was looking forward to spending time alone with Malachi, and would he mind if she stopped by after her son went to bed?

All of that was well and good, but wasn't what stole his breath. Disappointment had distracted him last night, but in the light of day, Emma's note was a revelation.

Her penmanship was exactly what one would expect from a finishing-school-educated aristocrat's daughter. Except, because she was Emma, she'd added extra flair to the mundane task of writing. The top of her *S*'s had a loop and the first letter of each new paragraph was slightly overlarge and slanted. Like an ancient illuminated manuscript, awaiting the addition of colorful unicorns or other such fanciful creatures.

Exactly like the journal he'd taken to sea with him. In fact, in the journal, the author occasionally decorated the first letter of a new entry, until the book felt like a combination journal and sketch pad.

"Holy hell," he breathed. Sure, he'd wondered when Roxbury had run his mouth the night before. This was solid, though. In his hand, he held irrefutable proof.

To consider explanations in which Emma and the journal author weren't one and the same seemed silly in light of this.

He knew far more about the lovely widow than she realized, which didn't sit well. The woman was entitled to her secrets, although, granted, she seemed to have more than her fair share.

Malachi stretched out to lie on his back on the thick rug, staring up at the white plaster ceiling as his mind raced.

The journal had documented her life, for her private use, so didn't elaborate on some things she referenced. Reading it had felt like picking up volume two of a novel without reading volume one first.

He had enough information to realize that Lady Emma Hardwick wasn't what she seemed, and that she had reason to keep some things to herself.

That didn't stop him from wanting to know everything. Discovering the author's identity was the culmination of every hour he'd spent poring over those pages while underway. Every stolen bit of honest emotion he'd feasted on between the covers of her journal to comfort himself while alone in the Baltic.

A bark of disbelieving laughter escaped. To think, he'd debated whether he should try to find and reconnect with Emma or to search out the journal's author the next time he was in Olread Cove. He'd lost sleep worrying over what to do with the book, contemplating if the writer might be as enchanting in person as her journal made her out to be.

The journal had seduced his mind months ago, and Emma had seduced his body with one smile. Discovering the women were the same was downright miraculous.

If you'd asked him last week if he'd leave the journal in London when he returned to sea, Malachi would have flatly refused.

Yet now he was planning to leave the journal's author in a few short weeks.

The clock on the mantel chimed, and he sat up off the floor. It wouldn't do to be late to his solicitor's office after demanding an appointment with such high-handedness.

Then tonight, it would just be him, the lovely widow, and the bed upstairs. If the experience lived up to his memories of her, he didn't know what he would do.

The Dukes of Trenton had used the same solicitor for decades. In part because of the man's competency, yes. But Malachi suspected another factor was the aversion of the previous dukes to making sweeping changes. The finances of the estate were sound, because the investments were low risk. The properties were maintained, but rarely had modern conveniences.

He'd have to do something about that. Address the farming methods. Renovate the landholdings. How the hell he was going to do it all from sea, he didn't know. More than likely, it would default to his mother to oversee everything.

Which didn't sit as easily with him as it had a month ago, or even a few hours before, when grief had swamped him in the study. Maybe it was the mischievous little boy in him balking at the idea of handing his mother control of all of his assets.

Mr. Hartfield had an office in an older but clean building close to the heart of the government buildings in London. He'd been in the office for decades, as had his father before him. Mr. Hartfield greeted Malachi formally and offered tea, which he declined. Taking a seat in the office, Malachi withdrew the leather-bound diary he'd found in George's desk.

"What can I do for you today, Your Grace?"

"I'm hoping you can shed some light on something I found in my brother's things."

"I can certainly try. And again, although I've shared my condolences in writing, I'd like to extend them once more in person. Your brother was a good man. He will be deeply missed."

Malachi cleared his throat of the emotion rising there. He'd heard those words dozens of times by this point. One would think he would be used to responding. And yet, every now and then the reality of the loss made it hard to breathe. "Thank you. I appreciate it more than you know. My question comes from a note he made in his business diary. He recorded his last appointment with you when he modified his will. And then, there's this additional line: *Father's secrets die with me.* What did he mean?" Malachi glanced up at Mr. Hartfield.

The solicitor leaned back in his chair and sighed, while the wood squeaked beneath him. "I see. The last duke's unique burial wish was intended to stay between us, Your Grace."

Malachi's eyebrows knit together as a sinking feeling in his gut made itself known. "You mean it's literal? Something was actually buried with him?"

The solicitor's lips tightened, and frustration replaced the sinking feeling.

Malachi bit out, "Need I remind you, my brother is no longer here? While I appreciate the sentiment, as the current Duke of Trenton, I am the one who requires your loyalty and pays your salary."

Mr. Hartfield's lips were white until he sighed out a gusty breath and color returned to them. "I wasn't told the contents. Your brother dropped off a leather satchel to be kept in our safe, with instructions to bury it with him upon his death. I followed his request to the letter and honored his wishes."

Bloody George had actually done it. Malachi pinched the bridge of his nose and tried to find the most pressing question amid his spinning thoughts. "Who else knows about the satchel?"

"Myself, your brother, of course, and the undertaker."

Malachi looked up. "The undertaker prepared the body?"

"Your mother was overcome. Women usually handle these things, but Lady Trenton was beside herself with grief. We hired an undertaker to prepare your brother for the funeral and arrange transport to the family tomb."

Mother didn't realize the bank book was gone. Assuming the book was in the satchel. Malachi sat back, staring at nothing in particular outside the window. Every childhood memory of his parents indicated a partnership between them. Father might have been the one technically in the diplomatic service, but Mother had known what was going on. Perhaps she had enough information to hold over the right people's heads, with no more than the threat of the book's contents. Wielding the right bits of intelligence, one wouldn't actually have to produce documents. Only bluff convincingly.

Which left him to produce the book so Mother wouldn't have proof to carry out whatever threats she'd made. With the powers that be aware of its existence, Malachi didn't expect them to rest until someone produced the book. Either Mother to carry out her blackmail or Malachi to secure orders to return to his men.

"Thank you for your time, Mr. Hartfield."

"Your Grace, there is one other order of business, since you're here." Hartfield lifted a stack of papers, then set them down again before opening two desk drawers and returning to a different stack of papers. "Here it is. I received a letter from your property manager. There's been an offer of purchase on one of your minor holdings. It's in the middle of nowhere, doesn't have a farm or profitable enterprise attached to it. In my professional opinion, you should consider the sale. It certainly wouldn't hurt."

Malachi reached for the offered paper. "How many properties does the estate have, exactly?"

"About a dozen, give or take."

A choked sound escaped his throat as a cough. "A dozen? What the bloody hell do we need with a dozen houses?"

"You own several properties like this one, Your Grace. Leasing a house without the worry of crops or extensive property is easy money. Less responsibility to the estate, higher profits. Our property manager handles the rents and business ends of things. With your father so often an absentee landlord, he molded the estate to be profitable with a different business model than the usual farms and tenants. Items like this do come up occasionally, but overall, we function quite well. Your brother enjoyed the hunt for appropriate properties and expanded on the family holdings. If you wish to pick up where he left off, you need only say so."

"Where's the property?" Malachi asked, skimming the paper. Two familiar words jumped out at him. "Olread Cove? I have a house in Olread Cove?"

"You've heard of it?"

"It's one of my favorite places to visit. Nice village, friendly people. Where is the house exactly?" The cave with his stored retirement plan was in Olread Cove, tucked along the beach where he'd found Emma's journal. A fanciful part of his brain marveled at the many treasures that beach held for him. Emma's thoughts, written in black and white, in addition to treasures gathered from all those years at sea.

If the house was even remotely close to the coastline, it would be a fortuitously convenient location for a residence. Close to his cave and a quiet village he already liked. If it happened to put him close to a certain widow, then even better. Having a place near Emma for his brief times ashore would be perfect.

Of course, should the worst possible scenario happen and his mother prevailed with the Admiralty—he suppressed a wave of cold fear at the thought of never returning to sea—nothing said he had to live in London. The estates could be handled from anywhere. Emma wouldn't appreciate being a consolation prize in his thoughts, but a small part of him couldn't help entertaining a scenario in which he and Emma lived near enough to have a legitimate relationship. Leading where, he wasn't sure. But the idea of seeing her on a regular basis took away some of the dread associated with staying in England.

Which, frankly, should terrify him in itself. What they were doing was short term. There was no way of knowing she would even want to keep seeing him back in the Cove if he was to stick around.

No, best to focus on finding Father's bloody bank book, enjoying the time with Emma, and then going back to the life he'd been building for so many years.

Thankfully, the solicitor yanked him from his thoughts and back to the matter at hand.

"I have a map of the properties somewhere. One moment, while I find it." More shuffling and shifting of papers, opening drawers, and muttered commentary from Hartfield as he located the information in question. A few minutes later, he said, "Here we are. This map notes all of your properties. And this more detailed map—" More shuffling, and Hartfield nearly upended his inkpot. "Ah, here. This shows the location of the Offred Cove property." Malachi handed back the paper from the property manager and exchanged it for the one in the solicitor's hand.

"Olread Cove," Malachi corrected absently, examining the map. By habit, he followed the squiggly line of the coastline, tracing the familiar dips and curves to find his inlet. There, the beach he knew so well, where he'd returned time and time again over the years. According to the map, he owned the property directly above it. "I'll be damned. The house is on the cliffside."

"If that's what the map says, then yes. I'm sure it's a lovely view." Hartfield referenced the paper in his hand. "The same tenant has rented for several years. They've kept the property in fine repair, and have made a generous offer of purchase."

Malachi stared at the paper with the dashed line detailing his ownership of the land above his stash of investment goods.

"They have cash in hand, Your Grace. I suggest you take it."

"Out of the question. Whatever the usual timeline of eviction is, double it. I don't want to greatly inconvenience the tenant with a short notice move. But please notify the property manager. I will not be selling this particular house, and the current resident needs to leave. This will be my primary residence."

Hartfield gaped. "Are you sure? It's several days' travel from London."

Malachi handed the map back. "Quite sure. Is there anything else?"

The solicitor collected himself, then rose and offered his hand. "As always, it's an honor to serve the Trenton estate."

Malachi barely stifled a snort. An honor indeed. Donning his hat, he closed the door behind him and made his way back to the busy street. Carriages rolled by in a congestion of humanity and wheels, while people surged on the street, mixing fine tailoring and ratty handknit shawls.

Olread Cove sounded like heaven right about now. Malachi sighed. If he had to, he could make a home there, and never set foot in London again.

See? He could adapt to life on land if needed. He just didn't want to.

Chapter Ten

Sweep me off my feet with passionate kisses,
kind words, gentle touches, and genuine laugh-
ter. With these things, I vow I'll be content.
                    —Journal entry, October 5, 1824

The Duke of Trenton's residence wasn't what she expected. Emma stood on the street looking up at the house, careful to not let her cloak hood slip off her head. If he'd been plain Captain Harlow, this house wouldn't raise any questions in her mind.

But this? Not in Mayfair. Not ostentatious or even particularly grand. A black painted door with a shiny brass knocker gleamed in the lamplights lining the quiet street. This was a perfectly respectable neighborhood, sure. But an odd choice for a duke. She checked the address he'd written down for her once more.

"Everything all right, miss?" the hackney driver asked.

"Yes. Apologies, I was wool-gathering." Emma paid the

driver, then stepped away from the carriage wheels as he set off down the street. Well, now she'd done it. Gone and committed to this. She took a deep breath and climbed the stairs, then clanged the knocker against the door.

It wasn't fear or doubt making her quake in her walking boots. More like realistic optimistic caution. If such a thing existed in conjunction with excitement.

Back in October, she'd spent the night with him on a whim. A delicious impulse. This was planned. Deliberate. She'd rubbed vanilla on her inner thighs, for him to find later, for goodness' sake. Their first night could be explained as a heat-of-the-moment fluke.

Tonight was a choice.

The door opened, and there he was, in his shirtsleeves and waistcoat.

"Don't you have a butler?" What a silly question. "I'm sorry. That sounded snobbish."

Mal leaned against the door to open it wider, inviting her in. "I keep minimal staff, and gave them the evening off. We can fend for ourselves."

He closed the door behind her as Emma looked around the snug entryway. Honey-gold wood, cream plaster walls, and a stained-glass chandelier nearly took her breath away. "Why, this is lovely."

"You sound shocked." Mal chuckled.

Emma placed her hand on his forearm. "Please don't take offense to that. I guess I'm pleasantly surprised. A person's home says so much about them, I think. And this place could say many wonderful things about you."

He dipped his chin, only slightly mocking. "I will take your comment as a compliment then. Can I help you out of this costume?"

Emma gripped the sides of her hood. "Costume? I thought

it wildly appropriate for a late-night assignation at a bachelor's residence."

He grinned. "Oh indeed. Anyone who saw you knew you were bound for some lucky bachelor's bed." Mal gently spun her by her shoulders one full turn. "I'm checking for a sign on your back saying 'On my way to my lover.' But you chose subtlety there, I suppose."

Emma laughed and stepped back. "I can find another bachelor's lodging if need be, Captain. Since clearly I'm dressed for the occasion." She peeked out from beneath the hood enough to wink.

He didn't appear too concerned at the teasing threat. "And miss out on all the fun we can get up to? How about I hang your cloak and convince you that this is the only man's bed you'll need for a while, milady?"

She unhooked the clasp at her throat and let the cloak slide like water into his hands. "Cocky."

Mal slung the garment over one arm and drew her close. "Confident," he argued, before dropping a light kiss on her lips that left her wanting more.

Which he probably knew, damn the man. It was impossible to not find confidence attractive.

Emma slipped the handle of her reticule over her wrist, taking comfort in her knowledge of the contents as she tugged her gloves off one finger at a time. Contraceptive sponges and the French letters she'd purchased were nestled inside the velvet bag, along with her tinted lip balm. She'd briefly considered bringing her tooth powder, but she didn't plan to sleep here. If all went to plan, she'd enjoy the captain, he'd enjoy her, and she would be in her own bed well before dawn. After all, Alton would wake not long after the sun. While she'd left instructions with Miss Lacey, and Phee knew where she was, Emma didn't want her son to miss her.

She draped one glove over the cloak on Mal's arm, then placed the other glove on top. Holding his gaze, she began to unbutton the pearl accented frogs along the front of her gown, and backed toward the stairs. "I assume this is the direction to your room, Captain?"

"If I say no, do you intend to undress in the foyer?"

Emma grinned wickedly and undid the last button, letting the simply styled gown fall open to show a whisper-thin chemise and embroidered stays. Watching his face, she unpinned her hair, dropping each hairpin into the reticule at her wrist. Those pale eyes followed each movement, lids growing heavy with desire as the pins released a fall of curls. Mal swallowed roughly when she ran a hand through the blond mass so it fell the rest of the way from the coiffure she'd worn to dinner.

Feeling like a siren luring this particular sailor to exactly where she wanted him, Emma shot the captain a wink. His wide chest rose and fell like a bellows, making her fingers itch to explore every inch of him.

As she climbed the staircase, she let the gown slip from her shoulders, then down her back. The fabric fell away from her body, and she caught it in her hand to let it trail behind her. Halfway to the second floor, she heard his grunted curse, then heavy footfalls on the stairs.

Emma nearly giggled. What a rush of power to affect a man in such a way. Lordy goodness, the look on his face before she'd turned to lead the way upstairs. He'd probably follow her through the gates of hell at this very moment, and they'd both have a grand time. Oh, how she'd missed feeling desirable.

At the top of the stairs, she paused, awaiting direction.

"To the right." His gravelly instruction coincided with his long hands gripping her hips. Mal tugged her against him, and Emma gasped when his hardness pressed into her bottom.

The captain wanted her as much as she wanted him, and the knowledge made her giddy with desire.

Emma turned her head and found his lips. It was supposed to be fast—a quick way of reconnecting on the way to the bedchamber. However, Mal didn't seem inclined to stop kissing her anytime soon, and frankly, she couldn't remember why she'd thought a short kiss was such a good idea in the first place.

He tasted divine. Heat, with a trace of brandy and a familiar flavor unique to him. She spun and twined her arms around his neck. With his hands under her bum, he lifted her higher, until her legs wrapped around his waist.

Sucking his bottom lip in a nibbling kiss, she let herself fall into the embrace as he carried her the rest of the way to his room. After a moment she felt a door at her back, then the hard surface gave way, and she raised her head enough to see a bedchamber done in dark wood, with draperies the colors of the sea. Grays and blues in varying hues. The perfect room for a lover of the ocean.

The world tilted as he laid her on the bed and followed her down. Having him so close, the weight of him pushing her deeper into the bed, was absolutely delicious. She wished she could stop time and wallow in the feel of him on top of her. Savor the scrape of his beard against her cheek and the way it sent tingles rippling down her neck as his kisses wandered. Relish the heat along every inch where their bodies met. Welcome the press of his arousal into the valley of her thighs. Instead, she registered each sensation in rapid succession and tried not to let the flood of pleasure overwhelm her.

"Perhaps we can set this down somewhere?" He slipped her reticule from her wrist.

Emma blinked and gathered her wits. "There's a prepared sponge and a French letter inside."

He smiled and dropped a kiss on her lips. "I have a French letter at the ready as well." He set the reticule on a table by the bed, within reach. "Now, I can't deny the view is delicious, but may I remove your stays, Emma? I'm dying to see you."

The rough timbre of his voice was another sensory tease, feeding the desire bubbling within her. At her nod, his long fingers went to work loosening the ties of the garment until she could shimmy out of her chemise and stays entirely.

"Bloody hell, Em. Nothing is lovelier than you," he whispered, and ran his fingertips across the globe of one breast.

When he traced the lines on her stomach left by her pregnancy, Emma studied his face. A slight smile tipped up the corner of his mouth as he took his time reacquainting himself with her body. It was oddly erotic to be nude while he remained fully clothed. But after imagining him so many times over the last months, she couldn't delay the satisfaction of seeing him for a moment longer.

"You're overdressed, Captain."

He made a vague noise, acknowledging what she said, but didn't deviate from his path of brushing his hands and mouth over her body.

"Mal," Emma's voice turned breathy when his lips grazed her hip, then rounded to her inner thigh.

"Do you want me to stop?"

A short laugh burst from her. "No, but I want to touch you as well. Get naked. I've waited long enough to see you."

His grin flashed white against her thigh before he sat back on his heels and stared at her hungrily. Emma propped herself up on her elbows and enjoyed the view of his tanned hands doing as she asked. Unwinding his cravat. Loosening his cuffs. Unbuttoning his waistcoat.

When he tossed the waistcoat in the general direction of a chair against the wall, then tugged his shirt from his breeches,

Emma held up a hand. "Slower. I've imagined this too many times to have you rush now."

"Imagined me naked, have you?" Mal teased, raising his bisected eyebrow.

Emma grinned, utterly unrepentant. "You've lived in my fantasies for a while, Captain."

The smile he gave her heated as he unbuttoned his breeches. "As have you in mine. Did you touch yourself and think of me?"

Emma sat up to caress the long line of his thigh muscle with one hand. Her teeth sank into her lower lip. The flexing bulk of his muscles showed through the fabric of his clothing. The man was utterly delicious. Slipping her hands beneath his shirt, she sighed when her fingers met hot skin and grooves along his torso. When she raised her lips for a kiss, he happily obliged her.

"I have pleasured myself over and over thinking of you." The ripples of muscle and bone under her fingers intrigued her as she pushed his shirt up, then off. Like the first time she'd seen him, she lost her breath.

"You've added to it. That's unexpected."

Mal cocked his head, and it struck her that this was the first time his confidence wavered. "Good unexpected or bad unexpected?"

His body was a piece of art. Not only the physique, which was remarkable in its own right, but the tattoos covering his chest and arms. Golden skin had been transformed into a literal canvas. Yet this canvas wasn't a static display, but a growing thing, as evidenced by the new sea creature inked in his skin.

"You're beautiful, Mal. It's like a storybook, permanently on display." Sea birds, fish, a mermaid who wore nothing but strategically placed swirling tendrils of hair, and the new addition—a creature she didn't recognize. "Is this a unicorn whale?"

He blew out a laugh, and she tore her gaze from the lines

covering his skin to see his eyes. "It's a narwhal. They're real. I've seen them only a few times, but they're remarkable."

"How fascinating. They look like they belong in myths, not our world." The flash of vulnerability she'd seen made her ask, "Were you scared I wouldn't like your new art?"

Mal shrugged one shoulder as if her answer didn't matter to him, which she didn't believe for a moment, then threw the shirt to land near the waistcoat. "I didn't know what to expect. Some people would question why I continue to add new tattoos."

With so much beauty in front of her, her hands had one clear impulse. *Don't stop touching him.* "It's your body, Mal. You own it; I just get to enjoy it. Now come here, and let me." She tugged him down to the bed and lost herself in his kiss.

Tangled limbs, open mouths skimming over skin, and breathy encouragements were all that mattered in the world. His fingers sank into her wetness, bringing a curse from them both.

When Mal dipped his head to suck her nipples, the open front of his breeches allowed easy access for her hand. Wrapping her fingers around his impressive girth made the need within her flare even brighter. "Perhaps now would be a good time for me to get my reticule while you finish getting undressed."

"Excellent idea." Mal went to work pulling his boots off while Emma ducked behind the dressing screen in the corner with sponge in hand.

When she approached the bed a few minutes later, he was waiting with his hands tucked behind his head. She paused to lean against the post at the foot of the mattress. Goodness, he was a sight. Dark beard, overly long hair, wicked grin. Broad, tattooed, aroused. And hers—for now, at least. Emma crawled onto the end of the bed, then kissed her way up his body.

"I could feast on you all night," she said, licking along the dark outline of an ocean wave cresting over one dark nipple.

Mal drew her hair over her shoulder to expose her neck and

pulled her higher. "Likewise. But Em, I'm dying to be inside you." His words were a hoarse confession between kisses along her shoulder to the sensitive place near her ear.

The way her inner walls clenched at his words confirmed Emma's eagerness. Desire burned bright from his expression as she straddled his hips, and she couldn't remember ever feeling more powerful. They inhaled together when he sank deep, then paused for a breathless moment.

A guttural groan sounding vaguely like a curse escaped Mal as his fingers flexed on her hips.

Words and coherent thoughts scattered in the wake of feelings, and for once, Emma didn't mind being out of control. Her head lolled back as she closed her eyes, allowing his hands to guide her movement, letting herself enjoy the sensation of his rough fingertips as they found all the places that made her body climb toward that peak.

When he was too gentle with her nipples, she covered his fingers to show him how she liked to be touched. The breathless words of encouragement he offered pulled her toward the edge. It didn't take long for her to tumble over, free-falling and crying her release as her body milked his.

Then he was rolling them over, sliding out of her to slip down toward her waist and cover her throbbing clitoris with his mouth. It was her turn to swear when his tongue urged her to climb one more time. Trusting him to bring her to climax, Emma let herself go. No working, no thought of how she looked, or what she should be doing. There were only feelings and instincts at the helm. Her inner walls were clenching anew when he plunged inside her once again.

Knitting their fingers together, he pinned her hands over her head in surrender. A random thought of pirates plundering made her grin up at him, and he smiled back, then nipped her bottom lip. It wasn't hard to imagine him on board ship with a cutlass, wind blowing his hair free of its queue—not when his body overwhelmed hers so powerfully.

Lordy, it was glorious. Instead of hurrying, he savored. The man actually slowed, going impossibly deeper, pressing the base of his sex against her, until that heat built again. Again? A shaking took over her inner thighs, and her body answered in the affirmative. Again.

With a relentless, steady pace, Mal pressed close, thrust deep, and carried her to bliss one more time before crying out against her neck and sinking his teeth into her shoulder. The light sting of his love bite made her clench around him and he answered with a moan.

"Holy shi—" he cut himself off with a groan as he rolled his weight to the side.

Breathless, she laughed. "Agreed." Emma turned her head to study the dark sweep of his lashes against his ruddy cheeks. That talented mouth of his hung open, gasping for air, while a relaxed bliss softened his face. As if he'd poured out his tension, his worries, and the cares of the world. Earlier, on the stairs, the power to lure him to bed had been a heady thing, but this? The ability to bestow peace was beautiful.

"I'll need a moment before I can walk," he said, a smile tipping up one corner of his lips.

Emma rolled to curl against him, letting their feet tangle together. "My legs probably wouldn't support me either." She traced the line drawing of a ship across his chest, then followed the inked ocean waves to his shoulder and down his biceps to where they turned into a twirling forest of seaweed and sea creatures. The ink was simple in some areas, more intricate in others. Some of the tattoos were more faded.

"That was from when I made captain and took command." He pointed to the ship on his right pectoral muscle, about three inches long, with tall sails open to catch curlicues of wind.

"And the sea monster under it?"

"Kraken. Always ready to take you under. To remind me to respect the sea; I'm never truly in control out there."

That inherent humility was so appealing. Having seen more than one naval officer strut down Bond Street as if he owned the place, it wasn't hard to admit she preferred Mal's perspective.

The narwhal swam up the inside of one forearm, and a mermaid holding a pearl in her tiny outstretched palm resided on the other.

"The narwhal is my favorite. To think, such a thing swims the seas. It's marvelous. Alton will be thrilled when I tell him."

Mal raised a brow.

"Not about you having one on your body, silly man. Maybe I can find an illustration somewhere, since I know what I'm looking for. He is bound to love the idea of a unicorn whale."

A lazy stroke of his fingertips along her spine nearly made her purr. "Mmm, feels good." Emma sighed, content. The lax relief of her muscles threatened to turn into sleep, and she forced her eyes open.

"Will you tell me about your day?" Mal asked.

A sigh escaped, followed by a yawn. "The boys are recovered from their fish debacle, I'm happy to report."

"Was it awful? Because it sounded awful."

"Mmmmm." His rough fingertips brushed a patch of skin on her shoulder and she shifted, silently asking him to linger there. "The truly horrific part happened while we were at the ball. By the time I got home, it was all over but for the snuggling. I didn't sleep well, between worry over the boys, the hard cot, and then some bad dreams."

"Will your brother arrive in the morning and challenge me to a duel over your honor, by chance?" He dropped a kiss on her shoulder, then flopped his head back on the pillow beside hers. "Not that I'd mind the chance to shoot him. I just want to plan my day."

Emma snorted a laugh against his chest. "He'd choose swords, not pistols. You can clear that worry from your schedule though, because he knows I'm here."

Mal jerked and stared at her. "You told him?"

Muscles tightened across his chest, and Emma couldn't help soothing away the tension with her hand. "I won't lie to my family. Lucky for us, his attention is focused on a situation with investors and a friend's brewery." In the end, Cal had returned cautiously triumphant from the meeting, having convinced the investor of the moral fortitude of Lord and Lady Amesbury. The damned blackmailer still had his money, though, so she had to wonder how much of a win it could be. "How about you? How did you while away the hours until I arrived?"

He shifted, then rolled to face her. "I dealt with my mother."

Emma settled, tucking her hands between the pillow and her cheek. "You mentioned her, but I've heard from others she's—"

"A dragon. She's a dragon with a coronet. And she's keeping me on land so I can marry someone especially fertile and sire strapping boys to carry on the Trenton title."

Emma stiffened. "I beg your pardon?"

He sighed, closing his eyes. "I know. It's ludicrous. But the Admiralty is on her side for now. My ship is dry-docked for maintenance, but my window to get back in command of the *Athena* is closing. I hate to think of it, but I might lose her altogether."

"You really love your ship," she said, aware of a slight pang of jealousy over the way he spoke of the ship as if it were another woman.

Mal was silent for a moment, but not distant by any means.

The weight of his gaze on her face might have been unsettling if not for him tracing the line of her eyebrows and then cheekbone with one fingertip. "My crew has become family. More than my blood kin have been over the years."

"It's understandable that you'll do anything to get back to them."

A pause. "I'll do anything to break free from my mother's manipulations. That's more accurate." He sighed, and the warm breath mingled with hers within the intimate cocoon his bed-chamber had become. Those wonderfully rough fingers ran a path from her shoulder, down her arm, then wrapped her closer until they were pressed front to front.

Tempting as it was to relax entirely into his embrace, it was impossible to miss what his words meant. "You'll be sailing away in no time at all," she reassured him, ignoring the sinking feeling in her stomach. It couldn't be disappointment. She'd fallen into his bed with her eyes wide open to the situation. Before he could respond, she opened her mouth in a giant yawn that began as fake, but quickly turned real. "You wore me out in all the best ways. I need to get home so I can sleep."

His hand on her back paused, then resumed its sweep over her skin. "If you must. I hate to let you go, though."

Emma bit her lip, wanting to ask when she'd see him again. She'd rather not come across as needy, even though everything within her wanted to see if he was as eager as she was to do this again.

"When will I see you again?" he asked.

She laughed. "I wanted to ask, but feared scaring you off with my eagerness."

Mal kissed her and she tasted herself on his lips. "I want you eager for me. Because I can promise, you'll be on my mind every minute until I can have you all to myself again."

Emma relaxed into his arms once more and buried her face in

his chest. "All right. I'll try to get away tomorrow, but I'm not sure how the day shall go. I'll send a note around."

"Then I'll remain flexible and wait for your message." Mal eased away from her to sit on the edge of the bed. He disposed of the French letter, and she knew it was time to go.

Back to the real world. But now she knew the real world held magical things like narwhals, and everything seemed a little brighter.

Chapter Eleven

*I'll never forget the moment I saw Ophelia's
headstone side by side with Adam's. All was
as it should be. Finally. It felt right to honor
him. He was a remarkable young man from
what I hear.*

—Journal entry, September 8, 1824

Adelaide cocked her head. "Rather uninspiring if you
ask me."

Emma turned to see what her friend was talking about, then
slapped a hand over her mouth to stifle the laughter. Alas, the
indelicate sound echoed off the walls of the British Museum and
caught the attention of the rest of their group.

The clicking of Lady Agatha's cane on the floor signaled the
approach of Lottie's godmother, which meant that Lottie and
Phee wouldn't be far behind.

"What are we laughing at?" Lady Agatha asked.

Emma silently pointed at the statue.

Lady Agatha raised a brow. "Poor, poor man. There are dogs more heavily endowed."

The laugh Emma had tried to smother escaped. No doubt, the sculpture was a fine example of Greco-Roman art. Rippling muscles were perfectly defined, polished smooth, and alabaster white. But the subject of their conversation dangling between his legs was... well. Lacking.

Lottie murmured, "It is rather sad looking, isn't it?"

Gesturing toward the statue in question, Adelaide asked, "Is this fellow normal? I mean, he seems rather proud of it. And the sculptor thought it was perfectly adequate."

Phee snorted, not bothering to cover the sound like Emma had. "Don't take this the wrong way, but I've seen a few in my day." Everyone shot a look at Phee, who rolled her eyes. "From my experience, they come in a variety of shapes, sizes, and colors."

"Like hats," Lady Agatha quipped dryly.

Lottie laughed. "Auntie, really." She composed herself into a semiserious face but her eyes still sparkled with mirth. "Miss Martin, we are happy to answer any questions you have. Although I don't have many real-life comparisons"—she glanced over at the statue in question—"my experience has been more inspiring than what the artist has captured in marble."

Adelaide sighed. "That's a relief. Because this..." Her voice faded as she held up a finger, comparing the length to the marble appendage. "Also, if we are to discuss penises, I give you leave to dispense with formalities and call me by my given name."

Emma said, "I've experienced one like this unfortunate chap, and, as Lottie put it so delicately, far more inspiring anatomy."

Having a conversation about penis size while standing in a gallery of the British Museum hadn't been on the agenda today. The British Museum had. In fact, Emma had gathered her favorite women in one place today because she'd needed the distraction.

After leaving Mal's bed in the wee hours of the morning, her emotions had yet to settle. The man upended her equilibrium, albeit in wonderful ways. But this sensation of having gotten in over her head wouldn't go away.

Last night had been passionate, lovely, and more than she'd expected. Mal's talking about his ship shouldn't have made her uneasy. Leaving his bed shouldn't have felt like a loss—not if she was keeping an emotional distance from him. And now here she was discussing his penis. Because what better way to get your mind off your lover, right? Emma stifled a sigh at her own foolishness.

Phee's eyes sharpened. "More inspiring, Em?" She quirked an eyebrow in a silent demand for more details.

Emma glanced around. Thankfully, the hall was empty except for them. "So inspiring. I have no doubt I'll be perfectly content for the next few weeks."

Lady Agatha cackled. "Well done. Who is the lucky gentleman?"

Lottie wagged her eyebrows up and down. "I think our darling Lady Emma has found herself a pirate."

Emma rolled her eyes at Phee. "Good Lord, do you tell her everything?" There was no heat in the question, only exasperated affection.

Phee shrugged. "I knew you wouldn't mind Lottie knowing. Besides, he earned the nickname while doing *her* dirty business."

Lottie said, "There is a certain symmetry to it all. Everything is coming full circle. Rather tidy. And we all know I love tidy."

Adelaide looked at the ladies, shaking her head. "I'm lost in this conversation. I think you're talking about Lord Trenton—who is terribly piratical in all the best ways. But how does he connect to the rest of you?" She waved a hand around the circle of women.

Lottie leaned closer, then everyone else did too, until their faces were mere inches from one another. She whispered, "I had a troublesome suitor several years ago. We needn't go into details, but he was an absolute beast. Emma's Duke of Trenton— who was not a duke then, but a captain—was most helpful in disposing of the suitor in question."

Emma interjected, "A delicate way of saying they paid Mal to ship the bastard off to the penal colonies."

Adelaide's mouth opened in a little O. "That is both the most brilliant and awful thing I've ever heard. Well done."

Lottie grinned. "It was my husband's idea. I wasn't even there. I think Ethan and I were pleasantly engaged in a bedroom somewhere while it happened."

Phee raised her hand. "It was my husband, Cal, Emma's brother, who hired the pirate."

Adelaide nodded, making the connection, then turned to Emma. "And now this man is courting you. Quite successfully from what it sounds like."

Emma started. "Oh, we're not courting. We're merely enjoying one another until he returns to sea." Between leaving his bed and now, she'd slept, played with Alton and Freddie, had a fitting for more wardrobe pieces at Madame Bouvier's, then made a batch of bread and biscuits before meeting her friends here. Yet still, an ache in her muscles and a tenderness in delicate areas ensured she wouldn't have a moment without thinking of Mal.

"Affairs have their time and place. But be sure, child, you don't mistake a man worth marrying for one who is good for nothing beyond an affair," Agatha said, absently polishing the brass head of her cane. With her tall, thin body clad all in black, the older woman made quite a picture.

Marriage? That wasn't something she could think about. Not now. Emma shook her head, perhaps too sharply, and rushed to correct Lady Agatha. "We entered into this arrangement with clear parameters. When he returns to sea, we go our separate ways with smiles on our faces and goodwill in our hearts. Nothing more, nothing less."

Lady Agatha raised an eyebrow, silently compelling Emma to honesty.

She tried not to squirm and continued. "Marriage is not something I'm looking for. What need have I of a husband? Besides, I believe he's already married to *Athena*."

In one movement, each woman turned toward Emma and said, "Athena?"

"Are you telling me that bastard is already married?" Phee demanded.

"I've disposed of one man. We can dispose of another," Lottie growled.

Emma grinned at her friends, who stood with clenched hands, ready to go to war for her. "*Athena* is his ship. He wants to get back to sea. Mal has no desire to be a duke or to live in London."

Lady Agatha tapped her cane on the floor and harumphed. "Fate rarely takes our plans into consideration. Lord Trenton would do well to remember that."

"Has there been a new law written forbidding sea captains from marrying?" Phee asked dryly.

Lottie added, "Like it or not, Lord Trenton holds the title. He has a duty to fulfill. Naval officers marry all the time."

Holding a hand up, Emma spoke. "I like Mal, I truly do. I enjoy him, and I certainly enjoy being in his bed. But I will not act like a simpering ninny over a man, hearing wedding bells where there are none. Not again. I'm determined to enjoy what I have right now, even though it's temporary."

She'd said her piece in a far more clean and concise way than her emotions felt at the moment. The women would pounce on the information if she told them marriage had crossed her mind more than once since seeing him last night, that she worried a couple weeks might not be enough to purge him from her system. Upon waking this morning, the first thought she'd had was to wonder if they couldn't have a sort of long-distance agreement. Then he would be hers when he stopped into port in Olread Cove. A part-time lover, so they didn't have to say goodbye.

"Help us understand. You're willing to take him to bed, but won't consider more. That's rather odd, love," Lottie said.

"I don't need to marry," Emma repeated, keeping her tone bland.

"Of course not. Choosing a partner is always a better option than taking one on out of necessity," Agatha said.

"Don't you…want him?" Adelaide asked.

Emma made a sound that was part laugh, part sigh. "Of course, I want him. He's amusing, and handsome, and wickedly intelligent…"

"And a duke," Lottie said.

Emma felt compelled to defend their situation, although she'd rather not delve too deeply into why. "It's not about the title. I like the way he looks at me. I feel safe, and…wholly myself. I'm not pretending or worrying over manners or being perfect when I'm with him."

"And he's a duke," Phee repeated with a teasing gleam in her eye.

"Does he make you laugh when you're in bed?" Agatha asked.

A warm bubble of happiness rose at the memory. "Yes. He does. It's rather wonderful, actually."

"So what is wrong with him?" Adelaide asked.

At that, the bubble popped. "Nothing, if we're being honest. There's nothing wrong with Mal."

His family had served the king and had borne their coronet without scandal for generations. Unlike her family, who historically had been the main course for every hungry gossip in London. She'd certainly contributed to the notoriety of their name, and if anyone found out all the myriad things she was hiding, her parents' picadilloes would fade in comparison. The previous Lord and Lady Eastly may have hopped through every bed in Town, but to her knowledge, they'd never killed anyone.

No, there wasn't anything wrong with Malachi. *I'm the problem, not him. He deserves better.* No matter how downright magical their night might have been, or how heady thoughts of him were, those were the facts. No man would want her if they knew the truth.

The rhythmic footfalls of boots hitting the marble floor made the women straighten like soldiers coming to attention.

Lady Agatha turned toward the interloper—an innocent bystander who didn't realize what he'd stumbled upon as he wandered into the gallery. The silence grew heavy and the footsteps faltered under the intense gaze of the older woman.

A confused expression crossed his face, and Emma nearly giggled. The poor man had no idea what he'd done to earn such a look. Some primal self-preservation instinct made him stop in his tracks. He bobbed his head, murmured, "Ladies," then turned around and left.

"Smart man," Emma said, turning back to her friends.

Adelaide gazed at Lady Agatha with huge eyes. "I want to be you when I grow up. Such a look. Masterfully done."

Lady Agatha sized up Adelaide with an inspection from head to foot and then back to head before she nodded. "You shall be. Eventually. One word of advice, Miss Martin. Simpering women do not get what they want. They may think they do. But anything easy is rarely satisfying. Complacency will get you nowhere, child."

Adelaide's lips twitched as if she wasn't sure if she was *allowed* to smile or if she was *supposed* to smile.

"In other words"—Emma grinned, setting aside her bitter-sweet thoughts of Mal—"next time Lord Marshall is nearby, let out your inner coquette."

Adelaide bit her lip. "I don't have an inner coquette."

"Every woman does," Lottie said. "It's the part of you that wants to stare when he enters the room or that thinks the naughty thoughts you don't have the courage to say. Those pieces of you are real, and they deserve some time in the sun— with the right partner, of course. It can be as simple as letting him catch you staring and giving a little smile to say you aren't sorry he caught you. If it's Lord Marshall you want, then we shall certainly do our part to give you a chance at catching his attention."

"Lord Marshall?" Phee scrunched her face a moment, then smiled. "Wait. Dark skin, perfect jaw, works in government?"

"Indeed. He dragged Adelaide out of the refreshment room to dance with her the other night," Emma bragged for her friend.

"Then you are halfway there already. Flirt, and be done with it," Lady Agatha said.

"I can't flirt!" Adelaide wailed, then froze when the sound echoed off the walls.

"Nonsense." Lady Agatha's voice bounced off the marble as well, but the older woman didn't appear concerned about it. "If you knew your every word and touch would be welcome, would you be bolder?"

Adelaide shifted from one foot to the other. "I suppose so."

"Well, there you have it." Lady Agatha clearly thought that was enough explanation.

"What my darling godmother means," Lottie said, "is if Lord Marshall is to fall in love with you, you need to let him see the real you. You've caught his attention. If you want more, you'll need to signal you're open to his advances. Let him meet the person you are with your close friends."

"Your suggestion is that I fool my shyness into subsiding. *That's* flirting?" Adelaide said.

"I think for you, it is," Emma said. "I know Saint Alban's taught us flirting was all fan language and fluttering our eyelashes. Your shyness probably makes it all feel terribly awkward and false. Pretend he's a close friend and be the version of yourself you are with me—with us. You'll enchant him more than you already have."

It struck her that the falseness of her training from their finishing school had always felt natural to Emma. Perhaps it should have been a warning sign from the beginning, when she was more comfortable constructing a facade than being authentic. Maybe that's how her mother's conscience had survived so many betrayals over the years. The endless line of affairs and flirtations. After a while Mother hadn't even tried to hide her romantic adventures, because discretion had never been the point. It had been about reacting to Father's last affair, and the two fought, reconciled, and betrayed in a painful cycle. Emma supposed it would be hard to harbor guilt about playing someone false when you yourself were false down to the core.

Honesty. Authenticity. Two ways Emma could be different from her parents. She drew in a breath to tell her friends she wasn't entirely convinced these few weeks would be enough with Mal, but Phee spoke first.

"Speaking from experience," she said, squeezing Adelaide's hand, "there's nothing better than knowing you're loved for who you truly are. We all have some version of a social mask. But the people in our inner circle get to see behind the mask. If you want to let him closer, you'll need to give him a peek."

Emma clamped her mouth closed. If she wanted more from Mal, she needed to give him a glimpse of the real her. The rollicking woman enjoying the assembly rooms in a tiny village was one part—but by no means all of her, any more than her society manners were. Fearing what he'd think if he saw Emma clearly in all of her messy, damaged entirety was another problem. However, it was possible to offer more of herself than she currently was.

Surely she could maintain a part-time lover. A marriage, with the terrifying intimacy expected with it, was too much to contemplate.

Adelaide wandered to the next piece of statuary with Lady Agatha. Emma and the others were following behind when one of their servants hurried down the hall toward them.

"Charles, what is it?" Phee asked.

The footman, clad in pristine livery, bowed. "I apologize for the interruption, milady. We found this in the coach. None of us were aware of a delivery, so I thought it suspicious." Charles held out a piece of paper, no larger than his palm, neatly folded and sealed with a glob of blood-red wax.

Phee reached for it, sending a worried glance at Emma and Lottie. The paper quivered when Phee opened the note, read it, then held it out.

Lottie took the note and read it first. "Oh dear God, not you too," she murmured, and handed it to Emma.

The vaguely familiar handwriting made dread flood her belly. *Not everything can be solved with money. One down, two to go. Who will be next?*

Emma opened her mouth, but Phee hissed. "Shh. Not here. Let's join the others. We'll talk at home."

Farther down the gallery, Lady Agatha commented in her echoing voice, "I have seen enough tiny penises for one day. We should go have tea."

Chapter Twelve

*How can I miss you so intensely, when I
don't even know what you look like?*
—Journal entry, December 4, 1824

his doesn't work!"

The toy wooden boat landed at Emma's feet. She crossed her arms and raised a brow at her son. "Well, it certainly won't work if you throw it about. Should you break your toy, I'm not getting you another. We take care of our things, Alton Hardwick."

He crossed his arms, mimicking her stance, and scrunched his face. The tremble of his bottom lip nearly made her laugh. "It's broken already."

Emma closed her eyes and prayed for patience. The Serpentine wasn't crowded today, thank God, so there were very few nurses and children about to witness her son's tantrum. He'd been like this all day—whiny, complaining about every little thing, with his temper on a hair trigger.

None of which helped with her rapidly disappearing well of

tolerance. Of course, it was possible Alton's temper and her own were fed by the tensions in the house. After receiving the note at the museum yesterday, Ethan and Lottie had been at the house for most of the waking hours talking things over with Cal and Phee. Emma caught bits and pieces of the conversations, and no one was actively excluding her. At the same time, Emma became aware she and Alton were a separate household unto themselves. So far she didn't appear to be in danger from whoever was behind these threats.

Assuming the other person the blackmailer referred to wasn't her. One down, two to go, the note had said.

The couples had brought together the books for all their financial ventures, comparing lists of colleagues they'd both done business with to find a common denominator somewhere. Some clue as to where to begin their search.

No one yelled or was short-tempered with the boys, but the air felt different. Heavier, as if the entire household carried dread with them as they went about their day. Everyone was irritable or distracted, right down to the miniature humans in their care.

A horrible feeling of impotence made Emma twitchy. She couldn't do a damn thing to help her brother, but at least she could help Alton. Children were simple in some ways, and in this, she knew what her son needed. His mood could be mended with a run. Back home, he'd clamber up and down the cliff trail by their cottage and frolic on the beach while yelling at the top of his lungs like the absolute heathen he was.

Here, they had to settle for a walk to the park—which was far enough away for him to complain about the distance, but not enough to actually tire him out. Alton had brought the toy boat with him, tucked in a basket of odds and ends Miss Lacey had packed for the outing.

"What do you mean when you say it doesn't work? It floats fine."

"But it doesn't run away. The sail isn't moving."

Emma squatted next to him, adjusting the brim of her bonnet to shade her eyes from the sun. "Darling, that's because it is not a breezy day. A sailboat requires wind to move. Besides, if it were to sail off down the Serpentine, you'd never see it again. Do you want to lose your toy?"

His shoulders slumped as he stooped and picked up the abandoned boat by her slipper. "I'll try it again," he said.

"You do that. Without the fit this time, if you please."

A shadow darkened her son's pale blond head. "Are we having sailing troubles? Perhaps I can help." Mal loomed tall and dark over them. While a flutter of awareness tickled Emma's belly, motherly instinct had her glancing at Alton. They'd met once before, but her son had been distracted by Phee. Truly, the captain presented a rather fearsome countenance. Even smiling, he was still large, wide, and rough looking. Which, judging by the warmth seeping through her body, was not a bad thing. But to someone Alton's size, he might be intimidating.

Emma rose. "Captain. Fancy meeting you here."

"Indeed. It's almost as if I had a detailed missive apprising me of your schedule for the day."

"What a happy coincidence." Emma winked and he grinned. After the small revelation she'd had at the British Museum the day before, realizing she might want to show Mal more of herself than merely her body, she'd sent a note around inviting him to a casual picnic in the park. If all went well, she'd stop by his house this evening—although Mal wasn't aware of that part of the plan.

Alton raised the boat between them. "Can you fix it?"

"Is it broken?" Mal asked.

"Well, it doesn't work. Mama says I don't want it to run off, but I want it to move."

Mal shot a glance at Emma, his pale eyes sparkling with

merriment before he looked back at Alton. "I do see your problem." Without further ado, the giant bearded man sat down in the grass. Alton immediately joined him, the two of them knee to knee on the bank of the Serpentine. The toy boat looked ridiculously tiny in Mal's hands.

"Do you remember me? We've met only once before, I believe. I'm a friend of your mother's." Mal's question was the perfect blend of casual and informative.

Alton studied Mal, tilting his head. After a moment, he brightened. "You said I can call you Captain!"

"Yes. What an excellent memory you have," Mal said.

With niceties dispensed, the men set to work.

Emma wasn't needed in the conversation, but she stood there enjoying it nonetheless.

"You see the sail? It's not catching the wind," Alton said.

"That is a problem. You know, when you are at sea and get stuck in an area with no breeze, we call those doldrums. Some sailors get stuck in the doldrums for weeks at a time, bobbing in the same place in the ocean."

"What can you do?" Alton asked.

Mal shrugged. "Not much. Some boats have oars. But I think our best bet for this situation with—what have you named your boat, lad?"

Alton shook his head. "It doesn't have a name."

Mal reared back with a hand placed dramatically to his chest. "No name? You're courting bad luck to launch a ship without a name." He handed the boat back to Alton. "No other efforts will be made to set sail until this ship has been properly christened."

Alton seemed to understand the gravity of the situation and nodded seriously. "What do you suggest, Captain?"

Mal glanced up at Emma. "How about the HMS *Beauty*?"

Alton followed Mal's gaze. "Because Mama is beautiful?"

Those light hazel eyes turned to her son. "Yes, because your mama is quite beautiful."

Emma smiled at the pair. "I'd be honored to have a boat named after me."

"The HMS *Beauty* it is! Now, how do we make it work without losing it?" asked Alton, handing the boat back to Mal.

Emma bit the tip of her thumb to contain a chuckle, and tried to ignore the sensation in her gut that felt like melted butter.

Mal turned the toy over in his hands. "Do you have a piece of twine?"

Emma raised a finger, pausing the conversation. "Let's look in the basket Miss Lacey sent along." The basket pinned one corner of the blanket they'd stretched out on the grass a few feet away. "You never know what you'll need when you're out and about with little boys."

"Ah yes," Mal said. "Our needs are many." He winked and she grinned.

"How about this?" Emma held up the ball of twine attached to the kite they hadn't been able to fly because of the lack of wind.

"Perfect." Tying off the kite string and snipping it with a pocketknife, Mal resumed his seat next to Alton. "This way," he explained to the boy, "we can let it bob down the river a ways, but it can never go beyond the line."

"What do you mean the line? It's string." Alton cocked his head.

Mal raised one scarred eyebrow at her son, and the melted butter feeling grew until Emma crossed her arms over her belly. "Rule number one of being a sailor, young lad. It's never string. It's line. Ropes on boats and ships are called lines. So, sailor. Secure the line." He passed it over to Alton.

"Make a knot?" Alton asked.

"Any kind of knot. Just make sure it's secure." Mal busied himself with unspooling a length of the string.

Alton placed the boat in Mal's lap. "I'm not very good at knots yet. Would you make a proper sailor knot, please?"

"Of course." Mal tied the twine to the mast of the ship, and a few moments later, the boat bobbed down the Serpentine, tugged along by Alton and cheered on by Mal.

If her heart was in danger of melting, this was it. Bringing Mal and Alton together might have been a misstep. Allowing Mal to see her in her role of Alton's mother was the biggest part of her personality he hadn't witnessed yet.

But nothing could have prepared her for this. Lordy goodness, if she hadn't already been wondering if she'd be happy to say goodbye to Mal in a couple weeks, seeing him handling Alton so perfectly would have done it. Again, the question of whether this affair should be as short-lived as planned rose in her mind. Emma tried to shrug it off, but the thought persisted.

No matter what, Mal was leaving to return to his first love, the *Athena*. Emma tightened her arms over her belly as if she could quell the butterflies there by barricading them from the man causing it.

What could she possibly lose by asking him to be her lover for longer than these few weeks? No, it didn't mean she would have him at hand all the time. There would be months and sometimes even years without companionship. But then, she'd already proven she could last years without the touch of a man.

However, keeping the captain around would mean Alton's dream of a papa would never happen. Not as if Emma planned to make that a reality anyway. Mal could be a great influence in Alton's life, in addition to Cal.

Emma watched the two, tall and short, dark and fair, as they jogged up and down the bank of the river, and a memory rose in her mind. Mother had shown up at their country estate unexpectedly when Father was in London and whisked Emma away to Paris. It had been right after the war, and all Emma had known at the time was that they were going to buy a new dress. Mother's attention was most reliable when Emma was her little doll, so she'd eagerly complied. Looking back, it hadn't occurred to her to question why Mother had arrived at bedtime and then whisked Emma away under cover of moonlight.

In Paris, Emma had gotten her dress. A confection of lace and pale blue satin with a matching bow for her hair. She'd also met her mother's lover *du jour*, a man claiming to be an Italian count. A count who, it turned out, didn't like children.

Mother hadn't even taken her home herself. Instead, she'd hired a chaperone to travel with Emma back to England. They'd left the day the dress arrived from the modiste. Within a half hour of the delivery, Emma had been packed into a carriage with the stranger calling herself a chaperone and the large box containing the blue dress.

The count had sent Mother away in her own carriage the next month, but Mother hadn't returned home to her family.

Emma had never worn the dress, and had never met another of her mother's lovers.

Alton's shriek of delight, followed by Mal's booming cheer brought her from her memories.

She turned her back on them and took a seat next to the picnic basket on the blanket. Perhaps a long-term lover situation wasn't the solution. Major life decisions shouldn't be made over the course of a picnic, anyway. They had time. A few weeks, at least, to settle this disquiet she felt at Mal's leaving.

Plucking an apple from the basket, Emma bit into it with more force than needed. *Get ahold of yourself. He's looking for a temporary lover. No more.* And Lord knew, no one had ever wanted to keep her long-term anyway.

With a grimace, Emma straightened her shoulders. Self-pity

would get her nowhere. Besides, it wasn't even true. There had been a line of men at the ball waiting for an introduction from Cal. Several had called since. The front drawing room had been full of flowers and compliments for the last several days from a parade of gentlemen. If Mal didn't want her, she would kiss him goodbye as he returned to his ship, and then proceed to replace him whenever she chose.

She took another bite of the apple and licked the corner of her mouth, where juice was trying to escape toward her chin. Bright and sweet and crisp, she did her best to enjoy the simple pleasures of fresh fruit and watching her son play. Familiar happy spills of laughter bounced off the water and made her smile in return. It was the base echo of chuckles from a man that was new.

A deep breath calmed the whirling thoughts and questions. It might be the first time she'd experienced seeing her son with a man other than Cal or their cottage caretaker, but it wouldn't be the last. "Come along, little love, before your lemonade gets warm."

"If you're offering lemonade, I'll answer to little love." Mal grinned and flopped down next to her, stretching those long legs over the blanket, while ensuring his boots remained on the grass. Propped on one elbow, he appeared at ease and happy in a way that sped her pulse.

"I doubt you've been called little anything since you were in leading strings," Emma teased.

Alton sat next to her on the blanket, then copied Mal's position. It looked like her son might have a case of hero worship. They were so adorable, grinning at her like opposite bookends.

Setting the picnic basket between them, she let them dig for their luncheon while she poured the lemonade.

"Captain, where is your boat?" Alton asked around a mouthful of ham sandwich.

Emma said, "Manners. Chew and swallow before speaking."

Mal waited for Alton to follow her instructions before answering. "My *ship* is currently undergoing maintenance in Portsmouth while I sort out some business with the Admiralty."

"Convenient that you were able to bring it back to port to wait for you," she commented.

"That took some maneuvering, I admit. But it was needed, because the king had essentially left us out to sea without any scheduled maintenance for far too long. Once the war ended, the fleet took lower precedence in the government's priorities. We've been limping along in many ways." Mal bit into his own sandwich, then washed it down with the lemonade. Emma had to wonder at everything he wasn't saying. He'd mentioned the sailors going without pay the other day in her drawing room. Life at sea truly wasn't as glamorous as some were led to believe.

"Have you ever fought pirates?" Alton asked—after a drink, mouth sans food.

"We didn't see as much action during the war as some ships, because of where we were stationed. But we've taken a couple prizes for the king over the years."

Emma cocked her head at the strange tone in his voice as she dismantled her sandwich, nibbling each element piece by piece. "You don't sound happy about avoiding battle."

Mal leaned his head back to look her in the eye. "Father was in the diplomatic service. He pulled strings and threw his name about to keep the *Athena* from action. My men signed up for conflict and prize money. Instead, they received iced lines and empty pockets because they were unlucky enough to serve with me."

Interesting. A theory pieced together in her brain and she had to ask if it held weight. "You said your mother wielded something with the Admiralty to pull you home. Is it connected to your father's service to the crown?"

"Yes."

Something powerful on a government level. Emma's eyes went wide enough to bulge and she could feel pressure behind them as she glanced around to verify that they were alone. Absently, she handed another serviette to her son to wipe his fingers as he pressed a small piece of cheese into the porthole of his wooden boat. That would need to be picked out later or it would attract rodents to the nursery. "You're searching for diplomatic secrets?" she hissed.

His pale hazel eyes avoided hers, but he nodded.

Worry for him made her stare in horror. "Isn't it dangerous?"

"No more or less dangerous than my mother claiming to have them and making herself a target to silence."

Her spine went soft. "It's not only about turning them over to the government and getting back to your ship, is it?"

Mal sighed. "I'd like to think it is. The emotions are confusing at best. But by claiming she has this thing and using the information for her own purposes, she's drawn attention to herself. There's a fine line between wielding your title for power and overstepping to make yourself a target. And Mother, well, she's never known when to stop."

"I can hit a target with my bow and arrow!" Alton interjected, then returned to his sandwich.

"That's a fine skill to have. Even I can't do that," Mal said with forced cheer.

"Do you miss the sea?" Alton asked, changing the subject in typical childlike fashion.

"Very much. I like having a purpose. Aboard ship, even in times of peace, there's always something to do. I miss that."

It seemed the conversation about Mal's search for his father's secrets would have to wait. Emma matched Mal's happy tone and said, "Today, your purpose is to play with the HMS *Beauty*, eat sandwiches in the sun, and drink more lemonade than a five-year-old boy. Otherwise, he'll need to wee on a bush half-way home."

"I will accept that mission," he said with a more genuine smile.

Emma grinned back and resumed eating. The cheddar in the sandwich was sharp enough to make her mouth pucker, and she savored every bite before moving on to the sweeter cured ham.

"Do you always dissect your sandwiches like that?" Mal asked.

Alton answered for her. "Always. She says it helps one to enjoy the different parts."

Emma smiled and shrugged. "It's true. Besides, what I really love is the bread. I don't want ham interfering with that."

Mal tilted his head. "Isn't the entire point of a sandwich to layer the flavors and textures?" He turned to Alton. "Your mother is a strange duck, lad. I like her. But she's not without her oddities."

Alton nodded, grabbing another sandwich. "Uncle Cal says they found her as a baby in a hollowed-out tree, and that explains everything about her."

A deep rumble of laughter came from Mal, as he rolled onto his back and threaded his fingers over his stomach. With his eyes closed, and a smile lingering on his mouth, Emma took a moment to enjoy the look of him. She couldn't help brushing a few stray hairs back from his forehead, and Mal opened one eye to look up at her.

"Would you like to see me later tonight?" she asked softly.

"Absolutely. Yes. A thousand times yes," he said, just as quietly.

She smiled, then turned her attention to Alton. "Wipe your mouth, darling, before that glob of mustard falls and stains your shirt—not with your coat sleeve. Lordy goodness, Alton."

Chapter Thirteen

 ❧

*Family complicates everything. Too bad I'm
so attached to mine. Well. Some of them.*
                                    —Journal entry, May 1, 1824

Someone was following her and they weren't being subtle about it.

Emma noticed the curricle back on Hill Street. It was hard to miss, with its bright blue paint and yellow wheels. The rig was even more out of place in Mal's neighborhood. Emma peeked around the edge of her hood as she stepped away from her carriage onto the pavement.

In Mayfair, the driver had been hard to discern, beyond a general impression of bulkiness under a driving cloak and hat. Distance kept her from discerning the driver's identity, so other than making note of the unfamiliar carriage, she'd thought no more of it.

What were the chances of two carriages leaving Hill Street at the exact same time, bound for the exact same place? The day after her sister-in-law had received a vague note warning of more blackmail and threats to come? A belief in coincidences could carry one only so far before one had to admit to being justifiably wary.

Ahead of her, the black door with the shiny brass knocker beckoned, alluring with its feeling of familiar safety. Cal's coachman, Hobby, murmured a good night to her and gave the horses their cue to pull away, heading back to the nearby mews to await her summons.

She'd made it up three of the four steps to Mal's door before she was yanked back with a rough hand on her arm.

Emma yelped in surprised fear and lashed out one foot to mule-kick whoever had grabbed her. The grip on her arm disappeared, and she whirled to see Roxbury bent over nearly double, gasping.

"What in the name of all that's holy do you think you're *doing*, Devon?" she shrieked.

Across the street, someone closed their window with a sharp clap. She glanced up and down the quiet street, illuminated by pools of light from gas lamps. Twilight transitioned to nighttime rapidly these days, and it was nearing dark.

Behind her, the black door opened, and a shaft of light spilled down the steps. "What have we here?" Mal drawled, bouncing down the steps with a loose gait she didn't mistake as casual. More like the way a boxer shook their arms and legs to keep them warm and limber between fights.

"I didn't touch her! I swear. I just want to talk," Roxbury said, holding up one hand, but not standing fully quite yet.

"Kicked him in the berry thicket, did you?" Mal asked her.

Emma lifted her hem enough to show her foot. "Walking boots. Wood sole."

"That's my girl," Mal said and brushed his thumb over her

cheek, then turned to Roxbury. "What brings you to my door, milord?"

"No desire to see you, I assure you. This is between myself and Lady Emma. It's a private matter," Roxbury said, finally straightening and facing them belligerently.

"If you've no wish to see him, then you shouldn't have assaulted me on his steps," Emma said.

"I didn't expect you to be calling on your protector," Roxbury nearly yelled. His cheeks were bright red, and the eyes she'd once youthfully claimed she wanted to fall into were dark and beady, nearly lost to the fleshy bloat brought on from too much alcohol.

Emma crossed her arms and glared. While she may not be ashamed of her relationship with Mal, she didn't want the details literally shouted from the street corner either. "Take your coarse innuendos elsewhere, if you please. I've already said I have no wish to speak with you. There is no relationship between us, and there never will be."

Mal placed his body between her and Roxbury. "May I hit him if he doesn't acquiesce to your request? It's not sporting that you got a whack in and I haven't." The grin accompanying the statement showed far too many teeth.

Roxbury stepped back one pace, but kept his gaze on Emma. "You sabotaged my last chance to marry the money I need, and you stole my heir. You owe me a dowry, you little bitch. You're not helping anyone by ignoring my attentions."

Anger, edged by dark fear, made her heart pound. But before she could register much beyond the flash of uncomfortable emotion, Mal's fist shot out in one clean move, cutting off any more ugliness from Roxbury. Devon had no stamina in a fight. With a nearly comical wheezing grunt, he fell to the pavement in a crumpled heap, leaving Mal standing over him with clenched fists, looking vaguely disappointed.

"Correct me if I'm wrong, but did I just witness the worst marriage proposal in history?" Mal asked.

Emma blinked in surprise at how quickly the situation had escalated, then been resolved. Mal hadn't even hesitated at Devon's claim that she stole his heir, but then, there hadn't been time to react. "I can explain. What he said—"

Mal held up a hand. "Tell me only if you want to. What he shouts while drunk on a street has no impact on our relationship. All right?" The expression he wore was so compassionate, and he was so calm about the whole situation, that Emma felt tears threatening. Emma nodded, hard enough that her hood fell off her head.

"Right then. Do you happen to know how he got here? Or should we leave him on the ground for the watch to find?"

Her finger trembled when she pointed. "The blue curricle over there with the grays. That's his, I think."

Mal shot her a smile. "Go ahead inside. I gave the staff the night off, so we're alone. I'll meet you in the house. You didn't want to attract notice, but this big lout might have done exactly that."

Mal didn't waver under the load of Roxbury's limp body as he hauled him toward the rig. When the black door closed behind her, Emma took a moment to collapse against it and take a few breaths. The soaring ceiling of Mal's foyer made her smile. Such a lovely little house. Even if she hadn't met a single member of the staff yet. He assured her they existed, albeit currently in a confused state.

Apparently, there'd been a fuss among the servants when they discovered they'd be serving a duke, only to find out he'd rather pay them to go away after half their usual schedule. When he'd shared the story with her, she'd laughed. No one knew what to do with the new Duke of Trenton. Not even the new Duke of Trenton himself.

The banister on the staircase was a lovely curved wood thing, polished to a high shine, topped by an overly large newel carved into a lion's head. Upon leaving the house after her first visit, Emma had named the lion Wilbur. Removing her cloak and gloves, she draped the outerwear over the handrail and patted Wilbur on the head. A fanciful gesture, but it made her smile despite her swirling thoughts.

Mal hadn't appeared concerned about Roxbury, but with Devon's accusations in the air between them, she couldn't ignore them. Yet some secrets weren't hers to tell, like Phee's years of impersonating her brother. In the museum, she'd determined to share more of herself. These secrets had never been on the list of topics she'd planned to discuss, but thanks to Roxbury's loose tongue, she would probably have to. Letting Mal believe she had stolen and hidden a man's child was unconscionable, even if the truth was twisted in the details.

The door opened and closed behind her. "He came to when we got to the rig. He'll be fine. Can't take a hit to save his life, but his skull is thick. I hope he'll leave you alone after this."

Emma nodded, clenching her fingers together in a knotted fist at her waist, while her heart pounded. "Adam knew. About the pregnancy, I mean. When I went to Roxbury, he turned me away. Said horrible things and refused to marry me. Adam—" her voice cracked, and she forced a calming breath. "Adam knew. He helped me. Saved me from myself in a lot of ways."

Mal's expression was unbearably sweet as she half lied, half confessed. Patient, accepting, and lacking judgment of any kind.

Guilt soured the nerves in her belly. He was being wonderful about this information, and yet she wasn't telling the whole story.

He held out a hand. "Would you like some coffee? Or perhaps a soothing herbal tea? The cook harvested fresh mint and chamomile this morning. I know it was chamomile only because I tried to help and put the flowers in a vase, and she laughed at me." Emma giggled, and he shrugged good-naturedly. "The servants are getting used to my oddities. I put a kettle on before you arrived, but it may have boiled out by now. Let's go check."

They walked through the snug house hand in hand toward the kitchen. Emma's shoulders relaxed when they entered the warm room. It smelled of home—yeast, a trace of sugar, and the mellow tang of herbs. While Mal busied himself with the kettle, she ran a finger over the wood work counter.

"Would you mind if we spent some time down here? Instead of upstairs, I mean," she asked. As soon as she said the words, Emma wished she could call them back. After all, she was here for sex. That was the whole purpose of her visit. Yet Roxbury's appearance had rattled her. Being followed across London was disturbing enough, but now Roxbury knew beyond a shadow of a doubt that not only were she and Mal involved, but where he lived. The possibilities of what he could do with such knowledge made her uneasy.

Then Mal's reply stopped her unease. "I want to spend time with you, Em. You aren't required to do anything when you visit. Sex isn't an obligation. It's you and your time I want."

The smile she gave him felt shaky on her lips, but honest. "Would your cook mind if I made something?"

Mal poured water into two cups and brought them to the wood plank table the servants used. "I would love it if you baked. If Cook has a problem with it, I'll handle her."

A flour-dusted apron hung on a hook, and Emma donned it, scanning the room. Butter and lard went into the icebox. Flour, salt, a cone of sugar, and some spices joined two apples and a sack of dried fruit. Emma glanced over, and Mal blew on the top of his drink, sipped, then kept watching her. A warmth crept over her face, and she knew her cheeks were pink. Alton watched her in the kitchen all the time, but it never felt like this.

"Do you have brandy? Or even whisky?" she asked. He rose and retrieved a bottle from the shelf.

"Fancy a nip?" he asked.

"Not exactly." Emma poured a measure into an earthenware bowl and threw the dried fruit in to soak. At the last minute, she tipped the bottle to her lips and winked at him as she took a swig. The burn of it traveled down her throat, and she welcomed the momentary shock of alcohol on her tongue.

Mal took a drink as well, then returned the bottle to the shelf.

The soothing, familiar motions of her hands on the dough calmed her as much as the brandy. Mashing the chilled lard and butter into the flour with tiny snapping flicks of her fingertips was practically instinctual at this point. While the pastry chilled, she sat and sipped the mug of herbal tea Mal had made for her.

"Did you love him?" The question seemed to come out of nowhere.

Emma didn't glance up from her mug. "I thought I did. But then, I was a headstrong young woman, determined to ignore all thoughts of consequences. I think it was the thrill of it. Clandestine rendezvous, sneaking away from watchful eyes. I felt so very adult and mature, and free."

"I think I understand."

"Do you?" she asked, finally looking at him.

"I ran away to sea when I was supposed to be going to Eton. The family coach stopped on the way to the school, and I bolted for the harbor. My family was going to be in England for only a short time. Long enough to leave me behind. So I made my own choice. Maybe I wanted them to raise a fuss and give chase. But a big part of it was needing freedom from the double standards they kept between George and me. He was attending Eton as well, and it was clear the Trenton name and reputation rested on his shoulders. I was not the spare to his heir, but disposable. The night before they put us in the coach, Mother told me not to make George look bad, because she wouldn't be around to bring me home. Even leaving for school, all that mattered was George. So, I left him and them behind."

"Did they? Come after you, I mean," she asked.

"Not exactly. I left while George slept. There was a ruckus when our parents discovered I'd enlisted, but no action beyond their histrionics over me changing the plan. George went to school and they moved on. There was business in Moscow, I believe. After that, Father kept his nose in the Admiralty's business and interfered with my career. I sometimes wonder if he did it as punishment for running away." A bitter smile twisted his mouth.

There was nothing to say to that. Not really. Emma squeezed his hand, then rose to roll out the crust. His gaze was a weight on her, but not unwelcome as she fit the crust into a small tin, stoked the fire in the stove, then set to work on the filling.

"Do you regret running away? Many men forge lifelong friendships at Eton." A paring knife sliced through the apples quickly, making neat slivers of sweet and tart filling. She set some aside and added the rest to the bowl with the brandy-soaked fruit.

"It was the right choice for me," Mal said. "Mother and I have never been close. George was her favorite, and I always knew that. With him gone, it's been messy. Mother didn't write to tell me he passed. Instead, she contacted the Admiralty and had me brought home. Used leverage of some kind, and now I'm dealing with the impact of that. Maybe our relationship would have been different if I'd stayed. I don't know."

"Parents are complicated. *Being* a parent is complicated," she said.

He sighed, then took a sip of his tea. "I enjoy seeing you like this."

"In a kitchen?" she asked, half-teasing.

"Relaxed," he corrected.

A flutter near her heart warned that her emotions were extending deeper than superficial. They weren't even lustful. Emma wasn't sure what to do with them, so she did the next best thing. She grated sugar, cinnamon, and nutmeg over the fruit, then added a dash of lemon zest, and poured it into the pastry shell. With the reserved apple slices, she created a spiraling curve on top that one might think looked like a rose. Maybe. If you squinted.

"Good enough," she muttered, and placed it in the oven.

While their dessert baked, she crossed to where Mal sat with his mug. Resting her bum against the table by his elbow, she leaned forward and placed a kiss on the top of his head.

"What was that for?" he asked lightly.

"Just because I could," she answered, then leaned down for a proper kiss. Mint lingered on his tongue from the tea, and the scent of baking crust in the air soothed the last vestiges of tension. Sucking his bottom lip fully, she gently raked her teeth over the plump flesh and welcomed his soft moan. "Thank you for tonight. This is nice. Not how I expected the evening to go, but nice." She tucked a lock of his hair behind his ear and studied him.

Heavy brows, sun-darkened skin, with pale streaks at the corners of his eyes from squinting at the horizon. Deep brown hair with enough wave to it to be unruly. Mal didn't move when she untied his queue so she could run her fingers through his hair.

"Why did you drop the honorific when you left London?" he asked.

Her hands froze, tangled in his long strands. "At the time, we were trying to avoid notice in the village and planned to stay away from London long enough to muddle the amount of time between our marriage and Alton's birth." Which was the god's honest truth. Another piece of honesty fell from her lips before she could catch it. "And I think, after Devon, I didn't *feel* like a lady. An aristocratic name carries expectations. I'd failed to live up to those expectations. Spectacularly so."

Mal took one of her hands from his hair and kissed her palm. "I understand all too well."

e~

He should have told her. Sitting in the kitchen, relaxed and sharing truths, Malachi should have told her to wait for a moment, then gone upstairs and retrieved her journal from his drawer.

But she'd been shaky at first from dealing with Roxbury, and then watching her take over the kitchen had been one of the most comforting, intriguing, oddly arousing experiences of his life.

The competence and surety in the way she moved in the room caught his attention first. Food came together under her hands as if for her, creating something delicious was an instinctive task, something she took joy in without having to dedicate much thought to it. More than anything, it was the way the manners and practiced gentility fell away like masks set aside, leaving only Emma, in her element. She was so beautiful, it stole his breath, his good intentions—and his courage. If he gave her the journal now, this night of confessions and pastry would end. And he wanted a little more time with this unguarded version of her.

A smear of flour dusted her cheek, and honey-blond curls turned to a darker treacle color as they stuck to her hairline from the heat of the stove. He could watch her all night. In fact, he wanted to. And not just tonight. He wanted Emma like this— creative and relaxed, and near him—tomorrow. And the next day, and the next.

As she rose to pull the tin from the oven, the sway of her hips caught his attention. Her movements held his gaze in a way that made it hard to look away. It was possible she was even more unguardedly herself tonight than she'd been two nights before when she came apart in his arms and cried his name in bed. This intimacy of sharing thoughts late at night fit so comfortably over them, he didn't want to spoil it. He didn't want it to end.

A suspicion awoke within him that he needed more than Emma in his bed for the short term. Especially when he craved more nights like this one, which had nothing to do with sex.

"Damn, this is delicious," he said around a mouthful of the best thing he'd ever tasted.

She sent him a quick smile and speared a bite on her fork, directly from the tin. No plates for them, which somehow made it taste better.

A knock at the kitchen door interrupted their peaceful late-night snack.

"Expecting someone?" Emma asked.

Malachi rose to answer the door. A footman in the emerald-green Trenton livery appeared taken aback by the duke himself answering the kitchen door, but he recovered quickly. "For you, Your Grace," he said, handing over a folded piece of paper.

A frown creased the bridge between his eyebrows as he read the short note. "Before you go, please notify the mews we will be leaving immediately." The footman tipped his hat and took his leave. Malachi glanced back at Emma. "My mother demands my presence, claiming an emergency. I'm terribly sorry, but it appears I need to cut the evening short."

She got up from the table and carried their pie tin and forks to the washing area. "If you'll get our cups and bring them over, I'll wash up."

Malachi grabbed both teacups even as he shook his head. "There's no time to wash up. I'll apologize in the morning."

She shot him a bemused look.

"What?" he asked, leading the way out of the kitchen toward the foyer.

"You're truly not very good at being a duke, are you? Dukes don't apologize to maids."

"They do when the maids did a fine job of cleaning the kitchen and the duke in question left a mess for them after they went to bed." Malachi smiled and handed over her gloves and cloak. "It's polite."

He slipped into his coat and plopped a hat on his head as she drew the hood of her cloak up.

"Would you like to share my coach or catch a hack?" Emma asked.

"I'll share, if you don't mind. Mother's place is only a couple blocks from your brother's." Malachi stopped her at the front door before she opened it and dropped a brief, but hard, kiss on her lips. "Thank you for tonight. The pie was delicious, but the company was better."

In reply, she raised on her tiptoes and kissed him back, with a short peck of her own. There was more sweet friendship in the gesture than there had been before tonight, but Malachi didn't have time to dissect how he felt about that.

Across town, he kissed her goodbye again in the carriage as it drew up to Calvin's house on Hill Street, before jogging to the family townhome.

Breathing heavily from the run, he stopped short when the door handle remained stubbornly closed. Malachi raised his fist and pounded on the wood.

When summoned by a messenger after two in the morning, one expected to see every window ablaze with light. Perhaps even on fire. But no, the door was locked tight, and the house appeared quiet.

The door swung open to show his mother, more frazzled than he'd ever seen her. Her dark, silver-threaded hair was in a long plait over her shoulder, and she wore a wrapper cinched tight at her waist. "Hush! Do you want to wake the servants?" she hissed.

Malachi raised a brow. "I assumed the servants were already awake given the note claiming an emergency. What is this about?"

She stepped aside for him to slip by, then carefully closed and locked the door.

A single brace of candles illuminated the foyer from the narrow table along the wall. She grabbed the candelabra and whispered, "This way."

"Why are we whispering?"

Eerie silence enveloped the corridor as his mother led Malachi toward the library. Their footfalls echoed against the marble, sharp and obscene, like a slap in church. No servants appeared. Not even the usual night staff. Unease slithered along his collar.

"Exactly what is happening here, Mother?"

Instead of answering, she opened the library, which proved to be well lit.

"Where are the servants? What's this about?" he asked again, closing the door.

"You and your questions, Malachi." Mother set aside the candles in front of a bookcase. Oh, good. Five seconds into the visit and he'd already been chastised.

Malachi rubbed his hand over his eyes. "Your messenger said there is an emergency. What are you doing? It's the middle of the night, if you hadn't noticed."

Mother finally took a seat on the sofa, gesturing for him to sit as well. "I'm afraid I need your help."

His face felt...strange, like it was experiencing an entirely new expression. Mother never needed his help. Ever. He couldn't remember her asking anyone for help, nor could he recall a single time she'd ever apologized or admitted she was wrong. Not even when she'd forced him to get rid of the puppy he'd rescued, claiming it was a filthy animal, only to turn around and give a dog to George the next month.

He slowly eased into a wingback chair, prepared to flee at any moment. "So there *is* an emergency." One involving meeting in the wee hours of the morning without servants to bear witness.

"Ivan was doing his rounds before retiring for the night, like he always does. He caught a prowler in my bedchamber. Although he chased the man through the house, the intruder got away through this window." Mother spoke, utterly stone-faced. However, her fidgety fingers and a tremor in her voice sent a ripple of alarm through him.

"Is anything missing? Did the butler see anything to help identify this person?"

Mother shook her head. "A man. Fair hair under a dark cap. I don't think anything is missing, because this wasn't a typical burglary." She stared across the room at the fireplace, composed as a statue but for the restless fingers in her lap.

A growing ache throbbed at his temple. "What aren't you telling me? What the hell have you done now?"

"Language, Malachi," she barked, finally looking at him.

"Don't worry about my language, worry about why someone is breaking into your bedchamber. Mother, what is going on?"

Her mouth pinched, but one hand fluttered near her neckline before returning to her lap in a white-knuckled fist.

"Your father kept a record book. The king wants it. Certain people think I am misusing the information within this book. Since I've ignored their demands to deliver it, they are clearly resorting to stealing it. I spent too many years with your father in service to not recognize the escalation of events."

A lovely way of saying her attempted manipulation was back-firing and biting her in the arse. Part of him wanted to laugh at the poetic justice of it all. But someone robbing the house was serious. Invading her bedchamber in the middle of the night was an outright threat. At least Malachi wasn't the only one who wanted to find the damn thing. "So give them the book."

"If I had it, don't you think I would?" she snapped.

"Then tell them you don't have it." He waited to see if she'd admit to her full culpability.

"I can't. I already claimed the opposite when I used the book to get you home to do your duty. It's unconscionable for them to treat me in such a manner." Mother avoided looking at him, focusing instead on picking a piece of lint off the lace of her wrapper.

No, Malachi thought that part was actually reasonable. When one threatened the British government, there did tend to be consequences. Not that he wanted his mother to suffer the sentence for treason. He sighed. "What can I do to help?"

"We need to find your father's bank book, so I can turn it over and prove my loyalty. Now that you're home, I have what I need from them." Mother rose and straightened her spine. "This room is the logical place to keep the book, but I've already searched here. I'm hoping fresh eyes will reveal a hiding place I overlooked."

His knuckles ached a bit where he'd landed that satisfying punch to Lord Roxbury's jaw, and the herbal tea and late-night snack he'd enjoyed were sitting in his stomach nicely, urging him to find a bed and sleep. The late hour chimed from the mantel clock as he climbed to his feet. "You aren't going to discuss the fact that you lied to the Admiralty to get my command pulled out from under me? Because that's what happened. And now you want my help to save your neck, in the middle of the night." The longer he stood there, the more aware he became of a headache blooming behind his eyes.

His mother huffed an exasperated sigh like she used to when

he disagreed with her as a child, and she claimed he was throwing a fit. "I did what I had to do, otherwise you'd have stayed on your blasted ship forever and neglected your title. You belong here, in London. You'll marry, sire an heir, and do your duty to the family. The time for playing sea captain has passed."

That ache at his temple grew to a pounding throb, thudding with each pulse of his heart. "I'm not *playing* anything, Mother. I am the captain of my ship, and I worked damned hard to get there. I don't give a flying frog fart about the bloody title. It can die with me for all I care."

She went pale. "You don't mean that."

"I mean every single word."

"George knew to protect the family line. The Trenton title was all that mattered to him." Her harsh whisper cut through the room.

The fight seeped out of him, replaced by the familiar dull, hollow knowledge that he would never be enough for his family. "George was perfect. I know."

"You were never supposed to be Trenton," Mother said, bitter grief soaking her voice.

"No. I wasn't. But we are all stuck with me being Trenton now. And I'll handle the title my own way."

Her lips tightened even more, making her face pucker as if she'd smelled something foul. The grief gave way to familiar disdain when she snapped, "Marry. I don't care who. Beget a son off a dock whore for all I care, as long as he's legitimate. But you *will* do your duty to the Trenton title, Malachi." Steel wrapped her voice.

"Like you are? Staining the title with acts of treason?" He let the jab fly, then turned. "Have fun finding Father's book. I'm going to bed. Tomorrow I'll coordinate with Ivan for more security. Intruders in your home is a threat I'll take seriously. The rest of this is your problem."

"Malachi, come back here this instant," his mother cried.

Turning, he pasted on a carefree grin he didn't feel. "Hush, or you'll wake the servants. You wouldn't want witnesses, would you?"

❦

It came as no surprise when Malachi felt like horse poop the next morning. The kind that had been smashed into the bottom of a shoe and tracked over uneven pavement, then scraped off on the edge of a step.

As the sun rose over London, making a valiant effort to bully through the morning fog, Malachi blinked at the walls of his bedchamber from his seat next to the window. A cold cup of coffee rested in his hands, long forgotten.

Burning grit abraded his eyes with every slow blink, but he didn't have the energy to rub at them.

It was a humbling thing, to face the boundaries of this relationship with his mother. Yes, he resented the hell out of her machinations and desired to see her face consequences for her actions. But crossing the British government—with a potentially deadly outcome—was another matter.

Last night's so-called emergency confirmed his suspicion that she'd bluffed her way into manipulating the Royal Navy. Whatever was in his father's journal was serious enough for the government to act without proof. Dangerous enough for George to hide the information *from* their mother.

At this moment, the only thing standing between Lady Trenton and a potential treason charge or, worse yet, a quiet accident, was him—the misfit son she hated, who was also her only hope of retrieving that damned book. And what stood between Malachi and said damned book? George's grave.

Being honest, he'd done some shady things in the past. Illegal things. Forging papers, smuggling goods as well as the occasional person, and anything else required of him to feed, clothe, and pay his crew. Those actions probably precluded him from ever being a genuinely good man. At least, in the strictest sense. In his mind, he usually termed those events as "adventures" to downplay the potential consequences on his soul.

Grave robbing his own brother was a new "adventure." God help him. Malachi let his head loll to the right and stared out his window. Across the street, the barrister's wife closed the door behind her while holding the hand of her son, who tugged impatiently. The boy appeared to be around the same age as Alton, which made Malachi smile.

Emma and her family had invited him to join them at the Ballymores' picnic today. A note from Simon confirmed he'd received a similar invitation, and he expected to make his interest in Miss Martin clear by staying by her side all day. Seeing Simon caught by the tall brunette made Mal happy. It shouldn't be a surprise to see his friend fall so quickly. Simon had a way of making up his mind and never turning back. Once, Simon had spent an entire year at Tattersalls looking at horses, only to purchase a bay mare after catching sight of her out of the corner of his eye. One look, bought. He loved that horse. Apparently, shopping for a bride was a similar endeavor. Who knew?

A picnic with Emma's whole family and friend group was a gesture. A legitimizing of their relationship. Moving it beyond the bedroom. Because she was a widow, no one would automatically expect a wedding announcement, but it was still a huge step. Essentially, her family was publicly accepting Malachi's interest in Emma, which, until he received the invitation, he hadn't realized he wanted. The fact that she wasn't hiding him from her family like a shameful secret was something he hadn't known he craved. After their evening in the kitchen, the idea of sitting with her family and being, well, accepted, appealed more than it had a few days before.

Normally, thoughts of seeing her would ignite excited tingles in his blood, but damn, he was exhausted. A nap would have to happen between now and then. Otherwise, his first outing with her family would entail her sitting on the grass watching him drool on himself while he snored like a great bear. So attractive. She deserved better, and her brother would never let him live it down.

When he shifted in the chair, stiff muscles protested. Setting aside the cold coffee, he rose and crossed to the writing desk. It took a moment to jot a quick note to Simon, apprising him of last night's events and of his plan. If anyone would understand the gravity of the situation and the need for extreme action, it was Simon.

He set aside the pen and sanded the note. There. One grave-robbing expedition in the works. Between them they could open the crypt and handle whatever was inside. Malachi's brain tried to supply images of dead bodies, and he shuddered. No. Best not consider the details right now. No good could come of that. The important thing to focus on was getting the bank book, handing it over to the king, and eliminating the threat to his mother's pale, bejeweled neck.

Sometime soon, he'd need to retreat to Olread Cove and check on his cave stash. Ensure the crates were still secure and protected from the elements. At the memory of the cave and the beach where he'd found the book that had kept him company on so many nights, Malachi glanced over at the journal on his dressing table.

Sliding a drawer open, he placed the book inside and closed it away. Last night would have been the perfect time to return it. In the warm kitchen, he'd kept his mouth shut, though. The night had been oddly delicate, created for intimate confidences.

During their time together, he'd hoped she would open up and tell him some of those secrets herself. And last night she had. Was it cowardice keeping him mum, or had it been not wanting to invalidate Emma's decision to finally tell him something of herself? There was no point in wondering about it now. He'd missed the opportunity.

With exhaustion tugging at his limbs, Malachi shucked his shirt and let it fall in a heap next to the bed.

Sleep first, violate his brother's eternal resting place later, and picnic in between. Then forget about all of it while in Emma's arms.

Oblivion could be found more than one way, and Emma was fast becoming his favorite.

Chapter Fourteen

Everyone lies. It's human nature. We protect and prevaricate with anything within our grasp, even if it means bypassing honor.
                    —Journal entry, October 1, 1824

"I didn't think this through," Emma murmured to Adelaide. Beside her friend, Lord Marshall muffled a laugh.

"I think it's fascinating. Like watching two peacocks prancing around one another." Adelaide sipped her lemonade, but didn't bother lowering her voice to hide her response from Calvin and Mal, sitting a few feet away.

"Saucy," Lord Marshall commented with a wink toward Adelaide. She grinned, then returned to what everyone else was watching—Emma's brother and her lover getting to know each other.

Both men had used those words in separate discussions with Emma. *Getting to know each other.*

Mal because he (correctly) thought things would be awkward

if he accepted Cal's invitation to sit with them at the Ballymores' picnic but didn't speak to her brother all day.

Calvin, because he'd resigned himself to Mal's being part of Emma's life for the next few weeks, and he admitted he might need to converse with the man a bit more before deciding he definitively hated him.

"I never should have told Phee about Mal." Emma picked a strawberry off Adelaide's plate and nibbled the sweet red flesh down to the stem. Almost immediately, Emma stopped chewing. The memory of the night she'd crawled in with Phee and Cal after her nightmare made her shoulders slump. Emma herself had let this particular nugget of information slip. Her and her damned determination to be honest with her family and deviate from her old ways.

"What is it? What's wrong?" Adelaide asked, concern making a groove between her eyebrows.

"I remembered that I can't blame this on Phee's big mouth."

Just then, Phee returned from the duck pond with a little boy clinging to each hand. "What's this about my big mouth?"

"That," Emma said, jerking her chin toward the two men who seemed determined to ignore the ladies' commentary as they swapped stories of their manly endeavors—otherwise known as foolish youth—and subtly tried to outdo each other.

"Oh, that. No, you're to blame. These are the rewards honest women reap, my dear." Phee swung one child-laden arm toward her, and Emma caught Alton around the waist, then pulled him down to her lap.

"Mama, I fed ducks. *Four* of them. They fought over the bread and squawked at each other and made us laugh." Alton dug around the edges of her skirts like a badger making a burrow.

"Little love, what are you looking for?"

"Food. I'm hungry. I tried to eat the duck bread, but Auntie Phee said no."

Beside her, Mal chuckled, proving he was still paying attention after all. Emma rolled her eyes at Phee. "Thank you, Auntie Phee, for not allowing them to eat stale duck bread."

Phee grinned in response as she settled beside Cal and appropriated his glass of ale.

"This is quite the gathering. Are we expecting anyone else to join us?" Lord Marshall asked the group at large. As it was, they had four quilts arranged in a giant square on the grass to accommodate everyone.

Cal answered, eyeing the fast-disappearing ale in Phee's hand. "Ethan and Lottie will be along eventually. Knowing them, they've been detained in a carriage somewhere."

Phee sighed wistfully. "Remember when we could be 'detained in a carriage' on a whim? Those were the days." They glanced at Freddie, then at each other, in one of those silent conversations married people had.

Emma had to smile at the pair before she caught Mal staring at her. She raised a questioning brow at him.

Leaning over to brush her ear with his lips, he asked, "Are you hungry? You haven't eaten anything except a few of Miss Martin's berries. I can fetch and gather for you and the lad."

The urge to kiss him swamped her, but they were in public, surrounded by members of the *ton*. Instead, Emma turned and buried her nose in the gold hair on Alton's head until the urge passed.

"I would like a sandwich, berries, and lemonade, please, Captain," Alton said.

"All of that sounds lovely. Would you mind?" she said, risking a peek at her lover.

Mal's smile made her toes curl in her shoes. It wasn't merely an "I'll ravish you at the next opportunity" smile. There was a new intimacy since last night. He'd sat with her. Listened to her confidences and handled them with grace. She'd baked for him—something she'd done only for those closest to her.

"I'll return shortly." Mal stood. For a moment, she was cast in shadow, surrounded by the scent of freshly cut grass, sunshiney little boy, and bay rum. Emma closed her eyes and breathed it in. Breathed *him* in.

On the neighboring blanket, Lord Marshall rose with Adelaide's plate in his hand, and the friends wandered toward the refreshment table, which left Cal alone with the women and children.

"So? What do you think of him?" Phee asked.

"I've met him before. This isn't a first impression situation," Cal said.

"But last time you met him you didn't know he'd seen your sister n-a-k-e-d. That changes things," Phee said.

Beside Emma, Adelaide muffled her laugh. Emma grinned at Cal's grimace.

"Must you remind me?" he whined, sounding alarmingly like his son.

"What does k-e-d spell?" Freddie asked.

"It's grown-up code for special friends who get sandwiches for you," Cal said, then stole his glass back from his wife and drank the last bit of ale in one rather desperate-looking swallow.

"Oh. I want a friend who brings me sandwiches," Freddie said.

"I'd love my special friend to get me a sandwich too. And more ale, please. Also, we should make sure to compliment our hostess on choosing the Amesburys' brew for the occasion." Phee grinned at her husband and Emma laughed.

Cal sighed dramatically, but he smiled as he kissed the tops of Phee's and Freddie's ginger heads, then headed toward the refreshment table.

As soon as he left, Adelaide collapsed in a fit of giggles. "Sandwiches," she gasped.

Emma and Phee joined her a moment later.

"What's so funny?" Alton asked.

Emma wiped tears from her eyes and said, "Your uncle Cal is a very funny man, that's all."

"Your aunt Phee is funny too," Adelaide added.

"My mommy and daddy laugh a lot. And I mean *a lot*," Freddie said seriously.

Lottie arrived, setting her reticule on the blanket beside Phee. "That sounds like an excellent testimony to what kind of family you've made, Phee. Is this seat taken?"

Phee craned her neck to look up at Lottie. "It is now. Where's Ethan?"

"He's been waylaid by the food table."

"Do we want to know why you are late?" Emma teased.

Lottie didn't respond to the jest as she normally would. Instead, lines of stress furrowed her brow. "We spent the morning in Kent dealing with getting the production line back on track. So many details, and workers to reassure, without knowing if the saboteur will rear his ugly face again. We got on the road later than expected."

"Have things settled down since the payment?" Phee asked.

Adelaide shot Emma a questioning glance. Emma wasn't sure if the blackmail was going to be openly discussed, so she shook her head.

The movement caught Phee's attention. "Apologies, Adelaide. I won't get into detail here with young ears and neighbors so close, but suffice it to say we are dealing with an outside threat. They targeted the brewery, and now appear to be going after our shipping investments with the same pattern. Someone, somewhere, is angry, and we have yet to determine who it is."

"So far, our odious blackmailer appears to be moving on to the next person on his list. I can't say that's a relief when you and Cal are the target, Phee." Worry colored Lottie's words.

"I have my urchins on the case, and Cal is hiring runners to look into the notes. Bow Street and my old contact, Frankie, and her crew of street children are patrolling the warehouses at the docks, keeping their ears open for mentions of the current investment fleet. Sooner or later, this saboteur will make a wrong move. Don't give me that look, Lottie. You needn't feel guilty when someone else brought trouble to our door. Family takes care of one another, and we are all family here," Phee said.

Everyone followed her gaze toward the men at the refreshment table. Objectively, Emma could appreciate the picture they made, but she couldn't stop drinking in Mal's dark, swarthy appeal. The way his coat stretched across broad shoulders and wrapped around the wide torso she knew by heart made the warm day several degrees hotter. Every muscled and inked line was imprinted in her memory forever.

"Seeing them congregating over there as if they're traveling in a pack is rather appealing, isn't it?" Lottie said, interjecting levity to the conversation. She made grabby hands at Freddie, who grinned and clambered off his mother's lap, then plopped into Lottie's.

"Wolves live in packs," Alton said to no one in particular.

"They do look rather impressive, as herd animals go," Adelaide commented. "The jawlines alone make them better candidates for ogling than that poor statue at the museum." She emptied her glass and said, "I hope Simon gets more lemonade."

"Simon, is it?" Lottie asked with a raised brow.

A flush graced Adelaide's cheeks. "He asked permission to use our Christian names. It's all very proper, I assure you."

"That sounds alarmingly civilized, dear. How go your flirting efforts?" Phee asked.

"He called her saucy." Emma grinned.

"Sounds like it's going swimmingly then," Lottie said.

"What's flirting?" Alton asked.

The women paused, looking at each other for an answer.

"Flirting is how you find a friend to bring you sandwiches," Emma said, fighting valiantly to maintain a straight face.

"What?" Lottie asked.

Phee covered her face as her shoulders shuddered, and Adelaide sputtered.

Freddie climbed off Lottie's lap. "I'm going to go flirt."

"Me too!" Alton joined his cousin and the boys made determined strides with their short legs toward another group with children.

"Dear God, what have we done?" Phee muttered.

"Keep an eye on Uncle Cal! Return when he does, so you can eat. And stay where we can see you," Emma called.

Phee shifted sideways on the blanket so she could keep an eye on both the boys and her friends.

"Sandwiches?" Lottie asked, still bewildered.

"Lord Calvin's chosen euphemism for lovers," Adelaide explained.

"Ah. Well, that clarifies things not one whit," Lottie muttered.

"What time are we meeting to deal with the bank book? I want to get this over with." Simon's voice was low, but Malachi glanced around to see who could overhear.

"Maybe now isn't the time to discuss grave robbing."

"Whose grave? Theft is essentially landlocked piracy. Moving things inland, Captain?" Calvin said mildly from behind them.

Malachi narrowed his eyes at Simon in a *look what you did* glare.

"Technically, it's not theft if it's yours to begin with," Simon said, completely undeterred by the arrival of another man.

"You're robbing your own grave? Isn't that a bit... premature?" Calvin asked.

The comment didn't warrant a response, although Simon was more than happy to laugh at the jest. Malachi went about dividing Emma's plate the way she liked. One pile of bread slices. Another of cheese, and one more of meat. Thankfully, she didn't mind mixing fruit. At least, not as far as he knew. He glanced back at the women where they sat with the children. No, Emma would have to divide berries on her own, or she should have stated her preference if it was so important to her. By comparison, Alton's plate was easy.

"What on earth are you doing to those poor sandwiches?" Simon asked.

Calvin appeared at Malachi's elbow and stared at the tidy piles of food. "Are you making a plate for Emma?"

Malachi shrugged. "She likes her sandwiches in pieces."

Something in Calvin's expression made him pause. The whole outing had made him feel like he was under a magnifying lens, while their friends and family watched Malachi and Emma like a particularly fascinating species of bug. This look was different, though.

Calvin squinted a bit, staring into Malachi's eyes as if trying to read his soul. "You'll do." He nodded. "Whatever this grave thing is, count me in."

"I didn't invite you," Malachi said, stating the obvious.

"It would be rude not to." Cal picked up a tiny sandwich from the platter on the table and popped it in his mouth whole. "Think of it as a friendship-building exercise. Like arm wrestling or getting drunk together."

Malachi raised one eyebrow. "We're friends now?"

"Afraid so. I can bring muscle with me." Calvin jerked a thumb toward a giant of a man approaching with a curvy dark-haired woman on his arm. "Surely bulk is an asset when robbing a grave."

The bulk in question wandered over and watched the brunette make her way toward where Emma sat. Somewhat distractedly, the man asked in a Scottish lilt, "Isn' grave robbin' illegal?"

"The more people we bring into this, the more likely we'll get caught," Malachi said.

"But you two have already done shady things together." Calvin waved a hand between Malachi and the newcomer. "Ethan, Viscount Amesbury, meet Captain Harlow of His Majesty's Royal Navy and the newly minted Duke of Trenton."

The name clicked in Malachi's brain. Yes, he did have history with this man. Simon looked confused, but no way in hell was he going to explain here. "Pleasure to finally meet you, milord."

Lord Amesbury nodded a greeting. "So, what's the plan?"

"What *is* the plan, Mal?" Simon asked.

Malachi cleared his throat. "When I think of one, I'll let you know."

"Lucky for you, I'm excellent at making plans," Calvin said, loading his own plate.

Malachi shook his head and juggled plates and glasses. "I might have liked you better when you were trying to outman me," he said.

"I can still insult you, if it would make you feel better," Calvin quipped, grabbing two glasses of ale and joining them. "You're giving me plenty of material to work with. Between the hair and the beard, you look like a dockworker, and the cut of your coat is appalling."

"I'll be along in a minute," Lord Amesbury said, eyeing the buffet table.

As they crossed the lawn, Calvin whistled a tune under his breath.

"Are you always so cheerful?" Simon asked.

"You'll get used to me," Calvin said over his shoulder. In the next moment, he tensed, then slowed.

The change was remarkable. A complete shift from joking to being wary. Malachi followed his stare and saw the problem.

Across the grass, near the copse of trees edging the lawn, stood Lord Roxbury with two other men. It was impossible to know if he'd spotted Emma, but Malachi wasn't going to let another minute pass before joining the others on the grass.

"I see him," Malachi murmured.

"I want to rip his gizzards out through his throat," Cal growled.

Malachi smiled darkly. So that's what Calvin's actual antagonism sounded like. "I like the way you think."

"Who are we talking about?" Simon asked.

"A problem," he answered at the same time Calvin said, "A cockroach."

"I'm surprised to see him out and about. He has to have bruises from where I punched him last night."

"You got to hit him? I'm jealous," Cal said.

Malachi glanced back toward the blanket, and a chill invaded his heart. "Where are the children?"

Calvin muttered an oath.

Maybe it was his years on board ship, always preparing for the worst-case scenario, but Malachi instinctively searched the space between Emma and Roxbury, looking for the boys. With typical childlike enthusiasm, the two children were running in a haphazard pattern toward the tree line.

"Damn it, they're heading toward him." Malachi lengthened his stride toward the blanket to set down the food, and Calvin kept pace.

"Back in a moment," Cal said to the ladies as they deposited plates and glasses on the edge of the picnic blanket, then headed directly toward Lord Roxbury and the two little boys wandering too close for comfort.

Malachi broke into a light jog, needing to get there faster but not wanting to alarm anyone or draw stares.

"My boots were not made for this," Cal said, jogging alongside him.

"Complaining?"

"Not at all. Merely making an observation."

"If that bastard says one word to Emma's boy..." Malachi wished looks could kill. If so, he'd take care of Roxbury from this distance and ensure he never said a foul word to the innocent child the blackguard now had in his sight.

"Freddie, come along now. Food is ready," Cal called. The unease behind the forced cheer rang through easily, but hopefully it would fool anyone within earshot. The young ones stopped and turned toward them, their eyes lighting up.

Lord Roxbury took a step toward Alton, and a primal rage roared through Malachi.

No. Way. In. Hell.

This man had laid hands on Emma the night before. If he expected to scare Alton the same way, Roxbury would end up with worse than a swollen jaw. Of all the people involved in their messy history, Alton was the only one completely blameless. In that moment, the only thing that mattered was getting Emma's little boy out of there.

Pasting a smile on his face, Malachi sprinted the last few yards and held out his arms to Alton. Bless the innocence of youth, because the child didn't question the affectionate gesture. Swooping Alton up in his arms, he said, "You look like a lad who needs lemonade."

"And sandwiches with berries?" Alton asked, looping his thin arms around Malachi's neck. An area near his heart clenched at the sweet, simple gesture. A few feet away, Cal did the same with Freddie, amid high-pitched squeals of joy.

"Of course." Malachi tucked his forearm under Alton's bum

and held the boy close. Goodness, Alton's feet didn't even reach Malachi's knees. One glance over his shoulder showed Roxbury watching them with the sharp eyes of a bird of prey. A satisfying bruise shadowed his jawline. Malachi let his animosity show on his face until Roxbury took a step back. It felt like a victory.

Between one breath and the next, Malachi sensed he'd passed some threshold. An invisible line past which he could no longer pretend to be in this relationship with Emma only for the sex. Not when he felt like a feral dog protecting her child, not when he was as content with watching her bake in his kitchen as he was with a tumble in bed.

This wasn't what he'd planned for their relationship, and yet, here he was doing the exact opposite of running away.

They headed toward the ladies sitting on the colorful blankets. Groups sat in clusters on the lawn, but no one besides their friends seemed to have noticed anything amiss. Emma and Phee rose to meet them halfway. The women smiled wide to mask their worry, then held out their arms to the boys, who happily let go of Malachi and Calvin in favor of their mothers.

Just that fast, the tension released. He glanced at Calvin. "Is this what parenting is? Always looking for potential dangers?" He found his place next to Emma and handed a glass of lemonade to Alton.

The blond man nodded, then settled onto the blanket next to his wife. "Essentially, yes. You get used to thinking in terms of 'what's the worst that can happen,' then heading off those eventualities before they can take place."

"Sounds exhausting," Malachi said.

"It is." Emma nodded and bit into a strawberry. The juice coated her pink lips, and all thoughts of parenting and evil men who would say horrible things to little boys fled his brain entirely. Completely oblivious, Emma licked her lips and reached for another berry.

Malachi blinked. The woman was a witch and had cast a spell. Like a fairy tale. Except, if he was lusting after the witch, perhaps he wasn't the hero of this story after all. Mildly unsettling thought.

Everyone shifted to make room for the boys. Freddie took his plate and made himself at home on Lady Amesbury's lap; she dropped a casual kiss on his head, then resumed her conversation with Miss Martin and Simon.

After witnessing Simon's interest in various women over the years, Mal found it interesting to see the difference in his pursuit of Miss Martin. There was an attentiveness wrapped in respect that Simon hadn't ever shown before. It was as if Miss Martin was a puzzle to endlessly fascinate him. Malachi glanced at Emma. He recognized the feeling.

Leaning back on his elbows, Malachi let conversation flow around him while he slipped one hand under Emma's hem. The sturdy walking boots she wore ended at her ankle, so he let his fingers rest right above where the leather transitioned to silky stocking. Strawberry lips or no, he wasn't going to disrespect her by groping her in front of her family and friends. But he wanted to touch her. And here, under the cover of her skirts, he could do exactly that.

The tiny point of contact—the tips of his fingers against her stocking-covered lower leg, soothed the lingering emotion from the threat of Roxbury. And it was soothing. Calming, instead of arousing. Malachi shot her a glance and caught her smiling at him.

This affair was supposed to be physical. Nothing more complex than enjoying how well their bodies clicked together and the general sense of fun Emma brought to every situation. That's all this could be if they were to return to their normal lives in a few weeks as planned. Under a warm blue sky, lounging on a quilt spread over green grass, the *Athena* seemed worlds away.

But then, if they were determined to limit this to a sexual liaison and nothing more, they might be doing it wrong. Friends surrounded them as they sat side by side in full view of the entire Ballymore picnic. Not only that, Emma's brother had just declared Malachi a friend before they rescued children from her swine of an ex-lover.

No, this wasn't merely sexual. Even with his hand under her skirt, knowing he'd tumble her into bed later, his body wanted to relax in the sun with Emma. This was potentially messy.

Simon said something, and everyone laughed, pulling Malachi from his woolgathering.

Alton scooted from Emma's lap, carefully holding his plate in front of him, into the narrow space between Emma and Malachi, then resumed eating. Wordlessly, the little boy offered a blueberry, and Malachi took it with a smile. Emma ruffled her son's hair in a casual caress, then brushed that same hand over Malachi's cheek, smoothing her fingers along his beard.

The blueberry burst, warm and sweet on his tongue, and he sighed.

This might turn messy soon, but at the moment, it felt . . . right.

Chapter Fifteen

❧

You won't lie to me, will you, love? You'll be honest and loyal. Kind. Generous with your laughter. I'll enjoy you, and you'll enjoy me. I'd like to believe that's in my future. Maybe.

—Journal entry, August 1, 1824

For you, guv." A child of indeterminate gender or age, covered in filth, shoved a piece of paper into his hand, then darted between a cart and a woman pushing a pram. Tracking the child's progress was fruitless as he or she seemed to have disappeared entirely.

The outside of the folded paper was grimy, but Malachi's fingers were darkly tanned against the clean white of the inside. One word in bold black letters sprawled over the page.

Consequences.

What the hell? Even though he knew it was useless, he glanced around for the child messenger.

Consequences of what? Who would send such an obscure and vague note? Maybe it wasn't meant for him. Malachi searched the street, but no one lingered nearby, signaling malicious intent with helpful clues like a sinister leer or heavy hooded cloak in the middle of the day.

There wasn't time for this nonsense. He crumpled the note in his fist and shoved it in his pocket before flagging down a hack. This day wouldn't get easier by avoiding it, and he had a group of men waiting to help him complete an unsavory task.

A half hour later, he paid the hack driver and joined Ethan, Calvin, and Simon at the gate of the cemetery. Headstones dotted the ground, with the occasional family crypt standing as a stone edifice showing off wealth in this area where material things no longer mattered.

"I imagined doing this in the dark." Calvin squinted at the sun, high overhead, as if disappointed at its presence.

"Me too," Simon said.

Ethan raised a brow at the lot of them and asked, "Is there an optimal time of day tae steal from the dead?"

Calvin shrugged. "The cover of darkness has to be an asset in this situation."

"Let's get this over with," Malachi muttered. The iron gate of the cemetery squealed a cry, as if imploring them to reconsider the reason for their visit. A gravel path wove through the lines of headstones and family mausoleums.

After several minutes, Malachi stopped before the structure with the Trenton crest. He rolled his shoulders, grateful he'd foregone a cravat this morning. Facing the granite building in front of him, adorned with the family seal over the door and knowing George was inside...well. The weight of it all meant that air was in short supply.

"Really, none of this is as I pictured it," Calvin complained.

"I clearly won't be needin' this." Ethan rested the shovel he'd brought against the side of the crypt.

Simon grinned, enjoying the other men's odd disappointment.

The humor, as misplaced as it might appear on the surface, cut through the emotions rattling in Malachi's bones. *The reasons for doing this are valid*, he reminded himself for the umpteenth time since inviting the men to join him on the expedition. "I was wondering why you'd brought a shovel."

"Because grave robbing implies an actual grave, no' politely entering a miniature castle. You probably even have a bloody key," the giant Scotsman grumbled.

"Would you prefer to break in?" Malachi shook his head, but found himself smiling as he withdrew the key from his pocket and fit it into the lock.

"I didn't bring a shovel. I brought a lantern," Cal said.

"Which will actually be useful. Do you need a flint?" Malachi lit another lantern flanking the door inside the crypt.

"This place is dark as the—" Simon began.

Malachi cut him off. "If you say grave, I'm making you leave."

Behind them, Ethan snorted. Cal lit his lantern and held it aloft. The light scared away some of the oppressive gloom.

The men took a moment to take in the ornately carved walls depicting a fantastical stone garden locked in bloom forever.

"It's beautiful. Like a fairy garden for dead people," Simon said.

In the middle of the room, an iron staircase spiraled down into the crypt beneath the building, where several stone boxes held Malachi's grandparents, father, and brother. The last thing he wanted to do was see those boxes.

"It's a monument to love, believe it or not. My grandfather adored my grandmother and visited her grave to talk to her every day. The family mausoleum used to be at our country seat, but when a fire ravaged the manor, my grandfather moved to London while the house was rebuilt. He couldn't bear to leave her behind in Essex, so he built this near the town house."

Ethan crossed to the staircase. "After you."

One by one, they descended into the belly of the building. The air grew stale, with a faint underlying of rot.

"Not to be disingenuous, but it smells like something died in here." Simon's voice carried through the room.

Calvin shone the lantern along the walkways between the stone coffins. In the far corner, a sizable rat had met its end. Rather a long while ago, by the look of it. Wordlessly, he illuminated the carcass, and Simon grimaced.

"How long has it been since you visited?" Simon asked, slowly making his way between graves.

"When Grandfather passed, I made Father move his coffin to lie directly beside Grandmother's." Malachi glanced at the two stone boxes pressed side by side. "That's where he wanted to be. Beside her always."

"So not only have you not visited George, but you haven't paid your respects to your father either?" Simon tsked.

Guilt tried to settle on Malachi's shoulders, but he shrugged it off. "I was at sea, serving in the frigid waters he consigned me to." He hadn't wanted to come home. Facing his mother's grief and his brother's calm competence as he stepped into the role he'd trained for his entire life, while Malachi had been all but forgotten in the Royal Navy—it was too much.

No, that wasn't true. Mal had chosen the Royal Navy. In part to get attention, and in part to run away from everything he thought was wrong in his life. While Father hadn't gone chasing after him to drag him back into the family fold by his ear, Malachi had hardly been ignored. The close watch and stifling control Father exerted on Mal's career was its own kind of attention.

And even that, Mal had chafed under. So no, when Father died, Malachi hadn't returned home. Perhaps it was the war, or a symptom of his family's pervasive dysfunction, but his views regarding death tended toward the heartlessly pragmatic. Father didn't realize Malachi hadn't been there to visit, any more than George was witnessing his absence from the Great Beyond.

"They're gone. I wish they weren't. Not much more to say." The words sounded true, but an unsettled sensation crawling along his skin hinted at feelings not so easily dismissed. He was deeply grateful his father and brother didn't know of his absence, but a slither of guilt over his refusal to attend their funerals wrapped around his heart and squeezed.

"What exactly are we searching for?" Calvin asked.

"My father's bank book. A journal of some kind, full of government secrets, with which my mother is attempting to blackmail His Majesty's Royal Navy."

"Correction." Simon raised a finger. "She's successfully blackmailed His Majesty's Royal Navy. Too successfully. They want the book."

"Right. I've torn the town house apart looking for it, but it's not there. And Mother was bluffing—which is a problem now, since there appears to be a push for her to deliver the book in question. A note in George's diary said Father's secrets died with him. Then, dear brother delivered a leather satchel with unknown contents to our solicitor with instructions to bury it with him."

"I'm impressed she could bluff so well," Ethan commented, pacing the perimeter of the room.

"Oh, I don't doubt she knows the contents of the book. Mother has enough information to hang over the appropriate heads. But the actual book? Signs point to it being here. Somewhere."

As one, they turned toward the nearest coffin, where George rested for all eternity.

"Let's look around before we take that step," Simon said, glancing uneasily at the stone rectangle.

The crypt echoed the sound of shuffling feet as they searched every nook and cranny of the room.

"Does Emma know about this?" Calvin asked.

"I've told her about the book. But not this particular expedition."

Calvin muttered a colorful curse directed at Malachi.

"Probably best to not blaspheme my ancestors when they're so close at hand," Malachi said blandly.

Working his way around the room, it became obvious that as fantastical as Grandfather's design of the building had been, he hadn't allotted for space to hide family secrets. Rather short-sighted of him, considering his son's line of work.

The men met back where they began, gathered around the stone box with its thick slab lid, and stared in silence for a moment.

"How do we do this?" Simon asked.

Instead of answering, Calvin withdrew a flask from his coat and passed it around. "Liquid courage."

One by one, the men took a swig from the metal canister until it came back around to Calvin.

"Crowbar, I think. Or shove it aside, maybe? Will a slide or a lift be easier?" Ethan crossed his arms and studied the coffin.

"How long has he been in there?" Calvin asked.

"Long enough to be...less than pretty." Malachi grimaced. Which was the part he dreaded. Beyond the ethical implications of going against his brother's dying wish and stealing from his resting place, seeing George postmortem disturbed him on many levels.

As if Simon read his mind, he turned. "Mal, will you be all right seeing your brother like this?"

When a rough swallow didn't loosen his throat, Malachi held

out a hand for the flask again. "I'm not sure. I'm hoping the satchel is by his feet. If we open this end, maybe it won't be so bad? If we shove, it will be easier than lifting." Taking another swig of liquor, he returned Cal's flask and nodded his thanks.

Malachi hung the lantern on the wall and rolled his shoulders. The brandy had left a warm trail down to his belly, but the heat cooled under the weight of chilly dread. "No time like the present, I suppose." He rested his hands on the slab and braced his feet. One by one the other men took places beside him until they all had their hands on the marble. "How heavy do you think it is?"

"Under a ton, by my estimate." Calvin glanced over at them and saw them staring. "Once you know how heavy an inch-thick square foot of marble is, the math is quite simple."

Simon shook his head and readied his stance. "On three?"

Malachi nodded. "One."

"Two," Calvin said.

Ethan finished the count. "Three."

The marble let loose a rough groan of stone against stone as the lid scraped out of place. The smell hit him nearly as hard as the sight of George's shroud. Silk, because their mother would never allow her son to be buried in wool.

Of one mind, the men stepped back and covered their mouths and noses with handkerchiefs, a coat sleeve, and in Ethan's case, the hastily untied ends of his cravat.

"Bloody hell, that's ghastly." Calvin's words were muffled, spoken into the crook of his elbow.

Malachi couldn't agree more. With his eyes watering, he tried not to breathe and avoided looking at the lump underneath the burial shroud. Snagging the lantern from the floor where they'd left it, he shone the light on the inside of the coffin.

"I think I see it," Simon said, pointing toward a shadowy corner beneath the marble lid.

Malachi handed the lantern to Simon, and Calvin came alongside to hold his light up as well.

"Here goes nothing." He shoved his hand into the coffin, keeping as close to the lid as possible. The occasional brush of silk against his palm made his stomach roll, but after an endless moment, his fingers brushed leather. "I'm sorry, brother," he murmured, withdrawing the satchel George had taken to his grave.

Closing the coffin was completed without further conversation.

Malachi held the bag, not touching the outside except for the strap. Setting it on the ground, he nudged the flap of the satchel up and pushed it open with the toe of his boot. Calvin craned closer to look, bringing the light with him.

Peeking from within the darkness in the bag was the binding of a book. Why his fingers trembled as he pulled it out, he didn't want to consider. The book was several inches thick, red leather, with a well-worn paper edge. In fact, the only thing noteworthy about it was its familiarity. All those years, this book had moved with them, and he'd been oblivious to the fact that its secrets were capable of manipulating His Majesty's government.

"I can't believe we did all this for a book." Calvin's voice rang out in the quiet room.

"My father's book of secrets. This is my best defense to allay charges of treason against my mother."

Calvin's eyes went wide. "Your life is far more interesting than I gave you credit for. Treason?"

"That's the fear," Malachi said. "The more real possibility is that she will have an accident. Or something appearing to be an accident. That's how spies work." Holding a book powerful enough to blackmail a government, the truth was undeniable. Father had been a spy. A good one. A spy powerful enough to have the influence to guide Malachi's career without ever setting foot on one of his ships.

Simon nodded. "I haven't heard anything through official channels, so you're probably right about the pending accident."

Smoothing the red leather cover with one hand, Malachi opened the book and flipped through the first few pages. Father's bank book. Government secrets. Columns of...gibberish. He squinted and tilted his head. No, the text didn't make sense sideways either.

"What's wrong?" Ethan asked.

"It's encoded." He slapped the book against his thigh. "Of course it's encoded. A proper spy would never leave damning information lying around where anyone could read it, if it wasn't in some code only he knew."

"So you admit he was a spy?" Simon asked distractedly, taking the book from Malachi's hands.

"Button your lip, Simon."

"Are you going tae turn it over? Whatever is in these pages is important enough tae code and threaten the king. You'll be giving away your father's work," Ethan asked.

"Do you have a better idea, Lord Bibliophile?" Calvin grunted. "Leave it to you to want to keep the bloody thing."

"Does anyone actually know what this looks like?" Ethan pointed to the book.

Simon let out a sharp laugh. "A decoy. You're thinking to make a decoy."

The idea made Malachi snatch the book back from Simon. This *was* his father's work. The dukedom had been a matter of birth. But this book, with every bit of damning information it held, had been Father's passion. "We find another red journal in case someone is familiar with what it looks like. And we burn it. Bring the Admiralty a box of ashes with enough pieces of red binding to be convincing."

"Make them think you burned it to protect everyone's secrets, and it could work," Calvin said.

A breath escaped on a sigh. "That's what we will do. I'll steal Father's book back from the government."

"What was it Simon said at the picnic? You can't steal what's already yours. This book belongs to the Duke of Trenton." Calvin swept an elaborate bow toward Malachi. "Your Grace."

For the first time, the title didn't grate on his nerves. Instead, he smiled and tucked the red book into his coat.

Chapter Sixteen

You're only a fantasy, aren't you?
—Journal entry, June 22, 1824

A re you trying to kill me?"

"I thought you were trying to kill me," Mal replied. Bless him, he sounded as winded as she did.

Emma rolled to her side and tucked her head into the cradle of his shoulder. He lifted his hand to rest it behind his head, making his biceps the perfect pillow. The bay rum warmth of his scent hit her nose, and she breathed in the mix of him and the smell of sex.

"You were on top and I was the helpless captive under your thrall. Therefore, you're killing me. Not the other way around." Mal ran his fingers over her hand, with which she absently followed the lines of ink on his chest.

Emma sighed contentedly, and waited for feeling to return to her legs. A yawn split her face, reminding her of the late hour. It would be time to leave soon, but she'd cling to these last few moments while she could. Alton's boundless energy had meant it was one of those afternoons when she'd been so grateful for the help of the nurse that Emma had nearly kissed the woman in gratitude.

"I've been thinking about the future," Emma began, gathering the nerve to broach the subject. "We said we'd end this affair when you returned to sea."

Under her cheek, he seemed to stop breathing. "Funny you should mention this. I've been considering the future as well."

She could hear the smile in his voice, and a glance up showed his pale eyes crinkling at the corners. The warmth there boosted her courage. Staying for the Season and entering into this affair was an exercise in honesty, in finding a way to live authentically without turning into her mother and replicating her parents' disastrous relationship. Which meant, in this case, asking for more. Vulnerability was knee-shakingly scary—good thing she was laying down.

"I'll be returning to Olread Cove in a few weeks. I'm putting down roots there and purchasing property for Alton. What if, when you returned to England, you and I made an effort to see each other? We could make this a long-term arrangement. At least, until your mother convinces you to marry some simpering miss worthy of your coronet."

He tilted his face down. "Do I detect a bit of jealousy, Lady Em?"

Emma rolled her eyes and huffed. "Of course not. I have no intention of marrying again."

Mal gently rolled over, keeping her in the cradle of his arms, so they faced each other. "I don't want this to end either. In fact, I've wondered if there is a path forward for us."

A light feeling in her chest made it seem that only her ribs kept her heart from floating away entirely. "I don't know what that path looks like. But I'd like to figure it out. With you, I mean."

Dropping a kiss on the tip of her nose, he agreed. "With you."

Joy bubbled up, but she didn't have any idea what to do with it. Did they make plans, or go on as they were, picking their way through their situation until they found themselves where they were meant to be? She had no idea, so she changed the subject. "Speaking of futures...do you think Simon plans to offer for Adelaide?"

"I'm not sure. But what is going on between them is different from anything I've ever seen from Simon. He won't toy with her, but he's never pursued a woman like her."

"You mean shy and quiet?"

"Virginal."

Ah. "I think they're great together. There would be many benefits to such a match. Especially with her father's influential role in politics, and Simon's place in the Admiralty."

"Playing matchmaker, Em?" He pulled her closer, until she was pressed against the length of him. When he nuzzled along her throat, he murmured, "Do I detect lemon tonight?"

She made a noise of agreement and wiggled when he found a sensitive spot on her neck. "Probably. I took over a corner of the kitchen and set Alton to work making lemon tartlets. We were both covered in ingredients by the end of it."

He reared back in mock horror. "And you didn't bring me any?"

"Blame Ethan. They're his favorite. That's why we made them. He and Lottie visited this afternoon."

The full bottom lip he stuck out made her laugh. "No need to pout. I'll bake a batch for you soon." She received a grinning kiss as answer, and Emma relaxed into the taste of him. Familiar, and growing dearer every day. It was such a relief to hear he didn't want this to end any time soon either. Yet their earlier conversation wasn't complete.

"Have you considered what you'll do if you can't return to sea?"

Heavy, dark brows met over the bridge of his nose. "Adapt, I suppose. Like it or not, I'm Trenton. I need a purpose, and managing the dukedom will certainly fill my days." The flat tone in his voice didn't make her think he looked forward to the prospect.

"Any luck finding out what your mother was holding over the Admiralty?"

The pause was heavy enough to make her study his face in more than the usual admiring perusal she enjoyed. Mal opened his mouth, then closed it, and opened it again, as if searching for the right words. Somehow, she knew whatever he settled on wouldn't be the truth.

Emma placed a finger over his lips. "Whatever you are going to say. Don't. Don't lie to me. If you won't or can't tell me, then just say so."

His expression relaxed. "I'd rather not say. It's a family situation, and I'm not sure what any of it means yet."

Well, that was clear as mud. But better she didn't know than he lied to her.

And no, the irony of demanding honesty wasn't lost on Emma. If her secrets and lies were bricks, she could build her own damn house.

Instead of delving into that, she took advantage of his closeness and nibbled his bottom lip until his length nudged insistently against her belly. A glance at the clock beside the bed showed it to be later than she'd thought. Every minute here was one less minute she could sleep in her own bed. It was also another minute her servants weren't in their beds. She sighed.

"Don't make that noise. That sound means you're leaving

soon," Mal grumbled, nibbling at the corner of her mouth and coaxing another kiss from her.

"The hour grows late. I need to get home." Emma ignored the way his hands flexed against her back, as if to clutch her to him as she slipped out from under the covers. She padded to the privacy screen and took care of herself, then crossed to the mirror to assess how much intervention her hair needed.

Behind her in the looking glass, Mal sat up, openly admiring her nakedness as she tried to style her hair into some sort of fashion that didn't make her look freshly tumbled. Even though she was. Wonderfully so. She shot him a grin in the mirror and he smiled back. "Can I borrow your hairbrush?"

"Top right drawer of the dressing table," he said, crossing his arms over his raised knees and looking his fill.

The brush was exactly where he said it was, resting inside the drawer atop a book.

A familiar book. The breath in her lungs stalled, and Emma went cold.

What the hell was Malachi Harlow doing with her journal? She glanced in the mirror and cleared her expression. Mal tossed the covers aside and rose, stretching his arms overhead. Showing off on purpose, and part of her wanted to enjoy the view.

Except he had her journal. She waited until he turned to the bedside table to remove the French letter before she used a finger to flip open the cover. Sure enough, there was her handwriting. A slip of paper tucked in like a bookmark caught her eye and breath left her lungs. Familiar script she'd recognize anywhere covered the page with one word—*Consequences*.

A shaking began with the hand gripping the soft, pliable cover, and she deliberately released her fingers. Dragging the brush through her hair, Emma kept one eye on Mal.

That handwriting had been on the blackmail note Lottie and Ethan had received, as well as the message Phee had gotten the day they went to the museum. No, it wasn't Mal's handwriting—but how difficult would it be to alter your pen strokes for anonymity's sake?

Her gaze flew to the drawer. Had she mentioned Phee's identity as Adam? Or the death of Phee's uncle Milton? Goodness, had she confessed to murder in those pages?

How much did he know?

Mal walked toward her, all distracting muscles, tattoos, and tangled hair.

Was he blackmailing her family? There was that business from a few years ago with Lottie's unwelcome suitor, but what did he have to gain from such a thing? Especially when he'd been involved.

Her heartbeat thudded in her ears as she tried to organize her thoughts. There were two problems here: Mal had her private journal and the note.

Damned if she knew what to do with either piece of information.

He dropped a kiss on her shoulder as he passed, and Emma forced a stiff smile. Inside her chest, anxiety made breathing quietly nearly impossible.

As soon as he stepped behind the screen and turned his back, she grabbed the journal from the drawer and darted to her pile of clothes. Damn, her reticule was far too small to hold it. The book disappeared into the folds of her hooded cape.

Emma scurried back to the dressing table and went through the motions, dragging the brush through her hair a few more times before setting it aside. With distracted movements, she jabbed pins into her curls and hoped the mass stayed put long enough to get her to the carriage.

She'd slipped into her chemise and was tightening her stays when Mal came out from the screen, cinching the belt of a banyan around his trim waist.

"You're in a hurry all of a sudden," he commented.

"I need to get home, and my poor footmen should find their beds soon." Emma tossed her gown over her head and hastily fastened the ties, to mask her shaking hands.

When she glanced up at Mal, he appeared slightly concerned, and so damned handsome, it threatened to break her heart. However, he didn't seem suspicious. Emma dropped a kiss on his cheek. "This was lovely. I'll see you later."

Emma closed his bedroom door behind her, then donned her cape and tucked the journal under her arm. She was several steps down the staircase when the door opened and Mal stepped through with a quizzical smile on his lips.

"At least let me walk you to the door and wait with you while the carriage is brought around."

Because he was a gentleman.

Who had somehow stolen her journal months ago.

It had to have been when they met in Olread Cove. The journal had disappeared in October, around when she'd spent the night with Mal. Questions buzzed through her brain, but Emma couldn't ask any of them without giving away that she had the journal back.

Was her identity clear within the pages? Perhaps he didn't realize the journal was hers?

That seemed as improbable as Mal sending threatening notes to the friends and family of the woman warming his bed. And yet, it wasn't impossible.

At the front door, Emma tugged on her gloves and avoided his gaze.

"Are you sure you're all right, Emma?"

"Of course. I'm just tired." She dimpled up at him, pulling on the unaffected and innocent air she used to ply on her father. "You wore me out, Your Grace. Oh, there's my carriage. Hobby must have been waiting for my summons. Good coachmen are worth their weight in gold, wouldn't you agree?" Emma opened the door herself and rose on her tiptoes to kiss his cheek one more time.

"Let's do this again soon," she said. No, they wouldn't be meeting like this again, but he didn't need to hear that right this instant.

The cool night air slapped her cheeks as she nearly ran down the stairs to the coach and the footman holding the door open. "Thank you, Charles. Let's go home."

Her breathing didn't calm until the wheels lurched into motion and the house with the black door and shiny brass knocker disappeared from sight.

Emma pulled the journal from her cloak and ran her fingers over the familiar dimensions. In the dark, she couldn't see the words, but as she opened it, she knew the pages fluffed open to the wrong place. The clean pages at the back no longer opened upon command, awaiting her pen. This book had been read, and often enough to have changed to greet someone else's favorite pages. A chill rocked her.

No, she could never see Malachi Harlow again. How she'd manage that, she had no idea.

⟡

"Good morning, Your Grace," Ivan said, opening the door to the Trenton townhome.

"*Dobroye utro*, Ivan. Is my mother home?" Malachi handed his gloves and hat to the butler.

"In the library, Your Grace."

Nodding his thanks, he strode down the hall toward the carved double doors. Inside, his mother stood on a rolling ladder, removing books from the shelves one by one. Now that he knew what the bank book looked like, it was obvious her efforts focused on those with red covers.

"Good morning, Mother. I trust you slept well. The night patrols report things have been quiet since the break-in."

Lady Trenton stepped delicately from the ladder and brushed her hands together in a gesture he knew probably indicated nerves. With his mother, one never knew for sure. But he'd learned from a young age to watch her hands. Like a gambler, her hands were always the tell.

"Malachi. I wasn't expecting you."

After his time in the family crypt, the plan he'd hatched with the other men had solidified in his mind. All he had to do was convince his mother.

Easier said than done under most circumstances.

Within reach of the desk, a shelf held the collection of daily diaries George had kept from his years as Trenton. And, as he remembered, several of them were the approximate size and color of their father's bank book. He slipped the stack from the shelf and placed them on the desk in a tidy pile.

"What are you doing? I've already searched those shelves."

Malachi opened the first, filled with his brother's neat handwriting and exhaustive details of the estate management. "We need to sacrifice one of them to get you out of the trouble you've made. Choose one to burn, and we'll take the ashes to whoever you threatened. You'll hand over the remnants and tell them it's the bank book, which you destroyed to protect everyone's secrets. And then, you'll apologize prettily, claim you were addled by grief, or some such excuse, and promise to never misuse your power in such a way again. Do what you need to for this to go away."

"But…those are George's." A crack in her voice made Malachi glance up. The stricken look on her pale face said it all.

The open book in his hands had his mother turning pasty white and shaky at the idea of getting rid of it. Malachi ran a hand over the page. It wasn't really the book though, was it? It was the handwriting. A remnant of his brother. That's what she couldn't destroy.

The old ache, the pain of knowing he'd never be as beloved as perfect George, reared its head, but he stopped it with one look at his mother. The grief on her face was undeniable. Yes, she'd loved George more. Yes, she'd been frequently cruel and dismissive to Malachi as a child. And as a child he hadn't understood why his mother favored one son over the other. At the end of the day, there was nothing he could do about it now. No way to earn her affection, or be enough in her eyes. The truth was, the Dowager Duchess of Trenton had lost the two men she loved most in the world—her husband and son. Her grief was real, and if he loved her at all, he'd recognize that.

"I miss him too, Mother. It's not the same as what you feel. I understand that. But, even if we gutted this entire room and erased all signs of George, it doesn't erase him. George knew how important Father's bank book was, and he took great pains to hide it from us. Don't you think he would throw this diary into the fire himself if it meant clearing a threat against you?"

To his shock, twin tears trailed down her cheeks. "Of course he would. You don't really think he hid the bank book on purpose? From me?"

"I know he did. I found an entry mentioning it in one of these estate journals. Mother, he loved you dearly. He probably hid the bank book to protect you from the potential danger of Father's secrets." Danger she'd found anyway. Mal offered the book to her. "Would you like to look through this? It appears to be livestock and dairy records from the estate in Essex. But there might be a few personal notations you want to save."

Marjorie sniffed and took the journal. "I'll see to it. As you said, a pretty apology and a token gesture on my part should clear the way to forgetting the whole thing if I bring them this.

Lord Clarey has a niece debuting next Season, I believe. Horse-faced little thing if I remember correctly. But if I sponsor her, I'm sure it will secure his assistance in making this go away."

That poor niece. Biting the inside of his cheek leashed a sympathetic grimace. "I'll leave this in your more than capable hands, then." Malachi bowed to his mother and left the library as quickly as he'd arrived.

Hill Street was only a short walk away. Emma's farewell had seemed strange last night. Distracted and not quite right. Their conversation about the future hadn't resulted in an actual plan, but their agreement that this affair wouldn't be a temporary thing had been lightening his mood ever since he awoke. A glance at his pocket watch showed the hour was early, but not obscenely so. Alton would have been awake for quite a while, according to everything she'd said about their schedule, so she'd be up for the day as well.

Tilting his hat at a jaunty angle, Malachi turned toward Calvin's house on Hill Street. It was hard not to whistle a tune as he raised his face toward the sun.

By resolving the threat to his mother, the reasons for the Admiralty holding him on land were eliminated. The last letter from his first lieutenant said the drydock repairs would be finished within the month.

Which meant he had a few more weeks to enjoy Emma before leaving. And this time, when he kissed her goodbye and sailed with the tide, she would be waiting for his return with open arms.

Finally, things were looking up.

Chapter Seventeen

⟋⟍

I sometimes wonder if the true measure of a family is in how they weather hardship. Mine splintered apart, leaving me with a reliable brother and parents who only occasionally pretended to care.

—Journal entry, May 8, 1824

After hours of restless tossing and turning, Emma rolled from bed. No need to stop before the mirror when she knew she looked like a gorgon. Inanimate objects confirming the situation wouldn't help her mood.

Emma felt like a little black rain cloud as she entered the cheery breakfast room with morning light bringing a glow to the yellow walls. Grumpily blowing a hank of hair away from the corner of her mouth, she blinked away the sleepy dirt and tugged at the neckline of her wrapper to make sure it covered the love bite from last night's doomed escapades.

Mornings like this made her infinitely grateful for her family.

No one talked to anyone until after their second cup of coffee. It was a rule. They hadn't exactly stated it in as many words, but it was a rule. A rule everyone respected when she flopped down in the chair like a rag doll. Her brother raised his brows, then slid the coffeepot toward her with one finger.

When Emma poured her second cup, Phee spoke. "I take it you didn't sleep well?"

"No." Emma's voice sounded dull and hollow. "I found something last night." Telling them hadn't been her intent, but the story had been bubbling inside her all night, and now it seemed determined to trip off her tongue no matter what. Besides, she'd decided honesty was the best way to break old habits. After a concentrated effort these past weeks, speaking the truth felt more natural, which provided bittersweet comfort.

"At Mal's?" Cal asked. She had to give him credit for not sounding judgmental about his little sister having an affair with a friend.

"At Mal's," Emma confirmed. "Do you remember last year when I wrote to you about misplacing my journal?"

Phee knit her brows together. "Yes. You thought Alton had run off with it."

Emma sighed and braced herself with another sip of coffee. "Right around the same time, I met Mal at an assembly in the village and we spent the night together."

Phee nodded. "I remember."

"If this story has a point, I'm not following it," Cal said.

Emma set her coffee cup down and stared into the dark depths. "Mal has my journal. Or *had* my journal. I found it last night in his room. I stole it back and now I can never see him again."

"Oh my," Phee said.

"Oh my, indeed," Cal said. "What exactly was in this journal?"

Emma leaned back in her chair. "A lot. One journal usually takes me about a year and a half to two years to fill. It was a daily or sometimes weekly accounting of my life and my thoughts. I didn't expect anyone to ever read it, so I didn't prevaricate while writing."

"So, he knows everything. Phee's history, all of it," Calvin said.

Phee grimaced. "I suppose that makes confessing all the family secrets rather anticlimactic."

"I told him about Alton's parentage, but left out certain details about you and Adam." Emma chose to ignore the raised eyebrows around the table at the news of her opening up to Mal. "It gets worse. I think I found the blackmailer. Mal had another note, already written, tucked into the journal," Emma said. Trying to determine why he would do such a thing had kept her up all night. What did he have to gain? There was no clear answer.

Phee froze, and her eyes went wide. "Shit."

"Precisely my reaction as well," Emma said.

"What did it say?" Phee asked.

"Consequences."

Cal shook his head. "What does that even mean? What's his motive? Why threaten your family while..."

"Having sex with me," Emma said. "Those are the words you were looking for, brother." Or making love to her—which is what it had begun to feel like. A dry piece of skin at her cuticle snagged on her wrapper and Emma gave it her whole attention while she spoke. "That's what I've been trying to figure out. Having one of those notes is pretty damning. But why would he do such a thing? *How* could he do such a thing? How do you threaten your lover, but be so convincingly *good* face-to-face?"

Now that the words were coming, she couldn't seem to stop them. "I'm not a fool. Sex does not equal love. Hell, our parents taught us that. We saw it over and over growing up. Lovers are disposable. But I thought..." She'd thought he was different. She'd thought she was finding her way to making better decisions about her relationships. Managing expectations, ensuring the person she spent time with was a decent person and kind to not only her, but to her son.

Phee reached over and covered Emma's hand. "Don't pick at your cuticles, Em. Not every lover is disposable. Some partners are made for keeping." Phee was using her soothing mommy voice, and Emma hated to admit it was working. The tension in her shoulders began to seep away. Maybe there was something to this deliberate sharing of secrets and honesty. It was hard not to wonder if her mother had ever tried it, or if she'd hopped from bed to bed thinking she'd somehow stumble upon this kind of intimacy and safety. No, it wasn't an intimacy that came from being naked with a lover. Even amid the heartbreak over Mal's betrayal, she could acknowledge a wave of gratitude for these members of her family.

"I don't know what any of this means. The note, the reason for stealing your journal—any of it," Phee said, pulling Emma back to the subject at hand.

"I think the timing is suspect as well. Didn't the problems with the Amesburys begin around the same time Mal returned to London? Unfortunately, it all lines up when you think about it," Emma said. Although no matter how she examined possible motives, she couldn't think of a reason that Mal would do such a thing. What did he have to gain? The blackmailer had demanded cash from Lottie and Ethan. And seemed to be focusing on the investment side of finances for Ethan and Phee as well, from what she'd overheard.

Malachi was a duke. He didn't need money. Which left one thing: a personal vendetta. Grudges were rarely logical, but damned if she could figure this one out.

A rap on the door brought their conversation to a halt.

"Pardon me," Higgins said. "The Duke of Trenton has come to call on Lady Emma."

She went cold at the name. Emma darted a look between Phee and Cal, shaking her head. "I don't think I can face him."

Phee swallowed so hard, Emma could hear it from her chair. "We can't just ask him to explain, I suppose?"

Cal shot his wife a disbelieving look, and Emma copied it, then addressed the butler. "Please tell His Grace I'm not receiving visitors today. I'm not feeling well and expect to be indisposed for several days."

Higgins nodded and closed the door behind him.

"You can't avoid him forever, Em. Society in London is too limited," Cal said, with a worried groove between his eyebrows. "As much as it pains me to say it, if the threat is here in Town, I'd sleep easier knowing you were far away in Olread Cove."

Phee rubbed her fingers over her forehead and sighed. "As a professional runner from my problems, I have to caution you. Running rarely works in the long term. But since this is a matter of safety, I have to agree with Calvin."

The door to the breakfast room opened and a footman entered with a salver. "Post, milord."

"Thank you, Charles." Cal flipped through the envelopes, then paused and examined one in particular. "Emma, you have mail. Looks to be from the property manager in Olread Cove."

"Perfect. I shall return to my house—one I'll own—and everything will be fine. Normal, even. No handsome pirate or reprobate Roxbury." She snagged the letter from her brother's outstretched hand and slid her fingernail under the wax seal as she smiled at Phee with a lightness she didn't feel. "See? It will all work out."

The note was shorter than she expected. Emma read it through once, then began again, digesting the words Mr. Williams had scrawled across the page.

"Are they counter offering?" Cal asked, spreading butter on a slice of toast.

Words felt nearly impossible, but Emma choked them out. "No. I'm being evicted."

Silverware clattered to the table and Phee whirled to face her. "What? Evicted? On what grounds?"

Being punched in the gut would hurt less. Tears pooled along her lower lashes as Emma struggled for breath. "Mr. Williams thanks me for my years of timely payments and being a model tenant, but the owner of the house intends to take up residence, so I'll need to move out."

"Who's the owner? Perhaps we can appeal directly to him with a higher offer," Cal said, already in a problem-solving frame of mind.

A tear splashed onto the letter, splattering ink into a smear. "According to Mr. Williams, the property is owned by the Duke of Trenton. I'm being evicted on the order of Malachi."

"Son of a bitch," Cal and Phee said in unison.

"What on earth have I done to make him hate me?" Emotional numbness set in, and frankly, it was a relief. Betrayal wasn't an unfamiliar beast, but goodness, this hurt. Out of nowhere, to be the victim of this level of duplicity absolutely took her breath away. The agony of it served only to highlight how deep she'd let Mal into her heart. Memories of his protectiveness with Alton, the deep rumble of his laugh, the wicked spark he'd get in his pale hazel eyes before kissing her. All of it had been a lie.

Yes, numbness was far preferable to all that.

"You won't be homeless. I'm sorry you won't have the cottage, but you can choose any of our properties, Emma. Make one your home. You and Alton will always have a roof over your heads, no matter what." Cal rose and threw his serviette on the table. "I'm going to Ethan's."

Higgins opened the door once more. "Pardon the additional intrusion, milord. You have several visitors claiming there is an emergency."

Emma rested her elbows on the table and cradled her face. "Can't a woman's life collapse in relative peace in this house?" she moaned.

"If I may make a suggestion, milord? Perhaps you could entertain these guests in here. I imagine they would appreciate breakfast, and if it's all the same to you, I'd rather not let them on the furniture," the butler said.

Phee sighed. "Are these visitors short, dirty, and young?"

"Er, yes, milady. Exactly right."

Cal motioned for Higgins to step aside and opened the door wider. "Frankie, bring them in," he called into the hall.

The summons brought the sound of scuffling footsteps, then the appearance of several scruffy children of indeterminate age to the breakfast room.

"Shall I stay, milord?" Higgins asked.

"No, thank you. They work for us," Cal said.

As soon as the breakfast room door closed, the children began speaking at once until their voices muddied together and not a word of it could be understood.

Phee raised a hand in the air. "Quiet!"

Like magic, they did as they were told. Emma blinked in bemused wonder. She'd known about the tiny urchin army who provided information to protect Cal's financial interests at the docks, but Emma had never met them. Phee began the relationship with street children back when she'd been impersonating her brother. Apparently, only their leader, Frankie, had known Phee then. Frankie was old enough now to lead her own crew, and she kept her mouth shut about Phee's previous identity out of loyalty.

"Frankie, would you mind summarizing?" Phee asked.

The oldest, probably thirteen or so, stepped forward. "We was on our way back from the pub and saw a light in the warehouse window. Then a man climbed out the window and ran off like hellhounds was at his heels."

"Did you get a look at the fellow?" Calvin asked.

"No, but we wondered what he was doing there, didn' we? So we broke in and found a crate on fire."

"Arson?" Emma said. A murmur of agreement went through the group of children.

"Not very good at it. Fool went for the wrong corner," piped up a boy who seemed made of equal parts grime and sharp bones.

The child Phee had called Frankie said, "Set a box of dishes on fire. Those don' burn well, or else he'd have done a better job of it."

"Chinese porcelain. Priceless Chinese porcelain," Calvin muttered, looking wide-eyed at the news.

"Now, if he'd gone for the cloth, it woulda worked a trick," said another boy, and the others nodded.

Emma glanced at Calvin for translation. "Hand-painted silk. Bolts of it." Cal sighed. "Frankie, how bad is it?"

"We put out the fire before it could spread. But someone's after ya, gov. This wasn' an accident," Frankie said.

Phee stood and placed a hand on the girl's shoulder. "Frankie, thank you for putting out the fire, but that was a very dangerous thing to do, and you could have been hurt. A warehouse full of goods is not worth anyone's safety."

Frankie shrugged, staring down at her feet as she rubbed the toe of one shoe against the carpet. "The boys actually put out the fire. I couldn' because I'm a girl. But I'm the one who spotted the man climbin' out the window."

Cal raised one brow. "What does your being a girl have to do with it?"

"We pissed on it!" a boy piped up, and the rest of the group beamed, so very proud of themselves that Phee's burst of laughter didn't seem out of place at all.

Emma covered her mouth to stifle a snort of amusement.

Calvin chuckled and ruffled the hair of the nearest child. "Quick thinking. And now I'm doubly glad the fire wasn't near the painted silk."

"Good work, everyone." Emma stood and crossed to the covered dishes on the sideboard. "Please help yourselves to breakfast."

She hastily stepped back to avoid the stampeding little feet, but their enthusiasm made her smile until Cal and Phee gestured her over.

"Start packing, Em. I would sleep better if I knew that you and Alton were away from this. Arson is a serious threat. What if they go after the house next? Phee, we should send Freddie to Lakeview with Miss Lacey," Cal said in a low voice.

Phee said, "Agreed. The country will be safer for the children." She linked her arm through Emma's and tugged her toward the door. "Let's go visit the boys in the nursery and tell them of their upcoming travels."

Leaving Cal to supervise Frankie and the others' breakfast, Emma let herself be escorted through the hall. "Phee, what am I going to do?"

Her best friend glanced over with a serious expression as they climbed the stairs to the family rooms. "You go on. You put one foot ahead of the other. Eventually you hurt less. You show up for your son and focus on being a mother for a while. Cal is right. Choose a house. Make it yours. I suggest an unentailed property, so we can give it to you. Alton will have his land, as you wanted. Eventually there will be an end to all this upheaval. In the meantime, take a footman with you everywhere. Charles is loyal, big, and will keep you safe until this is over."

The words settled on Emma, and she blew out a breath. Alton would be safe. He'd be taken care of. They'd make sure of it. Everything else was merely heartbreak, and she'd already proven she could survive that.

"Did you love him, Em?"

Emma didn't have to ask who Phee meant. "A little, yes. Or, I was well on my way. A slide from lust to love was happening, I think." Blinking back fresh tears, Emma reached a shaky hand out to grasp the door handle to open the hall to the nursery.

A rueful smile tilted Phee's mouth. "I'm glad you caught it in time, then. It wasn't a slide for me. More like a sudden drop of realization that it had been Cal all along."

How lovely it must have been. To wake up and realize you were already where you belonged. "I'm glad you have each other. Maybe one day I will find what you have. I need to stop letting rat bastards in my life first, though."

Phee placed her hand on top of Emma's on the nursery door. "Please don't blame yourself. We had no way of knowing. All of us liked him. Hell, he even won over Lady Agatha."

True. Mal had charmed everyone, slipping into their group of friends with an ease Emma had believed meant he belonged with them. With her.

Silly girl. Silly, stupid girl.

*

Something was wrong. Somehow, he'd made a mistake, and Malachi had no idea what he'd done. The note he'd sent Emma this morning sat in his hand, returned unopened.

The butler at Calvin's house had said she was feeling poorly and wouldn't be taking visitors for several days. The following day there was no reply to his concerned message. Which was fine. After all, the woman was a mother and surrounded by family and friends. It wasn't as if she was pining her days away for want of word from him.

Like he was for her.

Today's note had been returned unopened along with the

bouquet of flowers he'd sent to cheer her up as she recovered from whatever malady befell her. The blooms sat in a vase on his dressing table. Emma hadn't even taken his flowers.

What the hell had happened?

The only bright spots in the last few days came in the form of a summons from the Admiralty, and a note from Simon. A contact, who Simon simply referred to as Smith, had agreed to take a look at the bank book.

Mal should be thinking about the government information his father had left behind and returning to his ship before it left drydock. Instead, he was worrying about Emma's silence.

He'd had relationships end before, of course. But never this abruptly or mysteriously. Nothing else explained her silence—they were over, hours after agreeing they both wanted more from each other. It didn't make sense. The clock in the hall chimed, and Malachi rubbed at an ache under his sternum.

The clock's bells continued, and he glanced over. Damn it, he was supposed to have left a quarter hour ago. Simon was meeting him at the codebreaker's house.

The sun was obnoxiously bright against his face when he stepped outside to flag down a hack, and he glared up at the sky.

Fine, he was grumpy. Who would blame him, though?

Thankfully, the traffic gods were smiling down on him, even if the relationship gods were not. Although running late, he wasn't too far behind schedule when the hack arrived at the address Simon had given him.

The house was in a nice area of town with beautifully kept homes and swept streets. Having been on the receiving end of the king's salary for years, Malachi had to wonder who this codebreaker Smith fellow was that he could afford to live here. The sight of Simon pacing in front of a set of stone steps, thumping an impatient tattoo against his thigh with his hat, was confirmation that he had the correct address.

"Where have you been? We're late," Simon greeted him.

"Hello to you too. Sorry. I lost track of time." Getting into the intricacies of his suddenly dismal love life while standing on the street sounded like an appalling idea, so he gestured to the house. "After you."

A pleasant-faced butler answered the door, then ushered them into a cozy parlor without ceremony. The room appeared to be decorated with abandoned books and comfortable cushions. Every flat surface not designed to support a bottom had been turned into a bookshelf of sorts. No bric-a-brac or porcelain figurines for Smith.

Mal touched a finger to a stack of books on a marble-topped table and glanced at the titles. One in Dutch, four in French, and another in Spanish. He raised a brow. Mr. Smith was quite the eclectic reader. On the mantel sat two well-worn identical volumes, the gilt lettering of the titles nearly gone off the spine. He cocked his head and stepped closer. The books were obviously well loved, with fuzzy edged pages and bumped corners, and areas of the leather covers had split from frequent use. When he read the title, it only confused him more. Two identical, equally worn copies of nature poetry. Odd.

"Who is this Smith fellow exactly?"

Simon quirked his lips as if enjoying a private joke at Malachi's expense. "You'll see. I'm sure they'll be in shortly."

The door opened and a man about their age strode in. The newcomer had light brown curls and a wide smile. "Lord Marshall, so great to see you again. It's been an age. We were intrigued by your note."

The man—Mr. Smith, one had to assume—turned his attention Malachi's way. "And you must be Lord Trenton, the owner of the mysterious book."

"Indeed. I take it you are the Mr. Smith I've heard so little about."

The man laughed. "I am Edward Smith. But you don't want me looking at your book. You want my wife. Janie should be along shortly."

Mal glanced at Simon, who grinned. Jane Smith? No doubt a pseudonym given by a particularly unimaginative government agent.

"Did I hear Lord Marshall's name?" A woman entered the room with a welcoming smile. With auburn hair and an uptilted snub nose, Mrs. Smith appeared unassuming in many ways, and could probably move unnoticed in most places. Having grown up around agents and those in the diplomatic service, Mal could appreciate the benefit of this woman being rather unnoticeable.

Mal glanced over at the men. Unnoticeable, unless you were Edward Smith. The smile the pair exchanged was intimate and endearing, and given the current state of his love life, painful to observe so closely.

Strange how you could spot a love match once you knew what you were looking for. These two seemed to wholly embody the concept, and he'd been in the same room with them for only twenty seconds. Malachi's parents, for all their faults, had loved each other. Lord and Lady Amesbury, Calvin and his wife, Phee. Hell, even Simon seemed downright smitten with Miss Martin.

Surrounded by loving relationships, and here Malachi stood, wondering why he hadn't deserved a goodbye from his lover. Thinking of the happy couples made it nearly impossible to avoid thoughts of Emma, but he shied from that path out of self-preservation.

Mal dragged his mind from woolgathering back into the present.

Simon stepped forward and offered his hand to Jane. "Smith, it's a pleasure to see you again."

"Likewise, Lord Marshall. Now"—she shot a look at Malachi—"you must be the one with the intriguing puzzle. May I see it?" Her whole body vibrated with excitement and her eyes sparkled as she waved a hand toward the various chairs around the room, silently urging everyone to take a seat.

Malachi pulled his father's bank book from his pocket. He'd set it out to air in an unused room in his house, in the hopes that any lingering scents of the grave would dissipate. "It was my father's," he said by way of explanation, handing it over. "He worked in the diplomatic service."

"In Russia?" Smith asked, flipping through the first few pages.

Malachi knit his brows. "Sometimes, yes. How did you know?"

"Some of these notations share characteristics with the Cyrillic alphabet." Already, her voice sounded musing, as if talking to herself and not the room at large.

Mr. Smith crossed an ankle over his knee and leaned back in his chair. He sent a smile toward his wife but spoke to the men. "Well, she's gone now. Down a rabbit hole of research and coding only her brain will ever understand." He shook his head. "How she does it, I have no idea."

"Smith is a marvel," Simon agreed.

"I'm right here," she murmured but didn't look up from the book.

Simon and Mr. Smith grinned at one another.

"Shall I ring for tea?" Mr. Smith asked.

"Yes, please," Simon answered for both of them.

"Jane, are you hungry?" her husband asked. Smith didn't answer, wholly engrossed in the book. She pulled a notepad and pencil out of her pocket, scribbled something, then began flipping pages of the bank book, scanning the handwriting with a finger.

"It's been a bit since we ate. I'll ring for the cart," Mr. Smith spoke as if she had answered. "Maybe we still have some of those lemon cakes left over from last night."

Malachi couldn't help smiling as Edward Smith went about playing host while holding a one-sided conversation with his wife.

"How many children are there?" Jane asked suddenly.

Mal started. "Two."

"And their names?"

"George, my older brother. And myself, Malachi."

"Did your father ever refer to you by nicknames?" Still not looking at him, she was studying the pages intently as if they were bound to spill their secrets any moment.

"Georgie and Mal," he answered.

"Good, good," she murmured and offered no further explanation.

After a moment, Mr. Smith said, "If you both had three-letter nicknames it might be harder to distinguish between them. Sometimes," he elaborated, "breaking a code is as much about differences as it is commonalities. One symbol or letter that appears frequently could either be a stand-in for someone's entire name or a vowel. Right now, she's looking for characters matching possible common usage words and patterns."

"It looked like gibberish to me," Malachi said.

Mr. Smith nodded. "Jane sees things where others don't. She's probably the smartest person you'll ever meet."

"I'm right here," Jane singsonged again under her breath, and her husband grinned at her.

"And apparently she doesn't like being discussed as if she is not in the room," Malachi commented blandly. "Apologies, Mrs. Smith."

She glanced up. "I'm working, so it's just Smith, or Jane." Closing the bank book, she continued. "Since we don't know what kind of things we will uncover in this book, I have to ask:

Are you comfortable with my being privy to family secrets and personal information once I determine your father's method?"

Malachi swallowed a spike of unease and shifted in his chair. "I'm here because Simon says you're trustworthy. Honestly, I doubt there's anything personal in there pertaining to myself or my brother. Well, possibly George. But George wasn't the type to have damning secrets." Leaning forward, he rested his elbows on his knees. "We have reason to believe the book contains sensitive information our government would prefer to be kept quiet."

Smith raised a brow. "How delicious. You're correct in that I'm trustworthy and have the crown's endorsement. May I keep this book for a few days?"

"Of course."

"Thank you," she said, then focused her attention back on the pages in her hand.

A maid arrived with tea and Edward went about pouring for everyone, since the lady of the house was occupied doing her work. He set a lemon iced cake on a plate by her elbow along with a cup of tea.

As Smith sat immersed in her world of codes and character sequences, Mr. Smith made comfortable conversation with Malachi and Simon about the growing concern over the situation in Greece's war for independence and Russia's move to step in and take over more territory.

Malachi contributed opinions every now and then, as he pondered the possibility of being sent south to the Mediterranean. With his father gone, would the *Athena* see more action? Malachi might finally have a naval career to tell stories about when he was old and retired. The idea didn't send a thrill through him like it once would have.

He fiddled with the cup of tea in his hands, spinning the round ceramic bowl in his fingers while the heat seeped through and warmed his skin. All he'd wanted for years was the *Athena* and the life of a sailor. Now everything was back in reach, with the added allure of a possible maritime conflict looming on the horizon. One would expect he would be eager at the prospect.

Instead, his mind repeated the awkward smile Emma had given him when she left his house. The breezy way she'd said she had fun in his bed, and they should do it again soon. She'd been lying. At the time he'd felt something was off about the interaction, but he hadn't been able to put a finger on it. Hell, he hadn't been able to put a finger on *her*. As she scurried away from his bed with a casual peck on the cheek, Emma hadn't let him kiss her goodbye properly. It had already been the end and he hadn't known. What the devil had he done?

A clock on the mantel struck the hour, pulling him from the depressive ponderings. "Goodness, is that the time? I apologize, everyone, but I must go."

"The Admiralty?" Simon asked.

Malachi stood and set his cup on the tea cart. "Yes, wish me luck. I expect they'll finally have a date for my return to command. Smith, Mr. Smith, it's been a pleasure. Simon or I will be in touch regarding your progress with the book. I must take my leave now."

Simon rose. "Want me to go with you?"

"No, enjoy your visit. I'm sure the meeting will just be new orders and tedious paperwork. Farewell, everyone." Giving the room at large a bow, Malachi returned to the hall, retrieved his hat from the butler, then stepped out into the sunshine.

Surely this day could be salvaged. Woman troubles weren't the end of the world. He had Simon in his corner, he'd recovered Father's bank book and would discover its secrets shortly. On top of that, Malachi would have a command again. Hopefully the *Athena*, but ultimately his billet was the Admiralty's decision.

A hack stopped when he flagged it down, and soon he was surrounded by the oddly comforting normalcy of rattling wheels, torn upholstery, and the questionable odors of hired transport. The fact any of it was comforting at all made it clear that Malachi had been in London too long. Much longer and he'd lose his edge at sea.

It was not his destiny to be here or to be Emma's lover. He was a naval officer. And he never should have been anything else. Being Trenton was supposed to be George's job. His father's job. Soon, the day-to-day running of the ducal interests would be the duty of estate managers.

By the time the hack rolled to a stop in front of the government offices, it was Captain Harlow who stepped out of the carriage and rolled his shoulders. The persona of the duke would stay in London, and Malachi could hardly wait to be plain Captain Harlow once more.

Signing in and going through the motions, the salutes, the rigmarole required of reporting to his superior officers, was like donning a comfortable garment he'd somehow forgotten was an old favorite. If, in the back of his mind, thoughts of Emma lingered, well, they would go away soon enough.

In the end, Lady Emma would be no more than a squall in the sea of life. He'd foolishly thought he could handle her by letting the storm of emotions blow him wherever it led. The tactical error couldn't be clearer. Any captain worth his salt knew there were two ways to deal with a squall—turn tail and ride it out, letting the wind direct your course for the duration, or fight through the middle and pray your sails survived.

He should have fought it. Fought the attraction and the sizzle under his skin her nearness brought. Fought the wash of contentment he felt when her laugh swelled on the breeze, and when Alton rested his head on Malachi's arm, and everything had felt right in the world.

This is what a broadside knockdown felt like, and whether he wanted to admit it or not, his mast was in the water. But he'd be damned if she fully capsized him.

Squalls were temporary, no matter how beautiful the storm.

The halls of the government building smelled like floor polish and stale cheroot smoke. Muted conversations took place behind heavy wood doors. As he approached the desk of Admiral Sorkin's secretary, conversations in the hall paused. Ignoring the heavy gazes of the men he passed, Malachi did his best to keep his eyes locked forward.

The secretary rose. "I'll tell him you're here, Your Grace."

And so, he waited. One by one the conversations picked up around him, but they were quieter now, as if the participants were keeping their ears open for something. Their attention crawled like ants across his shoulders and nape until Malachi shifted uncomfortably in his coat.

"Admiral Sorkin will see you now, Your Grace."

The secretary stood straighter as Malachi passed, raising his chin slightly so he could look down his nose.

"Close the door, Harlow," Admiral Sorkin's voice commanded.

Malachi did as he was told, a ripple of unease skittering over his skin. He'd known Admiral Sorkin for years, and other than at official events, they'd never stood on ceremony with one another. But his commanding officer's tone had Malachi standing at attention and snapping a smart salute.

"Take a seat." Sorkin waved a hand toward a leather chair, then took his place behind a massive desk that could have qualified as a man-of-war purely for its size alone. "There's no need to beat around the bush. We have received disturbing information."

Malachi cocked his head. This was not how he had foreseen the interview going. "What kind of information? From whom?"

"The informant prefers to remain anonymous for now. However, the author of a certain letter in my possession details damning evidence against you and has offered to be a witness in any action we take as we investigate the matter. The gravity of the accusation leaves me no choice but to proceed."

The ripple of unease transformed into a wave of dread. "Sir, what is this about?"

In answer, Admiral Sorkin withdrew a stack of papers from his desk, then pushed the pile across the polished wood toward Malachi. "Effective immediately you are relieved of command, Captain."

Malachi drew his eyebrows together in a fierce frown. "I've already been relieved of command of the *Athena*."

"You will not be returning to the *Athena*. I doubt you'll see a command of your own again during your career. But as you are now a duke, I don't foresee an outcome where you serve a sentence in gaol. If nothing else, the memory of your father's duty to his country will keep you from especially dire consequences."

"I'm afraid I don't understand." Malachi reached for the stack of papers. Two words on the top sheet stole his breath. *Court-martial.* "What are the charges?" he managed to ask.

"We have reason to believe you forged transport papers in the name of the king and profited from the illegal transport of private citizens, treating them like prisoners and subjecting them to lives of hard labor. There will be an investigation, of course, during which time you will be on half pay." Sorkin lowered his voice to a deep murmur and Malachi had to lean forward to hear the rest of what he said. "I'll do what I can to lessen the consequences, but your father made enemies during his time. The chance to besmirch the title might have them circling like sharks now. Keep your head down, go through the motions, and we'll get through this."

Sorkin rose, forcing Malachi to stand as well, still clutching
the sheaf of papers in his hand. "Expect the investigation to
take several weeks. Your court-martial date will be sent to you
via messenger. Don't leave the country. And for God's sake, cut
your hair. You need to present to the jury as a competent captain
in the Royal Navy and a duke, not a ragamuffin privateer.
Dismissed."

And he was. As the heavy door closed behind him, the secretary refused to meet his gaze. Walking down the hallway toward
the exit meant traversing a gauntlet of stares and whispers.

An anonymous letter. Of all the cowardly ways to ruin
someone's life. But not so anonymous after all. The list of
prisoners he'd forged papers for and transported illegally was
extremely short. One. James Montague. And the only people
who knew about his involvement in that escapade were Emma;
her brother, Calvin; and the man who financed the whole thing,
Lord Amesbury.

Malachi had lost not only a lover but also, obviously, his
new friends.

Son of a bitch had a unique knack for revenge, he had to give
Calvin that. Emma might have left Malachi high and dry, but
her brother had sunk what was left of his career.

Chapter Eighteen

I had the dream again. His sightless eyes seemed to follow me, even though I knew he was dead. Why don't dead men close their eyes on their own? He watches me while I sleep, and no matter how much I remind myself it was an accident, I still see him.

—Journal entry, January 22, 1824

If the duchess heard about the court-martial through gossip, there'd be hell to pay. So the following morning, after washing away all signs of the bottle of brandy he'd drowned in the night before, Malachi dressed to visit his mother.

In the event that his future held more time in London, he should put a bit more effort into managing his expectations when it came to the dowager. A court-martial, no matter the circumstances, was a huge life event for a sailor. He'd foolishly thought she might greet the news with concern or empathy. In reality, she barely managed to garner credible interest, much less convincing emotion.

"Your duty is to the title now. Your life is here, not on some boat," Lady Trenton said.

"Ship," Malachi growled. He wasn't captaining a dinghy, for God's sake. Not that he was captaining anything these days. Or ever again. Even if he squeaked through this investigation without ending his career, his sea days were over.

He pushed away the useless frustration. "Did you deliver the book to the appropriate authorities?"

"Of course." With a languid kind of grace, his mother poured herself a cup of tea, then offered him one as well. "Lord Clarey was grateful for my offer to squire his niece about next year. By the end of the meeting, he understood my actions were merely the overenthusiastic efforts of a mother who needed her heir home safe. Anyone would have done the same."

He arched a brow. Sure. Blackmailing the crown was the first resort of mothers everywhere. Surprise was a wasted emotion. Her sons, even her beloved George, had always been pawns in her mind before they were people. George was the heir before anything and was treated as such. The grief she carried was genuine, but Malachi suspected there might be an element of anger on her part that God had dared change the plan for the title without consulting her first.

The nerve.

"I'm glad to hear the danger to you has passed, since I need to leave Town for the coast. There's a property I'm visiting before the trial. Distract myself with estate business and such." The phrasing was deliberate. Mother couldn't possibly complain about his leaving to carry out work connected to his godforsaken title.

"When do you leave?" she asked.

"Soon. I have a few things to finish in London. But soon. So, if you don't hear from me, don't be concerned."

His mother waved a hand. "I'm used to you disappearing to the ends of the earth, Malachi. I long ago gave up the habit of maternal worry."

He offered a tight smile. Of course. She wouldn't worry about him. Rather than let the knowledge hurt him, he imagined the words rolling through the air, but not touching him. Mother wasn't going to change. Just like his emotions toward her were a mixture of love and resentment, their relationship would always be complicated. The best he could do would be to protect his heart—oh, the irony, when it ached so much from Emma's mistreatment—and continue to honor his parent without letting himself be vulnerable.

Malachi set aside the untouched cup of tea, placed his hat on his head, and said his goodbyes. Ivan the butler showed him out, even though, technically, this was Malachi's bloody house. But he bit his tongue and murmured a farewell in Russian to the old retainer.

It was so tempting to walk out of the square and head for Hill Street. The need to confront Calvin and Ethan itched under his skin, but he stifled the impulse.

Instead, he flagged down a hack and directed the driver to Simon's bachelor quarters.

Malachi walked in after a cursory knock. "Simon!" he called out from the foyer. Raising his voice, he tried again, "Simon!" After receiving word of the court-martial, Simon should have expected a visit.

"Here! What do you want?" Simon padded barefoot out of the cramped room he used as a study. "Mal, stop yelling. Why are you here?"

"I need to borrow your valet." Malachi took off his hat, then untied the ribbon holding his hair at his nape. The long dark waves tangled around his fingers when he threaded his hands through the strands and drew them over his shoulder.

"If you were a woman, that might have been attractive."
Simon shook his head, but was smiling. "Are you getting rid of
the beard too?"

Malachi grimaced. "I'd rather not appear in front of the jury
with red bumps on my face like some green lad. Besides, we
have a few weeks before the trial."

Simon twisted his lips to one side. "Trim it, then. You'll
still be unfashionable, but at least you won't look unkempt.
Follow me."

Upstairs, they entered Simon's bedchamber and found a man
in the attached dressing room. "Wilson, are you up to a challenge today? We need to make Lord Trenton look respectable."
Simon jerked a thumb at Malachi.

Wilson looked him up and down. "I'll need a bit to
sharpen my scissors. Disrobe to the waist and take a seat,
Your Grace."

The valet left, then Simon held out a hand. "I'll take your
things."

Layer by layer, Malachi stripped. Did he want to cut his hair?
No. But the admiral was right. If he had any hope of convincing
a jury of his peers that he was an upstanding captain made of
strong moral fiber, he needed to look the part.

Never mind that he was guilty of the crime of which he was
accused. The irony was not in the act of committing the crime,
but that he wasn't alone in his actions. A good captain served
his men. No matter what.

During times of peace, when King George left his soldiers
and sailors to rot, those in command had to step in and do what
was necessary to see their crews taken care of. Sometimes, it
meant creative accounting methods. And sometimes, it meant
doing dirty jobs for pay. Such as getting rid of people who
hurt women, like James Montague. Oh yes, he remembered the
details. The transport of prisoner 8792–39 had paid for an entire

quarter's wages for his crew and refilled the *Athena*'s dry goods storage for the voyage.

As a duke and the son of a respected member of the intelligence community of England, Malachi would not hang. He probably would not even be ejected from the navy. But this cloud would hang over the rest of his career, giving him zero chance of ever holding the command of a ship. Since he hadn't joined the Royal Navy for the paperwork, manning a desk for the foreseeable future held little appeal.

Malachi cleared his throat and tossed his cravat to Simon, who draped it over the discarded coat. Bunching the fabric of his linen shirt in his fists, he pulled it over his head, then tugged the sleeves right side out again.

"Holy mother of…I knew you had tattoos, but I wasn't expecting this." If Simon's eyes opened any wider, his eyeballs would fall out of his head.

"Almost twenty years at sea documented on this skin."

"What is the creature with the horn?" Simon asked.

Malachi's smile slipped away. "Narwhal. It was Emma's favorite. She called it a unicorn whale. Was absolutely fascinated by it, and so excited to tell Alton such a creature existed." It felt like a layer of lead encapsulated his heart. The heaviness leeching humor and warmth from him day by day. Her absence made it clear exactly how much she'd become a part of his days and nights. It had been days since he'd seen her dimples or listened to her talk about whatever was crossing her mind at that exact second. Damn, he missed her.

"I truly am sorry for how that ended," Simon said.

Without a good answer, Malachi grunted and changed the subject. "Mother played her part and delivered the book ashes. Could you keep your ear to the ground for any lingering issues in the situation? She assured me it's taken care of, but it would be a relief to know you were on alert as well."

"Of course. If I hear anything, you'll be the first to know."

Wilson entered the room again, this time with shears in hand and carrying a leather roll of shaving accoutrements. The valet motioned for Malachi to take a seat, then draped a cloth around his shoulders. "I can trim up the ends, Your Grace. A neat queue at the nape is still worn by some."

"Cal wears his in a queue. Long hair can be fashionable if you don't want a drastic change," Simon said.

Fashion wasn't the point here. Malachi shook his head. "All of it. Take it off." The oval mirror in the corner reflected the truth of the matter. He didn't look like an upstanding citizen of the *ton*. His skin was darkly tanned, with pale streaks fanning from his eyes from squinting into the sun from the deck of a ship for years. The ink on his body was a pictorial history of his life—a life he wasn't allowed to return to. Dark waves of hair covered his shoulders, reaching down his back to his shoulder blades.

The admiral had advised him to show up to the court proceedings looking like a consummate gentleman, and he would. Of course, the only way to fully accomplish such a transformation would be to shed his entire skin. A haircut would have to do.

Malachi sighed. "Take it short. Extremely short. Clip the beard tight as well. As Simon said, I need to look respectable."

A flicker of concern flitted across Simon's face as Malachi repeated those earlier words in a tone lacking the original playfulness.

Like it or not, his best friend had the right of it. He needed to look like the opposite of a pirate. He had to walk into the offices of the Admiralty and pass for an officer who took orders and obeyed without searching for a loophole. To look like every other servant in His Majesty's service.

Individuality wasn't something the Admiralty or the king appreciated.

Wilson said, "Very well." The cold presence of metal near Malachi's ear made him flinch. At the involuntary movement, the valet froze. "Your Grace?"

He blew out a breath. "Apologies, Wilson. Carry on with your orders."

Palpable waves of concern wafted off Simon; Malachi closed his eyes against them.

Snip, snip. "No going back now." The valet tried to lighten the mood of the room, but from the draft hitting the back of Malachi's neck, the statement was accurate. "Do you mind if I collect the hair? Know a good wig maker who will pay well for it," Wilson said.

"Feel free. Keep whatever you can get for it."

It took less time than one would think to be transformed into a gentleman. On the outside, anyway. Wilson used a straight blade to rein in the marauding borders of Malachi's beard, then cropped the rest close to his skin before rubbing an herbal scented oil into the whole thing.

"To stave off the red bumps, Your Grace," Wilson explained, dusting his nape of little hairs.

Malachi tugged on his shirt, then shrugged back into his coat and stood.

"You look great, Mal. But your glower will scare children if you're not careful," Simon said.

A stranger stared back from the looking glass. Until now, he hadn't realized how distracting the hair had been or how often it had fallen in his face. In the reflection, he saw there was nothing to hide behind, or to take away from his sharp cheekbones and heavy brows—which were currently meeting over his nose on a scowl. Malachi shot Wilson a glance. "Thank you. It's exactly what I asked for."

"Are you going to debut your new look at the Claybourne soiree?" Simon asked.

Malachi continued to stare at his reflection. "I'll go if you tell me your intentions toward Miss Martin."

"Adelaide?" Simon's eyebrows rose.

A smile tipped Malachi's lips. "Yes. Adelaide. Are you going to offer for her?"

Wilson quietly withdrew from the room. Simon watched him go, then admitted, "I'm considering it."

"I've never seen you so happy, and she seems to return your regard." He wanted to shake his friend and tell him to marry the woman before Miss Martin walked away and Simon was cut to drift like Malachi had been. Instead, he said, "Hold fast to your happiness, friend."

"Wouldn't it be awkward for you? To toast at my wedding when you're…"

"A burnt-out husk of a man, pining after her friend? No, I would rather celebrate your happiness than mourn my loss."

Simon was quiet a moment. "I'll see you soon, my friend."

Taking his leave, he called his thanks to Wilson one last time, then headed down the stairs to the foyer. The butler offered his hat, and soon, a disturbing breeze brushed his neck where his queue usually lay.

Perhaps it was cowardly, but all Malachi desperately wanted was to get out of London until the trial. In Olread Cove, he could smell the sea instead of the ripe scents of the city. As he flagged a hack, he was seized with a longing to bury his face in vanilla-and-sugar-scented softness, making him wonder if the need for vanilla skin would ever fade.

Indeed, it was time to head to the coast. Check on the condition of his house, make note of anything he'd need to do before moving in, look in on his cave, and try not to turn every corner hoping to see Emma's smile. With the whole of England open to her, as well as her family's many properties, he doubted she'd returned to the Cove.

As quickly as she'd overtaken his senses and captured his heart, she was gone. Disappeared like a ghost.

$\sim$

"Mrs. Shephard, why is there a goat in the sink?"

"He's licking the dishes. It keeps him occupied, and out from under foot," the cook said. "Otherwise, he nibbles my hem while I'm baking. I've already stepped on the rascal twice this mornin'."

Leonard's two adorable babies hopped everywhere, stole into the house at every opportunity, and had yet to be convinced they weren't humans. Alton had named them Billy and Lily, but Emma could never remember which was which. She thought the one licking breakfast crumbs from her stoneware was Billy. Maybe.

Mrs. Shephard had fashioned little nappies for Billy and Lily out of rags. When Emma and Alton arrived home, they'd been greeted by a baby goat wearing a scrap of floral tablecloth, sitting on the sofa as if it owned the place. That was when Emma knew she didn't want to leave any of this.

Charles the footman fit in fine after a few days, and he now had the duty of diapering goats several times per day, since the duties within his normal purview simply didn't exist in this house. They didn't stand on ceremony in the Cove, so it took little convincing for him to leave the livery behind and settle into country life. Powder blue livery trimmed in silver braid would always be a poor fashion choice when goats were involved.

Leonard and her mischievous twins, Mrs. Shephard and her unflappable adaptability, Polly and her cheerful smile—all those things made a home as much as the cottage itself. During the first evening back in her room, listening to the surf crash against the rocks below, Emma had written to Cal and proposed the idea of finding a different property close to Olread Cove to purchase. It was either that, or somehow lure Mrs. Shephard all the way to one of the Eastly properties—which would be hard. No matter how modern a kitchen Emma promised, it couldn't compare to living near grandbabies. But staying in Olread Cove proper held no appeal if she'd have Mal as a neighbor. Even thinking his name sent a twist of emotion through her chest. Not longing or anger. More a sick sort of indigestion brought on by regrettably satisfying orgasms and poor choices.

That man had played his part like he'd been born to the stage instead of a coronet. Even knowing the duplicity he'd undertaken, it still didn't sit entirely right that he had betrayed her so entirely. The mark of a true liar, she supposed. When one could convince someone so thoroughly of one thing that, even when presented with evidence, they didn't wholly accept it.

"Can I help with anything?" Emma asked.

The older woman glanced over her shoulder, then blew a hank of gray hair off her face before it fell right back where it was to begin with.

"May I?" Emma asked, then tucked Mrs. Shephard's hair back under the white cap she wore.

"Thank you, dearie. I wondered when you'd show up." Mrs. Shephard pushed a bowl down the counter toward Emma. "Crust for meat pies." Which was cook code for "Get to work and spill your guts."

Emma smiled gratefully and went to the sink to wash her hands. She'd been in the garden collecting greens. No one wanted soil in their pie crust. "Pardon me, Billy. Carry on with your important work, but we need to share the space for a moment." The goat sniffed suspiciously at the soap, then returned to the waterlogged tea leaves he'd found on the bottom of the sink. When she splashed water over her hands his attention wandered back to her, so she filled a heavy earthenware mug with water and set it beside him. Today's nappy was a blue striped material and used to be an apron, if Emma wasn't mistaken. "Mrs. Shephard, have we considered putting Billy back outside?"

The cook placed the salt and a bin of flour next to the bowl she'd offered Emma. "Oh, he can leave anytime. Hops out of there easy as anything. But he likes the sink. If we throw him out, he'll find a way in again. We can either let him lick the dishes or gobble my roses."

Emma eyed the—frankly adorable—goat as he chewed tea leaves and then happily lapped water from the cup she'd given him. A sigh escaped. "Fine. Where are Leonard and Lily?"

"Playing with Alton. The boy will need new shoes soon, missus."

"Because he's growing like a weed, or because the goats ate them?"

Mrs. Shephard shot her a wry smile. "Both, I think."

Sinking her hands into the tub of cool flour, cutting in the lard, sprinkling in a bit of salt and water—all of it soothed Emma on a soul-deep level. It had felt as if she were carrying around a chest full of shattered glass since she'd found the journal in Mal's room. Pie crust came together in the bowl and she couldn't help feeling it glued some of those sharp emotions within her back into something close to normalcy.

"You seem gray around the edges since you came home, if you don't mind my saying so." Mrs. Shephard handed her the rolling pin.

"I met a man," Emma admitted.

The cook rolled her eyes at her. "It's always men, innit?"

"I trusted the wrong one. Then, the owner of this house wants to live here. We have a generous timeframe to move, but it pains me to think of leaving. Now I'm digging through the corners of this place, and I'm overwhelmed. How have we managed to collect so much *stuff*? Odds and ends and broken toys I never fixed. Why do we still have those? And the clothing! I meant to make a quilt out of Alton's baby clothes and never actually did it." A wail crept up her throat as she blurted, "I thought I had time. I thought he would grow up in this house."

Emma's gaze roamed the kitchen, where she'd learned to bake as Alton danced in her womb. Tears streamed down her cheeks. Wiping them away left streaks of flour over her face, but she didn't care. "It's silly. I know it's silly. It's just a house. Wood and plaster, and a back door you have to pull on extra hard when it rains. Why am I so upset?" The last bit was muffled in Mrs. Shephard's shoulder as the cook pulled her into a hug.

"Are you sure it's the house, Mrs. Hardwick? Or did the man dig in deeper than you want to admit?"

In her mind, the loss of the house was connected to Mal's betrayal, which was connected to her feelings for him and the undeniable fact that she'd picked the wrong man *again*. Like her parents, it seemed she was doomed to repeat choices, inevitably creating her own heartbreak. They'd chased love, pleasure, and lust—initially with one another, until monogamy wore thin. Father had left illegitimate children all over the country, and probably the Continent. Truth of the matter was, she'd followed in her parents' footsteps, right down to the fatherless son.

And she couldn't rail at her parents for their life choices and the damage they'd done to their family, because they'd had the audacity to die and leave their messes behind.

Leave her behind. Grief roared to life, claiming space in her mind after months of silence, and years of suppressing her mother's death. Finally, the tears she'd waited for flowed freely.

"I'm sure I speak for Polly as well when I say we'll follow you to the next house if you stay in the area. A home isn't only a house, missus."

Emma nodded and pulled back. "You've been a godsend, Mrs. Shephard. Thank you for all you've done. I'll inform you of our plans as soon as I figure out what the next step is." How had her parents done it? Bounced from relationship to relationship, without appearing to suffer from heartbreak? Perhaps they hadn't felt as deeply. Or they'd learned to guard their hearts more effectively than Emma had. She mustered a smile through the tears.

"You have a tender heart, missus. And you're a good mother. It will all work out somehow."

Emma felt deeply. She loved completely and threw herself into situations with an exuberance Cal had bemoaned more than once. Even her hiding here on the coast had been wholehearted, going so far as to leave her honorific behind.

But, exactly like her parents, she'd covered her mistakes with deception. Unlike them, she had the chance to change. Their stories were done—hers was not. The cook was right. It would all work out. There were places she could go. She and Alton wouldn't be without a roof or food, or comforts. Many mothers couldn't say the same if faced with a similar situation.

No matter how heartbroken she felt right now, Emma could still change herself and her life for the better. The tears began to slow as she hiccupped.

Living amid lies was exhausting. Honesty had one clear benefit in its simplicity. Lying took effort, and frankly, beyond the moral implications of breaking free from her previous destructive patterns, telling the truth was easier.

Besides, as she could attest, being lied to *hurt*. Lordy goodness, she hurt. While she'd love to understand why Mal had done what he'd done, she might never know. Emma couldn't easily reconcile the man she'd thought he was with who he'd turned out to be. There'd been no hints. No clues.

Which made Mal an exceptionally good liar. He'd certainly

fooled her. She wiped her face on her sleeve and sniffed. Swallowing down the bitterness, Emma focused on making the edge of the crust look pretty in the tin. Her fingers trembled, but at least she wasn't crying anymore. No, she was too angry. These last days had taught her the anger would be replaced by another emotion shortly, and she had to ride it out.

A thump behind them had Mrs. Shephard turning. "Billy, if you eat my broom, I'll whip your bum with it. Don't push me, lad."

The indignant bleat and skitter of tiny hooves on the stone floor answered the cook's threat as the kid dashed outside. Emma closed the half door behind the goat and said, "He's going to go tell Leonard you're a meanie head." Her voice sounded stuffy from the crying, but it felt good to smile again.

She latched the hook to keep the top of the door open to the sea air. The lawn was a vibrant green against the blue sky. It was a gorgeous day. The kind of day created to make you forget the cold rainy ones and make you think you lived on the edge of a sparkling fairy seaside kingdom. At least, until the next cloud bank moved in.

When she stuck her head out to look for her son, Alton wandered around the corner of the house with a barn cat tucked under one arm and a baby goat following behind. Polly was hanging the wash on the line, and linens blew in the breeze like landlocked sails. A pang near her heart made her sigh. This house was perfect. But Mrs. Shephard was right. Their home wasn't limited to a house.

Damn, but she loved this house.

Soon, the savory scents of baking pastry, meat, and herbs filled the kitchen and wafted down the hall toward the parlor, where Emma sat reading a magazine, after Mrs. Shephard had gently nudged her out of the room. A fashion plate caught her eye, momentarily distracting her from the gurgle coming from her stomach. The gown on the page had a cinched waist and puffed sleeves clinging to the edge of the shoulders, with a bejeweled brooch nestled in the cleavage. Emma glanced down at her chest. It would highlight her assets.

But where would she wear such a thing? Perhaps they'd spent too much time in London, if she was even considering such an impractical purchase. Still, it was tempting to take the illustration to the local modiste and see if elements of the dress could work in a less elaborate evening gown.

The Claybourne soiree had been last night, not that it mattered anymore. Emma had been looking forward to it, and no doubt she'd hear about it in letters from her friends. Had Simon danced with Adelaide again? An offer looked to be imminent, and she couldn't be happier for her friend. A trifle envious, perhaps. But happy.

Since the kitchen, her thoughts had been lingering and rolling over in her mind. Mother and Father were past saving. But Emma could change. If these past months in London had taught her one thing, it was that. Not the core of who she was—why would she want to change that, anyway? But the pieces of her parents she carried with her as an adult. Those broken little remnants of deception and entitlement could be left behind. Sometimes it meant doing the opposite of what her mother would have done. And sometimes it meant being true to her desires, such as beginning an affair with Mal, but refusing to hide it from those who loved her. Although the whole thing had ended in disaster, Emma could be proud she'd acted in a way she didn't have to regret.

There was a kind of peace amid the pain, knowing she'd survived a relationship without lying to those she loved about her actions.

Emma sighed. Introspection was exhausting. She glanced down at the magazine again. The picture was so pretty, she hated to bend the corner to mark the place. Setting the magazine aside, she searched the drawer in the table beside her for something to act as a bookmark.

Crinkling paper made her sigh and close her eyes, already knowing a bookmark wouldn't be necessary. Sure enough, Lily stood by her leg, happily chewing a sizable chunk of paper. The illustrated woman no longer had a head, and the edge was slightly damp from baby goat drool.

"You're a menace. How did you get in? I thought you were playing with Alton." Lily's nappy was yellow today, with a faint white check pattern faded from years of washing. The goat bleated a reply, then butted Emma's knee in protest when the magazine moved out of reach.

"Don't eat my papers. This came all the way from London, I'll have you know." Firming her jaw, Emma shot the goat the same look she saved for Alton's particularly bad days. A stare down followed, but Emma refused to blink. After a moment, the kid seemed to grow bored of the whole situation. Lily wandered over to the open window and hopped out, then pranced over the grass.

That explained how she snuck in, anyway. Jimmy, their caretaker and man of all work, needed to look into more functional penning options than the haphazard gates in the barn. The kids had outsmarted those within weeks, according to Mrs. Shephard.

Emma rose to close the window, then paused when Alton barreled around the corner of the house. The wide grin splitting his cheeks made her smile. If she could, she'd give him every last thing his little heart desired. Alton deserved it all. Everything she had, everything she could offer, even if it came by means of lying, cheating, and stealing.

Perhaps settling down in one place wasn't the answer. They could embark on a life of adventure and travel instead. With a companion and a tutor, she and Alton could explore the world.

See the pyramids and the Parthenon, and drink tea beside the Seine. Calvin could sign over property to Alton so they'd have a home to return to when the need struck, and the rest of the time, they could wander like nomads, discovering their place in the world.

Phee had warned against running away. But maybe this wasn't running away, but running *toward* something. What, she didn't know.

For the first time, the vastness of possibility stretched before her, bullying the heartbreak out of the way. Like a hallway of endless doors, and it suddenly dawned on her—she could walk through any of them. She'd been living small. Hiding with her secrets, fearful of discovery. No, she wasn't about to go shout her truths from the rooftop, but it wasn't fear holding her back anymore. The secrets she protected impacted other people, and Emma didn't have the right to expose them.

Sea air and the scent of savory meat pie filled her lungs when she sighed, clinging to a moment of contentment. A brief breath of peace amid the brokenness, but she relished it. Adventures with her son sounded more lovely with every passing second. No matter what path they chose—buying a house, moving to an Eastly property, or running away to Egypt, she needed to begin packing.

Alton poked his head through the window. "Mama, I found a fort!"

Emma bent down to kiss his warm cheek, then had to brush sand off her lips. "Did you? Was it full of treasure and pixies?"

His brown eyes sparkled with excitement. "Of course. It's a proper fort, after all. Want to go see it?"

"You'll have to show me tomorrow. Our meal is ready, by the smell of it. Come inside and wash your hands." She curled her lip at the dark sand coating his fingers and now the windowsill.

He slumped dramatically over the sill.

"No arguments or whining, please. Come inside."

Alton clambered through the open window, less gracefully than the goat had a moment before. When he tripped as he hit the floor, Emma sighed. "I meant through the door, little love."

Her son didn't answer as he bolted out of the room. Emma rolled her eyes and went to follow, when her slippered foot hit something hard. Only moments ago, there'd been nothing there, so it probably fell from Alton's pocket.

"Please don't be a dead animal," she muttered, moving her skirts out of the way to inspect the floor. Several heartbeats passed while her brain scrambled to comprehend what she was seeing.

A gold Russian Orthodox cross lay on the carpet, the metal gleaming in the sunlight streaming through the window. Each arm of the cross was bejeweled in precious gems catching the light with their facets in a way she knew wouldn't happen with paste stones.

"Holy hell," she breathed into the quiet room. Then, "*Alton Adam Walters Hardwick, get back here!*"

Chapter Nineteen

&

It took a while for me to stop looking over my shoulder. For the longest time, I thought I'd turn a corner and run into someone from London who would somehow see through the deception.

It's hard when you're scared of the truth more than the lies.

—Journal entry, April 22, 1824

The delivery of his father's bank book distracted him entirely until it was time to get ready to go to the Claybourne soiree.

Smith had included a key with a note explaining the coding system. She'd decoded several pages as examples, but since Malachi's father had used a simple enough method, she'd left the rest to him.

Instead of numerals to number the pages, Father had used a character system. It was a short leap of logic to realize there were only twenty-six characters in various formations, which clearly correlated to letters. Or so said Smith. Malachi would have stared at the bloody thing forever until his eyeballs fell out of his head, and still wouldn't have noticed that pertinent detail. In fact, Smith had sounded slightly disappointed the code hadn't been more of a challenge.

With the key in hand, Malachi had endless hours of work ahead of him to decode the rest of the book. Every symbol needed to be swapped out for a letter for any of it to make sense, and while fun at first, his head hurt already. Clearly, he didn't have a mind for code.

It was a relief when the clock chimed on the mantel, reminding him to get dressed for the evening.

One final glance in the mirror, and this time, the ducal image reflected back was less jarring than it had been this morning. He'd get used to seeing himself in this new way, he supposed. The coat was slightly looser than fashion dictated, but it had to be if he was going to dress himself.

Malachi slid a plain gold cravat pin into place. If he wasn't going to return to sea—even thinking it made his stomach clench—he'd need to get a valet. Eventually. Maybe. Or he could be a duke living incognito in a tiny coastal village, buy himself a boat, and spend his days harassing smugglers in the channel or something.

That sounded like so much more fun than going to this damned soiree. It also sounded like a solid long-term plan. A boat of his own. Not a huge ship.

He'd need to acquaint himself with the estate managers for the holdings. The solicitor would help with that task.

After seeing to the dukedom, he could gather a crew from the village, buy a mid-size boat, and sail wherever he pleased. No orders. No Admiralty. Captain of his own destiny.

The sick feeling in his gut eased, but he couldn't fully relax. The black armband was noticeably absent from his attire tonight. He didn't miss the slight pressure that had acted as a constant reminder of George. The dukedom had been in capable and competent hands with his brother. Malachi would do his best to direct the right people to honor his brother's memory. After all, their father had left the day-to-day business matters behind to travel in service to the king. He could do the same.

Except for the service to the king part. Thanks to Calvin, those days were behind him. Or they would be once the dust settled after the court-martial, and Malachi found himself with the options of working behind a desk in a cramped office or bowing out of the Royal Navy with a tattered reputation.

"Beg your pardon, Your Grace," one of the staff said from the doorway. "Messenger arrived with this."

Damn the flare of hope that roared to life at the sight of the missive. He inspected the wax blob seal.

"Will you be needing anything else before you leave for the evening, Your Grace?" the servant asked.

"No, thank you." Malachi searched his memory for the man's name. "Perkins, you may dismiss the crew for the night." He caught himself. "Staff, I mean." Not crew. Old habits die hard. When he was home, he tended to stay in his chambers. After so many years on board a ship, having an entire house to ramble about in felt strange. How much room did a lone man need, anyway?

Malachi blew out a breath and turned over the letter to examine the handwriting. Hope dashed on the rocks. It wasn't from Emma. At this point, he'd take a letter full of damning accusations against his character over this deafening silence. He just wanted to talk. Not even explain necessarily, because he had no idea why she'd left. But talk. Hear her thoughts, let her say whatever she needed to. He'd stand through any emotion she threw his way if she would fucking *talk* to him.

They'd agreed to grow their relationship. Didn't that imply

they'd work through things? Not if her complete abandonment was any indication. Maybe he should have brought up marriage. At least then they'd be stuck together and *have* to talk this out.

A bittersweet smile curled his lips. Emma would tease him about that. He could hear her mocking laughter. *Such a romantic, Malachi. How could a woman resist you when you put it so sweetly?*

The idea of marrying Emma didn't strike dread or fear into his heart. Quite the opposite. He missed her. Not just the sex, although they'd worked so well together physically, it would be hard not to miss that. But the quiet times. The conversations on the pillow, one precious memory of watching her take over his kitchen. The patient way she dealt with Alton, how she loved him so totally and could be a disciplinarian, while also keeping hold of her sense of humor. He missed his friend. He missed his lover. He missed the pieces of himself she'd taken with her when she left, that he hadn't even realized he'd handed over. Malachi rubbed at the hollow ache under his ribs.

This silence was killing him.

Sliding a finger under the wax blob, he opened the letter and began to read. He had to read it twice for the contents of the letter to sink in. "Son of a bitch."

Without bothering to gather proper outerwear, Malachi charged out of the room, down the stairs, and out the door. In a hack, he examined the note again and seethed all the way to Hill Street.

The absolute stones on Calvin to take things this far. Reporting him and bringing about a court-martial was bad enough, but this? Malachi was glad he hadn't grabbed his gloves before leaving the house. Punching Cal's perfect face with a bare fist would make such a satisfying sound when the time came. And the time was coming soon. A gentleman's resort might be to challenge the man to a duel, but Malachi didn't have the patience for all that pomp and circumstance. Not when he could simply smash Cal's nose and feel better right away.

The note was a crumpled ball in his fist by the time he knocked on the door and scowled at Higgins.

"Tell Lord Eastly the Duke of Trenton is waiting in his library." Malachi stormed past the gape-jawed butler and down the hall. It felt good to throw the title around for once. Because this—he clenched his fingers around the paper once more— would not stand. If Calvin thought he could manipulate Malachi, he was sadly mistaken.

"What the devil, Mal? How dare you show your face here?" Cal said from the doorway, a moment later.

Phee hurried to her husband's side within seconds, but she didn't stop at the door. With murder in her eyes, she already had her hands fisted. "Give me one good reason why I shouldn't bloody your nose right now."

Malachi raised a brow at the threat, even as he drew up to his full height and prepared to take a punch. Phee was a little thing, slender to the point of looking fragile. But she sounded like she would actually do it.

Calvin shot a hand out and slipped it through his wife's arm to stall her. "It's not an empty threat. She blackened my eye once," he said. Phee shifted her glare from Malachi to the hand holding her back. "Wait a moment, love. Let's see why he's here."

Malachi held up the paper. "This has to stop. You're hiding behind anonymous notes like a damned coward. Doesn't anyone in your family *talk* when there's a problem? What is *wrong* with you people?" Hurt and frustration over Emma mixed with this situation, until the hot emotions boiled over. "I demand an explanation. You claimed to be my friend, all the while plotting to destroy my career. Now this. You're not getting a single penny from me." There were more accusations to hurl at the man, but Calvin marched forward and snatched the paper from his hand.

"You're raving like a madman and making no sense at all." Cal glared, then read the letter. "Where did you get this?"

"Messenger. Why are you both looking at me like that?" Malachi said, questions breaking through the volcano of emotion.

"Mal, I didn't send this. Why would you think I did?" Cal handed the note to Phee to read.

"Is this the first letter they sent you?" The way Phee asked the question, Malachi sensed she already knew the answer.

"The second. Although the other was only a single word, and I haven't compared the handwriting. But I think it's the same person. The other message matched events Calvin brought about, so I thought he sent this as well."

"You're the third. Our note said one down, two to go. Then the fire happened. You're the third. Oh, hell," Phee said.

"What am I being blamed for? The writer mentions a court-martial?" Calvin asked.

Bafflement was so clear on the man's face that the wind went right out of Malachi's sails. "I need a drink," he muttered. None of this made sense if his initial theory was wrong. He rubbed his thumb at the aching pressure between his eyebrows. "You didn't talk to the Admiralty about our business from a few years ago?"

"And implicate myself and my best friend? Why would I do that?"

"Your part in the transaction was conveniently left out of the anonymous report." Malachi sent him an arch look.

"Consequences," Phee muttered, echoing the first note he'd received. She shook her head when Malachi glared at her. "Let's sit. This is making my head hurt, and you still have a lot to answer for, Your Grace."

Calvin crossed to a bar and poured each of them a drink.

When he handed Malachi the tumbler of liquid, he said, "This doesn't mean we are friends again. Like it or not, it appears we are in this muddle together. I might still let my wife hit you."

"At least you're willing to talk to me. Unlike your sister," Malachi grumbled into his glass.

"You stole her journal. Her private diary, full of extremely sensitive thoughts you had no right to read, Your Grace. On top of that, you have a note from the same blackmailer who had been harassing her friends and family. What was she to think?" Phee didn't daintily sip her whisky. She downed half the serving in one swallow, then stared Malachi down without a hint of being impacted by the alcoholic burn in her throat.

This all came back to that bloody journal he hadn't returned. Malachi closed his eyes and sighed. "A street urchin handed the note to me one day and I didn't know what to make of it. I shoved it in my dresser and used it as a bookmark until I had time and energy to figure out what to do with it."

"A bookmark in her journal, which she took back," Cal said dryly.

A rueful smile tugged at Malachi's mouth. Emma had grabbed the damn book. Because of course she had. Having read the journal and met the woman, he couldn't doubt it. Emma did what she had to do, no matter what kind of murky waters she had to navigate to find her way out of a situation.

Clasping his hands around the glass, Malachi stared down at his boots. They were the same in that regard. Both willing to do whatever it took to reach the desired result. Willing to lie, cheat, and steal. It made it easier to relax and fully be himself with her.

"For the record, I didn't steal the damned book. I found it on a beach the last time I was in Olread Cove. Emma and I were already involved when I began to suspect she might be the author. I should have handed it over right away, but to be honest, I was scared she'd run. And we all see how that turned out."

Any other week, he probably would have noticed the journal was missing. But this had hardly been a normal week.

"That explains the journal. Now tell me why you evicted her." Phee scowled at him.

"I have no idea what you're talking about," Malachi said.

"The morning after my sister found her *private* journal hidden in your room, she received word that instead of purchasing the home she's been renting for the last several years, she was being evicted—on *your* order."

The news stole his breath and he slumped against the back of the chair. "The Olread Cove house. Of all the damned luck. The property manager said someone had offered to purchase the place, but I planned to live there when I wasn't at sea. I had no idea Emma was the tenant."

Damn. Emma had burrowed her way into his heart, filling the crevices of his subconscious until he missed having her around in a way that felt elemental. Like she was his air or his water. Yet somehow, he'd bumbled into hurting her in the most personal ways possible.

No wonder she'd run, taking back those tiny bits of trust she'd offered, stealing his heart along with her journal.

It was an odd moment to admit he loved her. When she was gone and he was reeling at all of this new information. Yet, the realization didn't rock him. The earlier thoughts of marriage hadn't scared him either. Loving her had been creeping up on him. Inch by inch, one aching moment at a time, until he finally had no choice but to admit that she'd stolen his heart.

And he was the fool who'd hidden behind the guise of a no-strings affair. If he hadn't been vulnerable about his growing feelings, how could he possibly hold it against her when she didn't share all of her life with him? How was she to guess he wanted to know everything about her, unless he showed her?

It was bad luck she'd found her journal immediately after they'd agreed to take things further between them. Not only had he withheld her journal, but he'd failed to tell her when he first suspected his feelings were growing deeper. Now she was hurt and scared and probably terrifyingly livid, and it was his fault.

This tangled web of events was exhausting.

"Is that where she is? In Olread Cove packing the cottage?"

Calvin sighed. "She'll kill me for telling you this, but yes. It sounds like you two need to talk. She's painted you as the villain, but there seem to be a lot of misunderstandings in play."

"How does this tie in with a blackmailer demanding money to make my court-martial go away?" The note had been short and to the point. *Three down, the game is almost done. If you wish to save your career, deposit 15,000 pounds into the bank account below.*

"I hired runners, who checked into that bank account. We paid the money to buy time when the blackmailer demanded a similar sum from Ethan. The account belongs to an investment company out of Australia."

Malachi came to attention at the same moment the other couple paused, seemingly arriving at the same conclusion. "Australia? What are the chances?" he asked. "It makes sense though. There's only one person who connects me to you and Ethan."

"James fucking Montague," Calvin grunted.

"Three targets, aimed at what that rat bastard would assume mattered most. Ethan and Lottie's brewery. Our investments. Malachi's career," Phee mused.

"Will your career survive this, Mal?" Calvin asked, with a worried groove over the bridge of his nose.

"In the sense that I won't land in prison, yes. But I'll never command again." Damn, this truly was the day for his deceptions to come back around and haunt him.

Over the years he'd forged paperwork. However, James Montague was the only time Mal had forged transport papers to put someone in custody. He'd whipped up countless Freedom Papers, certifying individuals to be freemen. But Montague? He was the one man who had been placed in shackles at the wielding of Mal's pen. James fucking Montague, indeed. Malachi drained his glass of whisky and savored the burn. "I need to figure out what I'm going to do with my life beyond the Royal Navy. Whatever it is, I want Emma involved if she'll have me."

"You have your work cut out for you, my friend," Cal said.

Friend. It was good to have those.

"What do we do with Montague?" Phee asked.

"I'm not paying to ransom my own damn career. Whatever happens, I'll ride it out. It's no less than I deserve, after all. The note says he's almost done with us. What do you think the final act will be?"

Calvin drained his own glass. "I have a feeling we're about to find out."

Chapter Twenty

❦

I imagine what it will be like to love you, but
I come up empty with so many details. Or I
borrow things I see. Stolen moments between
others, claimed for myself.
                              —Journal entry, June 5, 1824

It had been a week since she'd found the cross and Alton had led her, Polly, Charles, Jimmy, and Mrs. Shephard across the lawn, down the rocky cliff trail, and into a cave she hadn't known was there. Now, wearing her oldest day gown and a borrowed mobcap, Emma wiped a dirty hand over her cheek and flicked a cobweb away.

Alton's fort did indeed contain treasure, although she had yet to spot a pixie. She rested her hands on her hips and surveyed the progress she'd made. Crates and barrels lined the cave walls. A few contained bottles of liquor, but most of them were valuables of other kinds. And oddly enough for this area, none of the items looked French.

Like the cross, with its distinctive three arms, many of the things stored in this cave appeared to be Russian. There were quite a few labels written in Cyrillic, and more than one crate labeled with the name *Athena*.

Son of a bitch. Mal had ordered her eviction so he could live on top of his smuggled treasure hoard like some mythical dragon. Emma kicked a lump of straw packing material aside and wished it were more substantial.

Couldn't he have been a normal, average, everyday smuggler who slipped a few casks of brandy by the excise men?

No, he had to be an honest-to-god pirate, stealing foreign treasures and hiding them in a goddamned *cave*.

Did he have a map to the cave? One marked with an X and little squiggly drawings so future pirates and treasure hunters could stumble upon his secret spot? *Walk three hundred paces away from the lovelorn widow's house and look for a rock crevice resembling a woman's lady bits.*

She certainly hoped such a map existed, because if Emma ever saw the man again, she was going to wring his neck until he turned purple, and this treasure would be lost until his crew came looking for it.

Oh Lordy, was she going to have to deal with a pirate crew too?

Alton would be thrilled if he knew such a prospect existed. Emma shoved aside the heavy wood lid of a crate and peeked inside. Framed paintings. She tsked. "These will mold, if they haven't already. Should have thought that through, Your Grace."

The last crate had been full of fancifully curved brass cups and a samovar covered in delicate metalwork depicting leaves and a harvest scene etched into the great belly of the piece.

It was all a bit overwhelming. This cave was filled with art. Beauty scavenged from other countries, then hidden away in this crevice on the edge of England. What did he plan to do with it?

The scratch of shifting pebbles and sand at the cave entrance had her turning.

"*Maaa*," Billy bleated in greeting and skittered over to her in his awkwardly adorable baby goat run. Today's nappy was a piece of last summer's picnic blanket.

"Did Mrs. Shephard send you to find me or are you wandering off from your momma? Leonard will worry, you little beast." Emma reached down to scratch between his ears. Billy leaned into her leg and exhaled in a gust. After a moment, he straightened and wandered over to the straw littering the floor of the cave.

"I should feed you the paintings. There are a few Russian saints in here you might like. Baby Jesus with his halo could be delicious, you never know."

Billy grunted in agreement and nosed at the lid of a wooden box full of liquor bottles.

Another slip of pebbles at the cave entrance told her she now had two baby goats to deal with, in a cave full of priceless no-doubt stolen art.

Emma threw her hands up and said, "Just eat it all. Every crate, every bit of straw. Wreak chaos and destruction to your heart's content. It would serve the rat bastard right."

"No thank you, I ate at the last inn. I will take a cup of coffee though."

꩜

The first brass cup hit him square in the forehead, but Malachi was quick enough to dodge the next. "There are only eight cups in that set. Use your ammunition wisely, my love," he said, advancing into the cave.

"I am *not* your love," she growled.

"I beg to differ," he said, sidestepping another cup, which flew by him to bounce off the wall with a metallic *ping*.

"Bastard."

Another cup careened toward his head, and this one Malachi caught handily, then tossed toward an open crate to his left. In her current state of raging fury, the chances of Emma really hearing him were slim, so he said the one thing most likely to cut through her anger. "Phee sent me."

Emma froze, then dropped her hands, still clutching brass cups. "Is she all right?"

A warmth formed in his chest. Oh, his Emma. With her prickly walls around her heart and fierce love for those she deigned to let in. He'd give anything to be one of the lucky few.

"I spoke to Phee and Calvin. They're a day or two behind me on the road. I convinced them of my innocence, and all I ask is the chance to do the same with you." He spread his arms wide, even though it made him a bigger target. "Please, Em. Let's talk. If you still hate me when we're through, I'll leave you in peace."

The neckline of her dress rose and fell with her breath, and a deep groove had formed between her dark eyebrows. "You mean, you'll leave me in peace for another four weeks. I have a month left in the period your property manager gave me." Hurt laced her words.

"You don't need to move, Emma. I didn't know you were the tenant. You want the house? It's yours. Free and clear. Take it. I might buy a place nearby, so I'll warn you now, you'll probably have an obnoxious neighbor pining for you for the rest of his life. But you can have the bloody house."

A sneer curled her lip. "I don't need your charity."

"Then buy it from me."

He didn't expect the next cup, which hit him on the shoulder.

"I *tried to*, you son of a bitch!" Her screech ended on a sob.

"Let's not bring my mother into this. The situation is bad enough as it is," he tried to joke. The sight of her distress tore at him, and Malachi reached for her. "Sweetheart, please don't cry. I'd like to hug you now, but I don't want you to throw anything else at me. All right?"

She didn't answer, but she dropped the cup in her hand, and he took that as agreement.

"I promise, on the grave of my perfect brother, I didn't know it was you. Had I been told the renter's name, I'd have gifted you the house, simply because you asked for it."

Slowly, keeping an eye out for rejection, he placed his hands on her shoulders, then moved in closer until she leaned in for those final few inches.

"I need to pay for it. I need to know it's mine." Her voice still wobbled, but she felt like heaven in his arms, even if she did hold herself stiffly.

"Fine, I'll sell it to you for half price."

"You're ridiculous. I'll pay full price, thank you very much. I'm only letting you hug me because Phee said you should come."

Malachi smiled and dropped a kiss on the dirty cap she wore. "I know."

She pulled away and crossed her arms over her belly. "Why did you have my journal? And explain the notes. Explain everything."

"I found it on the beach the last time I visited my cave. When I met you at the assembly rooms, I had no way of knowing you were the author. It wasn't until we were in London and I met Roxbury and Alton that I began to piece it together."

She sniffed and wiped her face with a hand. "Why didn't you say anything?"

Malachi sat on a crate and rested his elbows on his knees.

"I was afraid you'd run away if you knew I had such personal information. And, to be honest, I...didn't want to give it up. Your journal, your words—you kept me company on my last voyage. I have some entries memorized. The descriptions of your life—both the one you have and the one you want—became a dream. I imagined with you, and hoped to perhaps meet a woman like you. I wanted to sit at your side, sipping brandy by the fire while the wind howled outside. I think I fell a little in love with that mystery woman. Then I met you, and you were so much more than I could have dreamed up on my own."

He finally shifted his gaze from his interlaced fingers up to her face. This expression, he couldn't read. But she was still there, so he kept talking.

"I'm so sorry. I'm sorry I kept the journal. And I'm truly devastated I gave you reason to doubt me for even a moment. We both kept parts of our lives from the other."

At that, she sat on a crate a few feet away. "And the note I found?"

"A child shoved it at me on the street one day. I didn't know what it meant—*consequences*—until after you'd left. Turns out, I'm being court-martialed for my part in the transaction I made with your brother and Amesbury."

"Court-martialed?"

Malachi sighed. "Because of the title, I probably won't see a brig for it. But my career will be stained and I'll never hold a command again." He leaned down and plucked one of the brass cups from the ground and dusted off the sand and dirt from the metal. These cups and the samovar were some of the few pieces he'd collected for his own use. Funny that it was his personal favorites she chose to lob at his head.

"So, no *Athena*," she said.

He glanced at her. "No, my love. No *Athena*."

"You keep using that word."

Malachi quirked his lips. "What word? *Love*? I'm here apologizing and wearing my heart on my sleeve. Might as well tell you everything. I fell in love with you through your journal, and then gave you pieces of my heart bit by bit during our affair. But I was scared to admit it. I didn't want to admit you meant more to me than I seemed to matter to you. Our affair was supposed to be short and sweet."

"And if I ask you to leave right now, what would you do?"

The question stole his breath with the wicked sharp stab of an unexpected knife slipping between his ribs. "I'll respect your wishes, but I'll hate it. Regardless, the house is yours. It's the least I can do."

"If I forgive you? What happens then?" She sounded hesitant, then darted her gaze away from his, to watch a baby goat wander out of a maze of crates deeper in the cave.

"Is your goat wearing a nappy?" He waved away his own question. "Never mind. The goat can wait. If you forgive me for keeping your journal from you, then I'd hope every day you would fall in love with me too. And once you loved me, I'd ask you to marry me until you said yes."

Her dark brown eyes appeared black in the dim light of the cave, and he wished she were close enough to touch. Despite his declaration of love, she stayed where she was, and the worry that she'd send him away grew.

"You said Phee and my brother are on their way. Why?"

"Oh yes. Sorry, I was sidetracked with the *I love you*s and marriage proposal." He waited a beat, and she raised a brow.

"I didn't hear a marriage proposal. I heard a man hiding behind hypotheticals. Now, why are my family descending en masse?"

"I'll make a better effort at the proposal once we deal with the rest of this," Malachi promised. "I got another message from the blackmailer. I was the third target. Ethan, your brother, and then me—the only connection we share is James Montague."

She spent a moment in silence. "You think he's back."

"It's been what, six years? Almost seven? It's not beyond plausibility to suggest in that time he found someone to look into his case."

"And there is no case, just transport paperwork."

"Precisely."

She buried her face in her hands, but he could still make out her muffled voice. "What does he want? Cal paid him. The urchin army put out the warehouse fire. Now you. What exactly are we dealing with here?"

Malachi stood and crossed to where she sat. Kneeling before her, he took her hands in his. "I won't let you get hurt. And Calvin won't either. You and Alton are safe."

She looked at him. "Is that why you want to marry me? To keep me safe?"

Malachi leaned forward until his forehead rested against her shoulder. Beneath the dirt and sweat, he found a faint trace of her vanilla scent. "I wish I could say my motives are so chivalrous. Yes, I'll keep you safe. But I want to marry you because I adore you. Because you're smart and witty, and when I look at you, I'm turned inside out and laid bare."

Trailing the tip of his nose along the side of her neck, he felt her quake at the gentle touch. A soft kiss behind her ear, where the vanilla was stronger, made her sigh in a way he knew signaled growing arousal. Sure, he could capture her body and catalog the responses. It wasn't enough. "Marry me, Emma. Let me into your life, with no walls or secrets. I'll be honest with you; you'll be honest with me. Only say yes if you love me too. I want your body *and* your heart."

Emma stilled under his mouth, and the throat beneath his lips stopped moving entirely, even to breathe.

Pulling back, he asked, "Emma?"

"Do you mean that? It's all or nothing?"

If that was the source of her hesitation, then he might be foolish to hope. Swallowing through a suddenly tight airway, he croaked, "Yes. All or nothing."

Emma turned her head away. "Billy don't eat those. Come on. Let's go back to the house." She rose and placed a hand on Malachi's shoulder. "I need to think on it. And you still have to explain this cave, as well as what happened to your hair. You can stay at the cottage in the guest room. Until I write you a check, the house is yours, anyway. Alton will be overjoyed to see you, I'm sure."

It wasn't a no. But it wasn't a yes either. Malachi listened to the fading footsteps.

Crates surrounded him, filled with a decade of treasures and plans for his retirement. A brass cup lay on the ground by his boot next to a crowbar she must have used to pry open the boxes. Both were covered with a dusting of sand and straw. Priceless artifacts, art, and precious objects filled crates along the walls of this cave, amounting to an unimaginable stash of wealth he'd had to store here because—ironically—he hadn't had the money for a house of his own, and he'd refused to touch his father's properties.

All this gold, and the only thing of actual value had just left, taking a baby goat in a nappy with her.

Chapter Twenty-One

I feel bad for you sometimes. On days like today, when the sun is brilliant in the sky, and A— is a ball of laughter and smiles, and all seems right in the world. You're missing it. I hope you don't miss all of these days. I hope you come along while he still wants to cuddle and show you magic rocks he found in the garden.

—Journal entry, July 9, 1824

Somewhere on the other side of death, her father was laughing at her. Emma picked up her hem and scurried up the rocky trail toward the top of the cliff, Billy tagging along behind.

Could those in the Great Beyond, or heaven, or hell, or whatever awaited everyone, hear her? Had her father known when she determined to have a life different from his? She'd decided she would live the opposite way he had, change where he hadn't, and embrace honesty.

Then look what happened. A literal treasure hoard fell in her lap, her ex-lover showed up offering a ducal coronet and a house, and all she had to do to accept it all was to tell him she loved him.

Father wouldn't have hesitated. Mother would have jumped at the chance.

Which told her she needed to pause. Especially after deliberately shying away from examining her emotions when it came to Mal. Besides, the drastic swing from calling him a rat bastard to him on his knees proposing marriage was a bit much, even for her allegedly dramatic nature.

Time was called for here. And if that big beautiful man back there who'd poured his heart out loved her now, then he'd love her tomorrow. Or next week. Or however long it took her to figure out how she felt about him beyond lust and like.

She tugged the kitchen door behind her, leaving the top half open to the breeze. A dark head was barely visible cresting the top of the cliff, so Mal would be along shortly.

"Did the handsome gent find you, then? I told him you were on the beach," Mrs. Shephard said.

"Yes, he found me. He'll be staying in the extra room upstairs. Has Alton already greeted our guest?"

"The boy went to gather eggs with Polly and missed the arrival, I think. You're sure you want a man like that in the extra room? He looks like he might get cold all by himself." The cook sent Emma a saucy wink, making her laugh.

"You're a bad influence, although I appreciate the sentiment. He's proposed, but I need to think on it."

"Nothing says you can't lay on it and think on it at the same time. Not when he looks like that." Mrs. Shephard went silent when footsteps beyond the door interrupted their conversation. In an instant, she transformed into the formidable domestic goddess she was. "Wipe your feet before you come in my kitchen!"

Emma covered a grin with her hand. Should she tell Mrs. Shephard she'd yelled at a duke? No, that would ruin the fun. To her delight, Mal responded with a polite, "Yes, Mrs. Shephard," then wiped his boots and dusted the sand off his breeches and sleeves.

Mal held up his hands for inspection and the cook nodded. "You'll do. Mrs. Hardwick made ginger biscuits this morning for the lad. Missus, if you'd like to change, our guest can wait in the parlor and I'll bring refreshments."

Emma bit her lip and led Mal out of the kitchen.

In the hall, he whispered, "Should I have saluted? I feel like I should have saluted."

The laugh burst free. "Go through there and wait. I'll only be a minute."

He opened the door to the parlor and paused. "There's a goat in here. But I don't think it's the same one, unless someone changed his nappy."

"Red nappy? That's Lily. She will want to sit in your lap, but watch your cravat. She's fond of linen."

"Of course she is," she heard him mutter as she climbed the stairs.

Changing into a plain day dress and brushing her hair free of tangles after an afternoon under the cap prepared her to deal with Mal and the emotions he brought with him. She drew her hair over her shoulder into a braid and tied the end with a ribbon. It felt like a sort of defiance to not primp in front of the mirror for her suitor. The headmistress at Saint Albans would have a fit if she knew one of her former pupils would greet a duke in such a manner. Emma grinned ruefully at the reflection in the mirror before leaving the room.

Mrs. Shephard met her in the hall with the coffee tray. "I'm on my way in, I'll get it," Emma said.

The cook whispered, "I heard him talking to the goat. I like this one."

Sure enough, when Emma pushed the door all the way open, Mal was sitting on the sofa with Lily in his lap contentedly gnawing on his unwound cravat. The deeply tanned column of his neck momentarily distracted her. How long had she spent licking and kissing the skin usually covered by his cravat? And how long before she could do it again? Mal made a motion to rise, but Emma waved him off. "Don't get up. She looks comfortable."

"You were right about the cloth. But she's so happy about her destruction, I gave up and just gave it to her."

"Lily's finicky about fabric. Likes clothing, but won't touch the upholstery or curtains, thank God. Otherwise, I'd have to find a way to keep her out of the house, which would present a challenge. She and Billy are determined to wander at will. Thankfully, Leonard is content to stay outside and dominate the chickens."

The soft clink of the tray on the side table caught Lily's attention. Emma wagged a finger toward her fuzzy muzzle. "One biscuit. Only one. The biscuits are for the humans."

Lily turned to look at Mal, who shrugged his big shoulders. "Sorry, little one. When she uses the mother voice, she means it."

The goat took the biscuit, then hopped down with it in her mouth and skittered out of the room.

Without the cute distraction, Emma glanced at Mal and didn't have any words.

"Coffee?" she asked. Maybe her Saint Albans training would be useful after all, and she could stick to surface niceties.

"Please."

Emma poured and placed a biscuit on a plate, then handed it over. Several minutes later, the cup she poured for herself sat untouched, cooling as the swirls of steam rising off the surface dissipated.

"These are delicious. I see why they're Alton's favorite."

Without a word, Emma handed him the plate of gingery sweets and let him help himself.

"What part of my speech back in the cave is causing this strange silent version of you?" Mal asked.

Emma's gaze shot to him and she opened her mouth to answer, then shut it and sighed. "An hour ago, I thought you were ruining my life, and I was determined to hate you. Now you've proposed marriage and told me you love me. That is a drastic change. On top of that, I've recently made a decision to live differently than my father did, and you've come back into my life just in time to test me."

He settled back against the sofa and picked up another biscuit. "What was your father like?"

A simple question without an easy answer. "He loved me in his way, I suppose. But he never loved anyone as much as himself. Father liked money and women—especially if they belonged to someone else. I have half siblings scattered all over. In fact, I remember my mother saying I shouldn't marry a man with blond hair and dark eyes, lest he possibly be my brother."

"Damn. That's not the normal maternal advice given to young ladies, I imagine."

"In the last few years, Father finally turned over the family finances to Cal. Not happily, but after nearly bankrupting the estate, Cal convinced him. I'd like to think he'd learned his lesson and been a better man at the end, but the truth is, Father had an accident while climbing out a married woman's window. They found him in the garden the next morning, half dressed."

"And you're scared you'll end up like him? I promise to never make you leave my bed via a window."

That made her smile, but the heaviness settling on her as she spoke of her sire stunted it. "Father lied. All the time. Where he was, who he was with, how many cups of tea he'd had with breakfast. He lied about everything. It was as if he'd been born without a conscience. Mother was no better. They were quite a pair."

"Did you lie about your feelings for me?"

Emma grasped her cup of coffee and turned the cup on its saucer, making the dark liquid slosh. "The last time, at your house, I lied when I left. I already knew it was over, but said otherwise. Every other time, I withheld information. I didn't share much of myself with you—not really."

"I figured out that bit."

A curl fell over her eye, but before she could push it away, Mal tucked it behind her ear, dragging his rough fingertips over her cheek.

"If I did or said anything to make you think you weren't safe to be honest with me, I'm sorry," he said.

"I'm sorry too. When I found my journal, I should have confronted you right then."

Mal shook his head. "I may wish you'd railed at me and given us a chance to sort this out, but I understand why you ran. Between the journal and the blackmail note, it was pretty damning."

It had been. She'd run scared, and for good reason. Sitting across from him now, when he was being so vulnerable with his emotions, Emma wanted to run again. The initial urge was to scamper away until she had fully examined every nook and cranny of her heart and reinforced the walls she'd hidden behind for so many years. Which meant the right thing to do in this instance was to meet vulnerability with vulnerability. Be honest and open about her feelings.

She wished it wasn't so scary, but Emma took a sip of her tepid coffee and gathered her pieces of truth to share, offered up like sweet biscuits. "I tried to buy this house because I wasn't at ease in the *ton* anymore. I wanted to have someplace to retreat to. Society welcomed me when I debuted, despite my parents' scandalous activities. Cal cleared the way for me, making things as easy as possible. And I still made the wrong choices."

"Were they truly the wrong choices when they gave you Alton?" he asked in a low voice.

Her gaze flew to his.

"Roxbury is partly to blame as well, love. In the end, you have the most astoundingly loving little boy. You can't tell me Alton is a mistake."

Throat tight, Emma nodded. "You're right. He's not a mistake. Roxbury is a rotter, and he didn't do right by me. But I can't regret my son. Alton is only one part of my life though. I've done things, said things."

"Haven't we all?" He searched her face, then offered a gentle smile. "I swear on everything I hold dear, even if you throw me out on my ear, your secrets stop with me. I won't tell a soul."

Emma gulped, drained the cup of coffee in her hand, then glanced away from the man across from her. When she'd shared the details about her pregnancy weeks ago, he'd been nothing but kind as well. Yet, what he was asking of her meant confessing to more than Alton's parentage.

The heavy wood desk sat on the other side of the room, as immovable as ever. Phee had said once that talking about how her brother died lessened the guilt she carried.

In the cave, Mal said he wanted everything. All or nothing. If she couldn't offer the truth of herself, how could she begin to contemplate deeper feelings for him? Somewhere, under the fear that he'd be horrified by her confessions, a tiny part of her wanted to open up. Not to the world, but to him. If that little part proved to the rest of her that Mal could be trusted, talking about things like love and marriage would, by the default of logic, be easier.

"I killed a man. Right over there." She pointed with a biscuit toward the bulky furniture, then shoved the sweet in her mouth. Around the crumbs, she said, "Not on purpose. He came after me, I pushed him away. He was a bad man, but it doesn't really matter, does it? He bled out on the floor. Head wound from the corner of that desk."

Mal glanced at the desk in question, then raised a brow. "I robbed my brother's grave."

A chunk of ginger biscuit stuck in her throat and she choked out a cough. A confession of grave robbery wasn't the response she'd expected. The weight pressing on her chest lightened. Emma countered, "My marriage wasn't legal. The whole thing was a sham."

"My mother blackmailed the Admiralty to get me home, and when I was told she was in danger and facing possible treason charges, I had to think about it for *hours* before deciding to help her."

"I had sex in the Vauxhall Gardens paths." This conversation was ridiculous. A smile began to win over her anxiety.

Mal snorted a laugh. "Who hasn't? I once had sex in the throne room of a Russian palace, with only a velvet curtain separating me and a minor princess from a room full of people."

Emma gaped, and finally giggled. "If you were a woman, you'd be shunned for such loose behavior. What's the word for a promiscuous man?"

"A lieutenant," he said dryly.

Leaning forward, Emma snagged another biscuit from his plate. This was a competition now. "I'm keeping a man's heir from him."

"You forget, I've met the man in question. Alton and you deserve better.

"There's only one piece of stolen art in the cave, and I feel so bad about taking it, I'll probably donate it to the British Museum."

Emma rolled her eyes. "As if you'd be the first to give stolen goods to the museum. I tried to blackmail my best friend to get her to lie about finding me at Vauxhall with Roxbury."

"How'd you do that?"

"I kissed Adam, and then threatened to tell Cal about it and claim it was against my will." The truth about Phee had slipped out, and Emma froze, wondering if he'd catch what she'd said.

Mal leveled a look at her. "Badly done, Emma. I might need more information. Perhaps the next time Phee is here, you could reenact the moment so I can make my final judgment."

An incredulous laugh spilled free. Emma set down her cup and saucer and turned on the sofa to face him fully. "Does *none* of this bother you?"

For the rest of her days, she hoped she would remember the look on his face. Soft, amused, achingly adoring. "I told you. I love *you*. All of you."

The parlor door flung open and her golden-haired boy barreled in with all the care of someone being shot from a cannon. Alton skidded to a stop and gasped. "Captain! You came!"

As if it was the most natural thing in the world, her son threw himself onto the sofa, landing halfway in Mal's lap. He already had a mouthful of biscuit when he started chattering.

"Did you see the goats? Leonard is a good mommy, but my mama says Billy and Lily lack discipline."

"I've met both of them now. They're rascals." Mal handed him another biscuit. "Is that where you were? Playing with Billy and Lily?"

Alton nodded, chewing. "They like to chase the chickens, and then the chickens say, 'Bawk! Bawk!'" He flapped his arms in an impression of the disgruntled hens. "Then Barty, our rooster, tries to peck the goats. But I found seven eggs today with Polly. Have you met Polly? I'll go find her."

And just as fast as he'd arrived, Alton bolted out the door.

In unison, Emma and Mal sighed.

"He's a whirlwind," she said.

"He's a happy boy who knows it's safe to be himself. You've made a wonderful little human."

A warm glow had entirely replaced the dread she'd felt earlier. "Were you like that?" she asked.

He was quiet a moment. "No. But George was. I'm glad he had a good childhood. I ran off to the Royal Navy as soon as I could. When I didn't return after my first voyage, my father promised to buy me a commission once I was of age. He kept the promise, but he never stayed entirely out of my career afterward. The commission came with strings. Puppet strings."

"I'm sorry." The mood in the room had shifted to something less teasing and more pensive. "What will you do after the court-martial?"

"I'm still weighing my options." Mal returned his empty cup to the tray. "No matter what, I'll likely resign my commission. The estates will demand all of my time if I don't delegate, but the dukedom is a responsibility, not a joy. Once I have trusted agents in place, I might buy a ship of my own. Sail where I want, when I want. It all depends."

"On what?"

"On you and Alton."

Emma watched through the narrow crack between her door and the frame as Mal disappeared into the bedroom she'd assigned him. When he closed his door without looking back, she wilted against the wall, then shoved her door shut.

The room was as she'd left it, with the exception of the dirty clothes from earlier, which Polly had taken to launder. A collection of personal items littered the top of her dressing table. A holey stocking draped half in the sewing basket, awaiting her attention. The bed seemed bigger than normal. Emptier.

Ignoring the thought, Emma crossed to the window and flicked aside the curtain. Outside, the moon reflected off waves rolling like ink spilling from a bottle against the coastline. Near the horizon, a boat was visible only by its tiny flickering light. On the boat, it was probably a massive oil lantern, illuminating the deck and surrounding water. But up here, snug in her house, it was no bigger than a wink of flame.

Perspective. Emma turned from the window and shed her dress, following her nighttime routine as she always did before bed. Yet even as she brushed her hair, washed, and donned a night rail, part of her was attuned to sounds from across the hall.

The muffled thud of a boot falling to the floor. The thump of what she assumed was a traveling trunk. No matter how hard she strained, Emma couldn't hear the bed creaking, or anything else to enflame her senses, yet knowing he was there, close, and shedding clothes was enough to make her pace the length of her room.

Feelings were tricky things, yet the angst of earlier in the day had fled. Somehow, she was confident that no matter what sins she confessed to, Mal would not condemn her. Was it possible his love for her was the kind that Cal and Phee shared? An affection and passion rooted in friendship?

Lord help her, but he seemed to actually *like* her. The real her. The at-home Olread Cove version of her, and not the facade she put on when out in public. Even at the assembly rooms, there'd been a certain amount of society manners at play. Yet Mal hadn't blinked amid the little-boy jokes at dinner, the baby goats on the furniture, or even her cook taking him to task over wiping his feet. He fit her life here as well as he'd fit in London, and it was both exhilarating and terrifying. Not only that, but he'd made it clear that his future plans were on hold for her and Alton. Someone being willing to change their entire life trajectory for you was no insignificant thing.

Emma sank onto the bed.

The house grew still with the kind of silence found only at night in the country. The chirp of insects played their own lullaby, but she couldn't get comfortable. Restlessness wiggled under her skin, creating shivers and twitches in her limbs that prevented her from settling in.

After a while, the nerves won and she threw back the covers and slipped from her room. Navigating the halls by memory, she found the kitchen, then brought a glass of milk back to her bedroom.

And paced. Sipping the milk was soothing, and after a while, the rhythmic creak of the floorboards was its own kind of balm. A thought had occurred to her in the kitchen, and now that she was upstairs again, it was hard not to consider it.

She knew her body. This restlessness wasn't unfamiliar. Frankly, she should have predicted it, with Mal in the house being sweet and charming and heart-shatteringly attractive all evening. Damn the man, she'd asked for time, and he was giving her time. Which meant she hadn't even been offered a kiss good night.

Roger was tucked away in the same drawer as always. The smooth wood felt like ceramic under her hand, long and cylindrically phallic. After an orgasm or two, her body would sleep without issue. Years of living with this restless ache had taught her what worked and what didn't. She shot a look at the door. No doubt her houseguest was sleeping peacefully across the hall.

The bed shifted under her weight as she crawled atop the covers with Roger in hand. A tingle of anticipation threaded through her veins, and she ignored the fact that Mal was a few walls and doors away. Her night rail would only get in the way, so she removed it, flinging the garment toward the end of the mattress, without a care about where it landed.

With a contented sigh, she settled onto the pillow. Light from the lantern shone pink through her eyelids and she cracked one eye open. Blast, she'd forgotten to extinguish it. Oh well. She'd do it later. There were more pressing demands on her time right then. She smiled and closed her eyes again.

In her mind, she let herself drift as one hand caressed the sensitive side of her neck, across her collarbone, then down to the valley between her breasts. Mal had followed that path so many times. The skin warmed at the memory. A familiar fantasy began to play in her mind like an erotic theater act. The sun was a heated bath on her skin, as she lounged under the blue sky, with blades of grass tickling her through a colorful blanket. Her lover smiled wickedly, with his pale hazel eyes and—no. Not hazel. Blue. A blue-eyed lover would do fine, thank you.

A blue-eyed lover inched her skirts up her calves and over her knees, moaning in anticipation when the fabric pooled down her thighs and settled at her hips, leaving her most intimate parts open to his gaze. On the bed, Emma raised and spread her knees slightly, while one hand played with a nipple, exactly like she did on the imaginary blanket under the summer sky.

The man with the blue eyes raised one bisected brow in a smile that sent her pulse racing, then lowered his face between her legs.

Emma squeezed her eyes tight, as if she could reset the image in her mind. Fine, her brain wanted Mal. Her body wanted Mal. And yes, her heart was leaning in that direction too, but she wouldn't do anything so silly as walk across the hall and tell him at almost midnight.

Light hazel eyes, then. And a scarred brow, and a wicked mouth she knew so well. The scene coalesced, and she sighed, sinking into sensation. A hand stroked lightly over her breast, then pinched a nipple hard enough to send a spike of sensation straight to her core. The other hand traced the edge of her lower lips, then dipped in, seeking her own heat. A slick greeting welcomed her fingers, as she ran a finger up and down the imitate folds the way Mal's tongue had the last time they'd been in bed together.

Letting her imagination run wild, rubbing circles around her clitoris and slicking her fingers into her, in her mind, Mal's tongue lapped her up. A breeze from the open window tightened her nipples into tight nubs under the plucking motion of her fingers. A soft moan escaped through her parted lips.

Roger nudged at her entrance, and Emma was on the cusp of inserting the length of wood into herself when the door opened.

Chapter Twenty-Two

I have so many secrets, I tell lies about my lies. But you? What I will feel for you will be truth. I can't come to you unbroken, undamaged, or virginal. But I will come to you as myself. And for once, that will be enough.

—Journal entry, April 8, 1824

Malachi would swear his heart stopped from lack of blood. In between heartbeats, every chamber emptied and flooded his cock.

Holy hell. Emma was spread on the bed naked, with her hand between her legs, as if she was waiting for him. Maybe she was.

His gaze fell to the wooden phallus by her hip.

Fine, maybe not.

"I heard you pacing and thought you might still be awake. I...see you are."

Emma huffed out a sound that was part laugh, part sigh. "How do you always find me in odd moments?"

Closing the door behind him, he leaned against it and drank her in, since she hadn't moved to cover herself. "I wouldn't call this odd. Erotic as hell. Tempting. A little disappointed you didn't call me in to join, if I'm honest."

She rose to rest on her elbows and parted her knees a little more with a raised brow. The erection that had thrummed to life so fast now twitched in his breeches as if begging for attention.

"Like what you see, Captain?"

"You know I do."

"I was resisting the urge to cross the hall." The way her eyes drank him in, taking in his bare chest and the tent in the front of his breeches, was encouraging. A lifelong commitment may not be a certainty, but there could be no doubt that she wanted him in the bedchamber as much as he wanted her.

"Would you like me to leave?" He smoothed one hand over the hardness making his clothes uncomfortable, and Emma replied with a muffled groan.

"Not really." Her breathless answer made his cock jump anew.

"Want me there, or here?" Wrapping a hand around the length of himself, he squeezed.

A playful quirk of her lips was his only warning. Emma let her knees fall wide and swiped her fingers through her lower curls. "We've never watched each other before. Stay there. But I want to see you too. Fair's fair, after all."

With trembling fingers, he unfastened the placket on his breeches and sighed with relief when his cock sprang free. Emma groaned softly at the sight, then dipped her fingers into her wet heat in a move designed to capture his attention.

He knew that quim. The scent, and taste, were imprinted on him forever. Lantern light gleamed off the moisture on her fingers and he lost his breath at the sight. "Aw hell, Em."

"Touch yourself again," she demanded, and picked up the dildo beside her.

For the rest of his days, he would never forget the sight of that length disappearing inside her, or the way her eyes fluttered closed and her mouth formed a little O of appreciation. Sliding his hand along his cock as another lucky piece of wood slid into the woman he loved was a bittersweet pleasure.

Waves crashed outside in a familiar song. All those nights underway, he'd thought of her—the golden beauty he'd enjoyed for one night—and touched himself just like this.

"What were you thinking about when I walked in?" he asked, spreading a bead of moisture over the tip of his cock with his thumb. A surge of arousal shot up to his core at the movement.

"You," she panted, one hand working the wood, and the other thrumming her clitoris. "With your mouth between my legs, tasting me as we sprawled on the grass under the sun. You pushed my skirts up around my hips and I gripped your hair."

He grunted, matching his strokes with the rhythm she set. Heat built in his thighs, and he leaned heavier against the door. "I'm dying to touch you." The words sounded like they were made of gravel.

Although she smiled, she shook her head and stared right back at him. Her pace quickened along with her breath, but she managed, "I want to watch you tonight."

Then he'd let her watch him. This playful temptress was familiar. But then, she'd always given herself to him in bed, while hiding the rest of her. His lovely Emma spent so much of her life protecting parts of herself, in that moment, when she was open and vulnerable, it felt more important to ensure she believe he saw her—all of her—and loved what he saw. Especially after they'd both made such an effort this afternoon to be honest about everything.

"Right now, you look like a fantasy I've had for months. Ever since the first time I saw you, laughing on the street in the village, you've taken my breath away. I never dreamed I'd be allowed to be with you for more than one night."

She hesitated ever so slightly at his words. Emma liked a bit of dirty talk in bed—it was a proven fact between them. But this? Not an imaginary scenario, but the truth—he had to try.

"The sun hit your hair, because you were holding your bonnet at your side. Everything about you was warm, heartbreakingly beautiful. Your smile when you greeted the baker's wife stole my air, and I've wanted you ever since."

Recovering from that pause, one of her hands cupped a breast, gentling her touch with a fingertip across her skin, making her nipples tighten even more as a flush spread across her chest.

His fingers circled his cock in smooth strokes, but his real attention was on her, and how she responded to his words. "I see you, my Emma love. All of you. And you're perfect."

The column of her throat moved, like she was swallowing his words and taking them into herself, as her eyes fluttered closed. "You think so?" The question was huge, but her voice was small.

"I see you, Emma," he repeated, firming his strokes to match hers. "I've seen you and wanted more from the first moment. I want your heart, I crave your body, but what you write about—I want everything you described."

The movement of her hips made her breasts rock hypnotically.

Malachi continued, loving her with his words in a way he couldn't with his body. "Sit with me in this house and make love with me by the fire in winter. Two glasses of brandy because I won't make you share. Live with me. We'll keep each other's secrets."

Her breath went thready.

"And in the summer, I will spend hours outside on the grass

with my tongue buried in your sweet quim. You'll come apart under the sky so often, your chest will be pink from the sun, and you'll live every day knowing I see you and love what I see."

A cry rose from her throat, a low keening wail that shot fire through his blood and made his balls clench.

When she went over the edge, he followed. Because he'd follow her anywhere.

❧

Sunlight warmed her lids, and gulls cried outside her window. Emma shifted under the covers, then rolled over, smiling into her pillow.

She'd known last night, as his words flowed into her, honey sweet and warm, filling her limbs and taking over the fantasy she'd created in her head. The truth had been fragile yet, delicate in a way she didn't trust herself to say aloud, lest it dissipate into ether.

What he offered was real. More than sex. More than friendship. Mal's words had settled over her as she touched herself, sinking as permanently into her as the ink he wore on his skin.

It should have been an impossibility to believe him after growing up the way she had. Nevertheless, she did. He loved her. Wholly, protectively, with a clear vision of who she was and what she'd done. Accepting that, eliminating the fear of beginning the cycle she'd witnessed with her parents, had freed a fragile truth within herself.

Eighteen-year-old Emma would have flung herself at Mal the minute she realized she loved him. Shouted it immediately from the rooftops.

But the Emma who lay panting in her bed last night, swamped with myriad emotions overwhelming her ability to speak, had cradled the knowledge to her like the precious thing it was, marveling at the emotion, examining it from all angles.

The morning after brought even more clarity. What she'd felt for Roxbury once upon a time had been all sparkle and drama, laced with the fear that if she wasn't witty enough or pretty enough, he'd lose interest.

This? This felt warm and rich. Comforting like the soft quilt covering her, but solid and weighty like the gold ring he'd place on her finger. The truth of it no longer felt fragile.

A muted hum of conversation drifted through the walls, and the smell of sweet buns filtered up from the kitchen. A goat bleated from somewhere that was probably not outdoors, and her smile grew.

Washing her face in the chilly water in the basin at her washstand and using her tooth powder took but a moment. The wrapper from last night lay abandoned on the floor beside her bed, and she put it on, eager to find Mal.

Outside his door, she heard voices. One low and rough with sleep, and one higher. Emma paused and listened to their conversation.

"Why can't it be pink?" Alton asked.

"You can make it pink if you want to. It's your picture."

"What color were they when you saw them from your ship?"

"The young ones like you are bluish gray. Then they darken as they get older, until they're adults like me and your mommy. Eventually, they turn gray, and sometimes have spots. The oldest ones are white, and beautiful to see with their white horns."

"Old like Mrs. Shephard?"

"I wouldn't say so to her face, but yes."

Emma nudged the door open and leaned against the frame, taking in the sight before her.

Lordy goodness, if she hadn't loved the man before, this would have done it.

Mal, naked from the waist up, amid rumpled bedclothes and a little bleary-eyed at the early hour, lounged against the pillows. Beside him, Alton in his nightdress perched on the bed with his wooden kit of watercolors and a paintbrush.

The ship tattoo and waves had already been colored in with blues and greens, with a yellow ship and purple sails. A bright red kraken lingered menacingly beneath the waves. Alton was hard at work discussing the narwhal on Mal's forearm.

The hour was early, but Alton must have woken their house-guest a while ago to have already painted this many of the tattoos. She crossed her arms because, frankly, Emma's heart felt in danger of flying free from her chest and landing at Mal's feet.

He looked up and caught sight of her in the doorway. A crooked grin greeted her and the warm intimacy in his gaze sparked a flame low in her belly.

"Good morning, my love," he said.

"Good morning. I see I'm not your first visitor."

"Mama, the captain has drawings on him," Alton said, eyes wide.

Emma chuckled and pushed off the doorframe into the room. "They're quite beautiful, aren't they?"

She sat on the end of the bed, and Mal held out the arm not being painted, inviting her closer. As if it were the most natural thing in the world for all three of them to cuddle together on one bed, she settled into her spot on his shoulder.

"Sleep well?" he asked. That delicious voice near her ear sent curls of comforting warmth through her limbs.

Emma tilted her face up and offered her lips for a brief kiss. "I know it means waiting a bit, but can we do this right? Read the banns, marry in the local church, the whole thing. I want to be your wife, without a hint of anyone in London thinking I've rushed you into this. I love you. I choose you now, and

I'll choose you after your court-martial is final in a few weeks. Then we can get married."

The arm cradling her tightened, and she felt a sigh whoosh out of him. "I love you. I'm going to tell you so often, you'll be sick of hearing it, and I hope I'll hear it as often. As much as I want to marry you right this minute, I like the idea of finishing the court-martial and dealing with Montague before the wedding. Let's begin our life together fresh, without any of that spoiling our happiness."

Ah yes, because vengeful madmen didn't stop for things like declarations of love and wedding plans. "What does he want? When does this end?" she asked.

"He demanded payment from me and I ignored it, which won't go well with him. Calvin put his Bow Street Runners on the job of tracking the man down. Now we have a name, so it should be easier."

"My narwhal will be pink," declared Alton to no one in particular. Emma thought he might not have understood the conversation going on between them, but then he commented with a casual confidence only a child could have, "You were right, Mama. My new papa found us, even though we left London."

When Mal's breath caught, his chest stilled under her cheek, and she glanced up at him. His entire focus was on Alton, and the beginning of a smile curved his mouth. Those pale hazel eyes were wet, although a tear hadn't bridged his lashes yet. "Yes, I found you. And I'm not going away again."

Alton perked his head up from his painting. "What about your ship?"

Mal's smile quirked. "I'm going to get my own ship. Then I don't have to leave you and your mama when I want to sail."

"So, we can go on your ship?"

Mal nodded. "As long as your mama agrees, yes. You'll need a decent pirate name, though."

Alton's face scrunched in concentration. "I'll have to think on it."

Mrs. Shephard's voice carried up the stairs. "Leave that be, little rascal! Those are for the family, not you."

"I think breakfast is ready," Emma said. "Get dressed quickly, then we will meet you downstairs."

Alton set aside his paint case and scooted off the bed. As he left, he called out for Billy. An answering clatter of hooves sounded on the stairs.

Mal's chuckle rumbled under her ear. "I love this house."

"Is it everything you dreamed of when you read my journal?" she teased, sitting up to move the art supplies to the side table.

His hand cupped her cheek, then swept down her shoulder and arm to intertwine their fingers. "So much better."

They met for a kiss that made promises for them and curled her bare toes under the edge of her wrapper.

A little breathless, he said, "Are you sure about the banns? We could get a special license."

"And have everyone talking and watching my waistline for the next few months? No thank you." She ran her hand through his hair. "I miss it."

He shrugged. "It will grow back. I need to look respectable for the court-martial."

Sadness tugged at the bubble of joy she'd been floating on all morning. "I'm so sorry your career will end this way."

"Me too. I'd rather not think about it right now. Today is a day for happiness and planning a wedding with the most beautiful woman I've ever seen." He winked over his shoulder as he opened his trunk of clothing.

Watching him dress was a pleasure. Such a big body, wild with ink—and now watercolors—being confined in the trappings of respectability fascinated her.

He tucked in his shirt and then bent to grab his boots. "Will Mrs. Shephard mind if I come to the table in my shirtsleeves?"

She laughed. "Our house is terribly casual. Especially at breakfast. I'm just wearing my wrapper."

He eyed her up and down. "You're not wearing anything under that, are you, Em?"

She raised a brow and smirked as she stood. "Not a blessed thing. Come along, Your Grace. Wouldn't want your food to get cold."

"Bloody hell, woman."

Emma laughed as she skipped down the stairs to the kitchen, where she poured herself a cup of coffee and greeted Mrs. Shephard.

Absolutely nothing could ruin this perfect day.

So, when someone rang the bell at the front door, Emma said, "I'll get it," and carried her cup of coffee down the hall.

The contented smile she thought impenetrable fell from her face when she opened the door.

Once upon a time, she'd expected to see Devon Roxbury on the day she planned her wedding. But that was in a different chapter of her life story.

It was only a minor comfort that he looked as unhappy to see her now.

Her first impulse was to close the door on him, but he jammed a boot in the doorway before she could do so.

"I'm sorry, Emma. I didn't think he was this deranged." Roxbury looked like he hadn't slept all night, with dark circles amplifying his wild expression.

White appeared at Emma's knuckles where she gripped the door. "Devon, what have you done?"

Chapter Twenty-Three

⁓

A— likes adventure tales lately, and seeing those stories through his eyes has been enlightening. They're so very black and white at this age. Wrong and right, with nothing shady in between. I wonder sometimes how old he will be when he realizes people are rarely the hero or villain we believe them to be. Even ourselves.

—Journal entry, January 8, 1824

ow talk." Emma sat at the table, fighting against the trained guilt response at leaving her guest standing. She'd called up the stairs for Mal, and now Roxbury stood in the kitchen looking a little lost, facing people who clearly didn't like him.

Devon opened his mouth and shut it repeatedly, like a fish on a riverbank.

"Let's begin with the notes. The threats," Mal suggested. A

thunderous expression clouded the happiness from his eyes, as he stood beside her with his arms crossed.

"He wrote those. He paid me for information on your friends and family." Roxbury's gaze darted away from Emma to where Alton peeked around the corner into the kitchen.

"Mrs. Shephard, would you please take Alton out to Polly and Charles? Perhaps they could gather flowers for the dining table," Emma said.

The cook hustled out of the room, and they could hear her shooing Alton toward the door with false cheer.

"I thought I could kill two birds with one stone. Stay close enough to pass along inside details while getting back into your good graces. But you didn't cooperate," Devon said.

"Imagine that," Mal drawled.

"I need an heiress, otherwise I'll be left with no choice but to flee to the Continent. The duns are closing in. You already had my child. I thought if I could manage to spend time with you, you'd fall in love with me again. But you were determined to hold me at arm's length." He offered a pathetic shrug that was neither adequate explanation nor apology.

It took everything within her to not roll her eyes. "You say 'he.' Who are you working with?"

"I received a letter several months ago from a man claiming we had a common goal, who said he could solve my money problems, but I had to keep his identity a secret. He said he'd been gone from the country for a few years and only a few people knew he was back in England, and he didn't want his presence made public yet."

Emma and Mal exchanged knowing looks while Devon continued on, staring at his dusty boots.

"He offered money up front for help, and promised more when I provided everything he needed." Finally, Devon raised his face to watch Emma.

"I told him whatever he wanted to know," Devon admitted with an audible gulp.

"Such as the location of Calvin's business assets like the warehouse?" Mal said, but by his tone, he'd already guessed the answer.

"And the brewery in Kent," she added.

Devon nodded. "That's when I realized something was wrong. I provided details, but I didn't ask how they would be used. I heard about the warehouse fire. He hired someone and was angry about it being doused so quickly."

"You still haven't told us his name," Emma said.

"James Montague."

Mal rubbed a palm over his face. "I need coffee. Do we have coffee?"

Emma silently pointed toward the pot on the counter. He poured a cup, muttering a colorful expletive under his breath, then topped off Emma's cup.

"So why are you here, Roxbury? Why now?" Mal asked. He stopped next to Emma as he sipped his coffee, and she leaned into the warmth of his big body.

"Montague...he likes fire," Roxbury said.

Emma vaguely remembered something about a devastating fire on Ethan's estate the year before she debuted. She couldn't remember the details. Lordy goodness, she'd been terribly self-involved.

"When I left the inn, he was still asleep. I've been up all night, wondering what to do. I thought we were here to push my suit, but last night he was in his cups and talked of burning down your barn and cottage. Emma, I swear, I didn't know. But I fear I've brought disaster to your door."

"Did Montague mention a time? Any specifics that might help us?" Mal asked.

"Nothing I could discern amid all the ranting. He blames all of you for everything. He says you stole years from his life and destroyed his fortunes. This is about revenge, but he won't ever be satisfied," Roxbury said.

Emma leaned her elbows on the table and cradled her face in her palms. "What's the plan, then? Lay a trap for him here?"

"I prefer a more direct approach. He's asleep at the inn? Let's wake up the fellow and show him the error of his ways." It was hard to miss the threatening manner in which Mal flexed his hand.

"That would be the quickest way to head him off before he enacts his plan," Emma said.

"Let's dress quickly and reconvene here in a quarter hour," Mal said. "Roxbury, sit. You're not going anywhere. We don't know you won't alert Montague to our arrival, so you'll travel with us to the village."

Emma rose and smoothed a hand down her wrapper, acutely aware of her state of undress. Everything was covered, but still. Roxbury in her kitchen while she had her hair tumbling in disarray and nothing on besides a robe was unnerving to say the least. Playing hostess gave her something to do, so she said, "I'll make tea." Devon preferred tea.

Mal brushed his hand over her back in a soothing gesture, then kissed her forehead. "I can make tea for Lord Roxbury."

The gentle declaration—both the kiss and the subtle claiming of the kitchen—warmed a place in Emma's heart that had gone cold as Devon made it clear that danger lurked outside her door.

"Thank you, Mal. I'll get dressed and be down in a trice." Without another glance at their uninvited guest, she left the room, acutely aware of the weight of Devon's gaze on her back.

Upstairs, her hands trembled as she drew on a day dress trimmed in embroidered poppies and tied the cherry silk ribbons. The day's plans might have changed from wedding planning, but she wouldn't face her enemies looking less than put together.

Also, having enemies was still strange to her. Secrets? Yes. She had secrets aplenty. People who genuinely wished her ill, to the point of wanting to set her home alight? That was new.

She didn't like it.

But Emma would look beautiful and poised when she faced this Montague person. Who apparently hated her and her home because of her connections to Calvin, Ethan, and Malachi.

It made sense in an awful way. Montague wanted revenge on every person involved in his transportation. Take away Mal's role as captain. Destroy Amesbury Ale's project to expand their retail distribution and growth, which impacted both Lottie and Ethan. Hurt Cal's shipping investments.

After all that effort and months of pulling it together, the brewery was continuing on, the fire in the warehouse hadn't done significant damage, and Mal was ignoring the blackmail demand. The only one of the three targets Montague was successfully impacting in any long-lasting way was Mal. Seeing him lose anything tore at her heartstrings, no matter how unruffled and accepting he appeared to be about moving on from the Royal Navy.

Emma plucked the straw bonnet trimmed in red ribbon and clusters of silk cherries from her hat stand, then left her bedroom. In the hall, she paused.

They had no way of knowing what awaited them at the inn, except a man who hated them all so much, he had boasted about setting her house on fire. Emma slipped back into her room, carefully closing the door behind her. Dragging her vanity stool to the armoire, she stepped up and felt with one hand around the top of the wood wardrobe until her fingertips brushed metal.

The pistol was designed for a lady's hand. It had been a while since she'd shot it, but when she'd moved to the outer reaches of England, she had promised Cal she'd maintain the weapon and keep it handy for self-defense. In the years since she'd moved to the cottage, she had needed it only once. They'd had an unknown nighttime visitor lurking about the property, and she'd fired into the air and yelled that the household was armed and trained, so the trespasser should move along posthaste.

Knowing she could scare off strangers had been a blessing then. Now, the weight in her hand sent a wave of foreboding through her. Ignoring the sensation, she grabbed a cherry satin reticule from the wardrobe, loaded the gun, and tucked it inside.

A glance in the mirror showed what she wanted the world to see—a fashionable, composed, strong woman who would do anything to protect her family, and look good while doing it. Emma nodded at her refection, then cinched the reticule closed with shaking hands.

$\backsim$

The Barley and Bay Inn was a bustling hub of activity on the edge of Olread Cove, squatting in all its moss-covered stone glory next to the road travelers took south to Whitby, and eventually all the way to London. The last time she'd been in the building it had been with a head full of wine and desire for the handsome ship's captain who'd caught her eye at the assembly.

Emma glanced over at Mal, and knew from the way he winked at her that he was remembering that night as well. To think, when she kissed him goodbye the next morning and left, she'd never expected to see him again.

Stepping out of the carriage, Emma ignored the hand Devon offered and marched across the yard, deftly avoiding mud puddles and piles left behind from horses.

Beside her, Mal strolled toward the inn with long, relaxed strides, but the tense set of his shoulders gave him away. When the *Athena* had engaged in conflict, was this focused calm how he led his men to victory? The sheer size of him, along with his steady competence, made her grateful he was on her side.

"We're agreed?" Mal said in a low voice. "Negotiate first, see if he can be talked down. Avoid violence if possible. If he gets rough, we call the magistrate."

"Fine with me," she said, then turned to Devon. "Roxbury, lead the way."

Upstairs, Roxbury knocked on a door at the far end of the hall, but didn't wait for an answer before opening it. Inside the snug but tidy room, a man straightened from tugging on a tall boot, then calmly raised an eyebrow at them all and rose. Without a word, he turned his back on them to tie his cravat in the mirror. The reflection showed a man who kept his eyes on what his hands were doing, winding and twisting linen around his throat, not once looking behind him at the uninvited visitors.

When he finally spoke, after giving his clothing one final twitch and tweak in the mirror, his tone was relaxed. "I should have known you wouldn't have the bollocks for this, Roxbury."

A ruddy flush colored Devon's cheeks.

Emma tilted her head, taking a long inspection of the man who'd played puppet master behind the scenes to enact his revenge. Objectively speaking, James Montague was beautiful. Blond curly hair, exquisite face, and a trim figure showcased in good-quality clothing. Something was decidedly wrong with his eyes, though. Not so much windows to the soul, but windows to Bedlam. This man was unhinged in the calmest, coldest way Emma had ever seen.

"Devon did the right thing," she argued, keeping her voice mild. The old Emma would have done whatever it took to appease the bully. Perhaps tried to flirt, or reverted to determinedly cheerful chatter about nothing of importance. The new Emma didn't need any of that nonsense—not when a pistol weighed down her reticule, and the man she loved stood by her side.

"No, Lord Roxbury did the weak thing. And I have no use for weakness." Montague's calm demeanor gave no warning of what he did next. Drawing a pistol from his pocket, he pointed it toward Devon, and by extension, them. She and Mal stood against the wall, like the empty glass bottles Cal used to line up on their fence for her to shoot at in her youth. Targets.

Mal pulled Emma behind him, shielding her with his body. The hammer clicked on the pistol, and Emma flinched. Around the side of Mal's burly arm, she watched Montague. His focus never wavered. His hand didn't shake, and the same serene expression graced his face, at odds with his cold eyes.

Devon shook, though. A sheen of sweat glistened on his brow, and his breath came in short pants, as if he'd run all the way from the cottage.

Like it or not, the man who had once broken her heart and betrayed her had done the right thing today. And like it or not, without him, she wouldn't have Alton.

And Alton was waiting for her back home. No matter how she felt about Devon, she couldn't let the biological father of her child get shot while she stood by. It wasn't in her to allow that to happen. Not when her pistol knocked against her hip from within the silk bag on her wrist.

"You don't want to do that, Montague," Mal said.

"Are you averse to bloodshed, Lord Trenton? Would you prefer I sell him to the penal colonies instead?" Montague queried, still frightfully calm.

Behind the shelter of Mal's broad back, Emma eased open the top of her reticule and withdrew her pistol.

"Consequences happen, but you survived. You've exacted your revenge. Put the gun down and tell me what it will take to satisfy you," Mal said.

A rusty bark of a laugh exploded from Montague with the sharp percussion of a bullet. Emma flinched at the exact moment the muscles in Mal's back twitched.

"Satisfied? I've lost years of my life because of you and your friends. I'll be satisfied when I've destroyed your lives in equal measure." From around the edge of Mal's arm, she spied Montague swing the gun away from Devon and toward them. "I apologize for changing plans at the last minute, Captain Harlow. Or, rather, Your Grace. But when given the opportunity to either testify at your court-martial and destroy your career or to see you and your lady love burned to the ground in your little love nest, I couldn't resist. Well done, choosing the sister of some-one I loathe. It's all so very tidy." A smile, barely more than a bitter quirk of the lips, broke through Montague's reserve. "Rest assured, when I'm done with you, I will still burn your quaint cottage to the ground. I'll see you and all you hold dear reduced to ash. You took everything from me, and I'll do the same. It's only fair."

Alton was there, along with Polly, Mrs. Shephard, Jimmy, and Charles. Even those damned goats mattered in the grand scheme of things. This man, with his icy emotions, would not steal her home and family. The weight of the pistol settled in her hand as she steadied her grip and her nerves with a deep breath. There was one sure way to end this.

Phee's uncle Milton's face flashed through her mind. The way life had seeped from his eyes as his blood pooled around him. Emma had carried that guilt, for a man she'd never met before that day, for years. His death had been an accident. If she stepped around Mal with this gun, killing another bad man would not be an accident.

And yet, standing by while this man threatened her son wasn't an option either. And that—protecting Alton—was worth carrying more guilt. Another burden in a life of regrets, but she would make the best of it. Yes, an authentic and honest life was the ultimate goal, but not at that price. For Alton and her family, she'd lie, cheat, steal, and kill every bad man foolish enough to step in her path, and that was as authentic and honest as she got. Being true to herself did not make her weak. Because no matter how painful her childhood had been, it had instilled a ruthless survival instinct that was as much a part of her as her blond hair.

The weight of the gun in her hand grew slick against her palm.

Beside them, Devon shifted from one foot to the other. Movement, however slight, caught Montague's attention, and the pistol swung away from Mal.

Which gave her the split-second moment of distraction needed to slip around Mal and step between him and Devon, pointing her own weapon.

Time stretched with a heartbeat of shocked silence, before a slow, chilling grin spread across Montague's face.

Devon yelled, "Drop the gun, Emma!"

Emma didn't look away from her target, ignoring the slight tremor in her arm. "Why the concern? I can handle a weapon. I was taught to defend myself. And I am. This man wants to hurt everyone I love, even my son. Especially my son. What kind of mother would I be if I didn't protect my family?" With each word, emotion leeched from her until she too felt cold. Devoid of warmth, like the cliff top in December, where the wind cut through to your soul.

At least she still had a soul. A little murky in places, but she would live with it, like she lived with everything else. The tremor in her hand steadied.

Montague shifted his stance slightly—enough to point the gun at her instead of Devon—then raised a mocking eyebrow in challenge.

"The kitten has claws, I see," Montague said.

In response, she pulled back the hammer on her pistol.

Beside her, Mal spoke low. "Are you sure, Emma? Once you kill a man, it marks you for life."

A rueful smile tilted her lips. "Oh, I know. Give me an alternative, and I'll consider it. But this man won't go away. He's already proven that." Tension gathered in her arm the longer she held the gun out like this, and she tried to relax without losing her target.

It was true though. If they thought of another way out of this, she'd take it. No matter what might have happened in her past, Emma wasn't a killer at heart. She was a mother, a sister, a friend, and hopefully soon a wife.

The realization, although it was something she should have already known, sank deep. She wasn't a killer. There'd been an accident in her parlor years ago, when she'd been frightened and pregnant and defending herself, but she wasn't a killer. Would she protect herself and her family? Yes. Most people would, wouldn't they? She swallowed roughly, her eyes steady on the handsome man with the Bedlam eyes. "Mal, would you do it, if you had the gun?"

He didn't even hesitate. "Yes. Once he pointed a gun at you, he was a dead man."

Montague chuckled. The sound held a hollow finality, like rocks falling on a coffin. "Aren't you two adorable with your solidarity and hatred for me? It's touching, truly." The finger resting against the side of his gun shifted toward the trigger.

"Put down the gun, Montague. That's the only way I see this ending well for anyone." She sounded confident as she made this final plea, but Emma already knew his answer.

Between one blink and the next, Devon's hand covered hers, snatching the gun away and firing in one smooth move.

A blast of deafening sound struck Emma numb and she watched in disbelief as a red blossom spread over Montague's chest. No one spoke as he fell, gasping at the ceiling. Mal was the one who had the sense to cross the room and remove Montague's pistol from reach, and then release the hammer.

"You didn't ask me if *I'd* do it," Devon said. The skin around his lips was tight and pale, and now that he'd fired, his hand had a noticeable tremor. When he turned to face her, his expression was a bit shocked and wild. "I couldn't let him hurt you or Alton. He hated all of you. It twisted him. I'm sorry I was part of it. So sorry, Emma. Please forgive me."

Her feelings for Devon had run the gamut over the years. Attraction, lust she'd believed was love, then anger. Resentment over how he treated her. She despised the horrible things he said in London. Did this final desperate act at the very last minute erase all of that? Not a bit. But it had been an awfully long time since she'd felt anything positive toward the man, so gratitude now over such a massive act wasn't comfortable.

Instead, she said, "Does anyone have an idea of what to do with this body?"

The three of them looked at each other, then at Montague. The blood soaked his shirt in a distinctive way, and his face hadn't settled into a peaceful faux sleeping expression in death. Without the spirit in his body, there was an oddly empty, waxy element to his perfect face.

"I don't know," Devon said. "I haven't seen a dead man this close before."

Beside her, Mal dragged a hand through his hair and sighed. "I'll take care of this. I'll send for the magistrate."

"What will you tell them?" Devon asked.

"As much of the truth as possible. Montague was a deranged man obsessed with hurting me, who came to the village specifically to harm my family. When I confronted him, there was a struggle over the weapon. It's tragic, but accidents happen. In this case, it happened between a convict and the Duke of

Trenton. As the highest-ranking landowner in the area, I'll need to introduce myself to the magistrate anyway. This is as good a time as any."

Devon swallowed roughly. "Thank you for leaving me out of it."

Mal faced him and seemed to grow several inches before her eyes. "Montague threatened my soon-to-be wife and child, but so did you. Make no mistake, Lord Roxbury, I'm not doing you a favor. I'll leave you out of this, but on one condition. You will retire to the Continent. Live your life. Be a better man. Today cleans the slate, and we will part ways, never to see one another again."

Emma searched Devon's expression for a hint about how he felt about that ultimatum. It was fruitless, but she couldn't help looking for the man she'd once believed herself in love with. He might be in there somewhere beneath the ravages of alcohol. Once upon a time, she'd thought she would save him, reform him into a respectable husband. But heavy-lifting of that magnitude was entirely Devon's responsibility, and she wanted nothing to do with it anymore.

After a long moment, he agreed with a nod. "That is probably more than I deserve, considering the trouble I've brought on your heads."

"Do you have your own room?" Mal asked.

"Yes, mine is next door."

"Then I suggest you return to it and stay there until you hear the magistrate finish his business." Mal wrapped an arm around Emma's shoulders and kissed the top of her head, dismissing Devon. If she wasn't mistaken, Mal took an extra moment to breathe her in. She smiled as his face lingered in her hair.

At the door, Devon turned back. "Your Grace?"

They both turned to face him.

"He's yours. Please ... be the father I refused to be," Devon said.

Mal dipped his chin in acknowledgment. "I already am. He is, and will be, loved. I promise."

Emma burrowed her nose in his chest as a heavy sigh escaped. Lordy goodness, she loved this man. "Goodbye, Devon." The words felt as final as they sounded.

Chapter Twenty-Four

❧

Dear Mal,

You were worth the wait. Now hurry home and marry me.

All my love,
E

      —A note found in Malachi's uniform pocket

The hilt of his sword gleamed against the oak judgment table. Acquitted honorably. The words echoed in his head.

Without a key witness—since the Admiralty's witness had apparently been killed in an accident—the case unraveled. Even under questioning, no one on board the *Athena* could or would corroborate the witness's story. From the lieutenants and warrant officers, all the way down to the powder monkey, Malachi's crew denied knowledge.

"Take up your sword and return to His Majesty's service. Your orders will be delivered to you directly," Admiral Sorkin said, concluding his speech.

Malachi wrapped his hand around the familiar hilt and woven grip. The gold braid on the cuff of his uniform shone in the sunlight pouring through the window behind him. He spoke the words he'd gone over with the Admiral this morning. "I formally request to retain my commission in abeyance, Admiral. I continue to serve my king, but now in the form of a dukedom."

Sorkin jerked his head in a terse nod. "So it will be. Expect orders to arrive at your London residence within the next seventy-two hours. We hope to see you again in Town soon." The admiral bowed his head slightly. "Your Grace."

This time, when Malachi walked down the hall of the Admiralty, with his sword securely in its scabbard, the stares and murmurs were quieter. People would still talk, because people were people. But the presence of his sword said everything about his court-martial. Captain Harlow, the Duke of Trenton, remained in the king's service.

Ignoring the stares, he pushed through the door and out into the sunshine.

More than anything, he wanted to go home. To Olread Cove and his boisterous family and gorgeous fiancée. They'd reluctantly agreed that such a short stay in London wasn't worth uprooting everyone. Especially when Emma had a wedding cake to finalize. The rest of the details she'd not cared too much about, and delegated to Phee and Lottie when they arrived at the cottage a few days after their conflict with Montague. But the food? Emma was determined to have the perfect cake to begin their life together.

Instead of barreling straight out of London, Malachi gave a hack driver directions to the house he'd rented when he'd returned from sea a lifetime ago.

Simon had invited him to dinner and asked Malachi to wish him happy. Miss Adelaide Martin would be Lady Marshall in two months' time. Miss Martin's family remained a mystery to him beyond a vague idea of her father being in politics. From what he'd heard when Simon called yesterday, his friend enjoyed her family and was eager to marry. Of course, even if Miss Martin came from a family of trolls, Malachi would still show up to dinner and toast to his friend's happiness.

In a few days, he would leave London and head east with enough time to reach Olread Cove before the wedding. Miss Martin and her mother would follow behind, accompanied by Simon.

Seventy-two hours would pass quickly if he distracted himself.

And it did. The orders arrived, securing his place as a captain in His Majesty's Royal Navy, serving in abeyance. The uniform would still be his for special Royal Navy events, but Malachi would remain on half pay with no expectation or obligation to command another ship.

As he ran a finger over his last set of orders, a bittersweet smile curved his lips. How he wished he could repay his men for their loyalty.

Setting aside the documents, he wrote a note to his first lieutenant, thanking him for the years of serving together. With damp eyes, he sealed the letter, then penned a second to the coachman in the mews, asking for the travel carriage to be brought around the next morning.

There would be days of travel, but he had the bank book to keep him company. He'd applied himself to decoding it back at the cottage, while waiting on a date for his court-martial. The names and information revealed as he labored over each page with Smith's key were indeed damning to certain members of His Majesty's government. Some notations were merely scandalous, others made him question his father's moral fiber that he'd been involved at all. Spy work was messy business, even when it answered to the cleaner title of diplomatic service.

It was the personal entries that made him pause. Sometimes, Malachi would swear he read the text with his father's voice in his head. Those excerpts were brief, but enlightening. It had been a surprise to learn the atlas he'd seen in the library hadn't been George's. Not initially, at any rate. Father began the marking of it when Malachi enlisted, then George continued tracking his career after their father passed away.

Within the journal, Father followed Malachi's journeys and spoke openly about his military service. There were recorded anecdotes and highlights from Malachi's letters home. So far, he'd found two written prayers for gentle seas, a foul-mouthed rant about the Admiralty's incompetence, and no less than six mentions of both his father's pride and fear for Malachi's safety.

In fact, he'd translated an entire passage where Father weighed the benefits and consequences of speaking to the men in charge about keeping Malachi out of the fight with Napoleon.

Outrage and the old bitterness welled immediately from that familiar festering wound. Right there on the page in black and white, his father deliberated and ultimately decided to move forward with a plan to steal not only Malachi's fortune, but those of his men.

Yet the outrage faded under the other undeniable thing on the page—the worry. Paternal worry, which until very recently had been a purely theoretical idea for him.

It was something to mull over, and he had plenty of time to do exactly that.

Page by page, government secrets revealed themselves, interspersed with personal passages, which allowed glimpses of the man his father had been in private.

He'd thought he knew his sire, but Malachi hadn't seen

much—either because he hadn't been shown or hadn't wanted the knowledge.

Father had seen the favoritism Mother had shown between his sons. The frustration and pain rose from the text at times, acting as a balm to old hurts. Someone had not only noticed, but also cared, and it made a surprising difference.

As a child, Malachi had felt invisible. In fact, he remembered a period when he was around Alton's age, when he'd been convinced he *was* invisible, and had spent a week experimenting with standing very still in different rooms of the house and eavesdropping on conversations he had no business hearing. Painful to recollect now from an adult's perspective, especially when he had his own little boy to raise.

Growing up, he'd had a single summer of perfect happiness. Mother had stayed in London, while George, Malachi, and their father explored the Cornish coast from the seaside cottage they'd leased. It had been a whole month of the sea, their father's undivided attention, and boyhood bliss.

Perhaps his love of the sea had been born that summer. After a time, Malachi had refused to think about the fleeting feeling of home he'd reveled in. It was painful how quickly it expired once they returned to London, so the joy had been buried under the more plentiful memories from his home life.

Or at least, it was buried until he found a journal on the beach last October. Then, the world Emma had created with her words opened up those latent desires all over again.

Within the pages of the bank book, it was clear that not only had Father noticed the favoritism, he hadn't liked it. A few entries recalled arguing about it with Mother on several occasions. Often after they'd received a letter from Malachi.

The bank book and key occupied his hands and mind for the first two days on the road to Olread Cove. On the third day, he hit a point where he'd rather run to the coast than remain one more minute inside the carriage. No matter how lushly appointed the seats, it was a rolling box on wheels and he was tired of being stuck in it.

They stopped for a brief rest at an inn where the food was good, and where he'd boarded horses for the week, then it was time to resume the journey. With a sigh, he settled back on the seat and picked up the bank book and a pencil.

Two hours later, he narrowed his eyes, then flipped to the previous page and consulted the key in his hand.

"That's not right. That can't be right." The note on which Smith had provided the key had begun to fray around the edges from continued use. Nevertheless, the information didn't change when Malachi checked and rechecked his work.

Then he backtracked, as verdant landscape passed unnoticed outside the carriage window. Woven into several of the personal passages, a pattern revealed itself. Random capitalized letters and bold text started to make sense when Malachi reread the latest bit he'd translated.

By the fourth day, his eyes burned with exhaustion, and he could hardly believe what he was seeing come together on the pages.

His father had loved him. *Truly* loved him.

Father had known that by protecting Malachi from the war, he'd stolen the financial gains due a captain in the Royal Navy.

George was the heir, so most of the estate and holdings would go to him. As the younger son of a duke, Malachi hadn't been left out in the cold by any means when his father died, but the gap between the two inheritances was significant. Made larger by the resentment Malachi carried over the way he'd been forced to watch others earn riches and glory in their careers while he wandered about the Baltic Sea.

If what he'd found in this bank book was correct—and why

wouldn't it be—Father had found another way to see Malachi provided for.

A smile crept over his face. Raising his eyes to heaven, and ignoring the roof in the way, Malachi sent his first genuine laugh to his father in over a decade.

Through years of service to the king, Malachi had stashed away his treasures and hoarded them—like a dragon, as Emma liked to tease him. What he hadn't known was that his father had done the same. For him. Set aside an additional inheritance where no one else but his adventuring son would ever find it, unless they had a map.

The directions to his father's so-called treasure came together with the capitalized and fancifully drawn characters that made sense when paired with Smith's key. A simple system, just as the initial method Smith had figured out had been. Malachi could hear his father in his head saying in that pragmatic way he'd had, *Why make it complicated if it only needs to be effective?*

By the time the carriage rolled into the driveway in front of the cottage, and Malachi stepped down, bone weary, he'd figured it out. The key was tucked into the pages of the book to mark his place.

As exhausted as he was, his heart was light, and excitement buzzed through him. He put away the red book to deal with after the wedding. Coming home was so much more important. Father would agree, if he were here. For the first time, Malachi felt certain his father would approve of something he'd done. If only he'd lived to meet the little boy Malachi was lucky enough to call his.

"Papa! You're home!" Alton cried, running at full speed across the front lawn with two goats on his heels bleating their own hellos. The wedding date hadn't mattered one whit to Alton. And Malachi was hardly going to dampen the child's enthusiasm with a correction. The ceremony was merely a formality, making their family legal as well as binding.

Not for the first time, Malachi was grateful for Emma's widowed status. Had she been a debutante, their sleeping arrangement—nay, even his stay in her home—would have been disastrous for her reputation. As it was, Mrs. Shephard and Polly had given their seal of approval on the relationship, which somehow mattered to Malachi more than Calvin's cheerful congratulatory handshake. Anyone interested in the niceties would be deterred by the presence of her family.

When the London contingent arrived from Hill Street, Alton had been the one to share the news, joyfully telling his aunt and uncle and the Amesburys about having a new papa, and that had been that. Malachi had been Papa ever since, and his heart swelled every time Alton said it.

Malachi bent and opened his arms for his son. "I missed you, lad. How are you? I swear you've grown a whole inch since I left."

Alton wrapped his arms around Malachi's neck and hugged him. He smelled of sweat and sunshine, the remnants of a ginger biscuit, and a fine layer of goat. In other words, like Alton.

Like home.

༄

Their wedding day. Emma blinked to clear the sleep from her eyes, and yawned. Morning light warmed the bedroom and gulls cried outside the window. A faded quilt covered her bare shoulders. Snuggling deeper into the nest of bedding, Emma rolled into the heat of Mal beside her.

The man was a furnace, which would be useful as the nights grew colder. Bay rum soap and his unique sleepy smell made for a heady combination. Emma buried her nose in the shallow valley between his pectoral muscles and breathed him in. A hand absently caressed the lines of the kraken tattoo before his arms wrapped around her.

She dropped a kiss on the narwhal on his forearm. "Good morning."

He grunted what might have been a variation of "morning."

Muffled clangs from downstairs and the scent of baked goods in the air told her Mrs. Shephard was awake. Emma lifted her nose from the addictive smell of her husband-to-be and sniffed. Yes, rum and fruit. Their wedding cake must be either ready to come out of the oven or cooling on the counter.

She could barely make out the cook's voice saying, "Let them sleep, lad. 'Tis a big day."

"Bless Mrs. Shephard," Emma murmured.

A grunt from Mal, then "The door's locked?"

"Mm-hmm. I fell asleep before unlocking it after last night's…activities." The last word came out on a giggle as Mal rolled her onto her back and began kissing his way down her body.

Soft beard bristles woke up her skin inch by inch. Emma grinned and stretched her arms over her head, letting him do whatever he wanted.

"How are you so soft?" His muffled question didn't need an answer as his lips circled her navel, then continued down to the curls between her legs.

A languid sigh of pleasure escaped her mouth when his tongue licked the slit of her body. "I love your mouth. The rest of you is fine as well, of course, but I really love your mouth," she teased, only half joking.

Mal's response was to purse his lips around her clitoris and suck, which as far as early-morning communication went, suited her perfectly.

The sex between them had been great in London. Foolish

her, she'd thought the circumstances of their affair, the lack of expectations, had been a factor. Perhaps at one point it had been. But this? Every promise, every hope, every touch, bound them together in the antithesis of a no-strings affair. And it was glorious.

Emma's body arched beneath his mouth, while muscles low in her core fluttered in an intimate dance to her peak. When Mal surged into her softness, they moaned in unison. Her hands clutched him close, touching everything she could as their bodies worked together, chasing pleasure. Bunching muscles shifted under her fingers and his breath escaped in pants like a bellows carrying profanity and praise until he pulled her into bliss once more.

Mal raised his head from the pillow far enough to drop a kiss on her shoulder, then flopped back down as if his head weighed too much for his neck.

Another moment passed before he said, "I suppose we should go rescue Mrs. Shephard from the boy."

Emma sighed. "We should, yes."

Neither moved.

Finally, when their breaths had evened and the fine sheen of sweat cooled to a chill on their skin, Mal turned his head to stare at her. Pale hazel appeared more green than brown in the soft light and settled on her face with an adoring expression. "I'm marrying you today."

She grinned. "Damn right you are."

They were still smiling when they entered the kitchen a quarter hour later. Alton reached his hands toward them, and without a word, Mal picked up his sturdy little body as if he weighed nothing, and the two commenced a detailed discussion about her son's dreams the night before.

Try as she might, Emma lost track after Alton said something about a goose and a mermaid. Instead, she sat at the table and smiled her thanks when Mrs. Shephard placed a cup of coffee in front of her.

"Polly is gathering eggs, then I'll whip together a nice omelet," Mrs. Shephard said.

Joy filled the moment until her heart felt like it might burst. Their guests were still abed, and the house was quiet beyond her family in the warm kitchen.

A fruit-filled wedding cake sat on the counter cooling, with a bouquet of fresh picked flowers in an earthenware cup nearby for decorating the finished confection.

"This is going to be a good day," Alton said, wiggling out of Mal's arms. As soon as his feet hit the floor, he darted down the hall toward the stairs.

Mrs. Shephard hummed under her breath. The tune was always the same when she was kneading dough, because the song, sung through three verses, was her way of measuring the time to knead before shaping the loaf.

"Are you making bread without me?" Emma asked, not looking away from her coffee cup.

"You don't need worry about anything today but marrying that handsome devil," the cook said.

"Thank you, Mrs. Shephard. I'm fond of you as well, you beautiful creature," Malachi responded with a wink.

"Are you flirting with Mrs. Shephard? You can't have her. I've already claimed her affections," Cal said, padding into the kitchen and dropping a friendly kiss on the cook's white cap.

"Oh, go on with ye." Mrs. Shephard laughed. She offered a warm muffin to Calvin before he turned away, and he grinned.

"See? She likes me best." He held up the muffin triumphantly.

"Are the others stirring yet?" Emma asked. She held her cup out to her brother, who was closest to the pot of coffee on the stove. "Refill, please and thank you."

And so it went. Comfortable, warm, slightly chaotic once

Freddie and Alton let the goats in, but everything she could hope for. Emma smiled at Mal. "Are you sure you want all this? You have a limited window to run if you've changed your mind."

Malachi leaned over the table and dropped a kiss on her lips. "All the king's men couldn't drag me away."

Epilogue

❦

"But Mama, Freddie the Red *can't* win the battle with the Harlow Hellion. It's not fair." Alton crossed his arms and curled his lip.

Malachi bit back a smile as Emma stalled for time by taking a drink of lemonade and leaning against the railing of the ship, assessing their son.

Goodness, Alton had grown in the year since they'd married. The wind whipped through his blond hair, which had already lightened under the sun since their time at sea.

The *Beauty* had served them well for this voyage. The ship was barely large enough to comfortably sleep all the families, but a treasure hunt wouldn't be the same without everyone on board. The greatest selling point had been a deck large enough for the children to run feral. This resulted in daily duels to the death between the boys, so Malachi thought the boat suited their family fine.

"Who died last time?" Emma asked.

"I did," Alton said, but his tone made Malachi wonder.

Not to be fooled, Emma turned to Phee, who sat cross-legged with her back against the main mast as she whittled a piece of wood. "Phee, which of the boys died yesterday?"

"My only child died tragically at sea, I'm sorry to say."

"Serves him right for choosing a life of piracy," Cal called from the other side of the deck. Malachi laughed, then tried to turn the sound into a cough when Alton shot him an indignant look.

"Indeed. Where did we go wrong as parents?" Phee sounded bored as she raised the piece of wood to the sun and examined it, then resumed adding detail with her slim blade. The carving looked like a dragon, but he wasn't sure.

Malachi shot Alton a look, and his son slumped his shoulders, then returned to Freddie, where he'd presumably die shortly.

Calvin, Ethan, and Simon were tending sails, and doing a rather poor job of it. Their time at sea had been spent learning the basic skills of a sailor. Malachi was grateful for the crew he'd hired in the village. If he'd had to depend on this bunch of Mayfair men, they would have been in trouble at the first sign of weather. As it was, Calvin and Ethan were making progress and getting in the way of the crew in equal measure. Simon was utterly hopeless with sails, but could sing a shanty with the best of them.

At least they were trying.

Adelaide and Lottie leaned against the railing next to Emma, looking perfectly at home in their practical breeches. When Emma caught Malachi staring at her bottom in the snug clothing, she threw him a saucy wink and wiggled her hips. He offered her a wolfish grin in return.

"How much longer, Captain?" Lottie asked, shielding her eyes with a hand as she stared toward the tiny sliver of land on the horizon.

"Soon now," Malachi answered, making an adjustment to their course with the giant ship's wheel.

Their voyage had first taken them to Dago, an Estonian island on the edge of Russia's territory in the Baltic. The coordinates and riddle-like instructions revealed by his father's bank book had led them to a cave inland, tucked into the rocks and trees.

At first, Alton had thought someone else had beat them to the treasure, and the boy had nearly been in tears at the thought. But no, after studying the page in the bank book, Malachi spotted a line that meant something new in the cave. *You've grown into a man. Far beyond even my reach.*

Leave it to his father to not waste kind words on a mere single meaning.

With instructions to fan out in the cavern, they'd run their hands over the walls as high as they could reach. The rock had been cool and damp under his fingers. On a shallow ledge he would have missed if he hadn't been searching for it, the squared edge of a wood box brushed his fingertips.

Remembering the moment he'd found the box made Malachi smile now. As inheritances went, traveling all the way to Estonia for a box no bigger than his hand had been underwhelming. If he'd only known then, what he knew now, he'd have been giddy.

Three slim silver spinning dials had guarded the latch of the box. Tarnish blackened the letters on the dials, but he'd been certain of the combination. Yet, as his fingers spun the silver pieces until they spelled M-A-L, the box stayed stubbornly closed. It had been with a bittersweet pang that he'd spun the dials again and held his breath as he spelled S-O-N. The latch opened with a click, and breath had whooshed out of him with a sound bordering on a sob.

In the days and nights since, as Malachi clutched the contents under that weathered lid, he'd made those sounds more than once. Each night, he held Emma in his arms and they exchanged stories about their parents. Funny stories, sad stories, awful stories. They'd opened a vein of memories and let them pour out in the safety of the captain's quarters.

A clear emotional outcome might be too much to expect when it came to his parents and his childhood. But as he and Emma shared, much of the anger and pain had fallen away, until only grief remained. There'd been so much of his father he hadn't known.

Even with the entire bank book of countless secrets and anecdotes, the contents of the box were Malachi's most prized pieces of his inheritance.

Inside the box, a piece of parchment had been wrapped around an object with a blue silk ribbon. He would recognize his father's handwriting anywhere. Although to see it in English and not in damned code had been a surprise.

The words were forever imprinted in his mind now.

Malachi,

This was the only way I could think of to return to you what was lost. May you forever live in the joy of that summer.

Love, Father

Beneath the elegant script, punctuated by sharp pen strokes, his father had written coordinates. Presumably to go with the iron key resting in his palm.

No more codes or games, just the coordinates that led to a familiar port.

The castle atop Saint Michael's Mount loomed above the *Beauty* as they sailed through Mount's Bay toward Penzance and the house Malachi remembered from their long-ago summer in Cornwall.

At the railing, his friends and family took in the stunning view as he navigated toward the area he remembered. When they'd visited long ago, there'd been a private dock on the property, making an approach by sea possible. A smile tilted his mouth when he spotted the weathered wood and a roofline he'd almost forgotten.

Their motley crew of sailors and aristocrats made short work of securing the lines and sails.

"Do you think the house will be in livable condition?" Phee asked, and Malachi shrugged. If the house was a ruin, they'd repair it.

"If it wasn't on the list of properties tied to the estate, who has been taking care of it?" Lottie said.

Adelaide was gaping at the scenery. "Who cares what condition the house is in when its location is so divine?"

"I am going to have to find a place in Cornwall, aren't I?" Simon said.

"Immediately," Simon's wife answered, making Malachi grin wider.

The house peeked above the crest of the landscape meeting the dock. It wasn't the dukedom or the money in the bank that was his inheritance. This house, with its precious memories, was what Father had left for Malachi, and only Malachi.

Their merry party made their way up the stone steps from the dock toward the tall house, where every window stood dark against the midday sun.

In his pocket, the iron key thumped against his hip with each step. Freddie's and Alton's high-pitched giggles floated down the stairs as they ran ahead of the adults. Beside him, Emma squeezed his hand.

"Is it how you remember?" she asked.

At the top of the stairs, a rocky lawn area edged in overgrown gardens stretched toward the house. Built of gray stone during the last century, a serene solidity encompassed the building. It had become part of the land, as if there were no other places on earth where this house could have stood.

"A little more run-down. But beautiful, don't you think? We will give Alton wonderful memories of this place."

"I think we're already doing that," Emma said.

At the front door, Malachi pulled the key from his pocket. Everyone gathered around and a victory cry went up when the wood door swung open on squeaky hinges.

At his side, Alton vibrated with excitement. "Go ahead, son."

Inside, each room held furniture covered with drape cloths, as if waiting for his family to return. Room by room, he and Emma led their friends through the house. It wasn't terribly large, but the opulence of the décor withstood the test of time like a gracefully aging dowager.

By the time everyone had selected a bedchamber for the night and transferred their things from the *Beauty*, the sun was setting. Phee made a fire in the fireplace of a cozy drawing room where they'd removed the dustcloths from the furniture, while Adelaide fretted over whether or not the chimney would smoke.

Calvin, bless him, had identified a crate of liquor in the wine cellar, which held a bottle of what turned out to be exceptional brandy. They toasted the previous two dukes with the first glass. A mellow warmth soothed a path down to Malachi's belly like an internal hug.

For his contribution, Ethan had opened a box of books in the library and brought a selection into the drawing room.

As the daylight waned and the enormity of the day settled upon them, each couple claimed a seat. Malachi glanced around the room, remembering the summer nights he'd spent with his father and brother here.

The phantom memories were bittersweet. It wasn't hard to imagine more nights like this one, surrounded by family and friends, splitting their time between the cottage in Olread Cove and this house on a different body of water. Malachi could see a future of managing the dukedom on his terms, with the help of advisers. Mother could stay in her precious London with her showy town house. Emma and Malachi would visit Town when they wanted, then retreat to one of the coasts, where they were free to be themselves.

On the sofa across from him and Emma, Calvin and Phee passed a glass of brandy back and forth between them. Calvin read a newspaper from a decade before, and Phee worked on her wood carving. Apparently, she was making a whole set of figurines for Freddie. Knights, horses, and a dragon.

Ethan had a stack of books by his elbow, and he'd chosen one at random to read. Lottie curled up on the sofa beside him with her feet resting in her husband's lap. Ethan absently rubbed her feet with one hand and held his book with the other. Lottie settled a pillow behind her and draped a lap blanket over her legs in deference to the evening chill. A book rested in her lap, but she didn't appear to be in a hurry to read it. Instead, she rested her cheek in her palm and closed her eyes.

At a table by the window, Simon and Adelaide played chess. It was the same board George had used to teach Malachi to play, if he wasn't mistaken.

Freddie snored under a blanket in front of the fire.

Alton padded into the room with a red book in his hand. His hair stood up at odd angles, having dried vertically after his bath. "Papa, this looks like your treasure map book."

Malachi shifted to allow Alton to crawl onto his lap. "You're right. Where did you find this?"

The boy pointed to the far wall with its nearly empty shelves.

Malachi examined the book. It appeared to be the same as

Father's bank book. Oxblood leather binding, pages yellowed with age. He flipped open to the first page, read, then began to laugh.

Emma turned his way. "What is it? Another code to figure out?"

Malachi shook his head, still laughing in disbelief. "It's a literal bank book. A record of deposits into an account I've never seen before. Father built an account for me to replace the prize money I lost during the war. It's all here, along with a letter. No one knew I'd inherit, so he made sure I would have a financial future separate from the estate." Malachi continued to shake his head in amazement. "It's all here. He took care of everything."

The entries spanned years. Hundreds of deposits where his father made things right, little by little. It wasn't the money, but the forethought and effort, that covered Malachi in a feeling of peace.

Emma rested her head on his shoulder. Every few minutes, she sipped from her glass of brandy, but she seemed content to stare into the fire and smile occasionally at their son curled up on Malachi's lap.

The waves crashed on the rocks outside the house, creating a rhythmic lullaby designed to soothe the soul.

"It's like what you wrote about in your journal," he murmured.

"Mmm," Emma agreed. "Brandy, a fire, the waves outside."

"And us."

She raised her face and he kissed her, the brandy sweet and heady on her tongue.

"And us. I waited a long time for you, Captain," she whispered. Firelight lit the tips of her dark lashes and played across the bones of her lovely face.

"I love you, Em. I love our life."

A smile lifted her lips. "Is it what you imagined it would be?"

The fire crackled, and the waves crashed. Lottie giggled at something Ethan did under the cover of the lap blanket. Across the room, Adelaide declared checkmate. On the other sofa flanking the fire, Phee muttered a curse at the carving in her hand, until Calvin distracted her with a kiss that went on and on.

Malachi kissed Emma once more. "This is so much better than anything I could have come up with on my own."

Want more of the Misfits of Mayfair?

Don't miss Lottie and Ethan's story in

ANY ROGUE WILL DO

Available Now

About the Author

Bethany Bennett grew up in a small fishing village in Alaska, where required life skills included cold-water survival, along with several other subjects that are utterly useless as a romance writer. Eventually settling in the Northwest with her real-life hero and two children, she enjoys mountain views from the comfort of her sofa, wearing a tremendous amount of flannel, and drinking more coffee than her doctor deems wise.

You can learn more at:
  Website: BethanyBennettAuthor.com
  Twitter @BethanyRomance
  Facebook.com/BethanyBennettHistoricalRomance
  Instagram @BethanyWritesKissingBooks

Fall in love with more enchanting historical romances from Forever featuring matchmaking, disguises, and second chances!

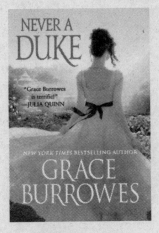

NEVER A DUKE
by Grace Burrowes

Polite society still whispers about Ned Wentworth's questionable past. Precisely because of Ned's connections in low places, Lady Rosalind Kinwood approaches him to help her find a lady's maid who has disappeared. As the investigation becomes more dangerous, Ned and Rosalind will have to risk everything—including their hearts—if they are to share the happily ever after that Mayfair's matchmakers have begrudged them both.

THE PERKS OF LOVING A WALLFLOWER
by Erica Ridley

As a master of disguise, Thomasina Wynchester can be a polite young lady—or a bawdy old man. Anything to solve the case—which this time requires masquerading as a charming baron. But Tommy's beautiful new client turns out to be the reserved, high-born bluestocking Miss Philippa York. with whom she's secretly smitten. As they decode clues and begin to fall for each other in the process, the mission—as well as their hearts—will be at stake…

THE HELLION AND THE HERO
by Emily Sullivan

Lady Georgiana Arlington has always done what was best for her family—even marrying a man she didn't love. Her husband's death has left her bolder—a hellion, some would say. When a mysterious enemy jeopardizes her livelihood, only one person can help: the man she left heartbroken years before. Once a penniless fortune hunter, Captain Henry Harris is now a decorated hero who could have his choice of women. Fate has given Georgie a second chance, but is it too late to finally follow her heart?

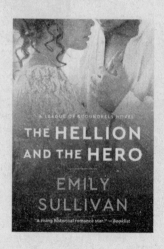

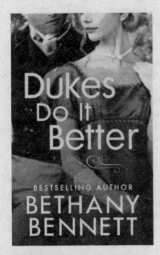

DUKES DO IT BETTER
by Bethany Bennett

Lady Emma Hardwick has been living a lie—one that allows her to keep her son and give him the loving home she'd never had. But now her journal, the one place she'd indulged in the truth, has been stolen. Whoever has it holds the power to bring the life she's carefully built crumbling down. With her past threatening everything she holds dear, the only person she can trust is the dangerously handsome, tattooed navy captain with whom she dared to spend one carefree night.

HOW TO DECEIVE A DUKE
by Samara Parish

Engineer Fiona McTavish has come to London under the guise of Finley McTavish for one purpose—to find a distributor for her new invention. But when her plans go awry and she's arrested at a protest, the only person who can help is her ex-lover, Edward, Duke of Wildeforde. Only bailing "Finley" out of jail comes at a cost: She must live under his roof. The sparks from their passionate affair many years before are quick to rekindle. But when Finley becomes wanted for treason, will Edward protect her—or his heart?

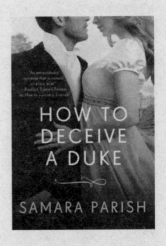

SAY YOU'LL BE MY LADY
by Kate Pembrooke

Lady Serena Wynter doesn't mind flirting with a bit of scandal—she's determined to ignore Society's strictures and live life on her own terms. But there is one man who stirs her deepest emotions, one who's irresistibly handsome, and too honorable for his own good…Charles Townshend isn't immune to the attraction between them, but a shocking family secret prevents him from acting on his desires. Only Lady Serena doesn't intend to let his propriety stand in the way of a mutually satisfying dalliance.

SEVEN NIGHTS IN A ROGUE'S BED
by Anna Campbell

Desperate to protect her only family, Sidonie Forsythe has agreed to pay her sister's debt to the notorious, scarred scoundrel dwelling within Castle Craven. But without any wealth, she's prepared to compensate him however possible—even if it means seduction. Yet instead of a monster, Sidonie encounters a man with a vulnerable soul, one that could be destroyed by the dark secret Sidonie carries. When dangerous enemies gather at the gates, can the fragile love blooming between the beauty and the beast survive?